THEATRE OF WAR

DOCTOR WHO – THE NEW ADVENTURES

Also available:

THEATRE OF WAR

Justin Richards

First published in Great Britain in 1994 by
Doctor Who Books
an imprint of Virgin Publishing Ltd
322 Ladbroke Grove
London W10 5AH

Copyright © Justin Richards 1994
'Doctor Who' series copyright © British Broadcasting
Corporation 1994

ISBN 0 426 20414 X

Cover illustration by Jeff Cummins
Typeset by Intype, London
Printed and bound in Great Britain by Cox & Wyman
Ltd, Reading, Berks

Acknowledgements

I should like to thank Craig Hinton and Peter Anghelides for their comments and suggestions, and Andy Lane for comments, suggestions and the use of a couple of ideas we discussed many years ago and promptly discarded as ridiculous.

Also, Martin Rawle for the internal illustrations.

I should probably also thank Shakespeare – but that's just forcing my soul so to my own conceit.

To Alison and Julian – with all my love.

Note

Justin Richards asserts his moral right to be identified as
the author of this work.

THEATRE OF WAR

The Rehearsal

The history of Menaxus took forty-three solar days to invent and, like all good lies, was grounded in truth.

The expansion of the Heletian Empire, by contrast, is not only well documented, but largely accurate. Its shortlived control of the Rippearean Cluster was as brutal as it was spectacular. Even after the Great Retreat *of 3985, it is doubtful if the Heletians would have remained contained if it weren't for the incident known as* The Dream Scenario.

The Dream Scenario, a Case Study in Virtual History – Al Jardine, 4123

Svenson looked down at the excavations, shielding his eyes from the burning suns. For as far as he could see, the carriers were sucking up the top-dust and spraying it out of the way, raising the sides of the valley like a giant trench and forcing the central pit still deeper to uncover the lower levels of the ancient building. He watched them crawl over the dusty ground, their movement giving away shapes which their camouflage tried to hide, their insignia catching the light as the vehicles turned and banked. In the middle of the activity, there was a flash as the light from one of the suns caught a facet of the thick transparent sheeting stretched high above the main auditorium of the theatre. The light subsided as unseen hands finished tying down the flapping material, securing both it and the excavation beneath.

Svenson ran his hand over his scalp, pushing his grey

hair into place, feeling the scars where the shrapnel had caught him. Lannic was a genius, no question – to predict so exactly the position of the theatre and its depth below the surface. If she wasn't so arrogant, then this posting away from the glorious battles being won at the front, to the back end of nowhere, chaperoning a team of whining archaeologists, might be half bearable. At least he was safe. But safety was hardly the issue, given the choice between the dust-hole Menaxus and being back with the Fifth as they continued their triumphant thrust into the Rippearean Cluster. He wiped a sodden handcloth across his forehead and the frustration from his eyes. Then he climbed into the jetter, slipped it into forward, and screamed down towards the activity.

Camarina Lannic and her team were at zone 26/G. Svenson was pleased to see that she too was perspiring in the claustrophobic heat, her face streaked and blotched with salty dust. A couple of the junior archaeologists were measuring the marbled floor of the admission gallery – or what remained of it – as he approached. Svenson could see why she had wanted the main theatre covered over, it was the only way to win against the swirling dust.

Lannic wiped her face with the back of her hand, smearing a new layer of grime across her cheek, as she directed their efforts. Her shoulder-length dark hair was tied back to avoid it getting in her eyes as she worked, but a few strands of it had worked loose and clung to her cheek – cracks across the grime of her smooth complexion. She frowned as Svenson approached – he knew that she saw him as just another interruption – and turned to examine the floor area beneath a collapsed column.

Svenson's tall shadows advanced until Lannic was caught in them. She could hardly pretend not to have noticed him now. She glanced up for a moment, irritated, then returned her attention to the marbled slabs.

A genius, maybe, but she was arrogant. Too aware that whatever the theoretical rank of the military personnel, she was really in charge. 'Lannic.'

2

She turned again, the irritation in her eyes turning to annoyance. 'Yes, Sub-Direkter?'

'A status report, if it isn't too much trouble.'

Obviously it was. 'Another one? Already?'

But Svenson needed to exert what authority he could. 'The Exec is keen to hear from us. You know his interest in the work here.' Svenson swept his gloved hand theatrically across the horizon. Its path described an arc which finished with it pointing at Lannic, his finger just shy of her face. 'He wishes to know if everything is still on schedule. He wishes to know when he will be able to inspect the more interesting finds.'

'The Exec is coming here? To Menaxus?' She seemed suddenly interested – almost excited.

Svenson's lip curled. A genius with no common sense: she would be lost on a battlefield. 'Of course not. The more interesting discoveries will be taken to him – to Heletia.'

'But – it is the whole site, the fact that it exists that is important.'

Svenson's eyebrows crept up slightly. She was being patronizing again, talking down to him like some overeducated strategy instructor.

'Don't you understand?' she went on. 'There is nothing here to take unless we uproot the whole theatre complex.'

'Nothing? So what is this amazing discovery that we've been boasting of for the last month?'

'The discovery is that the Menaxans had such a culture in the first place. I'd have thought any Heletian would marvel at the existence so long ago of another theatrologically based culture.'

Svenson just stared at her, holding back his anger.

'The papers and simularities I unearthed in the Braxiatel Collection documented a ritual regard for play acting. They even mention, and in some cases record, technologically enhanced theatrical ceremonies. But here we have the actual remnants and ruins – the real thing. An atomic-age theatre in which all the tracery and carving indicates a civilization with a high regard for theatricality. All the things that we believe make *us* civilized existed here centuries ago. We've even turned up an admission slip, complete with magnetic coding.' She held out a thin plastic card, about eight centimeters long and etched with a cluster of small leaves splaying out from a central branch. It fitted neatly into the palm of her hand, her fingers curling over the end of it, protecting it. Svenson made no move to take it, so she returned it to her breast pocket.

He was silent for almost a minute. Lannic watched, biting her lip. Svenson could see that just for a moment Lannic thought he was going to hit her. But instead he spoke, slow and deliberate: 'You are saying that as things currently stand, we have validated a theory and perhaps raised questions about the similarity of this dead culture to our own origins. But we have nothing material to show for it; nothing to take back to our beloved leader, however much he may wish to share in our discoveries? Nothing except a piece of plastic smaller than my fist?'

'I'm saying exactly that, yes.'

Svenson teased the black glove from his right hand, finger by finger, slowly pulling it free. When his hand emerged, grimy despite its protection from the dust, he flexed it, curling his fingers into the palm. 'Then you had better find something we *can* take back.' His voice was quiet, reasonable. He understood the situation and the only way to capitalize on it. He dusted his naked palm on the breast of his tunic, and watched the dust catch in the sunlight as it spiralled down. *Then* he hit her.

The spray eased the pain below her right eye a little, but it still stung like hell. Lannic washed the dust from the rest of her face, dabbing carefully round the swelling.

Larzicourt offered her a towel. 'He's dead.' If he had been less jittery, the threat might have been more convincing.

'Nice thought,' said Lannic through the towel. 'But a bit premature.'

'Can I get you anything else?' Larzicourt was more stung than Lannic. He rubbed his thin hands nervously

4

together now he that no longer had the towel to worry. 'Drink?'

'No. No thank you. I think I'll lie down for a bit.' She smiled faintly as Larzicourt dithered in the doorway. 'I'll be all right. Thanks.'

'Well, if you're sure.' Larzicourt's stooping form was silhouetted for a moment on the threshold. Lannic thought she heard him sigh with relief as he left, but it was probably just the servos hissing as they closed the door.

She dropped the towel into the laundry bin and picked up the spray again. The lettering on the plastic sleeve blurred as her eyes watered, and she hurled it across the room in the vague direction of the far corner, then sat down heavily on the bunk, cradling her head in her hands. And winced as she involuntarily touched her bruised eye.

The spray ricocheted off the wall into the mirror, cracking it across its length, then spun itself to a stop on the table below.

Svenson lay back on his bunk and closed his eyes, hoping that the nightmare would not be waiting for him. But it was. It always was.

Again he clawed his way over the top of the trench, using some of the sodden bodies as a ladder. He glanced across to see the rest of his unit also poised at the edge of the killing zone. Galaz smiled reassuringly, gripped his disruptor and leapt up the last step. He landed easily on his feet, the blast catching him across the chest and blowing away most of his face. Svenson ducked as the blood splashed past him.

When he looked up, still shaking, the unit was moving forward – running. He tried to pull himself out of the trench, to follow, to catch up. But the wide-beam blaster (which Intelligence had originally assured them the Rippeareans did not have) caught them while he was still bracing himself. The bodies glowed white-hot, then vanished, leaving just the ghosts of their images on his retina.

Once again he slumped back down into the trench, the

5

scream of the approaching sat-strike – targeters alerted by the blaster-flare – was the scream of his unit as their lives blinked out.

And again he put his head in his hands and closed his eyes tight – to find Galaz waiting for him, smiling reassuringly as his face disintegrated in a splatter of blood and tissue.

Svenson's eyes snapped open. He was back in his cabin on Menaxus. His uniform was still sodden, but with sweat rather than blood. Just the dream again. His jaw quivered as he choked back a sob. He would get no sleep again tonight.

Beneath the dust and sand, in a darkened room behind the main theatre excavations, a tiny red light blinked and pulsed into life.

Despite his doubts, Svenson had fallen into an uneasy, disturbed sleep. He drifted restlessly on the edge of waking, knotting the bedcovers between his clenching hands. Outside the noise of the desert night continued its soft murmur, wind sweeping dust against the prefabricated buildings.

The sudden brilliant flash of light roused him instantly. He was sitting upright on the bunk before the sound of the explosion followed. Automatic calculations based on the delay between sight and sound told him the burst was about three kilometers away. The angle of the light told him it was an airburst. As the chatter of disruptor fire started, he dragged on his tunic and grabbed his sidearm. The door hummed open and Svenson stepped out into –

'Here – Svenson.' He turned just in time to see the Plautus Strike-One that Galaz threw him. He caught it almost by reflex, both hands at chin level, and swung it towards the front of the trench. Edessa and Mursa were already down, Tibava was nursing a bloodied thigh, squeezing the pressure points so hard that the exertion as well as the pain showed in her face.

For a moment he was still, his brain struggling to cope.

Then it slipped into a well-worn mode which had been sleeping, not forgotten.

'How many of them?'

Galaz shook his head. 'Dunno. But they're about four clicks away.'

'Nearer three, I think.' They both ducked as the light burned across the killing zone and the thump of the explosion hurled mud and fragments of rock down into the trench. 'Make that two.'

Arlon dropped down beside them, blinking away the residue of the last flash. 'Space cover is due any minute. They caught the second flare. The satellite's being brought round to get a fix.'

Svenson thought for a moment. 'They must know that already. They'll see the signals to the bird.'

'They'll move position?'

Svenson nodded. 'They have to.' He looked to Galaz for confirmation.

'You're right. And while they're moving the blaster – '

'They can't fire it.'

Arlon had a chart of the area. It had changed considerably since the front had opened, but the basic geography was still intact. For the most part.

'There,' Galaz pointed, 'they're using that hill as the vantage point, moving forward along the ridge.'

Svenson nodded. 'And they have to move at least two clicks, at speed, to escape the sanitization.'

Arlon pointed to an area to the west. 'Here?'

Galaz nodded. 'That's where I'd go.'

Svenson agreed. 'So would I. So we'll strike – here.' His finger jabbed at a rocky area to the east.

Arlon frowned. 'They know what we would script, so they'll go the other way' Galaz told him. 'Get the rest of the unit. We're going out there.'

Svenson could see Galaz clawing his way over the top of the trench, using some of the sodden bodies as a ladder. Galaz reached the top and glanced across to see the rest of the unit also poised at the edge of the killing zone.

Svenson smiled reassuringly, then paused, puzzled. The scene was familiar, like déjà-vu – but different somehow. It was like watching himself in a cracked mirror. An incomplete image – something askew. He gripped his disruptor a little tighter, and leapt up the last step.

Just as his feet left the ground and he swung himself up and over, he realized the role reversal. But it was too late by then – his body was already swinging into the approaching bolt of disruptor fire. He landed easily on his feet, the blast catching him across the chest and the left side of his face.

Svenson fell back down into the trench; the scream of the approaching sat-strike was the sound of his own voice, as his face disintegrated in a splatter of blood and tissue.

Lannic was tying up her hair again, cursing as the clips refused to obey her sleepy fingers, when Larzicourt burst in. She fumbled for the clip she had dropped in surprise. He caught his breath, pointing back at the door as if she could deduce the problem from the insistent stab of his finger.

'What the hell's the matter?' She was annoyed. She was always annoyed before her second caffedeine.

'He's –' Larzicourt finally managed a wheezed phrase: 'He's dead.'

'Svenson?'

'You knew?'

'It seemed a fair bet. What's he done now?'

She could see Larzicourt in the cracked mirror as his mouth worked soundlessly for a moment. Then: 'He's – died. I mean, really died.'

She turned back to him, hair falling over her shoulders. 'You mean – he's died?' A silent nod. 'As in *dead* died?' Another nod. 'How – where?' Her hand automatically strayed across the loose coverall over her right thigh, instinctively checking the small holster and the obsolete percussion pistol nestling inside.

'I think you'd better see.' Larzicourt swallowed, his forehead furrowing for a second as he thought about it. 'It's not pleasant.'

Svenson was identifiable from the insignia on his torn and muddy uniform. The team's medic had covered the corpse's face with a silver insulating sheet which caught in the breeze, flapping up from the head and reflecting the morning suns' light. Lannic had caught enough of the bloodied mess beneath the sheet not to want it removed.

'I'll have him put in the sick bay,' the medic offered. Lannic nodded, licking her dry lips. The medic gestured to a couple of the crew standing at the edge of the hollow. One of them was leaning on a stretcher, its end dug into the dust.

Lannic tried unsuccessfully not to watch as the body was lifted onto the stretcher and carried away. The medic shuffled his feet next to her.

'How did it happen?' The stretcher disappeared over the lip of the hollow which Svenson's cabin occupied.

The medic shook his head. 'I've no idea. It's – ' he struggled for the word, and eventually settled on, 'bizarre.'

'How do you mean?'

'The mud on his uniform, the injuries . . .'

'Mud?' She had noticed the dried mud streaked down Svenson's body, but it had not struck her as odd. Until now. The medic gestured across the hollow. It was as dry a dust-bowl as the rest of the area. In the hot season there was no water anywhere but the tropical zone. In the wet season the constant rain turned the dust into sticky, cling-ing mud: impossible to wash off, all but impossible to excavate through.

'And there's the nature of the injuries.'

She had almost forgotten he was there, and looked back at the medic as his voice startled her. He misread it. 'I'll need to do a proper post-mortem of course, but if you want a preliminary outline?'

She nodded.

'He was caught in a high-disruption blast.'

'What?'

9

'A high-disruption blast consistent with that caused by a Rippearean wide-beam blaster.'

'Ground artillery – here?' She looked round nervously.

'I doubt it. Intelligence didn't think so. And anyway, the terrain's wrong for a wide-beam – no hills to get a proper siting.'

Lannic frowned. She could identify small arms, if she was pressed, but she knew next to nothing about artillery. 'You're sure?'

'I was on Zastaz Four when the sat-link went down. Nine hours without satellite support – oh yes, I'm sure.'

'But that doesn't make sense.' They had scanned before they came in. A lone Rippearean sniper they might have missed, but ground artillery was something else. 'You could be wrong – I mean, your diagnosis.'

The medic nodded, moving off a little. He sat down on a small bank higher up the incline and looked back down at her. 'Yes, I could. Although I don't think so.' He paused, either to give her time for what was coming, or to savour the moment. 'But then, there's this.' He reached behind him and lifted something from behind the bank. 'Svenson could have fallen from here to where we found him. If so, he may have dropped this.'

He held the gun up for her to see it, silhouetted against the sky, its shoulder strap dangling to his elbow. It was an old Plautus Strike-One – a weapon to which the Rippeareans would hardly have access. And even Lannic knew that the expedition didn't carry any.

The *Dunsinane* hung in geostationary orbit high above Menaxus. Her missile tubes were on stand-by and she was on full alert. This was not because her crew was aware of anything unusual to worry about, but because she was always on full alert. There was a war on, and Direkter Caralis would let no one forget that.

The tiny form of the Lander approached the *Dunsinane*. A door slid open in her underbelly for long enough to swallow the smaller craft. Then the door slid silently shut as the engines made minute adjustments for the change in weight and mass ratios.

'So, Sub-Direkter Svenson was shot by a weapon which is not on the planet, while carrying a gun which he didn't have. Is that right?' Direkter Caralis's eyebrows rose further up the forehead that stretched right over his scalp. But Lannic knew better than to attempt to answer. This much she had told him over the com-link. There was more than just his sarcasm and annoyance, more even than the death of his ground commander behind his summoning her to the orbit-ship. She swallowed, and waited, intimidated by the huge man as he opened his enormous palms towards her as if in supplication. She could see the vague shadows of las-burns on his right palm where he had gripped his disruptor too tightly when firing. 'I want a full script within one day. Otherwise I pull my people out.'

She had not expected a threat – a reprimand maybe, but not a threat. 'You can't do that – this dig is the most important theatreological –'

'It isn't. But you can stay on if you wish. *Your* team can take whatever risks you feel necessary. But my troops will exit if this incident is not explained. I wanted you to hear that from me, personally. I want you to understand that. No matter how important you or anyone else thinks this mission may be, *I* think I'm wasting time and properties away from the front. You have one day.'

Lannic bit her lower lip as the direkter turned away. She needed the military support. She needed the carriers, if nothing else. But one day would probably be enough to establish the prime objective. One more day might just be enough, then Caralis could take his troops and his carriers and anything else he wanted, and leave orbit for good. Just so long as she had enough to secure an audience with the Exec – her last and greatest ambition.

'I'll need to contact my people. To speed up the investigation.'

'Fine.' He didn't turn back to her. 'Stagirus will open a com-link for you.'

At the coms desk, Stagirus heard his name through the background noise of the consoles and punched a Ready command into the deck. The link to the ground base was established and the deck began to set up the encryption algorithms, passing codepage information down the link to the coms desk in the expedition's control centre.

'The link's established.' Stagirus turned up the output volume. 'Just a second while I get the cue signal.' He typed in a sequence and hit the process key. A bleep from the speaker; he frowned.

'What is it?'

Stagirus was typing again. 'I can't get an acknowledgement.' He hit the process key again. Another bleep. 'The link *is* established, but they're not answering.'

'Something causing wave variation?' Caralis reached across Lannic and typed a sequence. She hadn't noticed him standing behind her.

A sudden burst of static from the speakers, accompanied by a howling noise. Stagirus quickly reduced the volume. 'Sorry – feedback.'

'Well at least they're answering. Why aren't we getting them clearly?'

'We are, sir, it's just that there's nothing coming through.'

'Except the feedback.' Lannic didn't want to be left out completely.

'No, I've shut that off.' Stagirus was typing in another sequence.

'Then what's that?' Lannic reached across – if Caralis could, then so could she – for the volume control. The static got louder, but through the crackling and distortion the howling and shrieking was still there, muffled and distant but audible.

'Can't you tune that out?' Caralis was getting impatient. And Stagirus was getting frantic, typing like a demon and watching the read-out as it reported back to him. He shook his head.

'That's not feedback, sir. It's a real sound image.'

A pause. Stagirus turned in his chair to look at the

12

direkter. A moment's unspoken communication, then Caralis nodded quickly, swung round and returned to his command console. Stagirus started typing again – this time a different sequence.

'What are you doing?'

'Disconnecting. Otherwise we'll get white-out when the strike hits.'

Lannic swayed on her feet. 'Strike? What strike? Look, there are people down there – my expedition, the ground defence force.'

'I don't think so.'

'Because you can't make contact – that could be anything. A bit of feedback and – '

Stagirus was on his feet, the coms desk quiet apart from a flickering stand-by light. 'You don't understand.'

'Too right I don't!'

'This isn't feedback.' He opened the channel again. The screaming was louder now, almost drowning out the static.

'Then what is it?'

Caralis was standing beside her again, quiet, impassive, professional. He took her by the shoulders and turned her to face him, nodding to Stagirus to complete the disconnection. Lannic looked up at Caralis, confused and lost. 'That sound is the incoming signal from the command centre on Menaxus. What we heard is what is actually playing on the surface.'

She shook her head. 'No, that's impossible. What makes a sound like that?'

'How many people are there in your full complement? Excluding yourself.'

'With your ground crew, twenty-three. Twenty-two now that Svenson's gone.'

Stagirus was standing again, the disconnection complete, although it seemed to Lannic that the noise stopped before he hit the final key. 'We're soldiers. We've all seen service at the front. We all know that sound – we live it, dream it.'

Caralis let go of her shoulders. 'The ground-scan I just did counted seven active life forms on Menaxus.' She felt

13

faint, dizzy. 'I think if I scan again now, we'll find that the planet is down to just one.' He turned away. 'Arm tubes one through five with neutronic dispersers. Begin sterilization sequence three using ground control as target centre. Script-out to my console.'

Lannic's mind was blanking out. She tried to shout, to stop them, but could make no sound.

'Don't worry,' Stagirus murmured to her, 'we'll get that bastard sniper. Or traitor – whichever he is. And we won't even damage your precious excavations. Though you won't be going back to them for quite a while yet.'

The *Dunsinane* brought its weapons to bear at 11:59:04 on 15–9–3980. By 11:59:50 the area around the target centre had been sterilized. All organic material was shredded by the dispersement, but the excavations, the buildings and everything inorganic remained intact.

Lannic stood at the window of her cabin and watched the planet slowly recede into the blackness. It would be five years, they said, before the radiation levels dropped to a reasonably safe margin. In her hand she clutched a thin plastic card, about eight centimeters long and etched with a cluster of leaves. 'I'll be back,' she said quietly. 'We have things to finish.'

Source Document 1

Extract from *The Good Soldiers* by Stanoff Osterling

Braxiatel Collection Catalogue Number: 357EH
These two manuscript pages discovered: Mordee excavation, 2955–ref Prof. Zagglan Crichley

SPIDLER Was that a prologue – or a motto hid in verse?

REMEK 'Tis brief, good Spidler.

JORVIK As soldier's loyalty.

Enter the player soldiers, cloaked and hooded like Prologue and like Jorvik

SOLDIER 1 The enemy attacks, we are undone.

SOLDIER 2 To you we turn – our last great hope, good Kemer.

KEMER As Sergeant of this troop I know my rank,
And all know duty when its time has come.
Let's smite this mortal terror, hip and thigh.
To arms, my colleagues – death must have his due.

JORVIK	Remek – how like you this play?
REMEK	The sergeant doth incite too much, methinks.
KEMER	Thoughts apt, gun armed, take aim, all sights aligned. Once more atop the trench, my friends – once more. We smite the dreaded Pollacks in the eyes –

Jorvik acts as chorus

JORVIK	Kemer ascends, and outlined for a moment on the summit of the trench, his colleagues roused, his speeches stirring, he turns to face the enemy.

A shot – Kemer falls

JORVIK	But cruel deception – a Pollack sniper catches him, silhoutted, erect, against the evening light and blood-red sun. And noble Kemer, mighty Kemer, falls from on high into the muddy trench.
PRATOR	Remek rises!
JORVIK	What, frightened with Pollak fire? He who survived Limlough – a *hero* of that mighty battle? Oh Remek – consider the good soldier Kemer, who was once handsome and brave as you.

ACT 1

Chapter 1

An Archaeologist Prepares

One of the greatest talents which Osterling shared with Shakespeare was the way he layered the drama. The first scene of any of his plays lays down a metaphorical minefield. Images and references are charged, and left for later exploitation. For example, in The Good Soldiers *the opening scene introduces not just the future survivors of the battle of Limlough, but also the essential elements and imagery that will follow them through the plot.*

Similarly, in Shakespeare's Macbeth, *the first scene begins – like many of those which follow – with a question ('When shall we three meet again?'). There is immediate insecurity, doubt. Indeed, doubt is the dominant linguistic mode of the play. The imagery is set out as we are introduced to the world of the play through the weird and disturbing world of witchcraft. The second line, another question, sets out the aggressive, dark atmosphere. 'In thunder, lightning, or in rain?' It is as unsettled and chaotic as the political situation is destined to become. Everyone will be both a winner and a loser and the difference between good and evil becomes blurred and difficult to distinguish. This duality is already there in the language of the short opening scene: 'When the battle's lost and won'; 'Fair is foul and foul is fair.'*

The first name we are given is that of the central character – 'There to meet with Macbeth' – who is both named and doomed at once by the witches. The first scene on the blasted heath ends, merging into the next as the witches depart and Duncan and his men enter. The second scene also starts with a question, and the eyes of the audience which have so far been starved of colour (even in the imagery – 'Greymalkin', 'fog and filthy air'...) are shocked by the sudden introduction of a single, dominant colour – the colour that together with black defines the mood of the whole play: 'What bloody man is that?'

The Dramatist's Art – F. Van der Cleele, 2811

The flight disc was three months old, though it looked much older, and Bernice was bored. Still, the seemingly interminable shuttle trip gave her ample opportunity to update her diary with recent events.

Not that the diary was really a record of what *actually* happened – there was no time constraint in that respect. It documented not what had really happened, but merely an interpretation of events. Often it was an interpretation which Bernice knew was completely at odds with the real worlds. And whether it was right or wrong (whatever *that* might mean), she was quite likely to change her mind about what had actually been interpreted as having happened, and attach a sticky yellow label over the top with a new account. So when she came to read the diary – which was after all the reason for writing it in the first place – she could choose between the truth (on the sticky) or the *real* truth (underneath). After all, what actually happened was usually pretty boring and inconsequential compared to her interpretation, and anyway the past was dead, so why relive it?

Which of course brought her back to the two questions she wanted not to have to answer: why was she interested in digging up things from the past; and why was she even more interested in travelling about in it so often with the Doctor and Ace in the TARDIS? Certainly she wasn't ready yet to give that up. A short break, a sabbatical perhaps, but she would be back. After her once-in-a-lifetime expedition with Rhukk; and her once-in-a-lifetime trip to the Braxiatel Collection.

Bernice sucked the end of her stylus and considered. The TARDIS was a bit like her diary: from the outside it seemed rooted in the past – twentieth-century artefact versus the reassuring antiquity of paper – yet it was pretending to be something it was not. And like the TARDIS, her diary had more to it than was immediately apparent – her diary was not just a record of past events. Or was it not *even* a record of past events?

'Stuff it,' she said out loud, oblivious to the glance of the middle-aged man startled out of his disc-reader three empty seats away, and started to write.

Date: 3985, or something close. En route to the Braxiatel Collection to deliver findings and data from the Phaester Osiris expedition. I could have transmitted the data, but it's just as quick to come myself, and apparently it's quite a place. Doctor and Ace gone off to do something-or-other somewhere, somewhen. Sounded boring so stayed behind to do dig with Savaar and the famous Rhukk. Hope they enjoy it (whatever it is) as much as I am enjoying writing this. Probably best to get a rest from those two after recent events and tensions anyway – I could do with a break. Lots to say, don't know where to start. God, I miss them both.'

Bernice read back through it thoughtfully, wondering if she ought to try to include her own relative dates, if only to work out when her birthday was. Then she pushed the attendant call button, marked the page with the new yellow sticky she would need next time, and yawned.

The attendant, efficient in grey and light blue, hurried off to find Bernice a Craxiatanian Chardonnay. Bernice glanced round the cabin yet again. There was hardly anyone on the flight – it was less than half full – but that was a mercy after the overcrowded connection between Zincrast and Abadron. She pondered briefly which had been worse, the boredom of this final leg or the hot noisy atmosphere of the previous flight, complete with squalling

21

babies, at least half of which must have been born at some point in the queue to register that they were leaving Federation jurisdiction of their own free will. She closed her eyes for a moment and listened to the low air-conditional hum of the silence: no contest.

'Professor Summerfield.' The attendant was leaning forward just enough to be polite. He held out the small silver tray and Bernice took the goblet, smiling her thanks. The attendant inclined his head slightly further by way of acknowledgement, made the half-bow into a turn and headed off to an appointment with another small green call light. Bernice watched him go, and her eyes caught those of the man opposite as she turned back to her wine. He smiled at her.

Normally Benny would have responded. She would have made a point of ignoring him, or offered some sarcastic comment. But she knew he wasn't really looking at her. He was just as bored as she was and his eyes automatically followed any movement, his attention any sound. So she smiled back, and he returned his attention to his reader. Bernice was slightly surprised that he was perceptive enough to understand that she was behaving the same way, and not out to make conversation. She was also a little disappointed.

Not that he was at all attractive, but he had a kind smile and an intelligent look. The half-moon glasses glinting beneath the straight grey hair suggested a dislike or apprehension of implants and bionic surgery, so he also had some common sense. And that was not always the case amongst academics. The fact that he was an academic was of course a given – why else would he be on such a boring flight. Who was it who said 'It is better to travel hopefully than to arrive?' Well, whoever it was obviously hadn't been on the Yenvel-Braxiatel shuttle. Faster-than-light travel was all very well, but it didn't mean people spent any less time in transit – they just travelled further.

Bernice settled back with her wine and watched her distant neighbour's disc-reader over his shoulder. She couldn't hear it, but she could see the animated maps and knew from the contents listing of her own complimentary disc that it was showing the Heletian losses and withdrawal as it had stood about three months back. Since then they had sustained further losses and retreated even further. Not too long before they were forced back to their own systems – a couple of years, maybe. Perhaps even less according to some of the recent commentaries.

Bernice squinted to make out the detail on the map, not helped by the blur on the screen since it was angled away from her. Just on the edge of the image she could make out a small planetoid: Braxiatel. She had not realized it was so close to the Heletian territory, so close to the war. Still, close was a relative term, but it did seem to be on the nearest edge of the non-aligned clusters. A few years ago, with the Heletians in full advance, even Braxiatel must have been threatened with conquest.

The man shook his head as a blurred red arrow predicted the line of retreat and the cessations for the next quarter. Bernice could hear the clicking of his tongue as he switched off the reader and for the first time caught the slight greyness of his eyes behind the tinted spectacles as he leaned back. It couldn't be easy for him, to be so heavily in retreat after the years of expansion and conquest; suddenly to be losing after having the strategic advantage.

The reception area was away from the main complex. Bernice had no luggage apart from the satchel she was carrying over her shoulder, so she did not need to wait by the entrance for a trolley to deliver genetically coded possessions. The technology seemed to get rapidly more inferior as she moved further from the Federation, and she had not risked checking in her satchel – God alone knew where it might end up. She would not be staying long, just a few hours. However, all the passengers from her shuttle were obliged to wait while their invitations were checked, although they would never have been allowed to board the flight without a valid invitation. Bernice handed in the grubby plasti-disc to the receptionist cum security guard and wandered over to the huge picture window which dominated the opposite wall. It was easy to spot who had been here before; they were the ones not standing in awe alongside Bernice. She whistled softly in appreciation. Irving Braxiatel certainly had style.

The story was that Braxiatel had won the planetoid at cards. Whether or not that was actually the case was largely unimportant. However he had come by it, Braxiatel had set about terraforming the out-of-the-way rock with a vengeance. The only stories about Braxiatel which were more far-fetched than how he had acquired his home were those relating to how much it had cost him to make it habitable. All you could say for certain about him was that he had an awful lot of money, and that he had spent a huge sum transforming a barren wilderness floating through space with the designation KS–159 into the most desirable residence in the sector. But that was not what made it famous or brought people to it.

The Braxiatel Collection was arguably the finest and most extensive collection in the known worlds. *Collection of what*? was an invalid question – it was a collection of everything. It was rumoured that Braxiatel had a whole gallery devoted to Deauxob of Glanatanus; that Parry's original survey notes from the abortive Telos expedition had a small place on a long shelf in the archaeology archives; that somewhere in a dust-covered specimen cabinet lurked a complete manuscript (some people even said the original manuscript) of Osterling's *The Good Soldiers*. The claims were of course outrageous, and the increasing number of academics of the galaxy who had actually been to the collection found it easy to believe them all.

As a private collection it accepted visitors by invitation only, and sponsored research on a hundred planets and as many deep-space missions entirely at the whim of its brilliant, reclusive and presumably eccentric owner. The only condition attached to a grant or to the provision of research facilities was that the findings – both the theories and the raw data which fed them – be returned for storage

24

within the collection. A small price to pay for funding or access to such an archive.

Looking out over the ornamental gardens with the Mansionhouse soaring up behind them, Bernice decided she would have financed the entire expedition herself just to be assured of this visit. She had once stumbled across a holoschematic of ancient Versailles while looking for source documents pertaining to Thetalian transport systems. It was well known that Braxiatel had based the Mansionhouse and its grounds on the ancient Terran Palace of Versailles. But if Louis XIV could have seen what Braxiatel had accomplished he would have sacked his architects and landscapers and started again.

They called her name twice before she heard it, retrieved her plasti-disc and walked in a daze to the door which led out to the flyer.

The six-seater Ormand-Seltec flyer sat incongruously on the paved courtyard, a lovingly cared-for antique in an even older setting. The cedar trees towered above it and the dwarf crastions marked out the landing pad in a symmetrical formation of greenery. There were just two of them, excluding the pilot: Bernice and the Heletian man from the shuttle flight. He politely let her step up into the flyer first, ducking to avoid the rotors which drooped lazily over the doorway.

Bernice sat by the port window and her companion sat next to her on the bench seat, close but not embarrassingly so. 'You've not been before, I take it.'

She laughed. 'Is it that obvious?'

'Oh yes. It always is, not surprisingly. They almost had to drag me from that window in the reception area when I first came. You get a little blasé after a while.' Bernice must have looked surprised, because he went on: 'Yes, I suppose it's a bit sad really. Even this quaint form of transport loses its charm and just becomes noisy after a few flights.'

The pilot swung round in his chair and waved down the aisle at them. 'Two for Archaeology – right?'

Bernice and her companion exchanged glances. 'Right,' she called back.

The pilot nodded, and was about to turn back to the controls when the man beside Bernice coughed again, just loud enough for the pilot to hear. 'Could we perhaps take the scenic route? For some of our party this is the first performance.'

The pilot and Bernice both smiled at the formality. 'The scenic route it is, sir.'

The rotors' tips lifted as they began to turn, increasing speed until the flyer eased off the ground, the tail section lifting slightly before the nose. Then the flyer turned and rose, nose still angled towards the ground, perhaps for reasons of aerodynamics, perhaps to give a better view, before setting off over the trees and towards the Mansionhouse.

Bernice broke away from the view for a moment and held out her hand to her fellow passenger. 'Professor Bernice Summerfield. My friends call me Benny.'

With a smile, the man took her hand and squeezed it gently. 'Panactum Gilmanuk – also Professor. My friends use whichever they feel most comfortable with.'

Bernice laughed. 'Thanks – Professor.'

The archaeology section was in the main Mansionhouse rather than one of the outlying buildings. The flyer dropped Benny and Gilmanuk by the huge mock-Versuvial door and lifted off again almost immediately, the cool breeze from its rotors rippling Benny's sweatshirt as she shielded her eyes against the sun and surveyed the terraces stretching away into the distance. The curvature of the planetoid was such that they seemed to drop away ever steeper until they disappeared out of sight, the sculptured waterfalls spraying their last cascades out over the edge of the world.

Gilmanuk waited for her inside the door and led the way up the huge marble staircase.

It was one of the biggest rooms that Bernice had ever

seen, perhaps a hundred metres long and over ten metres wide. The polished floor seemed to go on forever beneath a ceiling which curved up to a glass roof. The sunlight shone in bands between the leading and soaked one side of the room in yellow. It was the sides that were the most impressive. They were lined from floor to ceiling with shelves, each shelf meticulously bar-coded and struggling to hold the weight of the documents, discs and optical spheres jammed on to it.

At intervals across the width of the room were pillared partitions with wooden desks against them. At several desks sat researchers fortunate to be granted access to the collection. They worked in silence, lost deep in piles of papers and storage media or engrossed in the graphics and read-outs which played across the desktop terminals. As Benny watched, one elderly man stood and, almost reverently carrying an optical disc, opened a door at the back of the partition and went into the darkened room beyond.

'Holographic simulation,' whispered Gilmanuk. 'Despite the somewhat, er, archaic trappings they have the most modern facilities here.'

Bernice nodded, and followed Gilmanuk down towards the nearest desk. The old man behind it stood as they approached. He looked how Bernice imagined the Ancient Mariner must have been – long white beard, face wrinkled and pale with age, and eyes full of experience with perhaps a hint of suffering. She felt that even if she had not met him in this storehouse of knowledge that she would have seen depths of learning and wisdom in him.

The old man nodded to them. 'Professor Gilmanuk, how nice to see you again.' Gilmanuk smiled. 'And this is – ?' The old man peered at Bernice. She felt suddenly out of place amongst the academics and researchers. Her jeans felt rough and her sweatshirt seemed rather informal in the context of the robed figures around her. Perhaps she should have brought one of her Parisian dresses – certainly it would have been less out of place.

27

'Professor Summerfield.' Gilmanuk answered for her.

The old man was silent for a moment. Then his face sprang into life as if he had found her index entry in the dark corners of his dusty mind. 'Ah yes. Welcome to the Collection. I am Archivist Elliniko, in charge of the archaeology libraries.' He paused, surveying Bernice again. His keen eyes gave away nothing, but his cracked voice was less tactful. 'What a shame that Rhukk could not bring the findings from Phaester Osiris himself.' He held out his hand across the desk.

Bernice thought at first he wanted to shake hands with her, but she instinctively knew that was not the case. There was an awkward pause. The archivist gestured with his outstretched hand, waggling the wrinkled fingers at her, and Benny realized that he was asking for the data discs. She pulled them from her satchel and put them on the desk. The archivist frowned and reached down for them, pulling them into a tidy pile by the unnecessary blotter.

'How do I apply for a research ticket?' asked Bernice, partly to continue the conversation and have the last word, and partly because she really wanted to know.

The archivist raised an eyebrow. 'You don't,' he said with finality.

'Oh. So much for scientific advancement and the enlightening of the masses.'

The archivist blinked. But Gilmanuk smiled kindly. 'They are available by invitation only, I believe.'

'That's correct.' The archivist seemed a little surprised that Gilmanuk had deigned to speak to Bernice, but since he had, the exchange had somehow been legitimized. 'We'll see what is on your discs, and perhaps next time you come we will discuss it again.'

Short discussion, thought Bernice. But she said, 'Thanks.' And she meant it.

The archivist nodded. 'If you will excuse us?' He turned back to Gilmanuk who pulled a couple of discs from his tunic and handed them over. The archivist took them carefully.

'Lannic's aborted expedition to Menaxus. What data there is.'

'The archivist looked at Gilmanuk and Bernice could sense a new intensity in his gaze. 'Tell me what happened.' His voice was almost a whisper. 'And when does Lannic go back?'

Gilmanuk took thirty minutes to relate the story, or what he knew of it, and to answer the archivist's questions about the new expedition. Bernice had listened in silence to the whole thing. There were things she wanted to ask, but was afraid that if she spoke the other two would be reminded she was there and become less animated – or even order her out.

More than five years ago Camarina Lannic had found the Menaxus files while researching something else entirely at the Braxiatel Collection. From related records and by some brilliant deduction she had pinpointed the position on the planet's surface where the massive theatre complex referred to in the documents was sited. Obtaining a grant from the Heletian ruler – the Exec – even at the height of their expensive advance into the Rippearean territories had not been a problem. Anything to do with theatre had top priority on Heletia.

Bernice knew something of the history of Heletia: a colony originally founded by a troupe of ambitious actors who wanted to set up a permanent playhouse to stage the greatest drama of the universe. They had come a long way since then. An expansionist race, though still centred in one small habitable area of their own barren planet, they were now finally being chased back to their homelands after several years of advance. But they were still heavily influenced by their theatrical background. They fervently believed that only cultures that had a history of sophisticated dramatic production were truly civilized. To find evidence of so similar a culture within the same sector must have been quite a coup for Lannic.

And now, Gilmanuk had said, with the radiation dispersed, Lannic was going back to finish the abandoned expedition. Even in retreat the Heletians were willing to fund and supply such an archaeological venture. So they couldn't be that bad. Certainly Gilmanuk seemed pleasant enough, all trace of his former diffidence gone as he furiously polished his spectacles on a handcloth and came to the end of his story. Lannic was going back, with a small team. And Professor Panactum Gilmanuk was going too. The team was almost ready to leave, all they needed was a week to be sure the rad-count was into the safety levels, and an expert in pre-Elziran artefacts.

Bernice knew almost nothing about pre-Elziran artefacts. But as they descended the marble staircase and she suggested that since they had hours till the next shuttle they could walk back to reception rather than bother with a flyer, she was already mentally preparing herself for the expedition.

'You seem to like it here,' Bernice said as they emerged into the bright sunlight.

Gilmanuk laughed quietly, leading the way across the courtyard. 'Yes, yes I do. Though I was dreading this trip, actually. Thank you for livening it up a bit.'

'Pleasure.' They continued in silence for a while, leaving the courtyard and starting along the path away from the Mansionhouse. 'What were you dreading?' Benny hoped the interval was sufficient for her not to seem too nosy. Here in the grounds, with the terraces stretching away in front of them, it was hard to believe that anything was other than serene and calm.

'Nothing here. I like Braxiatel – it's a break from the war, after all.' He paused, as if unsure whether or not to continue. Then he came to a decision. 'It's my wife. I visited her on the way. I do sometimes.'

Benny nodded. 'You're not together any more?' She realized as soon as she asked that this was not the most perspicacious or tactful of questions.

But Gilmanuk seemed to take the question well. 'Er, no. No we're not.'

Benny nodded again, unwilling to press him on the

subject, but unable to think of a way of changing the subject without it seeming obvious.

'We had a son. He kept us together for a while.' They turned off the main drive on to a narrow path towards a line of trees. 'If living in the same accommodation means together. He was called up on his eighteenth birthday, finished training before he was eighteen and a half.' Gilmanuk's eyes were moist behind his spectacles in the afternoon sunlight.

Benny knew what was coming next. She said nothing – she was not sure Gilmanuk even remembered she was there, as he stared into the middle distance.

'He was dead within a year. Revenwik filed for permission to visit a relative she never had on Panderian Major and left that week.'

'I'm sorry.' It was inadequate, and they both knew it. But Gilmanuk smiled sadly and they continued down the path in silence.

'Isn't the reception area back that way?' Bernice asked after a while. She had a good sense of direction so the question was rhetorical. They were at the top of an avenue of tall, thin trees which stretched down (everything was down, the planet was so small) in the opposite direction.

'That's the way we came, yes.' Gilmanuk's spectacles caught the sunlight as he nodded quickly, as if the question had startled him out of reverie. 'But we can carry on the way we're going. The scenery is more interesting – I should like to show you the Garden of Whispers.'

'Do we have time?' It seemed to Benny that they barely had time to walk the distance the flyer had brought them, let alone take some detour round a garden, however impressive.

'Oh yes, we have time. It's actually a shorter distance to keep going in our current direction than to turn back. But it's only a three-hour walk from the back door of the house round to the front.'

It took Benny a moment to work out what he was talking about. But looking down the length of the gardens ahead of her and seeing them dip away so steeply, she could believe that walking round the whole planetoid was not such a silly notion. She rather liked the idea of being able to walk away from the Mansionhouse and arrive back at the other side of it. 'Like *Alice in Wonderland*,' she muttered.

'I'm sorry?'

'Or was it *Through the Looking Glass*? Sorry – nothing. Lead me to this whispering garden, Professor.'

The Garden of Whispers was one of the most impressive areas of the grounds of the Braxiatel Collection. The centrepiece was a small lake, over which willows wept and oak trees towered. A perfect lawn stretched beyond the trees, bounded by the central driveway on one side and high hedges backing on to the parterres of the Small Trianon the other. There were statues – humanoid figures – positioned throughout the garden. Several were lined up along the hedge, facing back towards the Mansionhouse, the roof of which was just visible gleaming above the foreshortened horizon. For a second Bernice imagined the statues' arms poking through the hedge and emerging bodiless the other side, grasping for a hold on passers-by and feeling sightlessly for prey. The image seemed vaguely familiar – from a vis-cast or play she had seen.

At the far side of the lake, raised on a vantage point, was a summer-house – stone caryatids rising to a domed roof were the only walls. Inside the summer-house Benny could see several more figures, posed and immobile, as if some of the statuary that hid amongst the trees beside the lake had crept into the summer-house to admire the view.

Gilmanuk led the way through the trees towards the summer-house which, he assured Bernice, afforded an excellent view of the garden. 'Every single statue is visible from the summer-house, all forty-seven of them. And it's also the best place to hear the whispers.'

Bernice could already hear the whispers. It was the wind picking its way through the willow trees and playing on the lake's surface. Not real wind, she reminded herself as they passed a stone figure poised on one leg as he raised a sword forward and high above his head. Everything here was artificial, except for the raw data in the libraries and archives.

They paused outside the summer-house before going up the three shallow steps and stepping inside the ring of female figures which held up the roof for them. A single stone statue stood, ushering them in, and as they passed it seemed that it was she who was whispering to them. 'Mandrine – the Archalite goddess of plenty,' Bernice told Gilmanuk. He probably already knew that, and she hoped he had not seen her read it off the plinth. She had already impressed him with her understanding of pre-Elziran culture, secure in the knowledge that if he needed an expert in the subject he was not one himself. Now she wanted to make sure he knew her peripheral knowledge was also impeccable.

They turned from the three statues inside the summer-house without giving them a second look and stared out across the lake.

'Actually, it's pronounced *Marn-dry-nee*,' said a voice quietly behind them. Gilmanuk looked startled, and Bernice was sure her feet left the ground for a second.

She could see how she had mistaken him for a statue. He was wearing a close-cut grey suit, and he was standing perfectly still. His features were angular but attractive – Bernice thought *well-chiselled* was an apt description. He was tall, thin, appeared to be a little older than Bernice and seemed completely at ease.

'I'm sorry if I startled you.' He smiled, managing to seem both friendly and completely detached. 'I too was admiring the view, although I cannot stay long I'm afraid – I shall have to return to my researches soon.'

'It is quite a view.' Bernice was keen to show she had recovered from the shock, but the man hardly seemed to hear her. He pushed forward between Bernice and Gilmanuk.

'This summer-house was constructed by Dupok,' he con-

33

tinued as if she had not spoken. 'He worked from a holographic model. In fact the whole site was modelled as a simularity before construction began.'

'An interesting technique,' said Gilmanuk, 'although rather expensive on such a scale, I would imagine.'

'I imagine so.' The man turned to go.

'Hardly original, though.'

He stopped in mid-turn and looked at Bernice. 'Oh?'

'Much of the design is after all based on the ancient Palace of Versailles. Richard Mique worked from three-dimensional models when he created the small buildings in the grounds there. He gave the models of the Temple of Love and the Belvedere to Marie Antoinette.'

The man laughed. '*Touché.*' Then he turned and left, disappearing into the trees behind the summer-house without a backward glance.

'Professor Summerfield – Benny,' Gilmanuk had followed the exchange thoughtfully.

'Yes?'

'I'd have to check things with Lannic, of course. But – would you consider taking a part in our expedition to Menaxus?'

Bernice swallowed, resisted the urge to hug him, and said quietly, 'Well, I'd obviously need to sort out a few things.' She thought for a moment of the small round device the Doctor had given her. There was no reason why the TARDIS tracker/locator would not work as effectively from Menaxus as from Osiris – if she chose to activate it. And what could possibly go wrong on an archaeological dig? 'In principle I don't see any problem,' she said, and saw Gilmanuk's relief as he turned back to the view.

Then she remembered what he had said about the previous expedition, and she thought of her own experiences on Heaven. And she hoped the tracker/locator was still in her satchel.

Source Document 2

Plan of the Pentillanian Theatre of Menaxus

Loaned to the Stanarbrian Library by unnamed beneficiary

Sketch believed to be by De Witte, c2314. Not to scale.

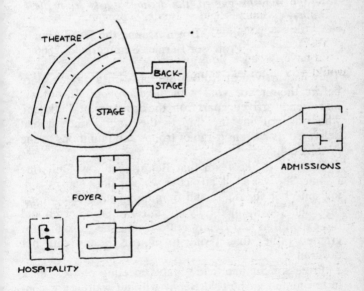

Chapter 2

A Bond Honoured

The first principle of archaeology is documentation.
It is the willingness – the passion – for recording
minutiae of excavation data to the point of pedantry
that separates the men from the boys. Or, in the case
of an excavation where material as well as historical
wealth may be gained, the archaeologists from the
looters.

Down Among the Dead Men
– Professor Bernice Summerfield, 2566

They had arrived at Kotosh Station with a day to spare
before their rendezvous with the *Icoronata*. The others
had already arrived, apart from the orbiter pilot, Lefkhani,
who was bringing the ship to the station once it had
delivered its current cargo of troops and munitions to the
Arfalla colonies.

The first of the team that Benny met was Camarina
Lannic. She was a tall, attractive woman, dark hair cascad-
ing onto her shoulders and framing a round face with a
firm chin. She seemed fully in control of both herself and
the expedition and Benny noticed that she took this for
granted rather than trying to impress Benny with her
position.

'Professor Summerfield? Status meeting on "C" deck
in ten minutes,' she told Benny without waiting for confirmation or acknowledgement.

'How do you do – you must be Lannic,' Benny said
quietly to her retreating back. She might not be impeded

36

by all the niceties of social etiquette, but everyone was on time for the meeting.

The agenda consisted mainly of Lannic going over the events and discoveries of her previous expedition, with precious little time reserved at the end for a few questions and rather fewer answers. They all introduced themselves briefly at the start of the meeting, stating their names and responsibilities. There seemed to be two camps; the military either knew each other already or were indifferent, and the archaeologists seemed at least to have heard of each other. Benny was the odd one out, and this was probably why she was asked to go first.

'Professor Bernice Summerfield. I won't bore you with qualifications and past experience, but I'm here to advise on any artefacts we uncover and generally lend a hand in the excavation work.' There was barely any reaction from anyone; either they were nervous about their own performances to come, or they were more interested in what Lannic had to say. 'My hobbies include bug collecting and poker,' she added with a smile. Nobody laughed, although several of them looked puzzled. Lannic glared at her, so Benny coughed politely and sat down.

Next up was Assok Bannahilk. It took Benny a while to work out that Assok was a rank rather than a name. Bannahilk was a well built man, stocky almost, with a moustache. Like all the soldiers he had close-cut hair, and like all the Heletians, his eyes were grey. 'Assok Bannahilk – in charge of the military side of things and responsible for safety and logistics.' He spoke in a quiet and authoritative voice, but the way his hands twisted together and his eyes darted round the room made Benny wonder what emotions he was bottling up inside. 'The military will already know me, and they'll know that I like things kept tight.' His small eyes swept round the assembled company, and only the tall man sitting beside him was anything other than indifferent – was he stifling a smile, or grimacing?

'The military will also know,' Bannahilk continued, 'that I share their view that this expedition is not necessarily the best use of our limited resources in these difficult times.' He paused again, this time to glare at Lannic. She met his gaze without flinching, and it was Bannahilk who lowered his eyes first. 'That said, we shall of course give our fullest support to this – this fool's errand.' He sat down quickly without sparing Lannic another glance.

'Thank you, Assok,' Lannic said without looking up from the notes on her clip-pak. 'We are grateful for your help. Though I doubt the Exec would think this a "fool's errand." It is on his patronage and for the greater glory of all Heletia that we undertake this.' She looked across the desk at him, and Bannahilk shuffled uncomfortably in her stare. 'Nothing that brings us closer to the Exec, nothing that enhances his standing in the eyes of the people – or ourselves in his eyes – is foolish. Nothing.'

Bannahilk looked embarrassed, but he did not respond. After a short pause, the tall man sitting beside him came to his rescue. 'Fortalexa,' he said as he stood and introduced himself.

Fortalexa was, he said, an electronics and communications expert. He towered over his commanding officer, and managed to get the only laugh of the meeting with an aside about keeping them up to date on the malquatch results (whatever that meant). He seemed to be about Benny's age.

Fortalexa finished up with comments clearly aimed at both Lannic and his commanding officer. 'I think we all share Assok Bannahilk's frustration at not being in the front line to contribute directly to the war, especially the way things are going at the moment. However, we are of course also conscious of the contribution we *are* able to make on a higher plane to the advancement of archaeology and our understanding of the dramatic arts.'

Benny wondered how he got away with it. A couple of times she saw Bannahilk twist his fingers in frustration or anger, but he said nothing. He even smiled his gratitude to Fortalexa as he sat down again.

The other military personnel Benny assumed to be the grunts, just along to do the fetching and carrying. Tashman

38

and Krayn were both muscle-bound troopers who could probably kill more efficiently than they could eat. Neither of them seemed as disappointed with this posting as their commander made out. Krayn seemed to be about twice as intelligent as his comrade in arms.

Cambri was short, dark, female, and looked like if she met Tashman and Krayn on a dark night she'd get the better of them both. She obviously *was* hankering for the battlefield, and Benny made a mental note to include the word 'psychotic' when she got round to mentioning Cambri in her diary.

Of the archaeologists, Lannic was by far the youngest. She was also the most self-assured. Benny had already met poor old diffident Panactum Gilmanuk, of course. The last one in the party was Leontium Klasvik. He was the expert in excavation and archaeological techniques – an archaeologist's archaeologist. He was about the same age as Gilmanuk, but tall and stooped. He came across as an officious dodderer whose nose was severely out of joint because he wasn't in charge.

'I am glad to be able to offer my humble services and expertise,' Klasvik offered – he sounded far from humble. 'I feel honoured to be the most experienced field archaeologist here.' He smiled round the room, his face cracked with the effort. 'I'm also very pleased that my old colleague Gilmanuk will be joining us – I know how difficult it has been for him to find time for any *real* archaeology since he has had his personal problems. I am sure we are all glad to see that they are now resolved.'

From the looks of the others assembled, it seemed that none of them had even been aware of any problems. But they were now. Benny kept her thoughts to herself, and waited to see how Gilmanuk would deal with the jibe.

Surprisingly, he acknowledged it immediately, and as a result regained at least as much respect as Klasvik had tried to strip away. As soon as he had introduced himself, Gilmanuk turned to Klasvik, and thanked him for the comment. 'I am – er – grateful, Leontium, for those few kind words. Things have not been easy, as you know, since

– er,' he broke off with a cough. 'Since my son's death and my subsequent problems. It is good of you to bring this to the attention of our friends and colleagues. I am sure we have all lost loved ones in this war, but that makes it no easier to bear the burden, of course.' He sat down and began to polish his spectacles. Benny reached across and squeezed Gilmanuk's shoulder. He smiled back at her weakly.

The introductions over, Lannic took the floor again and began to describe the previous expedition and what they could expect to find on Menaxus. As Lannic started to go through her slides, Benny wondered if she would have volunteered to join them if she had initially met any of the members of the team other than Gilmanuk.

'Ditch the recorders.' Lannic was firm. The lander would only take so much weight. The grandly but inappropriately named *Pride of Padrillion* was a lander cobbled together from a clapped-out satellite-hopper with auxiliary fuel tanks strapped and welded to its underside in the optimistic expectation that it would not have to land anywhere where the ground was uneven. It sat uneasily and incongruously in the landing bay of the slightly less dilapidated orbit-ship *Icoronata* – named after the bloody battle for that planet, which the Heletians had of course won.

Tashman and Cambri began loading the crates onto the carrier, and Klasvik glared at Lannic. They were his recorders. He had a passion for recording the minutiae of excavations, and insufficient assertiveness to object in front of the crew.

Tashman knew that too, but he drove the carrier back out of the hold, past the piles of provisions and the antiquated equipment spared grudgingly from Heletia's dwindling reserves, and into the orbit-ship without a word. A glance at Lannic had told him who would win the contest. Drive them in, drive them out again – that suited Tashman fine. Just so long as it kept him paid. And out of the front line.

He exchanged glances with Cambri as she drove the

other carrier past him, tense and upright as she negotiated the gap between Tashman's carrier and a pile of crates. A slight raise of one dark eyebrow signified she agreed with his reading. Tashman knew she would rather be at the battlefront, knew that she saw her attachment to the expedition as a diversion from the serious business of killing and (probably) being killed. It was a business Tashman was happy to leave to people like Cambri.

The war would catch up with them soon enough, the front line was already back to the moons of Dosardus. Optron would be next, and then Gluvene, reversing the order of their acquisition. Last in, first out.

Leontium Klasvik was still seething when he reached the flight deck. If anything, he was more angry than he had been in the hold. It was easier to be angry at Lannic when she wasn't there. She was brilliant – he had just begun to think of her as a potential protégée, although this said more about Klasvik's age than Lannic's youth. And now she seemed to be ditching the fundamentals of archaeology even before they had started on the excavations.

Not that Klasvik had worked with Lannic before. But he did know people who had ... and she certainly had a reputation. In the last five years her contributions to theatre history had been astounding. When he had discovered he was to work with her, he had scanned all her work. She had written a remarkable amount since her graduation, most of it covering new ground though she was never too proud to acknowledge any previous work in her fields of study. Klasvik was very much of the opinion that credit should be given where due – he had failed otherwise brilliant students for not acknowledging sources.

He had first heard of her about five years ago, but her papers went back five years before that. Some of them were quite brilliant, it was odd he didn't remember a stir when they were published. But then Klasvik was an archaeologist, not a theatrologist. His own papers had caused stirs enough. He sighed as he reached the end of the corridor to the flight deck. *New Brasiscan Discoveries*

41

from the Time of Corneille III – now there was a paper. First published in *The Archaeologist* in 3941. Or was it 3942, in *Brasiscan Diaries*?

'Everything on cue?' Krayn was strapping himself into the control seat.

Klasvik grunted and sprawled in one of the crew seats.

'That good, eh?' Krayn turned back to the deck, scooping a quantity of plasma-gel on to his index finger and applying it to the plastic suction pad on the pilot end of the com-connect. He glanced at the reflection of the lead archaeologist in the sightscreen above him. Klasvik was lying back in the seat, his eyes closed and his lips moving silently. Krayn smiled – he certainly wasn't praying, but he probably was cursing. Cursing Lannic.

Krayn attached the pad to his temple and keyed in to the com-net. His eyes glazed over and he sat back in his chair. The antiquated computer net fed antiquated data into the pilot's brain, which wondered why it was bothering to give him such basic information. The reason was simple enough – it was all the computer knew. Krayn ignored it, and followed his own thoughts instead.

As she boarded the lander, Bernice was beginning to have second thoughts about the whole thing. It seemed to be degenerating into a glorified treasure hunt rather than serious scientific research. And they hadn't even arrived at the site yet.

The scientists all seemed to know their stuff – well, all except for herself. But Bernice had taken the opportunity of the long flight back from Braxiatel to read up on Heletian history and get a basic grounding in theatrology and recent research. She had been grateful that the Braxiatel space dock had such an academically oriented disc library, although it was scarcely surprising.

As the members of the team drifted in and took their places in the lander, strapping themselves down in the flight seats, Benny went through their names to check she remembered them from the initial briefing.

Lefkhani was the final member of the team. He had not attended that initial briefing, and was afforded the dubious pleasure of remaining on board the *Icoronata* in orbit while the others were on the surface. He was a quiet, nondescript man who seemed happy to do his job and unhappy to be asked to do anything else. His look of anguish if anyone suggested he help in some task other than piloting the ship was so extreme that nobody ever did ask him. Benny was not sure whether this was just luck on his part or indicative of an inner judgmental ability of which there was no other external sign.

As she watched him on the main screen, counting off the last seconds before the drop, Benny began to wonder if perhaps Lefkhani had not got the best deal after all.

The lander dropped towards the surface of Menaxus like a well engineered stone. The auxiliary fuel tanks glowed a deep red despite their makeshift heat shield as the craft entered the atmosphere. Then the wing motors cut in and the ship started its powered glide.

'Glide' is a graceful word. It suggests a smooth, easy path through the air to a gentle landing. If any of the crew of the lander had been asked to describe their descent, only Krayn would perhaps have used the word 'glide.' But he had been taught the theory before experiencing the practice.

As the ship began its glide, it also began to suffer a buffeting from the Menaxan atmosphere. Lannic, sitting in the co-pilot's chair, staring at the sight-screen view forward, experienced no sense of *déjà-vu*. Seeing the surface loom closer through what she had taken for static and white noise but now could see was sheeting rain, she felt she was landing on a completely different planet.

'I'll need somewhere solid to put down,' Krayn shouted above the stress and motor noises.

'Solid?' Lannic wasn't sure what he meant. 'What's the problem?'

Krayn punched up a closer image of the ground below.

43

The computer had already seen it, and so therefore had Krayn. But Lannic was surprised.

The whole surface appeared to be a sea of mud, with water standing on it and the rain splashing in. 'There's no way to tell how firm it is, or how deep. No way without landing in it and that might be too late.'

Lannic reached across and keyed up a map of her previous excavations over the actual landscape. Everything they had uncovered was now buried in the mud. 'There – the roof of the Admissions Complex. It should be flat and higher than the surrounding land.'

'Will it be strong enough to take our weight?' Fortalexa was leaning over from his communications console.

'One way to find out.'

'Will the theatre itself have a stronger roof?' Krayn pointed at the semicircular area shaded on to the overlay map.

'It's an amphitheatre,' said Lannic, slumping back in her chair and letting the straps tighten across her chest. 'It doesn't have a roof.' The plastic sheeting they had stretched over it to keep out the dust – even assuming it was still intact – would never make a landing pad.

Krayn raised an eyebrow. Fortalexa shook his head and turned back to his console. 'Must have been difficult to bring the house down,' he said. Nobody laughed. He smiled humourlessly as another jolt pushed him forward in his seat by way of a reprimand.

Whether by skill or by luck, the *Pride of Padrillion* settled easily, her pads sinking a few centimetres into the soft mud and skidding slightly before gaining purchase on the roof of the complex. Her rad-counter began assimilating and analysing data derived from the heavy-metal content of the atmosphere, and her crew breathed heartfelt (and only slightly radioactive) sighs of relief as they unbuckled their safety harnesses. They were all grateful they were down and safe.

A space had been cleared in the centre of the hold. The

majority of the supplies and equipment were still waiting to be unloaded, but some had been dumped unceremoniously outside the lander, and more pushed back towards the sides of the craft. A long low crate containing flasks of purified water acted as a table, with most of the crew sitting round on smaller packages. Of the others, Krayn was checking the contents of the crates, marking them off on his clip-pak as he went. Tashman wandered after him like a lost dog. Cambri was checking off supplies in another area of the hold. Apart from them, only Fortalexa was absent, monitoring the newscasts over the com-net in the control cabin. The others were paying attention to Klasvik as he went over the maps and charts.

'Using standard techniques, and keeping records by hand as far as we can,' his voice echoed round the metal walls, catching in the plastic crates on the rebound, 'I estimate a ninety-seven per cent chance of complete excavation of the major area in thirty-four days.' He peered at the faces surrounding him, attentive to him. Even Lannic seemed happy to accept his plan and was nodding slowly.

Gilmanuk leaned forward a little and coughed politely. Odd for someone so knowledgeable about the extrovert world of the theatre to be so diffident. But Gilmanuk's expertise was not in performance, but in the structure of the buildings where the performances took place.

Klasvik glanced round. All faces were now turned expectantly towards Gilmanuk. Perhaps there was an element of performance after all. Klasvik frowned, but said nothing. If Gilmanuk felt he had to speak, then it was important.

'I don't wish to cause problems, you understand, but – well . . .' Gilmanuk paused for a moment, pulling off his spectacles and polishing them vigorously on a handcloth. He smiled faintly and his small round face seemed to wrinkle with the effort. 'Thirty-four days. Don't you think that is a little, umm – well . . .' He broke off, as if at a loss. Nobody spoke. Nobody ever interrupted Gilmanuk – if they did, he looked so embarrassed that it shamed them.

45

Gilmanuk started again; abrupt, hurried, keen to finish his soliloquy: 'Well, isn't it just a bit – don't you think?'.

Lannic was the first to gather her thoughts. 'It is an ambitious schedule, Gilmanuk. We do have to complete and leave before the war reaches us, after all. But you are the expert on the structure we intend to uncover. Do you think we should allow longer?'

'No – no – no. I'm sure Klasvik has his sums right, and I do appreciate the urgency of this . . . matter.'

'Thank you,' murmured Klasvik, and avoided catching Bernice's eye when he realized she had heard him.

'But you will be careful, won't you?' Gilmanuk shuffled on the crate he was perching on. 'With my theatre, I mean.'

Klasvik looked up abruptly, and found Gilmanuk already watching him.

'I'm sorry, Klasvik. I know you are in charge of the archaeology and you consider this to be *your* site – just as Lannic considers it to be *her* expedition. It's all a question of degree, really.'

'Go on,' encouraged Bannahilk. He smiled, having no proprietorial feelings about anything but his uniform and the military equipment.

'Well, I'm sorry to get possessive, and I understand you feel the same about your own areas of interest, but the theatre – the structure, the building itself – is mine. At least, to me it is.' He broke off and picked at a fingernail. 'I just want you to be careful with it.'

For a moment nobody stirred. Then Bernice pulled herself upright and walked round the crates to where Gilmanuk still played with his nail. She put her hand on his shoulder and he looked up. 'I know what you mean,' she said. 'We all do. Of course this is Lannic's expedition – and Klasvik's site and my artefacts, if we find any evidence of production or the things pertaining to it. And we are using Bannahilk's equipment. And it is your theatre.'

Gilmanuk put his hand up to his shoulder, covering Bernice's, and beamed. 'Thank you, my friends,' he nodded. Behind him Krayn grimaced at Tashman. And

Tashman's answering smirk froze as Fortalexa hurried in, eyes dancing in search of Bannahilk.

The others watched as Fortalexa bent and whispered in his officer's ear for a moment. Bannahilk frowned and stood up, drawing Fortalexa away across the hold. Klasvik gestured to Bernice as he caught her eye, but she shook her head – 'Don't know,' she mouthed across the crates, shrugging.

'Well, there's something going on.' Lannic was less worried about speaking aloud.

Bannahilk returned, Fortalexa following. There was a short silence as he stood stiffly in front of everyone. 'Gluvene has fallen,' he said, and the hold erupted with exclamations and questions. The archaeologists were all talking at once, Bannahilk and Fortalexa waiting quietly for them to finish. Eventually the noise died down enough for Bannahilk to have some hope of making himself heard. 'Fortalexa got it straight off the net – I'm afraid there's no room for doubt.'

'What about Optron? we never heard the Rippeareans had even reached it, let alone moved on the Gluvene.' Gilmanuk was even more nervous than he had been earlier.

'That's right,' Fortalexa answered. 'Unfortunately, the Rippeareans never went near it. They came through the wings.'

'They what?' Lannic was as aghast as the others.

'They came round it. Optron is still held by the Seventh Armoured. But they're cut off, they have nowhere to fall back to now that Gluvene's fallen. They've been written out of the war – surgically removed. All they can do is stay put.'

'Can't they break out – retake Gluvene?'

'No, Klasvik, they cannot. They're a buffer force. They're equipped for defence, not attack. Their strength is in their fortifications, the battlement satellites and antispace missile systems. They can't rescript the satellites as ballistics and the ASMs would make lousy space-attack weapons.'

47

For a moment nobody knew what to say. Nobody except Tashman. 'S'blood!' he said from across the hold. Loudly. Everyone turned to look at him and he looked down at his feet. 'Sorry.'

'His brother's with the Seventh,' Krayn apologized.

'I shouldn't worry about him, then.'

Tashman swallowed, his eyes glazing.

'I'm serious,' Bannahilk went on quickly. 'When I said they'd been written out I meant it. They can't move from Optron, and the Rippeareans won't go in after them – why should they bother attacking that fortress? All they have to do is keep going now till they reach Heletia. When the war is over, the Seventh will surrender, and Optron will cede back.'

Fortalexa smiled. 'If you want somebody to worry about, I should consider the sectors directly on the line of attack from the swing into Gluvene and on to Heletia. The whole dynamic of the advance just changed completely.'

'From the manner in which you went out of your way to mention that, I guess this is probably a silly question, but – ' Bernice paused, considering how best to phrase what she wanted to say. 'But are there any planets in particular which are directly in the attack line that you suggest we consider?'

Fortalexa looked at Bannahilk. His commander nodded for him to continue. 'Oh yes,' he said. 'This one.'

'And what do you suggest? We can't leave, not without completing the expedition.' Lannic looked across at Klasvik as she spoke. He nodded – he was not leaving now, not without some excavation at least.

'We can, and we will.'

'When? The danger can't be that imminent – this has only just happened, right?'

'That's true, Klasvik,' said Bannahilk. 'You just outlined a plan to excavate the site in thirty-four days. The absolute maximum I can give you now is eight.'

'Eight?' Gilmanuk was appalled.

'Eight. And that assumes a steady advance by the Rippeareans rather than a lightning strike directly at Heletia without worrying about pockets of resistance getting left behind.'

'In which case they wouldn't worry about us.' Cambri was picking at the plastic of a crate of dried foodstuffs at the far end of the hold. But her voice carried clearly.

Bannahilk rounded on her sternly. 'Want to bet your life on it?'

'Assok Bannahilk.' Lannic's voice was just as sharp. The officer turned back to her. 'How long if the Rippeareans do make such a strike?'

'Four days – at the outside.'

'And when would we know that's their intention.'

'Real soon now,' said Fortalexa. 'Today, anyway.'

'Is it likely?' Klasvik was already weighing up the alternatives, the risks of heavy-duty approaches to removing the top layers of ground.

'Likely? Who can say what their plans are now? But put yourself in their position. They have the choice of a steady advance to do things properly or a lightning strike and an almost certain quick victory. Given that choice in a war like this one, the choice between another few years or another few months of this carnage ... Well, I know which one I'd go for.'

Bannahilk waited a moment for a response, and when none was forthcoming marched out of the hold, Fortalexa in close pursuit.

'Okay everyone,' Lannic was immediately poring over the maps and schedules rolled out on the crates in front of them. 'I want a workable plan to get in to the main theatre complex, assuming a schedule of at most two days. That will leave us at least two days of real study, depending how generous the Rippeareans are and how many corners Bannahilk will cut for us. I want the plan and a risk assessment within an hour.'

Sitting on a crate swinging his legs and staring at an empty space on the floor, Tashman decided his earlier comment had been relevant after all.

* * *

The distant sun was sinking very fast now. Its violet light diffused through the gaps between the mountain tops and reflected off the slopes of snow and ice. After another moment the light dimmed a little, the shadows dipped and lengthened, and the snowy mountains became black against the rim of the sun. Then it was gone.

Darkness.

'So what happens now?' asked Ace.

The Doctor turned slightly to look at her, his back resting against the pestigogo tree. He raised his hat slightly as if to see her properly, his dark eyes still shaded. 'We wait.'

They waited.

'Then what?'

'Shhh. Be patient. There'll be another one along in a minute.'

Ace was patient. For a full five seconds.

'Another what?'

'Another sun.' She could not see his face, but she could feel the Doctor looking in her direction, and she somehow knew that he could see her.

A red glow touched the branches at the very top of the tree. It began to spread down towards them. Ace turned and peered back over her shoulder. Sure enough, a sun was rising behind her – a red sun this time. When she looked back the Doctor had gone. She jumped up, walked round the grey trunk and flopped down again next to the Doctor. It was as if he had been there all his life, waiting for the sunrise.

He pointed at the glowing disc with the handle of his umbrella, holding it impossibly by the very point. 'They follow the colours of the spectrum. You've missed infra-red, I'm afraid.'

Ace peered closer, and indeed it did seem that the sun was already glowing a little orange in with the red. 'How long does it take?'

'A day? From sunrise to sunset, oh, about . . .' He pulled out a gold watch on a chain, flicked it open and stared at it for a moment. 'Four gleebs.'

'That long?'

'Oh yes. In the summer.'

The sun continued its barely perceptible rise. It was more orange than red now.

'What's a gleeb?'

He didn't seem to hear. 'It slows down a bit as it gets higher, then speeds up on the way down.' He gestured, his hand playing the sun. They watched for a while longer.

'You've been here before.'

He smiled, but it was a dark smile with little humour in it. 'A couple of times. I staked my reputation on the beauty of the sunrise here once. Amongst other things. When I was young and fancy-free.'

'Young?' Ace was not sure the Doctor had ever been young.

'Well, younger anyway. Still young enough to bowl a good *Chinaman*, but not too old to appreciate the inexplicable splendour of it all.'

'Is that why you left?'

The Doctor turned fully to her. He leaned thoughtfully on the handle of his umbrella, its point dug into the ground in front of him. 'Left where?'

'Gallifrey. You know – to see the sights. Was it for "inexplicable splendour" like this?'

It was as if he had suddenly lost interest. The Doctor unplugged his umbrella from the ground with a flourish, laid it down beside him, then shifted down the tree, folded his hands theatrically on his chest and lay down. His hat magically tipped itself forward as he lay back until it covered his eyes. Ace tried to peer underneath it. Was he asleep? Had she offended him? Or had he *really* lost interest?

When he spoke, nearly a minute later, just as the very centre of the sun began to edge into the yellow, it took Ace by surprise.

'I left for lots of reasons, Ace.' She was all attention. The sun continued its cabaret without an audience. 'You know, there was one tutor who wasn't such a stick-in-the-mud as the others.'

51

'Like Mr Briggs. He was okay. Friday afternoon French – great fun. Or the weaponry officer on Belmos, not that he knew anything about weapons.'

The Doctor continued undeterred: 'I thought he might understand. So one day I went to him, after temporal engineering, and I asked him what it was all for. Why were we learning all these *boring* things? Why were we stuck in observation galleries and lecture halls, watching and learning rather than out there – *doing* it all?'

'Yeah. I used to wonder that. So I went out and did it all.' She clenched her fist and her teeth as she remembered the fire and the glory. And the death. She thought for a moment of the recent stained face of Julian Winmill's mother, holding his orphaned data-pad as the tears splashed on to its casing.

The Doctor raised his hat and looked across at her, as if he had forgotten she was there. 'Yes. Well, it was a bit easier for you.' He settled back into his former position. 'Anyway, he said that the theory was as important as the practice. He said that without knowing what you were doing, you couldn't know what you were doing.' His mouth smiled under the hat. 'He said I had a propensity for vulgar facetiousness. *Me* – can you imagine?'

His voice was quiet, almost soporific, and Ace found herself drifting off. She thought about school, about home, about killing Daleks in the Hai Dow system and about sponge pudding and custard. She tried to concentrate on what the Doctor was saying, but somehow the more she concentrated, the less she was able to focus her attention.

'I tried to follow their arguments, but I still felt it was all topsy-turvy. All backwards. All theory and no reality. However exciting and interesting it is for the first half-hour, just doing the same things repetitively gets tedious . . .'

It didn't help that they kept shifting round the tree; the Doctor edging round to keep pace with the sun he wasn't watching as it moved overhead, Ace following the Doctor to try to hear the words she wasn't listening to. She was just wondering if he was doing it on purpose, when she realized he had stopped talking.

She did a quick back-track, trying to remember what he had last said. She thought it was something like 'And do you know what I said to her?' but she could not be sure. So she kept quiet.

The sun was a flaming ball of indigo as it continued its descent. They were back where they had started, and Ace had seen it all before. Well wicked. She shuffled her position, but it was still uncomfortable. Funny that – the ground had been so soft and inviting when they had first arrived. When the sky was green and everything was new and exciting. She stole a look at the Doctor. He was leaning forward, staring intently at the mountains as the light shone off their slopes and played over their peaks. It looked as if he was set for the next thousand years.

Ace fidgeted a bit more, but there was no reaction. She coughed – nothing.

'Doctor?'

He turned slowly towards her, the brim of his hat shading his eyes so that all she could see were the points of the pupils as they reflected the darkness. 'Hmm?'

'I'm bored – shall we go?'

For a moment he was silent. Then he was suddenly on his feet, TARDIS key in hand. Ace leaped up too, dusting herself down. She hurried after the Doctor as he strode purposefully towards the TARDIS, key itching for the lock.

'You know, Ace,' the Doctor said as she caught up, 'that's *exactly* what I said.' The Doctor's eyes lit up and his face opened into a huge smile. He turned the key and the door swung open.

'No!' Benny was adamant. 'I can't accept that. I'm sorry. The damage to the fabric and whatever is actually within the theatre area, whatever artefacts remain, could be tremendous.' They were behaving more like Ace than like experienced archaeologists.

Lannic sighed. They had been through it a dozen times.

'You do accept that there is no other way? Unless we blast our way through the mud, we're not going to even get to the main complex in the time we have. Whatever artefacts there may or may not be will simply stay there.'

'Well maybe that's not such a bad thing.' Benny looked round the group, her eyes begging for some support. Gilmanuk was silent – had been for the last hour. Probably too embarrassed to say what he thought, and probably didn't think it would matter anyway. Tashman, Krayn and Cambri were unloading what they could into a temporary holding section immediately outside the ship. They had erected a prefabricated covered area to keep the rain off. It was set fairly securely into the mud. Tashman was driving a loader back and forth between the area and the hold, avoiding the debate. Cambri was sorting out the crates as they were unloaded.

Krayn occasionally wandered over, muttered unhelpful comments, then wandered off again, organizing Tashman's outbound loads. He had arrived in time to catch Bernice's remarks, and rubbed his nose on the back of his hand thoughtfully.

'I agree with Professor Summerfield,' Klasvik said, looking directly at Lannic. 'We are archaeologists. If we cannot uncover the past without destroying it, then perhaps we should let it lie until somebody else can.'

'Even the Rippeareans?'

'Yes, if necessary. Remember the damage Rumbelow and Proctor inflicted on the remains of Trajan Five – great discoveries, yes, but who can tell what was lost because of their ineptitude? I'm sorry, but Bernice is right.' Benny noticed how he paused slightly before using her Christian name. 'We are letting our enthusiasm cloud our scientific judgement.'

'What would you suggest then? That we leave, abandon the site, and maybe it will never be excavated? Or maybe the Rippeareans will destroy it as they pass.'

'What do you mean by "blast"?' Krayn was standing almost directly behind Lannic when he asked. His voice caught her by surprise.

'I'm sorry?'

'The mud's not *that* dense. It's not like blasting through rock. I should know, I've been wading about in it.'

Klasvik smiled humourlessly. 'So we can see.'

But Bernice had seen Krayn thinking. He wasn't muttering inane comments now – he had something to contribute. 'What do you suggest?'

'Phason bursts will blow your relics to bits, you're right. There's no way we could keep the impact to a low level in that lot and still make an impression. It's viscous, not solid.'

'So it wouldn't work anyway, is that what you're saying?'

'That's about it, yes. But you could use the water cannon to tunnel your way in.'

They were silent for a moment.

'Just a thought.' Krayn shrugged and turned away.

'Wait.' Lannic was on her feet. 'Would that actually work?'

'I don't see why not.'

'We'd need some way of shoring up the tunnel,' said Klasvik, 'to stop the mud just running back in again.'

'We've got loads of that prefab plastic sheeting. It seems solid enough. We should be able to slide that in as we wash the mud away.'

'How long would it take?' Lannic asked.

Krayn shrugged. 'Getting it shored up is the longest job. Using the cannon should be quick enough. And it's not like we're short of water out there to spray.'

'Ahem,' Gilmanuk coughed quietly. But it was enough: he had everyone's attention. 'A couple of points, if I may?'

'Of course.' Benny beat Lannic to it, and smiled an unfelt apology.

'First, I don't believe that we will need to shore up the tunnel for long. The surface is very fluid, but I imagine the mud gets quite densely packed very soon once you burrow through it. It will support itself, at least for a while. And we shan't be here for long.'

'That's probably right,' admitted Krayn. 'Might make the tunnelling slower as we get deeper, though.'

'Well, we can't have everything.' Lannic turned back to Gilmanuk. 'And the second thing?'

'Well, you are concerned about possible damage as you break through into the main theatre.' He was talking to Bernice. She nodded as he went on. 'I agree. And I think the water cannon may cause damage too.'

Lannic gritted her teeth, but Gilmanuk continued before she could interject. 'However, I think there is least chance of damage if we aim to break in to the area immediately *behind* the main theatre, beside the back-stage area – here.' He pointed at the map spread out on the crates in front of them.

Benny nodded slowly. 'Yes, I agree. There's not likely to be much there. In the backstage area itself, yes – prompt lists, props, even remnants of costumes have been found in previous excavations, but never anything of consequence *between* backstage and the auditorium.' She crossed her fingers behind her back, hoping she was right.

'And damage to the structure?'

'Would, I believe, be minimal, Lannic. There may be construction around the area that we need to get through, but it is not an integral part of the theatre. It's not marked on the De Witte sketch, so it cannot be of the original structure. I believe we can – and should – risk it.'

Lannic looked round the assembled group. There was an enthusiasm in everyone's eyes now – no one seemed to doubt that they should at least try it. 'Very well,' she said, and there was a general laugh as the tension was expelled. Gilmanuk reached across and actually shook her hand, Krayn slapped Klasvik on the back (much to the archaeologist's surprise) and even Tashman smiled across at them as he drove past on his way back for more crates.

'So,' Klasvik had recovered his composure and glared briefly at Krayn, 'what now?'

Lannic was already decided. 'We establish base camp outside the lander. Gilmanuk, will you work out a route for the tunnel with Krayn, and then he can get the cannon

56

set up? The rest of us can help Cambri and Tashman get everything we need unloaded and organized.'

'Yo!' Tashman shouted across to her. 'About time too. The other loader's at the far end of the hold – there's a mass of crates to be unpacked and sorted. And you'd better work out how you want the living quarters set up and let Cambri know – she's drinking hot blood out there.'

They had been excavating for what seemed like forever. Most of it involved spraying a high-pressure jet of water into the tunnel to hose out the mud, then scooping it into the front-bucket of a loader and driving it the ever-increasing distance up the sloping tunnel to dump it outside in the rain.

Krayn had been doing most of the drilling, most of the driving and most of the complaining. Tashman was responsible for shoring up the tunnel as they progressed, and the archaeologists were taking it in turns to sit on the water cannon and aim its hose. They had all had at least one break to get some sleep, although Krayn complained his had been shorter than everyone else's.

Bannahilk was permanently on the lander's flight deck where he and Fortalexa were monitoring every broadcast the com-net could find and plotting the Rippearean advance across a dedicated screen which had previously been an important part of the survey computer.

Fortalexa brought the others irregular reports, all of them delivered in his usual sardonic style and none of them optimistic. It was wet, cold, miserable, discouraging and they had nothing to show for it. Until they found the monolith.

Cambri was on the cannon and Krayn was drilling the loosened mud from the tunnel wall. Tashman had given up his shoring work – as expected, the mud was now packed hard enough for the tunnel to support itself – so Krayn was feeling more than ever that he had got the poorer deal. As a result he was setting about the mudface with an aggressive abandon that meant he was leaning quite heavily on the drill when it sheared away down the wall, taking a large chunk of mud.

Krayn swore as he released his hold on the power button and collided with the lamp which Cambri had left wedged into the mud floor. The lamp went out as it fell, and Krayn had to scrabble about for it.

'What the hell are you doing? Are you all right?' Cambri turned off the cannon and leaped down to the ground, skidding down the slope to where Krayn was pulling himself to his feet.

'I hit something – that's not just mud.'

'Well I hope you haven't damaged it. Here, shine the lamp over so we can see what it is.'

Krayn directed the light at the far wall, and Cambri peered at the slab of stone that had been uncovered. 'See if you can clear any more of it,' she said. 'I'll get Lannic.'

Krayn nodded and moved the light for a better view. It was only after she was beyond earshot that he realized he had neglected to argue about it.

Lannic, Klasvik and Bernice had been discussing progress against the timetable Bannahilk was imposing as a result of his projections of the enemy advance. They did not wait for Cambri to give them details: any find was important at this stage. They needed something to convince them they were getting somewhere, it hardly mattered what.

But *what*? was a good question. Krayn had freed the edges of the huge slab of stone so that it stood out against the mud behind it. It was almost the size of the tunnel, and was jutting across it at an angle. Actually, Klasvik pointed out, it was almost vertical, but the angle of the tunnel was such that it seemed to loom over them, precariously top-heavy.

'What do you make of it?' Bernice asked them.

'It's natural. A native type of igneous stone.' Klasvik ran his hand across the muddy surface. 'And rough – it's got indentations in it.'

Lannic leaned past him and wiped at an area with her

sleeve, dislodging slivers of mud. They fell away to reveal dark shadows beneath.

'They look like cuts.' Krayn turned the lamp slightly so that the light caught the edges of the indentations.

'They *are* cuts.' Lannic wiped a bigger area. 'They're deliberate. Maybe letters even. Can we clean it up?'

Krayn nodded. 'Stand back a bit, I'll hose it down for you.'

It only took a few seconds for the jet of water to wash the mud from the front of the monolith. Then they gathered round it again, the water washing up against their feet as the pumps began to pipe it back up to the surface.

Krayn lifted the lamp from its tripod and held it up as they leaned forward to peer at the inscription. Lannic's shadow was cast across it in an elongated manner, distorted by the angle of the slab. The lamp was the only light source apart from a faint glow from the tunnel mouth up and behind them.

'We need better lighting, really. It looks like one of the Cluster dialects. An old one, too.' Lannic straightened up. 'It's not one I know, I'm afraid. Mean anything to you, Klasvik?'

Klasvik looked pale, even in the subdued light. His voice was quiet and grave: 'I can't see much of it, but what I can see – yes. I'm afraid I can read it.'

Krayn turned the light full in Klasvik's face and he blinked. 'My Volanthan is a little rusty, but a loose translation of what I can see would include *Those unbelievers who disturb the rest of your temple of dramatic art shall suffer death for their blasphemy.*'

Source Document 3

Original Text of the Menaxan Tablet and Translation by Leontium Klasvik

*Library of Curios, Thrastus 3 (ref 2699/E) – Original text
of the Volanthan engraving on the slab at the entrance to
the Pentillanian Theatre of Menaxus*

Leontium Klasvik's translation (3985).

Great god Dionysus, father of all thespians, read these words from the humblest of your company:

For any desecration of your theatre, you will be avenged. Those unbelievers who disturb the rest of your temple of dramatic art shall suffer death for their blasphemy. Though it take years of empty time, I know you will find, in your Art, the instrument of your revenge, as was ordained.

Death shall come on swift wings to him that touches the tomb of the drama.

Chapter 3

Ghosts

The problem that most students have in studying drama is one of immediacy. In many cases this lack of appreciation of the application and practical worth of the texts disappears when the student is involved in performance. But for some the feeling that the study of ancient drama is irrelevant is not purged.

The lucky few discover the true worth of the drama in later life – often under the strangest circumstances and in situations where an interpretation of, say, Hamlet is the last thing on their minds. The moment of revelation is often coupled with the realization that Shakespeare and Osterling wrote not about fictional characters, but about real people in real situations. They were interpreters of life.

The Dramatist's Art – F. Van der Cleele, 2811

Tashman and Cambri were the most concerned by the discovery of the monolith. The archaeologists were more interested in the scientific and historical implications than the alleged curse. Lannic was slightly peeved that her previous expedition had missed it but, given they were now digging into the theatre via a very different route from the initial excavations, that was hardly reprehensible. Bannahilk and Fortalexa took it all in their stride: unless people were actually dying then they were not concerned.

Bernice was more worried than the other archaeologists, although she did not believe in the inscription in the way that Cambri in particular seemed to. At least, she believed it existed: she had seen it. And her expertise told her that it was old, although she also noted slight inconsistencies in the wear on the upstrokes of the lettering and tentatively put that down to meteorological erosion while it was still 'in use' as it were. Her concerns were more to do with the existence of the stone in the first place. The others seemed overjoyed to have found something; Benny was more interested in why it was there at all to be found. The whole thing seemed bizarre. It was melodramatic and, as they were proving by ignoring its words, ineffective.

That was perhaps what really niggled at her. Unless the threat was sustainable, why make it? A deterrent based on fear and superstition alone would suggest a primitive and impressionable culture completely at odds with the sophisticated and civilized theatre complex they were here to excavate. Even the curses on the ancient Egyptian tombs of the pharoahs had turned out to have a deeper, extraterrestrial meaning – as she knew very well since she had just finished excavating the source of it.

Only Gilmanuk appreciated her worries. His explanation was straightforward. The slab was either a prop from some noted production or was purpose-built to be a welcoming curio at the side entrance of the theatre. Bernice didn't like it, but she had to admit that this was a simple and plausible explanation. After all, it was no more pointless or eccentric than posting a sign saying *Abandon Hope All You Who Enter Here* above the gates of Hell. Or writing *Police Public Call Box* above the entrance to a time and space machine.

Cambri was drilling away at the tunnel wall while Klasvik aimed the water cannon. She hated every moment of it, she would rather be on the battlefield, where she belonged. She would rather be wading through slime towards the Rippearean front line on Frauton Five than splashing about in this mud-hole. She was a soldier; combat infantry. She had signed up on her eighteenth birthday (the day before her conscription notice arrived), and had seen action in eleven battles in three campaigns. She was concerned with the recently deceased and the soon-to-be dead, not the long-decayed. She ran her grimy hand through her short dark grimy hair and dug the end of the drill viciously into the mudface. She felt it give.

She paused, confused, then pushed again. It was certainly giving, the whole of the centre of the tunnel wall was bowing in slightly as she leant on the drill. She almost turned the drill on, but if there was an opening up ahead then she might fall through into it, and there was no knowing how deep it might be. It could be a small air-pocket or it could be a whole crevasse.

She turned back to Klasvik, waving for him to stop the water. But her arm froze in mid air.

Klasvik saw Cambri turn and raise her arm. Then she froze, like a statue. What was it now? She was forever muttering and complaining under her breath. He wished she'd come right out and say what was on her mind, however forthright. She could take a lesson or two from Krayn there.

He stemmed the flow of water to the main hoses. But Cambri still didn't move. Then, suddenly, her arm fell to her side. She was staring past Klasvik, her mouth half open. Then she blinked and shook her head as if to clear it. Klasvik turned and looked behind him up the tunnel. It was empty.

Cambri was still standing looking past him. Klasvik called out to her but she made no sigh of having heard, so he climbed down from the cannon and, placing his feet carefully in the slurry, he slithered down to her. 'Well, why have you stopped?'

For a moment she still did not acknowledge him. Then she shook her head again. 'Didn't you see it?'

'What?'

'The figure.'

'What figure?'

'You must have seen it.'

'Seen what?'

At last Cambri turned to look at Klasvik. 'A character. Dressed in armour. He was standing right behind you.'

'Armour?' Klasvik had a thought. 'Must have been Fortalexa – or Bannahilk. I didn't see him. He must have gone back before I looked.' He peered back up the tunnel. He could see now that there was a figure picking its way down the slope towards them through the dimly lit tunnel, one hand on the wall to steady itself. But it looked more like Professor Summerfield than one of the military.

'No. It wasn't either of them. He just disappeared – faded away. And anyway, it wasn't that sort of armour.'

Bernice arrived just in time to catch the end of the exchange. She was due to relieve Klasvik. 'Wasn't what sort of armour?' she asked.

'Military – combat armour.'

'Oh?' Klasvik was getting bored with this. 'And what sort of armour was it then?'

'It was ceremonial armour. Metal. He had a metal helmet covering the top of his head. He had a breastplate and leggings. I could see as he turned sideways against the lights – just before he faded away.'

Klasvik snorted in disbelief, but Bernice was attentive.

Cambri turned to her. 'He also had – he was holding – ' Her voice tailed away and she stared down at the tunnel floor, her foot making circles in the viscous liquid.

'Yes?' encouraged Bernice. 'He was holding . . .?'

Cambri looked up. Her eyes held Bernice's for a moment, before they faded into vacancy. 'He was holding a sword.' Then she turned and walked off up the tunnel, splashing muddy water with each automatic step.

Cambri told her story three times, and still Bernice was the only one to give it any credence. She and Klasvik had followed her back up the tunnel. Cambri had not answered their calls, but had headed straight for the hold. The whole area, now almost devoid of crates, had been converted into an operations room with computer terminals linked through from the main deck and the com-

65

net control centre. Cambri was slumped in one of the chairs when Bernice caught up. She was staring into space.

The others did believe that Cambri thought she had seen something but they were betting on shadows and tricks of the light. They did not believe that it could be put down simply to an over-active imagination; *that* was a failing from which everyone tacitly agreed Cambri did not suffer.

Bernice was not sure exactly what Cambri had seen either, but she was sure it was something more substantial. Her whole demeanour, her transition from frustrated warrior full of pent-up emotion into placid dreamer suggested at the very least a shock. And it took more than shadows and tricks of the light to shock an experienced soldier.

But whatever Cambri had seen, the whole incident was all but forgotten when she recovered enough to mention that the wall at the far end of the tunnel was thin enough to yield when pushed. Lannic was certain that this meant they were about to make progress.

'A breakthrough?' Fortalexa suggested with a smile in his voice. It was lost on Lannic, but Klasvik frowned at the electronics officer's levity.

'More likely a dirty great crevice,' offered Krayn gloomily. He hated to think his work at the tunnel face might have been wasted.

Tashman however found the thought amusing: 'Yeah,' he laughed, 'we'll either have to go home, or you'll have to dig us another tunnel.'

'Only one way to find out,' said Bernice. Lannic nodded, and led the way out to the tunnel. Benny paused in the doorway for a moment and looked back at Cambri.

She was sitting in the chair still, her hands cradling a hot caffedeine solution.

They crowded round the mud wall at the end of the tunnel. They were all there except for Cambri. Fortalexa and Bannahilk stood at the back, deferring to the archaeologists. So did Krayn, but more out of boredom than politeness.

Tashman was setting up the drill on a tripod so that he could inch it forward rather than relying on his weight and the mass of the drill to do the work. Benny and Lannic were pushing at the mud to determine the point where the wall was thickest. Gilmanuk was silent, his hand to his mouth. Klasvik offered the two women unsought advice, which they mainly ignored. But he kept offering it so as not to have to admit that he knew they were ignoring him.

Eventually Lannic and Bernice agreed on a point about chest-high on the wall and Tashman manhandled the drill into position. The water which cooled the drill-head splashed into the muddy slurry around their feet as Tashman slowly pushed the drill forward in its mountings. It bit into the damp mud, dark tapeworms spiralling from the hole and tearing under their own weight.

Tashman lurched forward suddenly, managing to regain his balance just before the drill-head disappeared completely into the wall. 'We're through,' he said unnecessarily. Everyone crowded in closer as he reversed the spin of the drill and eased it out of the wall. It came free, leaving a perfectly round hole just too small to squeeze a hand through. There was a glimmer of light visible through it.

At once Lannic was squatting before the wall, her eye to the opening. She did not say anything.

Klasvik knelt beside her. 'Can you see anything?'

'Yes, yes,' she replied. 'It is wonderful.' Then she stood aside and Klasvik peered through after her. They all heard his intake of breath.

Benny exchanged looks with Gilmanuk, raising an eyebrow. He nodded, and gestured for her to go next. Eventually Klasvik moved aside, his face giving little away, and Benny bent down and put her eye to the hole.

She was looking out into the huge auditorium of the amphitheatre. It seemed almost as if she was on the stage, the curved rows of steps where the seats had been stretching away and up from her. In fact they were offset from the centre of the theatre, the stage area was below and to the left, out of Benny's line of vision. But what she *could* see took her breath away. Their vantage point was quite high above the theatre floor, there was a drop, she estimated, of about twenty feet from the wall of mud. Mud seemed to have pushed out into the theatre, probably covering the stage area, but had not filled it. The excavation from this point would be comparatively easy.

And it was light – good enough for Benny to make out the view once her eyes had become used to the muddy illumination, but no brighter. It took Benny a moment to realize that the amphitheatre was covered over. An enormous sheet of transparent plastic was stretched across the whole area, supported at intervals by metal posts stuck up through it, from which ropes held the sheeting in place. Lannic's previous expedition must have roofed over the structure to keep the elements out, and against all the odds the makeshift cover had held. Benny could see a thin layer of mud across the top, rain splashing onto it and running down from the raised centre and off the sides. Where the mud was thinnest the light of the suns shone in, grimy and broken.

Benny was beginning to feel a tightness in her chest, and could hear a rushing in her ears. She realized with a start that she had been holding her breath, and let it out in a low whistle. Then reluctantly she stepped back from the aperture and allowed Gilmanuk to take her place.

They all took a turn at peering through the small hole. Even Tashman seemed moved, managing a grunt as his eyes adjusted to the dim light on the other side of the wall. Fortalexa and Bannahilk were more impressed with the fact that they had bought a day from the time allocated to tunnelling into the theatre and excavating it, but they were also staggered by the size of the structure.

Only Lannic seemed unmoved. She had after all seen it all before. And in contrast to the others, she was annoyed that they had wasted time tunnelling through the mud when it now appeared they could have walked round and cut a hole in the plastic sheeting. The only reason she was not blaming the others for this oversight seemed to be that it had never occurred to her either that the flimsy covering could have withstood the battering from the rain and the wind.

Bannahilk went back to get ropes and grappling hooks so they could get down to the theatre floor, Fortalexa went with him to check on Cambri and the com-net. Tashman drilled a patchwork of holes through the thin wall, and Krayn knocked the mud from between them with a sledge-hammer. Before long the opening was wide enough to squeeze through. The only obstacle remaining was the drop into the theatre.

'Once we're down there we can rig something up,' Tashman offered with uncharacteristic enthusiasm. 'Maybe use some of the mud from the stage and build steps up to the tunnel.'

'Not a bad idea,' Lannic leant out, holding on to the edge of the wall to balance herself. 'It looks pretty solid. We can probably cut out chunks with a low-intensity burst from a disruptor.'

'How did the mud get there?' Benny was concerned at once with the archaeological practicalities. 'I mean, why just the stage area?'

'There's probably a skene,' Gilmanuk was thinking aloud.

'There is.' Lannic of course had seen it. 'The central opening is fairly large.'

'Then the mud must have seeped in through there. More mud kept pushing through as your previous diggings filled in, but the mud at the front dried out a bit and set, blocking the doorway.'

Benny nodded. It was a plausible explanation. The similar theatres she had studied on the Braxiatel disk had a flat wall across the back of the stage area – a skene (pronounced *skaynay*, apparently) – with doors in it. Typically there were three doors. They were used in production as entrances and exits. She knew Gilmanuk had a theory that the design of the skene in any particular theatre often influenced the drama written for it. The ancient Pranchens of Golrargos had concerned themselves with plays centred round different households; each door in the skene, Gilmanuk was certain, representing one of the houses. Benny could well imagine the dust, drifting through the uncovered doorways, then turning to slurry and mud as the rain started; drying under the heat of the sun as the plastic covers kept the interior of the theatre dry. Slowly silting up like the mouth of a river.

Gilmanuk and Klasvik were pressing Lannic for information about the skene, despite having seen the simularities shot on the previous expedition. There was no substitute for actual, physical experience and first impressions.

Bannahilk was soon back. He had ropes wound over his shoulder and was carrying two toughened plastic grappling hooks. He and Krayn quickly attached the ropes to the hooks and dug the hooks into the floor of the tunnel, far enough back from the edge to prevent it crumbling under the weight. Krayn hammered them into the packed mud and threw the ropes out of the tunnel mouth. Benny peered over and watched them snake down, jolting as they reached the end of their play and jumping back upwards slightly before slapping slowly against the uneven walls of the mud bank.

Almost as soon as the ropes were still, Lannic wiped her hands down the front of her coverall, grasped the nearest rope and swung herself out and down. She abseiled easily the twenty feet to the muddy floor, slipping slightly as she landed. She did not look back, but headed off to inspect the stage area.

Tashman shrugged and pushed his way through the others to the tunnel mouth. He grabbed the same rope as Lannic had used and lowered himself after her.

Benny chose the other one and leapt out into the auditorium. She reached the bottom with no applause, her hands a little sore from her over-enthusiastic speed down the rope.

Lannic was examining the base of the huge pile of mud covering the stage. It reached up almost to the plastic ceiling, like a damp mountain. Tashman was nowhere to be seen. Benny wandered over to join Lannic.

'Is there any damage?'

'Can't really tell yet. There doesn't seem to be. With luck the seepage was relatively slow and the weight was applied over a period of time.' Lannic stood and moved round to examine another area. 'If this lot came through too quickly, then at the very least the floor will have cracked.'

Krayn had joined them. He ran his hand down the side of the mud closest to the tunnel, then glanced back up the tunnel opening. Benny followed his gaze, just in time to see Klasvik make his way nervously down the rope. Gilmanuk was just picking himself up from a slippery arrival at floor level. She turned back to Krayn. 'What do you reckon?'

He shrugged. 'Tashman's the engineer. But I think we could take slices out of the side, cutting the base of each slice higher than the previous one. They'd make steps when they fell. Not ideal – several short climbs rather than one big one. The real problem will be getting the equipment down here to being with.' He was looking into the depths of the dim theatre, trying to locate Tashman. His eyes swept across the tiers of the auditorium in front of them.

'Equipment?' Benny was confused. 'Surely a hand disruptor will cut through this like butter.'

'Like what?'

'Well, quite easily.'

'Yes, but that's no good. The beam's so tight that the mud will just stay in position with a thin slice through it. Like an upright pillar. We need to loosen the base so it will fall. I think the water cannon would do a good job. We can direct it reasonably accurately and wash away the foundations of each "pillar". We could cut chunks out with a disruptor, but we'd have to be sure the angle was right or the whole thing could fall in the wrong place.'

Benny agreed. 'That could screw things up good and proper.'

Krayn nodded, still looking for Tashman. 'Where the hell is he?'

Benny looked too, but she could hardly see to the back of the theatre where she had last seen him heading. She was about to suggest they go and look when they heard him call out.

Fortalexa left Cambri in the hold. He guessed she was still coming to terms with her hallucination; with the fact that the crazy curse had got to her. She failed to respond to a couple of quips, so he was happy to leave her to it. Especially as he was in a hurry. He had to find Bannahilk.

His mind was still on what it had found in the com-net when he reached the end of the tunnel without having seen any of the others. He lowered himself down one of the ropes almost on instinct.

Fortalexa looked round. Everyone was running, making their way hurriedly up the steps of the area facing the stage, where the audience had sat. It occurred to him that it was not the landing at the base of the rope that had jolted him out of his reverie, but a sound. A man's voice calling out urgently. He followed the others.

When he caught up with them – in fact, he overtook Gilmanuk and Klasvik on the way – they were gathered round Tashman. Tashman's eyes were wider than usual, and not just from the dim light. He was pointing at an area of the stone wall at the back of the theatre.

'Well, there's nothing there now.' Fortalexa noticed that Professor Summerfield seemed less out of breath even than he was. She must be very fit, especially without the military background as an excuse. She noticed him as she turned back to Tashman. 'I see the army got here at last,' she offered sarcastically. 'Were you waiting for an invitation?'

'We aim to please.' He could see from her eyes that the pun was not lost on her. But she ignored it and addressed Tashman instead: 'Tell us again.' Gilmanuk and Klasvik had joined them now and they all listened attentively.

Tashman sighed and looked round them. 'Look, I didn't believe her any more than you lot did.'

'Who?' asked Lannic.

'Cambri, of course. I mean – ghosts. Well, whatever. But he was here – there.' He pointed.

Lannic was losing her patience. 'Who was here?'

'I don't know. A figure. In metal armour, like she said. An old man, standing tall – like he owned the place. He had one of those helmets that used to cover the whole head.'

'How do you know he was old, then?'

'He wore the front up. And he walked – through there.'

They all looked. Tashman was pointing at a blank section of wall. There was nothing remarkable about it at all. Certainly there was no door.

'You saw his face?' Bernice was curious.

'Yes, that's how I knew he was old.'

Fortalexa decided this was not getting them anywhere. 'Yes, well, I have some sad news too. It looks like they're going for it.'

'You got that off the net?' Bannahilk was suddenly animated, his moustache twitching with excitement. Here was a problem he could understand and deal with.

'Straight off. The Rippeareans have crossed the Charasian Line. They're heading right for Heletia, and we're in their way.' He looked Bernice in the face. He could tell she resented their presence as soldiers and the fact that the war interfered with her business. But that was life, and she would have to come to terms with that. 'I wouldn't invite anyone else to the matinée in a hurry.'

She frowned for a moment. It was as if she were considering something important. Then she seemed to come to a decision. But before she could say anything Lannic was pushing past.

'Right, let's get moving then. Tashman and Krayn, see if you can get us easier access to this place from the tunnel. Klasvik, Gilmanuk, Summerfield – come with me. We've got to get started.' She paused as she passed Fortalexa. 'Shouldn't you be busy too?'

'Very probably,' he conceded.

Bannahilk drew him aside for a moment. 'Warn Lefkhani – he may not know.' Fortalexa nodded and followed the others down towards the stage. He got half-way before he realized that Bernice was not in front of him. He turned and looked back. She was bent examining the wall where Tashman's ghost had disappeared.

It was just a section of wall, old and scratched and made of stone. Completely unremarkable, but it fascinated Bernice. It was the age, the history – what the wall had seen – that she found so captivating. An unremarkable wall, maybe, but it had a remarkable view of the stage. She looked down at the mud-face covering the central area below, catching Fortalexa's eye for a second as he turned away and continued down after the others.

Benny smiled. He wasn't so bad, for a soldier. At least he had a sense of humour and didn't take himself too seriously; a contrast to the quietly efficient Bannahilk. She could easily see how the officer had got his stripes (or pips, or whatever) while Fortalexa had remained on communications and electronics. Attitude was everything to the military; and it was the military attitude that she had trouble relating to.

She patted her satchel to reassure herself that it and the small green globe it contained were still safely with her. Not that she would be calling for the Doctor and Ace just yet. A few spooks in the minds of impressionable grunts who'd got fazed by a phoney curse were hardly enough to motivate a cry for help.

Benny continued her examination of the wall, following it to the corner of the amphitheatre where it joined the side wall. She ran her hands over the wall, feeling the stone rough and cold against her skin. But there was something else – it seemed almost to shrink away from her. Benny thought for a moment, her eyes searching the surface for a clue. There – a line that descended the bottom section of the wall where the stones were not interlaced, but all ended at a given point. A doorway. She pushed hard

74

against the outside edge of the section of wall, guessing that it pivoted in the corner where it joined the other wall so that the hinges would be better hidden. She was right, and the heavy door swung slowly open, grating with the sounds of age and disuse. Benny went through into the blackness beyond. She stood still for a moment facing into the dark, waiting for her eyes to adjust.

Eventually she could see a little way ahead. She was in a corridor with real walls, not excavated mud. She picked her way slowly along, one hand against the wall to guide her, the other held out in front to ward off any obstruction her dim eyes might miss.

After a while she stopped. This was silly, the corridor was leading nowhere. Better to get a light and come back with the others, explore and record the whole thing properly. She turned back towards the dim rectangle of light that was the doorway she had come through. And as she did so, Benny caught sight of another doorway in the opposite wall. Just for a second, then it was gone.

She blinked. And it was back. A low red light emanating from within. Then abruptly it was gone again. She frowned and when it reappeared moved cautiously towards the light, almost losing her footing when it disappeared yet again.

Then she was on the threshold and she went into the room beyond.

The room was behind the back wall of the theatre. It was stone-walled on three sides like the theatre and the corridor she had just come along. The fourth side was filled with a bulge of hardened mud which jutted into the room. It was lit intermittently by a flashing red light which was over by the mud wall. It was a tiny light, but seemed very bright. And it was on what looked like the control panel of a machine.

When she got up close to it, Benny could make it out rather better. The machine was square, about a meter along each side, raised on a wheeled trolley so it was at waist height. From one end projected a short rod, not unlike the barrel of a gun except that it had no bore and was ringed with transparent circlets within which Benny could see fine wiring. It was pointing at a tinted window in the wall.

Benny moved round the machine, examining its far side. She squeezed between the machine and the mud behind it, running her hand along the smooth plastic exterior. The panel at the back was the only set of controls on it. Was the machine something left by Lannic's previous expedition? Or had they not found the hidden doorway that she had stumbled upon before they had to withdraw?

Benny looked through the low window: it afforded a green-tinted view down into the theatre. She was looking directly at the stage area. She wondered why they had not been able to see the winking light from the other side, and reached out. Her hand touched something solid. So that was it. Some sort of one-way glass; she could see out, but the outside world could not see in. It was like being in the holographic projection chamber of the TARDIS cinema, she thought with a smile.

And a thought began to form in her mind. A thought cut off by the damp hand that closed over her throat.

It caught Benny by surprise. She would have screamed had the hand not been choking the breath from her windpipe. She flailed at her attacker, forcing her elbows backwards in the hope of catching him . . . or her . . . or it, but they met with no resistance. She could feel the life slowly draining from her body, her toes and fingers were tingling with the lack of oxygen. Her ears were rushing with blood and the red of the light got redder each time it flashed.

But she still heard the noise. It was an old noise. A noise Bernice knew from handling ancient weapons in museums and on digs. It sounded like a sword being drawn from a scabbard. It frightened her enough to give her the impetus and strength to lunge – not backwards at her attacker, but forwards.

She knew she could not break the hold on her neck – her hands had been scrabbling at the damp slippery fingers since they had closed round her throat – but if she had something heavy, a club, she might be able to reach over

76

her shoulder and batter at her attacker. So she lunged towards the stubby barrel of the machine in front of her. Her hands closed over it and she summoned her last resources of strength to try to snap it off at the narrow base where it joined the main part of the machinery.

But just before she heaved on the potential club, she was free – the hand had left her throat. Benny dived away, past the machine and across the floor, keeping low to avoid the blow of the sword. But it never came. There was no rush of air past her face as the sword swept by. No biting pain as it connected with her. Nothing at all.

Benny rubbed her bruised neck and gasped in air as she stared past the machine. There was nobody there. Just a dark wall of mud reaching up to a stone ceiling.

She sat there for a few minutes, getting her breath back, too faint to leave the room despite her fear. Then she came to a decision. Ghosts were all very well, but when they somehow became corporeal and started throttling people – particularly her – then it was time to call in the experts.

Bernice pulled her satchel round and cradled it in her lap as she drew herself up into a cross-legged position. Her hand moved in slow jerks as the light flashed, frame by frame like an old movie. She undid the clasp and reached inside for the tracker/locator.

Well, now's the time to see if the theory works, she thought as she felt for the slight indentation in the base of the sphere. A moment later a low green light pulsed unevenly with the red one for a few seconds. Then it was gone. Bernice refastened her satchel, pulled herself to her feet and, still breathing heavily, made her way back to the dark corridor.

Source Document 4

Extract from Intelligence Report XV117 from Analyst Ezira to Rippearean War Cabinet – 3978

Braxiatel Collection Catalogue Number: 219FD

But that is not to say that the Heletians rely on words. On the contrary, if they can show the event on the stage, then they will. I saw a production of *Dratus and Tomark* where Palmera's speech about the arrival of Tomark's spacebarge at the battle of Actinium was augmented by the *actual arrival* of the barge. They want concrete images all the time; they have lost their appreciation of the abstract. This applies not only to their theatre – although there it is most manifest – but also to their paintings, similarities and literature. Seeing is believing, and they do not believe until they have seen.

Analysis: So far as I can discern, the Heletians believe that if they can understand the nature of acting and production, then they can better understand themselves. To this end they want information and facts (they also of course want to spread the word and bring nonconforming systems into line, as they are doing so ruthlessly). They see theatre as inextricably linked to history: plays are chronicles. Plays with an historical setting *must* be accurately staged. To a very real degree they see Shakespeare as an historian rather than a story-teller.

The other principle to which they adhere (ironically) is the notion that theatre is beautiful, even to the detriment of the historical detail. There must be a visual beauty in the settings, the actors and the language. This is why Osterling is the perfect choice, since he combines the historical chronicle with visual splendour and linguistic finesse.

Chapter 4

A Dream Play

JORVIK	*And so the once noble Leet, now a common criminal, is tried for the murder. And as a common criminal his head is spliced from his body.*

Teel rises in horror

JORVIK	*See, Teel, see where the axe-man's blade pauses at its apogee. Then gravity gives it one more little pull and the blade continues over and down.*
PRATOR	*Teel stands amazed. The drama works its vicarious spell.*
JORVIK	*It gathers momentum as it goes and slams into his neck . . .*

The Good Soldiers – Stanoff Osterling, 2273

'So where is she?' Ace watched the Doctor as he moved round the control console, tapping this dial, flicking that switch, checking the other read-out.

He frowned for a moment, clicked his tongue and reversed his direction round the console. 'Not where she's supposed to be, that's for sure.' His frown turned into a wide grin. 'Which is normal – for Benny.'

'So where's she supposed to be?'

'Phaester Osiris. Probably more interesting now it's ruined than it ever was when Horus was at home.' The

80

Doctor stared off into space for a while and Ace took the opportunity to check over the controls the Doctor had been inspecting.

The Time Path indicator was locked into their present time – 3985 – and the reading gave the offset from their present position in space, paused above Phaester Osiris to take a bearing on Bernice's signal. Or rather, to reverse – calibrate the bearing that Benny's tracker/locator was taking on them. That would enable them to take the TARDIS right to her.

It was a little more complicated than that of course. With the Doctor it was always a little more complicated than you might expect. Since they had not arranged an exact time for Bernice to operate the tracker, they had been drifting forward in time, waiting for her signal to appear. That way Benny could be picked up when she had had enough, and the Doctor and Ace could avoid the wait.

Ace moved round to a panel of the console which the Doctor had not yet reached, fed the calculated co-ordinates into the navigation computer and leaned forward to read the result.

'Menaxus,' said the Doctor, still staring into the middle distance.

'Bless you.'

He snapped round suddenly as if she had nudged him in the ribs. 'No no no no no.' His eyes lifted momentarily to the heavens. 'The planet Menaxus – just off the edge of the Rippearean Cluster.'

'So what's wrong with that?'

'In 3985 there's a war going on there, that's what's wrong with that.'

Ace nodded. That sounded like the sort of archaeology Benny would appreciate. 'Great,' she said. 'Let's go.'

Bernice was still feeling decidedly shaky. She made her way back to the auditorium, using the corridor wall for support. Thankfully the door was still open and afforded some illumination. The light at the end of the tunnel, she thought as she stumbled slowly towards it.

She sat for a moment on the top tier of the auditorium. According to Gilmanuk there had been benches here – probably wooden – although nothing remained of them now. She looked along the floor for areas of wear or signs of how they had been fixed, but could see nothing. After a minute she gave up and raised her line of sight so that she was looking down at the stage.

It was a good view. She could imagine the actors playing out their drama below, tiny figures on a distant stage. Clever how the eyes were drawn to the centre of the theatre by the inward slope of the walls and the stacked tiers of seats.

There were no actors there now. Just Klasvik and Gilmanuk working in different areas at the front of the theatre and Tashman and Krayn manoeuvring the water cannon into position facing the huge mud slide. She could hear them swearing at each other as they lowered the heavy equipment into place beside a tripod-mounted disruptor and swung it towards the stage.

Bernice smiled as Krayn's voice floated up to her, clear and insistent: 'No, not the top of the mud – aim it at the bottom. We're not going to wash the whole thing away, just take it off its mark.' Whatever else the Menaxans might have got wrong with their theatre, the acoustics were superb.

She pulled herself to her feet and set off down the wide steps towards Gilmanuk.

A small blue box swam through the eternity that exists in the gap between the past, the present, and the future. She floated through the space where space itself does not exist, and curved her way towards an appointment in the real universe. The dematerialization circuit began to reverse-phase as the outer plasmic shell of the TARDIS emerged into normal, finite-dimensional space. The police-box exterior slowly appeared in the gloomy corridor, lit almost exclusively by the flashing of its own light as it pulsed to the same unholy grating rhythm as her engines as they echoed round the deserted castle.

A pause. Utter silence again. The gloom receded slightly as the dim light from the narrow slits of the high windows gained the shadow of a foothold in the darkness. Then the TARDIS door swung open, spilling light onto the stone floor and silhouetting two figures.

'Cold and dark,' said Ace. 'Can we try again?'

'It wouldn't be so dark if you took off your sunglasses,' the Doctor's voice called from behind her.

Ace wrinkled her nose in the gloom as she pulled off her mirrored sunglasses and held them out. The Doctor sniffed cautiously at them as he examined the sunglasses in the gloom. Then he snatched them from her hand and stuffed them into a jacket pocket.

'They obviously couldn't afford the electric bill.' The Doctor pulled the TARDIS door closed after him and locked it.

'Don't be facetious, Doctor.'

The Doctor peered through the semi-darkness at Ace. 'I'm not being facetious.' He touched her lightly on the nose and Ace flinched. 'It takes a lot of power to heat and light a big place like this.'

'Not in the middle ages, it doesn't. And anyway, nobody lives here now.' Ace drew her finger down the dusty wall of the corridor to make her point. It came away clean, and she inspected it in the gloom for a moment, then looked quizzically at the Doctor.

'Yes.' The Doctor stood stock-still, his hand held up to keep Ace quiet. His dark figure looked like a statue waiting for night to break and the sun to rise over a distant courtyard. Eventually his hand dropped to his side and he turned. Ace could see one side of his face where the light caught it. Her eyes were getting accustomed to the darkness. 'It is very quiet,' murmured the Doctor. 'Except for that hum.' He cocked his head to listen again. Ace could hear nothing. She shuffled her feet impatiently in dust that did not move or stick.

Then the Doctor was off, striding down the dim

corridor, his umbrella catching what light there was as it swung in time to his steps.

'Oh, Doctor –' Ace had to walk quickly to catch up, stubbing her foot on the raised edge of a flagstone. 'I can hardly see!'

The Doctor continued undeterred. 'Light thickens,' he said mysteriously, as he rounded a corner Ace had failed to notice. She caught her step and hurried after him.

Tashman had managed to carve a thin slice down through the edge of the mud. Steam rose from the crack and the damp edges were dried and fragile, lumps crumbling off where the disruptor had lingered. A web of veins spread out from the narrow gap between the main mass and the relatively thin pillar which now stood beside it.

Krayn was aiming the water cannon at the base of the mud, preparing to wash the foundation from under the sliver which Tashman had detached. Benny joined Gilmanuk as he watched uneasily from a safe distance. His face brightened as she approached. Then he saw the serious look in her eyes and his demeanour changed to concern.

'What is it?' he asked as she reached him.

Benny shook her head and gestured at the tunnel mouth. 'Come with me, will you?' She remembered all too well how good the acoustics were. She was not sure she was ready to publicize what had happened: already she was beginning to doubt it herself. Then she felt the constriction in her throat as she spoke, and she knew it had happened.

'I think we should wait a moment.' Gilmanuk nodded towards the water cannon. A jet of white water shot out from the nozzle, taking away the outer bottom corner of the new mud pillar. It worked its way slowly inwards and downwards as Krayn made minute adjustments. The mud was very damp, but it remained a solid lump as it peeled away from its parent and toppled slowly towards the floor under the tunnel entrance. For a moment it paused on its newly cut corner, then gravity gave it one more little pull and the mass of mud continued over and down. It gathered momentum as it went and slammed into the ground with a slapping squelch that echoed round the theatre and within Benny's head. The bottom half of the newly formed step splayed out under its own weight, but the whole thing held together.

'Well done,' called Benny, and Krayn answered with a smile and a wave. 'We'll test it for you.'

Mystified, Gilmanuk followed her as she went towards the step. It came up to just below her waist – a little tricky, but not too difficult to clamber up. They would need a total of six steps probably to reach up to the opening above. She was not prepared to wait until they had finished.

Luckily this first step was slightly away from the back wall so the ropes still swung loose. Benny helped Gilmanuk up onto the slippery surface of the mud. It was solid enough for her feet not to sink in, but she almost slipped over several times as she leant over to pull the nearest rope towards her. She grasped it at last and started to climb up out of the theatre.

Blackness. No moon. No stars. Nothing. Ace peered up at the dark opening a few feet above her, a slit of black in the murky grey of the wall.

'Heavy cloud?' she suggested.

'I'm not sure.' The Doctor shrugged. He stared up at the window pensively, his eyebrows tight and his forehead creased.

'Well, there must be something out there.' Ace squatted down in front of the Doctor, knitting the fingers of her hands together to make a cradle. 'Here, I'll give you a bunk up.'

'Thanks.' He lifted his foot into Ace's hands and reached up for a hold on the ledge at the bottom of the narrow window. He could just reach, fingers scrabbling for a purchase, as Ace stood upright, hoisting the Doctor up as she did so.

'What can you see, Doctor?'

'We're in a sea of nowhere.' The Doctor's voice floated down to her.

'Why do they make these windows so narrow?' Ace asked him. If he was not going to be any more helpful then the least he could do was come down and let her have a look.

But the Doctor seemed unaware of the hint. 'To keep the arrows of the opposing archers from raining in. Or the rain from arrowing in. Defence – you should have known that, Ace.'

'I did. So what can you see?'

The Doctor jumped down easily, dropping his umbrella first, then dropping after it in time to catch it as it balanced on its point for a moment. He gestured up at the window, and Ace scrabbled up the wall to it and looked out.

Below her, she could see a courtyard jutting out into the night. It was lit by two flaming flambeaus, one at each extreme corner of the area. Each was held by a figure in a shining metal helmet. The soldiers were standing stock-still, dressed in breastplate and rough trousers. Their helmets, now that Ace peered closely at them, were little more than hard hats covering the crown of their heads and brimming out about level with the brow. The flames from the torches reflected in the polished metal, but the soldiers were standing so still that the reflections were unbroken, unflickering. But there was something even more still about these men. It took Ace a moment to realize what it was. Partly it was the fact that nothing moved round them. They were standing absolutely alone, in an empty courtyard outside an apparently deserted castle which stood in a sea of blackness. Beyond the confines of the castle and this outer bailey, there was nothing but matt blackness. It was as dark as the view into the night sky from below the window. Unbroken night. Weird.

But not as weird as the complete lack of movement. The fact that the soldiers could stand so motionless was something Ace could cope with. And if it was so dark, so cloudy (or foggy?) that it was impossible to see beyond them, fair enough. But the flames of the soldiers' torches were as still as their bearers. Ace had seen enough flames – many of them dancing around the blackened remains of burning Dalek shells – to know that fire is never still. These flames looked like the fake torches that Mrs Parkinson had got the class to make for the school concert one year: cardboard flames, cut into tongues, painted and stuck to the end of a broom handle. If they could have cut out real fire and stuck that on the top of a staff, it would have looked exactly like this. Like a photograph. No flicker or spark – still flame. Frozen fire.

Ace jumped down. The Doctor was looking at her, waiting for her to say something.

'The world just stopped.'

The Doctor leaned back against the wall and pointed his umbrella at Ace. 'Do you mean that the world ends at the castle, then there is nothing more, just the black emptiness of the void? Or that the world has been stopped, so that we can get on?'

Ace looked at the Doctor. 'Both?' she hazarded.

The Doctor nodded slowly and pointed his umbrella down the corridor. 'Let's try this way.' Then he was off again before she could ask further, a silhouette receding into the gloom.

Bernice had largely glossed over the attack in her account to Gilmanuk. They were both more interested in discussing the machine she had found. Lannic had been even more enthusiastic than Gilmanuk, as if this was the find that her two expeditions had been searching for. To Bernice's surprise she seemed entirely happy that it was Benny who had made the discovery rather than herself or her previous expedition.

They were in the operations room (as Bannahilk now insisted on calling the hold). Lannic was haggling with Bannahilk for more time, using Bernice's discovery as proof that it was worth staying on as long as possible. Bannahilk was firmly opposed to any extensions to the schedule, and Gilmanuk was trying to make the not unreasonable point that they should examine the machine before making any decisions. If they could hear him above their own voices, then they were not listening to him.

Cambri, almost back to her old self as far as Benny could tell, shook her head in disgust and wandered out of the room. Benny took her place in the spare chair beside Fortalexa. He glanced at her and smiled, then returned to his scan out of the com-net.

'Any news?' Benny asked.

Fortalexa shook his head. 'Nothing good, anyway.'

'So no extension to our stay?'

Fortalexa grinned and they both looked over at Lannic and Bannahilk. Bannahilk was shaking his head and holding up his hand as Lannic kept on at him. He walked away from her off into the piles of crates not worth unpacking. Lannic followed him.

'No chance.' Fortalexa told Benny.

Cambri had had enough of the operations room. She felt fine now – must have been tired. Should not have made a fuss, just got on with the job. It was the boredom that had got to her. It might have been more dangerous on Magvel Seven, or in the advance on Basfonal, but it had never been as mind-numbingly boring as this.

She grinned in the dim light. Magvel Seven: she could see herself now, looking down at the woman she had found cowering in the burnt-out wreckage of a civilian airbus. The woman was in her mid twenties, her face streaked with blood and dirt and her hair hanging matted round her face. Her clothes were torn and grimy and she was trying to shelter a child in the remains of her cloak. The cloak had once been red and was clasped at the throat with a gold brooch. She had looked up at Cambri, standing over her, her eyes wide and damp, appealing for mercy. Cambri had shot the child first and taken the gold clasp from her cloak afterwards. She left the woman with her eyes still wide, but now unseeing.

The light dazzled her as she rounded the corner. Instinctively Cambri put her arm up in front of her face as her eyes smarted. Through the glare she could make out the walls of the tunnel ahead of her. It was still part of the shored-up section but it seemed to be lined with wooden panels rather than sections of plastic. She shuffled forward slowly until her stomach touched the low wooden wall in front of her.

Her eyes were clearing now and Cambri could make out the silhouettes of the two counsels: defence and prosecution. Across the room from them the head of the Critics was standing. He turned to her and answered the judge: 'We have. On both of the charges of unprovoked murder of civilians while on campaign, we find the defendant guilty.'

Cambri gasped. How could they know – nobody had seen, she was sure. She was on the edge of the advance, an outrunner, outside the sat-link surveillance envelope.

The judge turned slowly towards her and Cambri grasped the brass rail along the top of the dock for support, her knuckles whitening as she blinked back the light. The judge was in her mid twenties, her face streaked with mud from the courtroom floor and her wig hanging in tresses round her face. Her robe was red and was clasped at the throat with a gold brooch.

Cambri looked over at the judge. Her eyes were wide and damp, appealing for mercy.

The judge said nothing, just nodded to the two warders flanking Cambri. She felt her arms twisted up behind her back, and her head was thrust forward over the edge of the dock. Through the gap between the brass rail and the wooden top of the dock Cambri saw the executioner step forward. His eyes were slits in the dark hood as he raised the axe high above his head. Cambri's scream echoed round the tunnels as she saw the axe begin to swing slowly towards her. For a moment it paused at its apogee, then gravity gave it one more little pull and the blade continued over and down. It gathered momentum as it went and slammed into her neck with a slapping squelch that echoed round the courtroom.

They left the woman with her eyes still wide, but now unseeing.

It was a high-ceilinged room. The Doctor marched across the floor, his shoes slapping against the ornate tiles. When he reached the centre of the room he spun round on his heels. His umbrella somehow found itself leaned against his shoulder as he stood almost to attention and looked back towards the doorway as Ace followed him in. 'Smooth,' he said.

Ace looked round. They were in a bedroom, albeit a rather large one. The bed was tucked away in the far corner. The room seemed to be fashioned entirely out of doorways, huge roman arches with heavy tapestries hung over them. Probably they were not really doors, but rather alcoves. 'I don't think I'd rate it that highly,' Ace muttered as she pushed past to examine a tapestry in more detail.

'I was referring to the floor, not the ambience.'

Ace looked down. The Doctor was right, the room was laid not with the rough flagstones of the rest of the castle that they had seen, but with smooth pale tiles. They were laid in a pattern, a circular border around the inside of the alcove walls. In the middle of the floor was a tiled mosaic, a cluster of small leaves splaying out from a central branch.

'This cost serious money.' Ace was already kneeling and running her hands across the tiles, feeling the expensive finish. 'Why's it so much better than the rest of the dump?'

'Why do you think?'

'Because someone important lives here – in this room?'

'I think you're right,' the Doctor said.

'I dunno about their taste in curtains, though. Look at this stuff.' Ace pointed at the nearest tapestry and they went closer to examine it. It depicted a scene, or rather a tableau, intricately woven in muted colours. The scene was of a section of a courtroom. A figure stood centre-stage, in the dock. Her head was bowed over the top of the wooden wall of the dock, forced forward by the figures either side of her. Behind, another figure, tall and hooded with slits in the dark material for eyes, raised an axe high above her head. The blade was paused at its apogee, about to continue over and down.

The only light source seemed to be from directly in front of the scene – as if it were bleeding in from the room where the Doctor and Ace stood. The background and foreground were an empty brown, as if the world of the figures consisted only of the figures themselves and the stone. As if the world just stopped at the edge of the tableau.

'An execution.' The Doctor rubbed his chin thoughtfully. 'Remind you of anything?'

'Yeah, some cheap horror movie.' Refusing to be drawn, Ace turned away. She was suddenly bored with the tapestry.

'Certainly horrible. I have been in similar situations myself, even before Peladon. I remember once in Italy – ' He paused for Ace to interject. Either she had heard it all before, or it was dead boring. But there was no response. 'Ace?'

'Sorry Doctor.' Ace's voice was strangely quiet.

'What is it?' The Doctor turned and looked over towards the far side of the room. Towards the shadows where Ace was staring.

'Maybe we should ask *her* what it means.' She nodded at the figure standing still and silent beside the bed.

'Maybe we should,' murmured the Doctor, walking slowly towards the figure. She was a woman in her middle years. Still attractive, but with lines of worry on her face. She was wearing a long green gown of a heavy fabric – velvet maybe. It had a wide white lace collar and sleeves which hung loose to the cuffs. The woman's hair was auburn and tied up in traces, swept back from her forehead and away from her ears. Her eyes were brown and stared unseeing into space.

Benny led Lannic, Gilmanuk, and the two soldiers back down the tunnel towards the theatre.

'Sounds like it could be a tight-beam projector of some sort.' Fortalexa was still on at her for details. She had not realized how into the technology of it all he was. Not just a wisecracker but a techie as well. He wanted to know everything about the machine, whereas Lannic seemed strangely disinterested. Probably keeping her ideas and views to herself until she actually saw it.

They rounded the last corner of the panelled section of the tunnel.

'Stay here,' Bannahilk said quietly but urgently to them. Then he pointed at Fortalexa and jabbed his finger back up the tunnel. Fortalexa nodded and turned. His disruptor was already drawn as he darted back to the nearest corner, braced himself, then leapt out to cover the passageway behind them. Bannahilk was moving ahead in similar fashion, covering the shadows and crevices. Benny and the others were left alone. With Cambri's decapitated body.

Gilmanuk had sunk down at the sight of it. He was sitting propped against the mud wall of the tunnel, his head in his hands. Lannic was still standing, the colour drained from her face and her hand over her mouth. Benny gagged. It was not the sight of death so much as the smell of the fresh blood as it trickled from the neck and ran down the sloping floor towards the tunnel mouth. She could imagine it dripping into the theatre, forming a small congealing puddle on the topmost of Tashman and Krayn's steps before running over on to the next one and repeating the process.

A hand touched her shoulder from behind and Benny flinched even though she instinctively knew it was Fortalexa.

'Nothing behind us, at least so far as I can tell.' He looked down at Cambri. Her eyes were grey, and stared unseeing into space. 'And I thought she'd lost her head when she started seeing ghosts.'

Bannahilk was back before Bernice could respond. 'We need to get back to the theatre and check on the others. If all's clear I want to see this machine. If not, we get back to the operations room and prepare to leave immediately.'

Benny looked round. Gilmanuk pulled himself slowly up. Lannic, surprisingly, was nodding agreement. She must be even more shaken than she looked.

'I'll take front of house,' Bannahilk continued. 'Forta-lexa – you take the back.'

Benny hung back so that she was immediately in front of Fortalexa. 'I just hope you can shoot straight,' she told him.

'I don't believe it.'

The Doctor turned to see what Ace was talking about now, and froze. Across the room, almost where they had just been standing, in front of the execution tapestry, stood an old, white-bearded man. Like the woman he was perfectly still and his eyes stared blindly across at them. Ace was about to go over to him, when she heard the distant thud of footsteps – boots on stone – from what seemed like miles away down the hallway.

'Someone's coming!' Ace tugged at the Doctor's sleeve. For a moment she thought he was going to go on tapping the arm of the woman, who was showing no reaction at all to all the attention. But the Doctor seemed to hear her a few seconds after she had finished speaking, and suddenly he was skidding across the tiled floor towards the nearest tapestry. He pulled it back so that it almost swamped him, and held it out with his umbrella until Ace had dived behind. Then he joined her.

'An android?'

The Doctor shook his head. 'No, stranger than that.'

'Oh?'

He turned to face her, the light from the room filtered in behind the tapestry and lit one side of his face, throwing the other into sharp relief. 'They're real – real people.'

Ace grabbed for the tapestry and pulled it back to look at the statue-like figures again. But the Doctor snatched it away from her and smoothed it into stillness, his finger to his lips. They both peered out from behind the edge.

The footsteps that Ace had heard down the corridor were still a long way off, the sounds echoing louder as they approached. Suddenly they seemed to galvanize the old man into action. His eyes blinked once, and then he hurried over to the woman, his steps taking him almost sideways across the room as he glanced nervously between her and the door.

The woman blinked too, her gaze focusing on the old man as he approached. She seemed almost as nervous as he, the serenity of her stance broken in a split second.

Ace strained to hear the old man. He was speaking hurriedly, obviously wanting to finish what he had to say before they were interrupted. But while his voice was in a hurry, his vocabulary was working against him:

'He will come straight. Look you lay home to him;
Tell him his pranks have been too broad to bear with,
And that your Grace hath screen'd and stood between
Much heat and him.' He was standing by her now, almost tugging at her dress in nervous excitement, except that he seemed worried to touch her.

'I'll silence me even here,' he went on with another glance at the door. About time too, thought Ace. Whoever was coming would be in the room in a second, 'Pray you, be round with him,' the old man finished.

The Doctor leaned towards Ace in the gloom. 'I think I know where we are,' he whispered.

'Where?'

But before he could answer a voice called out from the corridor: 'Mother?' The footsteps stopped, and after a moment it called again 'Mother?' The footsteps started again – almost into the room now. 'Mother!'

The Doctor nodded as if this confirmed his theory.

'Well?'

But the Doctor shook his head. 'If I'm right, we'll know in a moment.'

The woman was speaking now, nervous, almost shrill: 'I'll warrant you. Fear me not. Withdraw – I hear him coming.'

Ace would have commented on the woman's poor sense of hearing, except that at that moment the tapestry in front of her was pulled back and the old man dived in at them. Ace gasped, and even the Doctor seemed taken aback. Oh well, she thought, on with the bracelets. But the man ignored them both and turned back to face the room, peering out through the gap that Ace and Doctor had been using. Ace and the Doctor exchanged glances. When they looked back towards the man, he was gone.

'Doctor – I don't like this.'

But the Doctor just nodded at the back of the tapestry. Ace could hear the man who had been approaching for so long walk across the room towards the woman. His voice was quieter and more reasonable now, but it still had an edge. 'Now, mother, what's the matter?' Ace could imagine him taking her hands in his.

'Hamlet, thou hast thy father much offended.'

She stared at the Doctor. He nodded.

'Mother,' came the voice from behind the curtain, rising in volume, getting angry, 'you have *my* father much offended.'

'Yes, Ace. We're in Elsinore. And I don't like it either.'

The room seemed much smaller with them all crammed into it. The machine was the centre of attention of course. The whole party stood round and examined Bernice's find.

Fortalexa was the only one who had actually dared to touch it, running his fingers over the control panel and tapping the barrel-like extension. Klasvik was talking about using thermoluminescence to establish the machine's age. Gilmanuk was advocating fission-track dating while Lannic was more concerned with its purpose. Behind them, Tashman and Krayn were talking in low voices about Cambri's death.

Fortalexa was ignoring them all. He was now lying down under the wheeled trolley, poking at the machine from underneath. 'He gets like this with machinery – can't stop tinkering,' Bannahilk said quietly to Benny.

'Do you think he can work it?'

'Oh, he can work it. I think he's more concerned with finding out what it's for.'

He was right. In a moment Fortalexa was back on his feet, dusting the palms of his hands against each other. 'Well,' he announced, 'I've no idea how old it is. But I know what it does.'

The other conversations stopped.

'But, *Hamlet*'s just a play – it isn't real. I know, we did it for English in the fifth year.'

'Really?' Now he knew what was happening, the Doctor seemed amused by the whole notion. 'But it's happening.'

'Yes – but –'

'Oh just enjoy it, Ace. This is a pivotal scene, and you won't see it played for real like this again.'

The Doctor tweaked the tapestry back a fraction and sneaked a look at Hamlet and his mother. Over his shoulder Ace could see Hamlet in mid flow:

'You go not, till I set you up a glass
Where you may see the inmost part of you.'

Ace prodded the Doctor in the shoulder. 'Do you remember what happens next?' she asked him. She was suddenly worried that she could recall this scene quite clearly. Like the way one's life was supposed to flash before the eyes.

'Yes of course.' He was irritated. 'This is the bit where –' He broke off, his mouth still open, worry creasing his forehead.

'What ho! Help!' screamed the old man's voice from beside them. But he was nowhere to be seen. 'Help – help!' the voice screamed again.

'I think we should have hidden somewhere else,' the Doctor murmured almost audibly. 'When I say run, run.' He hooked the handle of his umbrella round the edge of the heavy material, ready to haul it aside so they could escape.

But before they could move, Hamlet's voice shouted from immediately beyond the tapestry: 'How now! a rat?' Ace heard the cloth rip, the threads breaking one by one as the blade sliced down through it. She leaned back against the wall as the knife continued down towards her and Hamlet screamed in triumph. 'Dead for a ducat, dead!'

Source Document 5

Transcript of Report from Jarnus Lox, captain of the *Lime Light* to Rippearean High Command

Central Rippearean Registry, originated 19–10–3985

As expected, the Heletians are withdrawing on all fronts. They are sustaining heavier casualties than anticipated by sim-prog enactment 509, mainly since their retreat is slower than predicted.

This tardiness is due almost entirely to the fact that they are destroying every emplacement as they leave it. This includes those based in civilian areas and on populated planets. There is, regrettably, much loss of life amongst these communities.

Art and cultural treasures (especially those pertaining to theatre) are removed and transported back to Heletia under heavy guard – more security than the troop carriers are afforded. This is entirely in accordance with projection 509 and with the *Dream Scenario*. There is no reason to suppose that their imminent evacuation of the team on Menaxus will be other than according to this pattern.

Chapter 5

Three Characters in Search of an Author

> *Devereaux Watkins, on the other hand, is an example
> of a playwright driven almost entirely by the medium.
> Whereas Osterling and Shakespeare considered the
> story generally as a way of eliciting character, Watkins
> drove his characters in response to the plot. And the
> plot was dictated by the effects currently available.*
>
> *To be fair, the early twenty-first century was rife
> with innovation. Theatre had become a sensation
> rather than a catharsis. The amalgamation of cinema,
> music concert and games machine was never an easy
> partnership. Watkins merely played to its advantages.
> So his best-remembered play,* Death's Bane *features
> statues that are seen to come to life and take over
> from their living counterparts – not, as Osterling
> would have proposed, as a final condemnation of the
> failures of the flesh, but simply because this was
> the effect which Rumbelow had devised for the Drury
> Lane theatre that month.*
>
> *Watkins used the technology because it was there.
> It is no surprise that the accounts of the time, and the
> memories of all of us who have seen a revival of his
> work, dwell on* what *happened rather than* why *it
> happened, or* to whom.
>
> **The Dramatist's Art** – F. Van der Cleele, 2811

The others all watched as Fortalexa examined the control
panel. His fingers brushed over the buttons and read-outs
until they rested on a button below the flashing red light.
He tapped gently beside it several times, then looked

round the expectant faces. 'Well, here goes,' he said. Everyone craned a little closer.

He pressed the button. The light went out. It stayed out. They all waited, and Fortalexa rubbed his hands together proudly.

Benny sighed audibly. 'Is that it?'

'Well, yes. I've switched it from stand-by to off.' Fortalexa seemed to think this was a major achievement. Judging by the expressions of the others, he was alone in the assumption. He busied himself about the controls again. 'Now we can get this cover off and really see what's going on inside.'

Benny exchanged an exasperated look with Gilmanuk. Lannic leaned forward, her face intent. 'You said you knew what it was for.'

'What?' Fortalexa stopped his efforts at prying away the metal cover for a moment. 'Oh, yes. It's how it does it I'm interested in.' He went back to work and managed to pull the cover clear of the controls.

'Look,' Bannahilk was getting impatient. 'Will you just stop that and tell us what it is?'

'Sorry sir.' He was crestfallen. 'I thought it was obvious,' he hazarded, then went on quickly: 'It's a crude virtual reality projector. You program in the subject from a pre-packaged set, and the result appears down there.' He pointed down through the window towards the stage.

'What sort of subject?'

'Oh, theatre – you know, plays.'

Klasvik shouldered his stooped way past Benny and pushed through to face Fortalexa. 'Plays? What plays? This could be extremely valuable, if it contains a lost work by Brachnid or some of Tergenev's earlier experimental drama.'

'Yes, well, as I say you select the one you want on the panel from a predefined set.'

'But what is in the set?' Benny was not sure if he was being deliberately obtuse, or whether his enthusiasm had genuinely got the better of him. She suspected the former.

'Well, how should I know? You stopped me before I could trace which button punches it up on the read-out.'

Now Benny knew she was right. 'I've got a friend you should meet,' she told him. 'You'd get on like two Arcturans in a goldfish bowl.'

'Er, excuse me.' Gilmanuk had been looking down through the window, as he spoke he seemed to rise up over the machine. Benny blinked in surprise and Fortalexa took a step backwards. Gilmanuk was undeterred: 'You say this machine projects an image, an image of a pre-programmed play, at the stage down there.'

'A holographic representation, probably according to a set of performance criteria. Like I want to see *The Weavers* in thirty-first century dress with a Crotist interpretation, or whatever.'

'You also said you had switched it off.'

'Yes.'

Gilmanuk leaned towards the window again, pushing his glasses up his nose. 'So who are they?' he asked, pointing at the two figures standing at the front of the stage.

Ace was somewhat confused, although she had to admit that she was probably no less confused than was usual when keeping company with the Doctor. The knife had just nicked her left ear as she dived away from it, expecting to smash her head against the stone of the wall behind her. Instead she had thumped it into some sort of muddy sculpture, parts of which seemed to compose a badly proportioned makeshift stairway to heaven. Or rather, to a ragged hole in the wall above them.

She shook her head to clear it and looked round – partly to see where she was, and partly to see where the Doctor was. She eventually found him crouched behind her, examining the floor.

'We're on a stage.' She tried not to sound surprised.

The Doctor was equally calm. 'All the world's a stage, Ace,' he proclaimed as he stood up and dusted his hands

100

together. 'And it seems that all the men and women were merely players.'

'But where did they go?'

'They have their exits and their entrances,' he said, widening his eyes in surprise as if amazed by the lyrical flow of his own turn of phrase.

'I think there's somebody making an entrance up there.' Ace pointed towards the back of the theatre. Several dark figures were emerging from the gloom as they ran down the auditorium towards them.

Ace and Doctor watched them draw closer. 'It's raining,' said the Doctor, as if that explained everything. He gestured at the makeshift plastic-sheet ceiling high above them. 'Don't do anything rash, will you Ace?' he continued as she reached towards her pocket, his umbrella colliding with her right hand and slowly helping it back down to her side. He was probably right, the two nearest figures already had weapons drawn. The taller of the two men dropped to his knees and levelled his disruptor at them. He gripped it in both hands, combat-style.

'Stay exactly where you are. Do not move. Do not attempt any aggressive act.' The words had an automatic ring about them. Which meant that these people were professionals. Ace and the Doctor stood as still as statues.

The kneeling soldier kept them covered while his companion came up to them. Behind the soldiers, Ace could see more figures approaching. But these were less assured, nervous almost. One of them was not nervous. She moved with a more confident gait, lacking the tense caution of the soldiers. There was something familiar about her figure and her movements. Her body language.

The soldier standing beside Ace looked her over for a couple of seconds. 'I think we may be about to get some explanation for what's been happening here, don't you think, Fortalexa?'

But before the kneeling figure could reply, Benny said, 'I don't think so, Bannahilk. I know these two, and they're just archaeologists I'm afraid. They're colleagues of mine.' She paused for a moment, as if trying to think of some-

101

thing to say. 'I expect they just dropped in to see how we were getting on,' she finished lamely.

'Hello, Benny,' said the Doctor raising his hat in greeting. 'We just thought we'd drop in and see how you were getting on.'

The soldier Benny had called Bannahilk still had his gun levelled. His eyes narrowed as he turned to examine the Doctor.

The Doctor returned his stare. 'A discerning fellow – I can tell.' He looked down at his white linen suit and muddy trousers. 'Surely you can see I'm an archaeologist?' He leaned forward and whispered conspiratorially, 'I have been told it's written all over me.'

Slowly Bannahilk lowered his disruptor. After a second Fortalexa raised his sharply upwards, set the safety and re-holstered it.

'Hi, Benny,' said Ace.

Benny hugged her tight for a moment, and Ace could feel the tension in her arms. 'I'm so glad you're here,' she murmured to Ace.

'Now then,' said the Doctor, smiling round the group gathered in front of him, 'what exactly *has* been happening here?'

It never ceased to amaze Bernice how quickly the Doctor could win over a crowd of people and persuade them he was a friend come to help. With only scant character and professional references from Benny he was able to impress Gilmanuk, Klasvik and even Lannic with his comments on the theatre; he was able to persuade Bannahilk to give him a summary of the situation and events of the expedition; and he was able to convince everyone that he and Ace had crash-landed at the far end of the tunnel, just out of sight of the lander, while coming to visit their old friend Benny and see how she was getting on. The fact that they were virtually in a war zone, far from the established space routes, and Benny had had no time to tell anyone where she was off to was quickly glossed over and shrugged off to everyone's satisfaction.

The Doctor had listened carefully to Bannahilk's account of events, his brow furrowing deeper with each revelation. 'Tell me some more about this machine,' the Doctor asked.

'Well, Fortalexa's the expert.'

'I'll show you, that's probably easiest.' Fortalexa led the way back up through the theatre. The others followed. Benny and Ace waited till last.

'I must say this is very good of you.' The Doctor's voice floated down to them.

'Well I suppose we'd better hear the pearls of wisdom. Then I'll tell you what we've been up to.' Ace made to follow the others.

Benny caught her arm. 'You're right. But before we go, there's something else. Let me tell you what happened when I found the machine – what finally persuaded me to call for you.'

The Doctor was enmeshed in a tangle of wires spewing out of the machine's control panel within a moment of Fortalexa agreeing to let him have a look inside. 'You know, this is fascinating,' he said somewhat redundantly as he hooked another wire over his ear. 'Hold this a minute, would you?' He shoved a transparent circuit cube vaguely in Krayn's direction. Krayn took it, surprised.

The Doctor's face appeared for a brief moment from within the mess. 'Thank you so much,' he grinned, then went under again.

From the far side of the room Benny and Ace watched as they discussed recent events.

So it's a sort of dream machine, I suppose,' Benny finished.

'Which projects plays.'

Benny nodded. 'Like *Hamlet*.'

'You think there's a connection?'

'Don't you?'

'Must be. We'll ask the Doctor.' Ace glanced over to where the Doctor's hand was reaching up from beneath the machine, groping for a particular switch out of sight above him. 'If we ever get the chance,' she added.

With a flurry of activity the Doctor was back on his feet, wires and circuitry disappearing miraculously back inside the machine's casing. 'That should do it!' He peered at one of the read-outs. 'That should give us a list of the plays programmed into this thing.'

Lannic pushed forward. She had been watching nervously as the Doctor tinkered with her greatest treasure. Ace heard her sharp inhalation across the room. She looked at Benny and they joined the others.

'This is incredible.' Lannic was reading down the list, scrolling through the titles by drawing her finger down the read-out screen. 'All three plays of *The Oresteia, Death's Bane, Love's Labour's Won*,' she read out.

Ace craned to see as Lannic kept reading, but the screen was just a blur from where she stood.

'You're right, Fortalexa, there are about fifty plays, including *Hamlet* – ' She broke off. For a moment she was silent, then she turned to face the others, her face drained of colour.

'What is it – what's wrong?' Gilmanuk was immediately concerned.

'The list.' They could all hear the disbelief in her voice. 'One of the plays is *The Good Soldiers*.'

The commotion was immediate and prolonged. The archaeologists crowded round noisily, each wanting to see for themselves. Even Fortalexa and Bannahilk seemed impressed.

Ace shook her head, confused. 'What's so interesting?'

Benny was surprised. 'You've never heard of *The Good Soldiers*?'

'Afraid not, though I've met a few.'

'*The Good Soldiers* was written by Stannoff Osterling in 2273.' The Doctor was suddenly standing between them. 'It was universally acclaimed as the greatest ever work of one of the two greatest every playwrights. Accounts of the first performance and some critical reviews survive, but the manuscript has been lost for centuries. Except for

104

some pages found on Mordee by Zagglan Crichley in the mid-thirtieth century and extracts quoted in the reviews and critiques, little is known about it save a brief outline of the plot in a children's story-book.' The Doctor smiled at Ace and she could tell he was limbering up for the full lecture. It could take a while. 'The story concerns six survivors of the battle of Limlough –'

'Thanks, Doctor. I get the picture.'

The Doctor looked hurt and Benny turned away to hide her smile. 'You don't want to hear about it, Ace?' He seemed genuinely surprised.

'Perhaps another time.'

He considered this. Then he nodded pensively. 'Another time it is. We have lots of those.'

'I'll examine it here.' Fortalexa was insistent. 'It will be less noisy and I'd prefer to figure it out alone.' He looked to Bannahilk. 'If you can spare me, sir.'

Bannahilk nodded. 'Yes, let's get this sorted out, then we can finish up here and be away before things get too hot.'

Fortalexa went on quickly, 'I'd like your help, Doctor, if you can spare the time.'

The Doctor seemed surprised. 'What me? Oh of course. Thank you.' He beamed round at everyone. 'But I should like a short time to talk with Professor Summerfield, if I may. We've so much to catch up on. And it must be time for tea.'

The Doctor commented on everything they passed on their way to the lander. He was especially scathing of Tashman and Krayn's attempts at steps, pouring sarcasm on their efforts as he hauled himself up each huge block of compacted mud.

'I wouldn't like to have to climb that in a hurry,' he commented to Lannic when they reached the top. He glared at Tashman, who shrugged his indifference. 'Or while transporting anything bulky or valuable,' the Doctor continued. 'Like that machine, for example.'

It hit home immediately. And while the others continued their journey, Tashman and Krayn found themselves back at the water cannon. Benny threw them a backwards glance as she hurried down the corridor after everyone else. She had been tempted to stay with Fortalexa, but she doubted he would accept that, and anyway she was the Doctor's excuse for a tour of the excavations and the lander. Ahead of her she could hear the Doctor muttering criticisms about the uneven tunnel floor to anyone within earshot.

In fact the only thing the Doctor was not critical of was the strange and sudden presence of another artefact standing a foot deep in water just outside the end of the tunnel, a short way from the lander. Instead he suggested that they had all missed it initially because the rain had been heavier. Lannic was enthralled and sent Bannahilk off to get a loader so they could carry it into the hold.

'Oh I wouldn't bother,' the Doctor told her in a dismissive tone. 'After all, it's only a Terran twentieth-century police telephone box.'

The fact that he failed to convince Lannic and she insisted on dragging it into the lander's hold made Bernice wonder if that had not been his intention all along.

But whatever the Doctor's intentions, he was soon sitting in the lander, perched on a crate with Benny and Ace just outside the TARDIS. From somewhere in his voluminous pockets he had produced several crumpled teabags and three sachets of powdered milk. Now Benny was drinking what she reckoned was the worst-tasting cup of tea ever made, listening to the Doctor telling her she was on a badly organized treasure hunt rather than a serious archaeological expedition. As if she didn't know.

'So why don't we just slip away?' asked Ace.

'No.' The Doctor shook his head. 'There's something happening here – something rather odd.'

'You're telling me,' muttered Benny.

'The dream machine?'

'Yes, Ace. It's not as simple as it looks.'

Benny frowned. 'What do you mean?'

'The componentry is too sophisticated for a glorified

magic lantern. There's more to it than that. Then there are these deaths. And Ace's ear.'

'My ear?'

'Yes. Somehow the TARDIS got caught inside one of the – what did you call it, Ace?'

'The dream machine.'

'Hmm. Very precise. Anyway, we got caught up inside one of its performances. That's theoretically possible. It's obviously theatrically possible. We were in amongst the holograms, except they're more than that – there's a virtual reality element to it. We could touch the characters, feel the texture of the set walls.'

Bernice shrugged. All that was feasible: she knew that from her own experiences, just as Ace knew from her space corps training exercises.

'But it doesn't matter how real you make such a scripted projection, how much you *think* you feel and experience, you are not actually there – it never *really* happens.'

'Obviously.' Ace could not see the point either. 'Otherwise you could die in one of those training simularities. And that's not how they work.'

The Doctor nodded. 'That's right. You can't get shot. You can't get bombed. You can't get killed. And you can't get your ear sliced by a non-existent dagger.'

Ace's hand went instinctively to her left ear, and Benny could see the thin trail of dried blood that ran down the back of it.

Tashman and Krayn still had not decided what to do to enhance their makeshift staircase. They were wandering round the stage area, occasionally making each other laugh with frivolous suggestions. Krayn was in favour of blasting the corners and edges off the steps and converting it into a steep ramp. Tashman suggested trying to precision-blast smaller steps out of each of the large ones. Neither of them thought either would work.

Tashman leaned heavily against the dried edge of the mass of mud on the stage. Chunks of it crumbled away under his weight and he rubbed his back against it in an attempt to get comfortable. There was still a solid lump sticking in his spine. It refused to break loose. He turned to examine it, perhaps he could smooth it down with the heel of his hand.

But what he found was not a lump of mud. It was more rigid; colder. It felt like stone, and what little he could see of it looked as if it had been deliberately shaped into a rounded corner. 'Hey, Krayn – there's something in here. Buried.'

Krayn came over and they tried to push the mud back from the edges of the lump. It was soon apparent that this was the tip of a larger structure.

'What is it, do you reckon?'

'I don't know.' Krayn considered for a while. 'I'll go and find Lannic, she'll want to see this – and it might take her mind off the steps.'

'Right. What shall I do?'

'See if you can clear some more of it. Try the water cannon, but keep it very gentle – we don't want to break anything.'

Tashman smiled. 'No chance of that,' he called after Krayn, 'she'd kill us.'

Krayn smiled, reflecting as he pulled himself up on to the tunnel floor that the steps *were* actually a bit too steep. But that was hardly important now. He peered down the gloomy tunnel. He could just make out the pale pool of light spilling from the nearest lamp. Beyond it the tunnel curled slightly as it rose towards the lander. Still out of breath from the climb, Krayn set off up the tunnel towards the lamp.

It flickered as he got closer. Typical – probably the fuel cell. They had skimped on that as well as everything else on this lousy expedition. If it were not for the Exec's obsession with their theatrical past they would not be here at all. They would be fighting the Rippeareans on the front lines, taking orders from losing direkters who had no time to send for more experienced advice, or even to co-ordinate responses between each other. Krayn had been there, had seen it, and was glad he was stuck on a lousy, skinflint archaeology mission. He had fought in space battles where he never even saw the enemy, and in the streets of Flastapor where he had stared his enemy – and death – in the face.

The light went out. He was almost at it when it guttered and died, almost as if a huge dark hand had grasped it. The bend in the tunnel meant he could see nothing ahead, and behind him the tunnel mouth was a torn grey oval a lifetime away. But when the arm grabbed him from behind, the crook of the elbow locking round his throat, it was all he had to turn to.

Krayn swung savagely back at his assailant, unable to break the grip round his neck. But his fists failed to connect and he flailed uselessly in the air. He staggered back towards the mouth of the tunnel, trying to free enough breath to shout – perhaps Tashman would hear. But just as he began to think he might manage to slither back down the tunnel dragging his attacker with him, his legs were kicked away at the knees and he fell forward into the darkness.

The clammy arm tightened its grip as Krayn's fingernails tore away at the mud floor and the grey of the tunnel mouth misted over with red.

Tashman found the body. He was so excited by what the water cannon had revealed that he decided not to wait for Lannic and the others, but to meet them in the tunnel. Instead he found Krayn. He could see him immediately since the body was lying almost directly beneath the first of the lights. Krayn's eyes were bulging, his throat crushed. The tips of his fingers were almost embedded in the tunnel floor.

There was no sign of anyone else. Tashman was alone with his comrade's body, and a mud-spattered lamp.

When he broke the news to Lannic and Bannahilk in the operations room, their reactions were not what he expected. Tashman had assumed that they would both decide that enough was enough and they should exit straight away. But he had overlooked one fact which struck both of them immediately. Krayn was the pilot.

Ace listened to the conversation with increasing amazement. She had gathered from Benny and the Doctor that the archaeological side of things was pretty messed up. Now it seemed like the military were equally disorganized.

'Can you help, Doctor?' asked Gilmanuk once the initial noise had abated.

'Well, we landed with quite a splash,' the Doctor answered without missing a beat. 'And even if we can find where our vehicle sank, you'd soon see that it looks like it can only carry two at most.'

Ace wondered why he was avoiding helping them – no doubt he had reasons.

As if in answer to Ace's thoughts, the Doctor said, 'You must help yourselves. Why don't you ask your friend in orbit to come and get you?'

'He can't,' Lannic admitted. 'This is the only lander.'

'And Lefkhani hasn't piloted a lander, so far as I know,' Bannahilk added. 'Big stuff like the orbiter, yes. Lander – no chance. I doubt he's ever flown in an atmosphere, let alone the sort of weather out there. It's quite a skill.'

That was enough for Ace. 'Doesn't look too difficult,' she said confidently. 'Give me a couple of hours and I'll figure out how to get this heap off the planet.'

The Doctor frowned at her, and she smiled back. 'I'm going to do it, Doctor,' she whispered to him as the others launched into a round of self-congratulation and relief.

He nodded. 'I know, Ace. I know.' He beckoned Benny over and latched an arm round the neck of each of his companions. 'Ace, you keep everyone out of here for a while if you can – at least, away from the area where the TARDIS is parked. Benny, you and I are going on a little journey.'

Ace led Bannahilk off to the flight deck, the others following behind. They were still not sure that Ace was serious

110

and wanted to see how confident she was once she had seen the control systems.

Once the hold was clear, Benny asked the Doctor, 'So, where are we going?'

'I was rather hoping you could tell me.' He set off for the TARDIS, swinging the key round his finger on its chain. It wound itself up into his hand, increasing speed with each revolution.

'Doctor, I haven't a clue.'

'Clues – yes, that what we need.'

She still did not follow.

The Doctor sighed and put on his do-I-have-to-explain-everything look. 'There is something distinctly odd happening here, Benny.'

'That much I had noticed.'

'Then you've been asking yourself questions. Questions like: how come the Menaxans died out in such a hurry but left their theatre behind? How come there are buildings but no other material evidence that anyone ever lived here save the dream machine, as Ace rather quaintly calls it? And how come the acoustics in the theatre are so odd?'

'The acoustics? Doctor, I've sat at the back and heard people talking quietly on the stage. The acoustics are brilliant – they couldn't be better. The place is built to optimize the hell out of the acoustics.'

'Exactly. But why would a race of theatrical experts optimize the hell out of the acoustics when the theatre is empty? Fill that place with the thousands of people it would hold and the acoustics may not be so good. That would make an interesting experiment, don't you think?'

Benny considered for a moment, annoyed she had not thought of this. 'What we need are some clues,' she told him.

'Good. So where can you get at the initial survey material, and at the source documents which led Lannic here in the first place? Where can you look for clues?'

'Of course.' She saw what he was driving at, and

wondered if he had the answer already, or just knew that she would know it. 'The Braxiatel Collection.'

The Doctor beamed.

'There's just one small problem, Doctor.'

He looked crestfallen, as if she had just robbed him of his favourite toy.

'They won't let you in without a research ticket. And I don't have one.'

'Ah.' The Doctor looked round nervously, then stage-whispered, 'But I do.'

Ace knew what most of the main controls for the lander were and how to operate them. Some could have one of several functions, others she really had no clue about.

'Fortalexa probably has lines on some of them,' Bannahilk told her. 'He's into engineering and all things electrical. I've appeared with him several times – he knows his stuff.'

'But he is not a pilot,' Klasvik pointed out.

'No. He's not a pilot.'

'Is he still examining the machine?' Lannic wanted to know. 'More to the point, has he worked it out yet?'

Bannahilk turned to Tashman. He shrugged. 'I don't know, I haven't seen him. I was in such a rush to meet you – ' He broke off, his eyes widening.

'Meet us? I thought you came to tell us about Krayn.'

'I did. That is, I was on my way when I found him. He came to get you – to tell you what we'd discovered.'

'Discovered? What have you discovered?' Ace thought Lannic was about to grab Tashman by the shoulders, but she managed to restrain herself.

'In the mud. There was a hard edge, like stone. Krayn came to tell you while I tried to see what it was that was buried. It's incredible.'

They stared at him. Ace was the first to recover, perhaps she thought to herself because she was the least interested. 'And what was buried?'

Tashman seemed unsure whether he should be apologetic or proud. 'It's a hand. A human hand.'

Benny watched the TARDIS fade away, glancing round nervously to see if the noise of the engines had attracted any attention. But there was nobody in sight.

The Doctor had dropped her off in the courtyard just outside the doorway into the archaeology department. She felt a little more prepared this time – she knew what to expect indoors, and she felt she was rather better dressed for the surroundings. This time she was not wearing jeans and sweatshirt, but had searched through the TARDIS wardrobe until she had discovered a full-length scarlet dress in light velvet with lace trim around the cuffs and collar. She had had half a mind to search through for a suitable wig, but decided there were limits.

Well, she thought as she picked her way up the staircase, holding her dress just above the floor with one hand and the crumpled plastic card the Doctor had given her in the other, so long as old Elliniko isn't on duty this should be a breeze.

But he was.

For a moment Benny thought he might not recognize her. But he did. 'Professor Summerfield, how pleasant to see you again.'

She nodded, 'Likewise, Archivist.'

'But I am afraid you have been misinformed. Ticket applications are handled at reception. Perhaps you were misdirected here?' His tone assured her that this could not be the case.

'Oh no.'

'Then perhaps you would like an escort back to reception.' This was not a question.

'I don't think that will be necessary, thank you. I was hoping to look at the material you have on Menaxus – both Lannic's data and the original sources she worked from.'

'I'm sorry. No research is possible without a research ticket.' He was unapologetic.

'You mean like this one?' She smiled in what she hoped was an angelic manner as she handed it to him, and his face fell.

Then he frowned, puzzled more than angry. He ran the plastic strip through a reader on the side of the desk. A green light winked in response and his frown deepened. 'One moment, please Professor.' He waved her to a reproduction Louis Quatorze chair and reached for a call-set. It sat incongruously over his ear as he spoke into the microphone. 'I'm sorry to disturb you, sir, but I have a research ticket here that I haven't seen before.'

Benny strained to catch the response, but all she could hear was a tiny vibration as whoever Elliniko was talking to answered.

'Well, that is part of the problem, sir. The ticket does read valid, but there is *no* name on it. It was presented by a Professor Summerfield, who was here recently. From the Phaestor Osiris expedition.' He paused for the reply, turning the ticket over as he listened and squinting at a worn area of print on the reverse side. 'That's another odd thing, sir. The number is zero zero zero one.'

Benny watched in amazement as Elliniko's jaw dropped. The laughter from the call-set seemed loud to her, and she was a desk away.

Elliniko listened for a while longer, then he thanked whoever he had called for their time and help, and broke the connection. His smile was broad and appeared totally genuine. He reached across the desk and shook Bernice's hand as if she were an old and treasured friend. 'Professor Summerfield – welcome to the Braxiatel Collection.'

Benny stood, perplexed. But Elliniko was not to be stopped now. 'I shall allocate you a workstation and simu-larity studio immediately. The VIP suite is free, I believe.' He started off down the room, pausing politely to allow Bernice to catch up. 'I shall have the data you requested delivered to you as soon as we possibly can, Professor. Will you be with us long? I can arrange accommodation, although the VIP suite does of course have its own lounge and washroom facilities if those will suffice.'

Ace was waiting for him when the Doctor emerged from

the TARDIS. It was back in the lander's hold and Ace assured the Doctor that it had not been missed.

'They're too busy chasing after Tashman's hand. I said I'd stay and finish working out the controls.'

'What happened to Tashman's hand?'

'It's only his on a sort of finder's-keeper's basis.'

The Doctor was still confused. 'You mean he *found* a hand?'

'Oh yes. In the mud.' The Doctor seemed unenlightened. 'He thinks there's a whole arm in there,' she offered helpfully.

'In where?'

'In the mud – on the stage. Where we arrived, or whatever it was we did.'

The Doctor pondered for a moment, his eyes defocusing and his face slackening slightly. Then he blinked and fixed Ace with a steady stare. 'The stage. Yes. That will be the focal point.'

'Focal point?'

'The most dangerous area, if I'm right. Come on.'

'What if you're not right?' Ace asked him as they ran to the tunnel.

The Doctor stopped in mid step, and Ace went flying past as the law of momentum refused to stop. She stopped as soon as she could and waited for the Doctor to walk up to her.

He wore a hurt expression. 'I'm always right,' he told her, shouldering his umbrella and marching off down the tunnel.

They could see the archaeologists crowded round the stage. In the middle of the little crowd was the side of the huge mass of mud. It was only two thirds its original size, the steps having taken the rest. And in the otherwise smooth-cut side was a rough indentation where Tashman had gouged out the dirt. From the middle of the resultant crater protruded what looked like a human hand.

The Doctor assumed control as soon as he was on the stage. Before long he had them all gathered round as he

115

examined the hand, pushing the mud back from the wrist with a scalpel that had mysteriously appeared in his grasp at some point.

Tashman leaned forward to see what the Doctor was up to now. He appeared to be examining the edge of a cuff attached to the hand's wrist. 'I thought about blasting away the remainder of the mud with the water cannon, but it might damage the stone. If it is stone.'

'Oh it's stone all right.' The Doctor seemed preoccupied. He scraped more mud away and fixed a jeweller's glass in one eye. He prodded at the hand's wrist, moved round to give himself better light from the distant lamps which Tashman and Krayn had set up earlier, and frowned in concentration. After a long moment he looked up, the jeweller's glass dropping into his open hand and from there into his jacket pocket. He stared round at everyone. Ace could see him looking carefully at their arms.

Suddenly he caught hold of Bannahilk's jacket sleeve and pulled it towards him. Shocked, Bannahilk took a step forwards. But the Doctor dropped his arm in disgust and disappointment. He sat down heavily on the edge of the stage, unhooking his umbrella from his wrist, resting in on the theatre floor and leaning his hands on it in front of his face. This brought his cuffs level with his eyeline, and Ace saw him do a prize double take.

Then he was on his feet again, his eyes sharp with worry. 'Tashman,' he called across the stage. Tashman turned in response, and the Doctor's instruction was clear and loud: 'Do it!'

They cleared the stage and sat on the tiered steps of the auditorium as Bannahilk and Tashman adjusted the angle and range of the jets.

'What's going on?' asked a voice from close behind Ace. She looked round to find Fortalexa standing behind her.

She told him. 'It'll be a wash-out,' he responded immediately, and she grimaced.

'How are you getting on with the machine?'

'Not bad, I suppose. I know exactly how to work it.'

'But?' She could tell from his voice that there was a *but*.

'But I need the activator key.'

'And you don't have one?'

Fortalexa shook his head. 'No, I don't. So keep your eyes open.' He slumped down beside her. 'Where's your friend, professor Summerfield?'

Ace was not sure what she should tell him, so she asked instead, 'What does this key look like?'

He seemed not to notice the change of subject. 'It's a rectangular card with an internal magnetic strip. Probably plastic. About so wide.' He held the thumb and forefinger of his right hand about as wide apart as they would go to demonstrate.

'I'll keep a look out,' Ace told him, but her words were drowned out by the sound of the water jets hitting the wall of mud and burrowing inside it.

The Doctor was on his feet and staring towards the stage even before the jets had stopped. They could all see the three figures standing on the stage, vague shapes through the haze of water droplets, but distinct enough to be discernible – characters waiting for a cue that would never come.

Ace joined the Doctor at the edge of the stage. The mist was clearing a little now and she could begin to make out more detail in the figures. They were posed, unnaturally upright like typical stone statues. But there was something more familiar about them. Two female, one male. Strangely she recognized the least familiar one first.

The rightmost figure was Lannic. She had seen this herself and was standing beside Ace, her mouth open in surprise. On Ace's other side the Doctor nodded grimly.

And at last Ace recognized the other two stone figures. One was herself, and the other was the Doctor.

ACT 2

Source Document 6

Account of the opening performance of *The Captain's Honour* at the Pentillanian Theatre on Menaxus

Braxiatel Collection Catalogue Number: 882PA

Fragment. Author unknown. Date presumed to be c 2295

On Menaxus, as the capital of the most flourishing society, theatrical representations without end prevail throughout the calendar in the Pentillanian Theatre.

The performance that it was my good fortune to attend was *The Captain's Honour*. This play by Osterling is not, in this reviewer's opinion, one of his most keen. Yet the interpretation of the Menaxan players was hailed as being as fresh as it was profound and I remember it with particular clarity. The majesty of the huge theatre lent the proceedings an air of spectacle I have not discerned in other versions.

Chapter 6

Ace You Like It

But for all the papers and posturing from Brett and his cronies, it remains unproven that a computer can think, even on a conscious level. Nagler's assertion that a computer is somehow capable of unconscious heuretic thought – can discover and invent from the data fed to it – is completely implausible. It works only in controlled experiments where the learning path is clearly defined before the data is provided. There is absolutely no way to prove Nagler's famous example of a computer choosing, apparently at random, a passage of text which reflects upon and illuminates a current, unspoken context.

The Myth of Artificial Intelligence
– Phil Houseman, 2009

Ace followed the Doctor as he stepped up onto the stage and began to fade into the mist.

'What are they, Doctor? How did they get here?'

'They're statues.'

'I can see that.'

Lannic was with them, appearing out of the mist as it thinned and dropped around them. 'It's incredible,' she said, rapping her knuckle against the arm of the statue of Ace. It gave the dead thud of stone. She turned accusingly. 'Do you know anything about them?'

'Nothing, I assure you.'

Lannic shook her head in disbelief and went over to examine the statue of herself. Ace followed the Doctor over to his statue.

'Are you sure you know nothing about this?'

The Doctor examined the hand that had originally projected from the mud, tracing his finger back along the wrist and arm. 'Quite sure, Ace.' He stared across into his own face and was met with stony indifference. 'Do I really look like that?' He explored his own features with his fingers, drawing the skin tight on his cheek as he pulled at it. 'Yes, I suppose I do these days.' He stared across at the other two stone figures for a moment. 'They've been here a long time, Ace.'

'You can say that again. But how did they get here?'

He shrugged. 'Someone put them here. Long ago. Before the theatre collapsed into ruins; before the mud came; before the archaeologists started digging.'

'So – why? They look just like us.'

'They are us, Ace. Or statues of us, rather. And they look exactly *as we do now*.'

Ace considered this. 'The TARDIS?'

'Possibly.'

'Must be. We travel back in time, to when the theatre was in use. You, me and Lannic.'

'And we do something that leads to these statues being erected – something outstandingly good. Or bad.' The Doctor prodded his stone midriff with the point of his umbrella. 'I'm sure Blinovitch would have an opinion to voice.'

'Who?'

'Oh, temporal theorist. Nobody important.' He turned to the statue of Ace and patted it on the shoulder. 'But it is puzzling, don't you think?'

Bannahilk found the various reactions to this new development interesting. He and Fortalexa both stood back and watched the others, periodically scanning the dim recesses of the theatre for any signs of movement. Surprisingly, Lannic and the two strangers recovered first. It somehow seemed less of a shock to them to find life-size stone replicas of themselves than it did to the others.

Tashman seemed as indifferent as ever, shrugging the whole thing off and sitting in the front of the auditorium to watch. He showed no signs of appreciating the possible threat, no wariness or real interest at all. Typical – no wonder he had been selected for a routine mission like this rather than a front-line role. *Routine*. Bannahilk almost laughed out loud.

Gilmanuk and Klasvik seemed the most affected. The diminutive Gilmanuk was wandering around in a daze after the Doctor and Ace who were examining the Doctor's statue. Lannic was similarly interested in her own. Klasvik was slumped down close to Tashman.

Bannahilk looked round at the sorry team he was left with. Only Fortalexa had any real combat training or experience, although Tashman could probably hold a gun the right way round. And the woman, Ace, looked like she might be useful. He watched her as she moved round the stage after the Doctor. He saw the tenseness of her stance; her almost cat-like movements – as if she could smell the blood on the wind, hear the blood in her ears; the athletic outline of her body moulded into the dark combat suit. Yes, she certainly could be useful.

'Right,' Bannahilk's voice echoed round the theatre; he need not have shouted but it had the desired effect. They all turned to him. The cantankerous old Klasvik, he noted with satisfaction, almost leapt out of his costume with surprise. 'I want everyone back in the operations room now. We're going to get some answers, or at the very least a direction for exiting this place.'

Klasvik was the most in favour of leaving immediately. Ace had not thought the old man would have so much noise in him, but he had insisted that there was obviously a whole army of Rippeareans down in the theatre complex waiting to rush out and slaughter them all.

'Why don't you contact the orbiter and get help from Lefkhani? He is a pilot after all,' Gilmanuk wanted to know.

'Fortalexa can give Ace as much help as Lefkhani can,' Bannahilk told him. 'And with the Rippearean advance so close now, I'm not breaking communications silence for anything. I want to get out with my skin in one piece.'

Ace left them to argue and went forward. She might as well get on with it – the sooner they left the better. But she knew not to rush things. 'If you get a moment in your busy schedule,' she whispered to Fortalexa as she passed him, 'I'd appreciate some help understanding the anti-quated com-net equipment you have.'

Fortalexa nodded. 'Give me a couple of minutes,' he told her. 'I want a word with Bannahilk.'

Ace glanced back. The meeting seemed to be breaking up into smaller conversations. She caught Bannahilk's eye as she turned to go. Their gaze locked for a moment, but she could not read his expression.

'What do you think is going on, Doctor?'

The Doctor had been on the periphery of the conversations, both by keeping his thoughts to himself and by sitting away from the main group. He had seen Ace leave for the control deck, and had noticed Bannahilk watch her go. Fortalexa had followed soon after, whispering a few words to his commander on the way.

He looked up from his present study of the mud on the floor. 'Ah,' he said. 'That, Lannic, is the question.'

'You must have some idea.'

'I have an idea –'

'Yes?' she interrupted him eagerly.

The Doctor continued as if she had not spoken: ' – that we should get off this planet as soon as we can.'

Lannic nodded. 'You're probably right. Looks like we have an hour to get together what we can from the exca-vations before we leave.' She turned to go.

'We have an hour,' the Doctor called after her, 'to stay alive.'

Gilmanuk came over. 'Doctor?' He gestured at a spare crate close by. The Doctor waved him to it. 'I hope you will not feel me impertinent, but I must ask you something.'

'She's quite safe,' the Doctor said, quiet and distant.

'I'm sorry?'

125

The Doctor looked him in the eye. 'You were about to ask about Benny.'

'Yes. I thought, since she is a colleague of yours . . .'

'Indeed.' The Doctor took Gilmanuk's hand in his. 'I must ask you to trust me. Professor Summerfield is doing something for me, something important. She is quite safe, but I would rather that as few people as possible knew where she is and what she is about.'

Gilmanuk considered for a moment. 'Very well, Doctor. I will take my cue from you.' He stood, slightly embarrassed as he realized his hand was held by the Doctor. The Doctor smiled, and turned the grasp into a friendly handshake. The archaeologist smiled faintly.

'None of the others have asked after her,' the Doctor said. 'Thank you for your concern. Benny will appreciate it.'

The com-link seemed easy enough: a simple plasma-gel to stick the suction cup to her forehead and then Ace would be at one with the machine. For what it was worth.

'Krayn told me it slowed him down,' Fortalexa told her. 'But you have to link in or you might miss something important.'

The interior door slid open.

'Lannic.' Fortalexa nodded politely and stood almost to attention, towering over the dark-haired woman.

Ace went back to her study of the equipment. She had little time for Lannic, who struck her as cold, aloof and interested in nothing other than the dead past. At least Benny had some appreciation of living people, of technology, and of hard liquor.

'How are you getting on here?'

'Just about done, actually. Aren't we, Ace?'

Ace answered without looking round: 'Give me a while to get plugged in, then I can start the pre-flight checks.'

'Good. Since we still have some time, I have a request, Fortalexa – I need your help.'

'Oh?'

'Bannahilk is ready to leave as soon as possible. I agree

126

that seems the best course of action, although obviously we'll be leaving most of our work here undone. I want to salvage something from this mess. Despite the problems, we have the chance to create quite a performance when we get back. Will you help?'

'What is it that you want?'

Ace held her breath: here it came.

'That machine. I want to know if it can be moved.'

'And if it can?' Ace could tell from his voice that Fortalexa already knew the answer.

'Then I want it back here – I want to take it back to Heletia. I want to present it to the Exec.'

Bannahilk was supervising the work troupe which was reloading the lander from the base camp. The troupe consisted entirely of Tashman, who was not wasting any opportunity to point this out.

Fortalexa smiled as he approached. It seemed almost as if Tashman had taken over Krayn's role of chief moaner. Bannahilk seemed to welcome the opportunity to get away and they moved to the start of the tunnel and spoke in low voices. Fortalexa told his officer about Lannic's request.

'Seems fair enough, I suppose. Get that Doctor to give you a hand – he seems to know his stuff.'

'Perhaps too much so, sir.'

'He is supposed to be a colleague of Professor Summerfield.'

Fortalexa nodded. 'And she was a late member of our cast.'

'So she was.' Bannahilk thought for a while. 'Have you seen her recently?'

Fortalexa had not. 'She may have wandered off like she did before.'

'Or she may be dead.'

Fortalexa did not think that likely. But then again, so many of the others were dead now – why should the professor be any luckier?

'No,' Bannahilk told him. 'We have to trust the Doctor.

And the woman, Ace. She is after all our only hope of getting out of here.'

'True.' Fortalexa had seen how Bannahilk watched Ace. And he knew what that meant; he had served with Bannahilk before. He shook his mind to clear the images he remembered from shore leave on Avidos, and the sounds from his commanding officer's cabin after they had over-run the Pletillon quarter of Cortasplay. They all tried to cope with the stress in their own ways. He favoured humour, diffusing the emotion rather than giving it free rein. Bannahilk, he knew, had other methods. Fortalexa took a deep breath. 'I'd be careful of her, sir.'

Bannahilk snapped his attention back to Fortalexa. 'What do you mean?'

'Just that I think the Doctor is a man to be reckoned with, sir.' He searched for a way of expressing what he meant without seeming insubordinate. 'I think we should help him see that nothing happens to her.' Bannahilk's eyes narrowed as he took Fortalexa's meaning. 'And, as you say sir,' Fortalexa went on, 'she is our only hope of getting out of here.'

Bannahilk was about to reply when a voice from behind startled them: 'Ah, there you are.'

They both whirled round, in time to see the Doctor replace his hat.

'I was thinking, perhaps we should take advantage of this lull in the proceedings to have another look at our dream machine.'

The two soldiers exchanged glances, both wandering how long the Doctor had been standing behind them.

The VIP suite was certainly plush. Bernice had installed herself at a workstation in the corner of the spacious lounge. The lounge walls were lined with red silk and hung with portraits framed with heavy gilt. One wall was dominated by a huge marble fireplace, another was almost entirely taken up with a bay window which looked out on to the main lawn as it sloped away from Mansionhouse.

Doors led off to a washroom, a simularity chamber and back into the main area of the archaeology department.

Bernice had kicked her shoes off and was curling her toes into the deep rug which ran almost to the sides of the room, the onyx floor just visible as a margin round the edge. She was impressed by what the research assistants had managed to dig out for her – a '59 Chardonnay. She sipped at it appreciatively as the computer on the desk in front of her chewed its way through millions of facts and figures from Lannic's original survey, generating a simularity of the Menaxan theatre.

'Done,' said the computer. She had given it a deep male voice. It was attractive and sonorous, and the hint of an extinct Scottish accent was somehow comforting.

'Okay,' Benny told the machine. 'Feed that through to the simularity chamber and give me a direct voice link and control.'

'Done.' She might have to do something about the vocabulary and personality.

The simularity chamber was just a dark room, until a simularity filled it. Benny stood in the doorway. 'Play-back,' she commanded, and at once the room stretched out and down before her. She was standing at the back of the theatre, looking out over the seats and stage below. It was bright, twin suns shining in – no canopy of plastic, no rain, no mud. Exactly as it had been when Lannic's team had first uncovered it. Rather than the dark oppressive place she had seen on Menaxus, the theatre was bright and welcoming. She could imagine comedy playing here, the walls echoing with laughter. On Menaxus she had assumed that the only performances given were tragic.

'Are you familiar with *Hamlet*?' she asked.

'Yes,' replied the deep voice from above and around her.

'Good. Give me Hamlet, on the stage. Play back a soliloquy – something to test the acoustics. Normal human volume for an actor.'

'Done.'

Far below her a man appeared, standing centre stage.

He was wearing traditional doublet and hose. He walked slowly forward and began to speak. His voice was the same as the computer's.

'O, what a rogue and peasant slave am I:
Is it not monstrous that this player here,
But in a fiction, in a dream of passion,
Could force his soul so to his own conceit
That from her working all his visage wann'd,
Tears in his eyes, distraction in 's aspect
A broken voice, and his whole function suiting
With forms to his conceit? And all for nothing!'

'Stop.' Benny could hear the words clearly. She wondered how the computer had decided on that particular speech, how it had decided at what points the voice should break slightly and the character shake his head in near despair. 'Add seats, wooden ones,' she said. 'You decide the size and shape, but fill the auditorium with them.'

The seats appeared, low wooden benches. 'Adjust the acoustics to compensate and replay the soliloquy. From the top.'

'O, what a rogue and peasant slave am I,' Hamlet began, snapping back to his original position and replaying exactly the intonation and gestures. His voice was still clear but slightly deadened, quieter, because of the wood.

'Stop. I want an audience now. Put someone on every second seat. Human, half of them male, half female. All adults.' She laughed as she watched the theatre fill from the front as if an invisible hand were pointing to each seat in rapid succession. Throughout the theatre, Hamlet sat a seat away from Professor Bernice Summerfield.

'Done.'

'Not much imagination but it will do, I suppose,' said Benny as she made to pat the head of herself sitting in the back row. Her hand passed through. 'Adjust the acoustics to match, and then play it again, Ham,' she said.

The result was interesting. Although the audience was still and silent, she could barely hear Hamlet. If she had

130

not heard the words a couple of times already it would be a real strain.

'Stop. Raise the actor's volume to the loudest reasonable level. Also add background noise from the audience, at the lowest realistic level. And change the words – give me a different soliloquy.'

'Done.'

Hamlet started again. His voice drifted up to Benny as she strained to catch the words above the slight murmur and rustle of the unmoving audience. It was near impossible. She started to walk down the centre aisle. The feeling was slightly odd as the theatre rose up past her, the simularity matching her movements to the generated image.

Odd words began to resolve themselves into meaning: '... thought ... wisdom .. : coward ... I ... say ...' As Benny moved closer to the stage, she managed to decipher more and more of the speech. When she could hear it all clearly, she stopped. She was over two thirds of the way to the stage. The Doctor was right: the theatre, the whole premise of the Menaxan civilization just did not work.

In front of her Hamlet continued undeterred:

'... to my shame, I see
The imminent death of twenty thousand men,
That, for a fantasy and trick of fame,
Go to their graves like beds, fight for a plot – '

'Stop.' Benny carried on down to the front of the theatre and stepped up onto the stage. She was so deep in thought she hardly noticed Hamlet, frozen into a grey statue, as she walked through him. Then she turned and looked back out over the unreal audience. Somewhere in the pile of material that Elliniko had brought her, was a clue – something that would tell her what was going on, would explain the contradictions of a race that disappeared with no explanation, and a theatre that only worked when if was empty. 'When a play is performed to an empty house, does it make a sound?' she murmured.

'More information needed,' the computer answered.

'You're telling me,' said Benny, and made her way back up through the silent seated figures.

Bannahilk looked round the hold. The only equipment on his manifest which was not yet back on board was the water cannon. Tashman was getting that now. He would probably need help on the ropes. Bannahilk took a last look round, and went out to the tunnel.

He was about half-way to the theatre when he saw a figure in the dim light ahead. He stopped, reaching for his side-arm. The figure was approaching, walking a little unsteadily as if afraid of slipping. As it reached the lamp immediately in front of Bannahilk the figure paused, as if it had seen him. Bannahilk could make out who it was now – it was Ace.

Bannahilk grinned, and he could swear that the young woman smiled back at him. He remembered what Fortalexa had said, but he was in charge. She was a soldier; she would do as she was ordered. Just so long as she could fly the lander afterwards. Bannahilk moved his hand from the disruptor at his side to the hilt of the knife at his belt, then down to his side. Time enough for that later, on the way home.

Ace came closer, her body swaying heavily as she made her way carefully towards him. Her face was a wide grin, grey in the faint light.

As she drew level with him, Bannahilk said, 'Hello there.' Then he paused, puzzled. 'I thought you were on the flight deck – how did you get here ahead of me?'

But she shook her head slowly, almost ponderously, and reached out to him.

Bannahilk felt his stomach yawn. This was easier than he could have hoped. He opened his arms and let her reach around him, her face coming close to his own. Any moment now he would feel her breath on his face. He reached for the clasp on her combat suit, and in the same moment as he realized that she was not breathing, he felt the clasp moulded and solid with the suit. And cold.

He pulled back, but her arms held him tight. He could see her face close to his, the mouth stretching across, lips slightly parted as she pulled him back towards her. And as her cheek closed coldly on his, he realized that the

132

edges of her mouth were cracked slightly – as if her whole face were made of stone.

The pressure on his body increased to breaking point. He could feel his ribs cracking as he struggled to break from the cold embrace of the statue. Then suddenly the stone form seemed to melt, to give way, as if the outer shell had split open. Bannahilk was pressed relentlessly into the soft mud inside. He felt his face crack through Ace's cheek, and the dark slush behind it smothered his nose and poured into his mouth as he gasped for breath. His hands clawed at the soft innards of the lithe female figure as it moulded itself round him, pushing him down to the ground in a parody of an embrace. The remains of her mouth was over his as he choked his last desperate breath and a long tongue of mud blocked his throat.

The figure lay prone and still as the mud slid away from it, disappearing into the floor of the tunnel, raising it imperceptibly. Then the body too began to sink away. Silence. Then a slight squelching noise as the wall of the tunnel bowed outwards. A female figure formed from it, and stepped free. She stood silent and still for a while, then started cautiously up the tunnel. The light from the lamps seemed almost to be absorbed into the dull grey of her sleek combat suit as the figure made her way towards the lander.

Source Document 7

An eyewitness account of Hagan's acting

Braxiatel Collection Catalogue Number: 117GPR

Fragment. Written by George Lichbergh. Dated 2407

Hagan was without doubt the greatest Menaxan actor of the time. I was fortunate enough to attend his version of *Hamlet*, hailed as the most profound interpretation of modern times.

I remember with particular clarity the scene in which Hamlet first encounters the ghost of his father. The theatre was darkened (it being an evening performance) and the whole audience of thousands was quiet and motionless, as if painted on the walls. At Horatio's words: 'Look, my lord, it comes,' Hagan turned sharply, and at the same moment staggered back several paces, his knees giving way under him. His whole demeanour was so expressive of terror that it made my flesh crawl even before he spoke.

Finally, not at the beginning, but at the end of a deep breath, his voice trembling, he said the line: 'Angels and ministers of grace defend us!' These words completed the tension and fear inherent in this scene and made it, in this writer's opinion, one of the greatest and most terrible that will ever be played upon a stage.

Chapter 7

Saint's Day

It is not often appreciated that, in archaeology, to see the big picture, it is necessary to examine the details and minutiae. This is one science where it is often better to extrapolate from detail than to look for supporting evidence.

Down Among The Dead Men
– Professor Bernice Summerfield, 2466

'We won't get much further without an activator key,' Fortalexa said again. He hated to admit defeat, but he replaced the main cover and thumped it home.

'Perhaps we could make one,' the Doctor suggested, raising an eyebrow hopefully. But they both knew that it would take forever to decode the encryption sequence.

'Oh well, at least it's mobile. There doesn't seem to be any problem with getting it back to the lander.' Fortalexa wobbled the wheeled contraption experimentally to and fro. 'Look,' he quipped, 'travelling theatre.'

The Doctor laughed. 'We'll have more time to look at it once we're away from here.'

Fortalexa nodded. 'I'll get Tashman to drag it back to the lander for us. He should have finished with the water cannon by now.' They had both enjoyed an interlude of several minutes watching through the concealed window as Tashman tried to raise the dismantled elements of the water cannon one by one up to the tunnel mouth using a rope and pulley. They could hear him cursing volubly as he tried to swing it onto each successive step.

As they got back to the main theatre, they paused and

looked down towards the stage. Tashman was just visible dragging the tied-off rope precariously holding the water cannon's main nozzle assembly into the tunnel mouth. It looked like the nozzle was the final component. Below him Gilmanuk, Klasvik and Lannic were frantically scribbling notes on their clip-paks as they examined various parts of the theatre construction.

'She's taking everything she can,' Fortalexa said. 'She'll get a good review for diligence.'

'You mean the water cannon?' joked the Doctor.

'I meant the statue, actually. Look.' He pointed down at the stage. There were only two statues there now – those of the Doctor and Lannic.

'Are you all right?' Fortalexa asked after a moment. The Doctor was still staring at the stage, his mouth half open. He seemed entranced.

'Lannic,' the Doctor suddenly shouted down the aisle. Fortalexa took a step back in surprise at the strength of the Doctor's voice.

Far below them, Lannic paused and looked round for the source of the sound. She found the Doctor at last and waved up at him. 'I'm rather busy,' she called out, her voice clear despite the distance as it travelled up from close to the stage.

'Did you move the statue of Ace?' the Doctor shouted back undeterred.

She looked up again, annoyed. Then she registered the meaning of his words and turned to look at the stage. 'S'blood!' she exclaimed, and from across the theatre Klasvik and Gilmanuk also paused to look.

The Doctor and Fortalexa continued their descent, Lannic and the others joining them at the base of the stepped aisle.

'Sit down,' the Doctor told them. They sat in the front row, and he stood at the base of the stage. 'I have a theory. Not pleasant, not proven. But I think I know what is happening here.'

'You think you know?' Klasvik was on his feet, pointing

past the Doctor. 'The statue has been removed and you *think* you know what is happening?'

'What is the point you are trying to make, Klasvik?' Lannic's voice was weary, resigned.

'I'll tell you the point, although I would have thought it was obvious. Someone is playing games with us. The Rippeareans are here, picking us off one by one.'

'Not the Rippereans, I'm afraid. Something far worse.'

'Worse? You don't know what you're talking about.'

The Doctor leaped down from the stage, umbrella held out in front of him so that it pointed directly at Klasvik's chest, stopping just short of touching him. 'I know infinitely more than you ever will, Leontium Klasvik.'

Klasvik started. 'How did you know – '

But the Doctor ignored him. 'I have been to the Eye of Orion, have been caught in the clutches of the black hole of Tartarus, been hunted through the universe by the Daleks, and played backgammon with Kublai Khan. And you say I don't know what I'm talking about? Have you ever seen the skies above Metabelis Three, tried the experiential grid on Argolis, or watched the space yachts of the Eternals race against the stars?' He turned away in contempt. 'Of course you haven't.'

After a moment the Doctor turned back to face them, tapping the handle of his umbrella thoughtfully against his chin. He opened his mouth to speak, and Klasvik screamed.

'I may have been a little harsh,' the Doctor seemed taken aback, 'but that does seem a somewhat extreme reaction.'

But Klasvik was not the only one to react. Lannic and Gilmanuk were already on their feet, as Fortalexa reached out to the Doctor. Tashman and Klasvik were backing away from the stage. The Doctor took a step backwards, but Fortalexa grabbed his sleeve and pulled him into the front row.

And the arms of the Doctor's statue closed on the empty space where his throat had been. Its eyes snapped upwards to see where its quarry had gone, a tear of mud

137

streaking down one cheek as the stone shell cracked with the movement. The Lannic statue joined the stone Doctor at the edge of the stage and together they watched their prey scurry away up the aisle.

'You're right,' the Doctor said breathlessly as he raced Fortalexa and Klasvik through the auditorium. 'I don't know what I'm talking about.'

Bernice leafed through the pile of documents for a few seconds, then checked the optical sphere's index on the screen for the umpteenth time. 'Strange but true,' she muttered quietly. There was something odd about all the documents. Some detail that was evading her.

She had noticed the obvious problem almost at once. All the documentation was about the theatre. It had taken her a while to realize that this actually was a problem, though. Since she was interested in the theatre she was initially overjoyed that so much material existed which related to it. Lannic must have had the same reaction, she thought.

But then Lannic had not drunk enough Chardonnay to get to the point where you suspect any euphoria, however mild, to be alcohol-induced. So Benny had looked for the down-side. And the down-side was that there was no material relating to any other aspect of life on Menaxus. None.

That was when she had first called Elliniko. He must have understood her only to be interested in the theatre, and not provided whatever other documents there were. But no, this was it. A whole planet's history from (she leafed through a pile of half-sorted papers to check) universal calendar date 2176 to (she glanced at the index) UCD 2542. And all of it related to a tiny geographical area significant only because someone called Pithess had built a theatre there. It was almost unbelievable. Almost – she clung to the idea that maybe the eccentric Braxiatel was not interested in anything else about the planet: not interested in any other area or nation, not interested in medical or political or geographical information. Just theatre. And just this one theatre.

But that was not what worried Bernice. What worried her was whatever she was missing. She had almost had it as she again read through the fragment of an anonymous account of the opening performance of *The Captain's Honour* at the Pentillanian Theatre on Menaxus, but it had escaped. She had come even closer when she reread Georg Lichbergh's eyewitness account of Hagan's *Hamlet*. But again it had eluded her. It was not something particular to those documents, but they were somehow a part of it – whatever it was.

'Stuff it,' Bernice said out loud, and went back to the simularity chamber. She might as well try a completely different approach.

The theatre was still there, waiting for her. The audience of Hamlets and Bennys still sat waiting for the Hamlet on stage to begin a random soliloquy.

'Cancel this lot,' said Bernice, and they disappeared, the whole theatre folding up and fading away in front of her. 'Reference Lannic's data – measurements and holograms. Show me the admissions complex as it was when she saw it.'

'Done.' A set of ruined buildings swam into existence. The main building was largely intact apart from a side wall which lay where it had fallen across the sand. The wall opposite it no longer existed at all – or maybe the entrance had been completely open. The roof still balanced across the top somehow, and Benny wondered briefly how it had managed to take the weight of the lander. The other buildings were in varying states of disrepair, many being little more than piles of stones laid out where walls had once been.

Benny walked down through the ruined stone buildings, picking her way needlessly round the walls and rubble. She had been to a thousand similar sites, yet they never ceased to amaze her. She could stand for hours and lap up the feelings of the past.

Except there were none.

She put it down to the simularity for a while. But then she began to notice consciously what her subconscious had seen all along. This site was different – the lie of the stones and rubble; the way the wall of the main building had fallen away from its neighbours.

'Stand this wall up again,' she said on a whim. The computer obliged and stones rose of their own accord until the wall slotted neatly into place, completing the building like a jigsaw. Bernice walked up to the wall and looked at it, cocking her head to one side. It seemed odd that just a single wall had gone without apparently affecting the others. 'How did it fall?' she asked herself.

But the computer heard, and the wall crashed down at her. She yelped and jumped back, then immediately looked round to see if anyone had seen her leap out of the way of a non-existent wall. Her stomach settled and she turned back to the ruin. An idea was forming in her mind. She did not yet know what it was, but it was close.

'Show me again, half speed.' The wall slowly toppled forward and crashed into the sand, remaining largely intact on impact. 'And again.' Benny watched it through three more times at various speeds. After she was sure that the middle of the wall bowed outwards first, the top tearing away a moment later from where the roof had been. She thought about the problem, then said, 'State basis for calculation of the way the wall fell.'

'Simularity animation consistent with spatial arrangement of stones on site. Pressures applied to match dispersal on ground impact.'

'You mean you can tell how the wall fell from the way it was lying afterwards. Very clever.' She considered. 'Are you clever enough to run the animation again, at twenty-five per cent speed, with the other three walls of the building removed?'

In answer the standing walls faded away, and the square of stones on the ground rose slowly into position. Bernice moved so she could watch from behind. 'Okay – go.'

The wall fell impossibly slowly, curling away from her. She shook her head. It was still not quite right. 'Give me

140

a light source, angled at ninety degrees to the wall and at forty-five degrees elevation.' The light appeared, and Benny stood so she was end-on to the wall, a short distance from it. 'And run it again.'

It was all too obvious this time. The shadows thrown onto the falling wall by the light source clearly illuminated the slight bulge in the middle of the wall just as it started to fall. But how could she find out what had caused it? The answer, when she reached it after pacing round the ruins for several minutes was equally obvious.

'Why is there a bulge in the middle of the wall just as it starts to fall?' she asked.

'Simularity animation consistent with spatial arrangement of stones on site. Pressures applied to match dispersal on ground impact. The bulge referred to is the main point of pressure.'

'The wall was pushed over?'

'Yes.'

'What by?'

In answer a rectangular surface of metal materialized in the air before Bernice. The wall rose to meet it, and the metal square fitted into the slight bulge as the wall reached a near-upright position. The animation froze.

'Put the other walls back.' They duly appeared in place. Benny walked round them, and looked in through the open end of the building at the newly erected far wall, the metal sheet still pressed against it.

She could not prove it, of course, but it looked to Benny as if someone had driven a bulldozer through the open front of the building and knocked down the back wall, leaving the rest of that area of the complex intact.

She walked over to one of the completely ruined buildings. It was just four piles of stones where the walls had been once. 'I wonder . . . Show me that wall intact.' She pointed to the nearest part of the ruin.

'Not possible.'

Oh well, everything must have limits, she supposed. 'Can you tell if this wall collapsed in the same way – from similar exertion of pressure?'

'Impossible. That is not a wall.'

'I beg your pardon?'

'That is not a wall. None of the sections in close proximity are walls.'

'Then what are they?'

'Piles of stones.'

Benny frowned. 'I can see that. But they used to be walls – like that one we just looked at.' She waved vaguely in the direction of the main admission block.

'No.'

'Explain.'

'Collapsed stuctures can be recreated mathematically from their constituent elements if the dimensions of all elements remaining are known and at least fifty-five per cent of structure is still on site.'

'You mean most of this one is gone?'

'This represents four sets of stones, one with ninety-four constitutes, one with one hundred and five constituents – '

'Yes, yes – all right.'

'The constituents are not related. It is impossible to assemble a coherent structure from any of the sets using more than one third of constituent stones.'

'So these piles of stones are just piles of stones?'

Benny held her breath; she was not sure whether things were becoming clearer or whether the whole thing was getting out of hand. There was still something she was missing.

'No coherent structures have stood in the areas now illuminated in green,' the computer said dispassionately.

Benny looked around. With the exception of the main block and the theatre itself, just visible behind it, as far as she could see the reconstruction was bathed in green light.

Tashman was the slowest. While the others turned and fled up the steps of the main aisle, he backed slowly away from the stage, eyes wide and mouth open.

'Tashman – get up here,' yelled Fortalexa. Only he and

the Doctor had spared a backward glance to see where everyone was.

The sound of the soldier's voice echoing round the theatre galvanized Tashman into movement at last. He swung his huge body round almost as the statue of Lannic reached him, and started up the steps two at a time.

But they were too steep. Fortalexa and the others were far enough away from the ponderous statues to risk stopping to get their breath back. So they all saw Tashman miss his footing, his ankle turning on the crumbling edge of one of the steps. He crashed to the ground, his head connecting with a dull thud.

Fortalexa already had his sidearm drawn, but the blast did not even slow the lumbering forms. He holstered it and started down to help Tashman immediately, only to find the Doctor holding on to his sleeve.

'We're too late,' said the Doctor, although Fortalexa had not seen him make any move to help. But the Doctor was right.

Below them, Tashman lifted his head slowly, shaking it to clear the pain. As he started to pull himself to his feet, the Lannic statue reached him. Its shadow fell over the steps where Tashman was sprawled, and he rolled onto his back to see what was above him. And screamed.

Fortalexa watched helpless as the statue reached out, almost in slow motion, and grabbed Tashman's hair, pulling his head forward and up. Then it pushed its other hand into Tashman's face. He thought at first that the force of the deceptively slow blow had smashed through the man's face, but he could see now that the hand had squashed against it, cracking and fracturing. The outside was a thin shell which cracked open to release mud which oozed out and over Tashman's face, burying it.

Tashman's scream was choked off. He writhed for a few movements, as if impaled on the statue's wrist, then the figure of Lannic let go of his hair and Tashman's dead weight dropped him back to the ground, allowing the mud and stone to reform into a female hand.

Fortalexa looked away. Behind him the real Lannic

was pale with shock, her lower lip trembling. The Doctor caught Fortalexa's eye. 'We are become death,' he said quietly. Then he turned suddenly and sprang up a few steps to join Lannic. He patted her gently on the shoulder, but she hardly seemed to notice.

The two statues were approaching them from different angles. Lannic was continuing up the aisle, but the Doctor's statue was clambering up the tiers of the auditorium where the seats had been.

'The problem as I see it,' Fortalexa said, surprised at how calm his voice was, 'is to get past them and to the tunnel. Then we can get back to the lander and hope that Ace is ready to leave.'

'I think they realize that. Which is why they've spread out – to block our exit.' Gilmanuk's voice was equally calm, his hesitancy gone.

Klasvik looked at them both as if they were mad. Lannic seemed not to hear. The Doctor had produced a small abacus from his pocket and was flicking beads across it frantically, pausing only to measure up angles and distances like a draughtsman up against a deadline.

'What we need is a diversion – they're not very fast.' By way of demonstration, the Doctor ducked out of the way as the statue of himself drew level and swiped an arm at him. Its weight carried it past and swung the figure's body away.

'Allow me, Doctor.' Fortalexa jumped down a couple of steps so he was in the statue's line of sight. It saw him at once and changed direction to follow as he stepped backwards, into the Lannic statue's way. As Fortalexa backed away up the steps, both the statues followed him, as if locked on to his path.

Fortalexa backed away up the steps towards the back of the theatre. The Doctor ushered everyone else across through the auditorium. When they were well clear of the statues, he all but pushed them down towards the stage. 'Thank you, Fortalexa – you can join us now!' he shouted over his shoulder as he ran after the stumbling Klasvik, overtaking him in a moment and grabbing his surprised hand to drag him along faster.

Fortalexa was beginning to think he might have left it too late. He had reached the back row and was almost at the wall. Both statues reached out towards him, toothless smiles breaking their faces. Their hands were all but on him when he sprang forward, pushing himself off the back wall with his right foot and diving through their arms. He felt cold fingers tear at his uniform as he crashed through and the ground flew up to meet him.

Just as he hit he curled his shoulder down so it hit the ground first, rolling him over and down the steps, drop-chute style. After two complete rolls he was on his feet, the momentum carrying him down to join the others.

Lannic and Gilmanuk were already up the first of the huge steps of mud. Lannic seemed to have recovered from the shock and was pulling Klasvik up after her as the Doctor pushed him from below. Klasvik's hands were scrabbling to get a hold on the slippery surface. Fortalexa added his shoulder to the Doctor's and together they heaved the old archaeologist up.

Fortalexa scrabbled up after him. A hand reached down to help him as he straightened his arms and pulled himself up. He was about to offer thanks, but he was too surprised – how had the Doctor managed to get up the step so quickly?

Painfully slowly they scrambled up the remaining steps. Fortalexa was last to reach the top, having pushed the others up ahead of him – all except the Doctor who seemed somehow just to arrive at the next level with no help from anyone. He looked back down into the theatre.

And saw the stone eyes of the statue of Lannic looking back at him from the step below. Surely that was impossible – how could it have climbed so fast, especially weighing what it must? But before he could speculate further, the head of the statue of the Doctor appeared at the top of the steps, seeming to rise out of the mud of the tunnel floor.

Fortalexa turned and ran up the tunnel after the others.

'We made it!' Klasvik was almost euphoric. But he was right, the open door of the lander was now within sight. He hurried towards it.

Gilmanuk looked back down the tunnel. There was no sign of their pursuers.

Ace was waiting outside the closed door. She was standing quite still, watching them approach.

'Thank Dion,' said Klasvik. 'Are you ready to leave?'

There was no reply, although the woman turned to face him, silhouetted against the light spilling from the hold.

'Ace?' called the Doctor. 'Ace, are you all right?' When there was still no reply he stopped dead. 'Klasvik – come back.'

'What?' The old man stopped, puzzled and annoyed.

'Come back here, Klasvik.' Lannic's voice was calm and authoritative. 'The Doctor's right.'

'Right? What about?'

Gilmanuk strained to see, peering through his muddy spectacles at the figure ahead. Even at such a disadvantage he could see, as Klasvik now could, that it was not Ace.

It was a life size, perfectly formed statue of Ace. It was completely grey, as if made of stone, except for the dribbles of darker fluid where the joints had stretched and strained with movement. And it was starting down the tunnel towards them.

'Doctor, I think we have a problem.' Fortalexa pointed the other way. To where the two statues from the theatre had just rounded a bend in the tunnel and were advancing.

'If only we knew what they were,' muttered Lannic, 'we might have a chance.'

'Oh, I know what they are,' the Doctor said dismissively. 'But I don't think it helps much.'

'It would help me,' Fortalexa told him. 'The whole thing seems to be someone's idea of *Death's Bane* on a limitless budget.'

'They're mud. The outer shell is dried and hardened, but it's still mud.'

'Mud, Doctor?' Klasvik seemed interested in spite of himself.

'The surface of this planet is a living thing – maybe many things. In the dry season it's dormant, disconnected. Its parts are scattered around as dry sand with no constituency. Add water, and it bonds together. Comes to life.'

'Are you sure?' Fortalexa was pushing forwards into them as the statues approached from behind.

The Doctor pushed backwards as Ace stepped slowly closer. 'No, not *sure* as such. But I like a good theory, and you probably haven't time to disprove it to my satisfaction.'

'Does it help us?' Gilmanuk could see what was probably the only way out. But he would rather have an alternative, if there was one.

'Help?' The Doctor seemed surprised at the question. 'No, it doesn't help us at all.'

Gilmanuk shrugged. 'That's what I thought.' He leaned across to the Doctor and whispered, 'You are sure that Professor Summerfield is safe?'

The Doctor looked deep into his eyes, and Gilmanuk could tell that he sensed what he was thinking. The Doctor's hand closed on his, squeezing it slightly as he said, 'Yes, I am sure.' He held Gilmanuk's hand for a moment longer. 'You're a brave man, Gilmanuk. Thank you for caring.'

Gilmanuk smiled, a tear coming to his eye. 'Well, this is where I make my exit.' Then he walked forward, into the arms of Ace.

Her embrace was as cold and tight as he had expected. Her cheek was hard against his for a moment, then he felt it give way and a sticky mess covered his face, oozed behind his glasses and against his tightly closed eyes. He felt the grip tighten round him and was unable to move. Images flashed past his sightless eyes: of his wife; his son; and of Professor Bernice Summerfield.

As his body sank to the ground he heard the sound of metal on metal and knew that the door to the hold had opened for his friends. And although his whole face was set in a muddy death mask, in his mind he was smiling.

Source Document 8

Cover letter accompanying application for post as Admissions Overseer at the Pentillanian Theatre on Menaxus

Braxiatel Collection Catalogue Number: 831 CPH

Extract. Written by Di Pietro Palladio. Dated 2315.

Sir,

Please find enclosed an application form for the post of Admissions Overseer. You will appreciate from my qualifications and experience that I am eminently suitable for the position under offer. I am available for immediate interview.

You will note from the *Comments* section of the form, which I have completed with particular clarity, that I have suggested profound changes to the standard admissions procedures which could, in this applicant's opinion, increase the throughput of ticketing and the accuracy of fulfilment.

Chapter 8

The Infernal Machine

> Verbal *communication is by contrast much harder to interpret. Indeed, as far as the written word is concerned, it is almost impossible. The author will have taken time to disguise their automatic and subconscious mannerisms through revision and rewriting – and may even have introduced deliberate confusion.*
>
> *In fact, the most one can reasonably hope to say about written material is that it was – or was not – written by the same person. Stylistic and linguistic habits are difficult to lose even though their meaning and intention may be obscured. In* Macbeth, *for example, it is easy to see which sections were added to the 1623 folio by Middleton. What is rather harder to fathom is why he added them. Or, come to that, why they are rarely removed by an editor.*
> **Verbal Non-Communication** – Vyse Plaquet and
> Hughes Frost, 2137

'You got this from a cheap "B" movie, didn't you?'

The Doctor looked hurt, but Ace went on, 'From the people who brought you *Attack of the Fifty-Foot Poodle.*'

'You're not taking this very seriously, Ace.'

'I know, I know – people are dead and the killer zombies are at the door.' She turned back to the flight controls. 'Still, we can be out of here in a couple of minutes. I just need to run the motors up to speed.' She adjusted a dial, and squinted at the read-out next to it.

'Well done, Ace. I'll get back to the others – I left them in the hold nursing their credibility.' He paused in the doorway. 'And anyway, poodles don't have fifty feet.' But she did not hear. So he turned, disappointed, and set off down the corridor.

'Doctor!' Ace's voice reached him before he had gone ten paces.

The Doctor frowned and returned to the flight deck. 'It was just a joke.'

But Ace still was not listening to him. She pointed to the read-out, flashing red as power-to-inertia ratios rolled past. 'That's not right – what could cause that?'

The Doctor watched the figures for a while, then stared past Ace into the far wall, his lips moving as he out-thought the flight computers and leaped at explanations.

'Mud!' he exclaimed at last. 'Lots of mud, packing into the engine pods for the lateral thrusters and blocking the drive feeds.'

'You're not serious?' He scowled. 'Okay, you are serious. We've got to clear it, then – the readings are way above tolerance already. I'll have to shut it down. And we can't take off in this weather with no lateral control.' She reset the engine controls. It was only as the sound of the drive died away that either of them was aware that it had been there, straining as the power fought in vain to express itself. 'Much more of that and the whole lot would go up.'

The Doctor nodded. 'Which is where we want to go. But in one piece. We must clear it out and try again.'

'Doctor, what if something's waiting for you to do just that?'

'Waiting for us?' The thought did not seem to have occurred to him.

Ace nodded. 'Something out of a "B" movie.'

'Well.' The Doctor's face brightened a little. 'Let's hope it's a poodle.'

Fortalexa had assumed some sort of authority. All he could do however was issue a status report to the survivors. 'And since we cannot locate them,' he concluded, 'we must assume that Assok Bannahilk and Professor

Summerfield are also amongst the casualties. So that leaves just us.'

'And Ace,' the Doctor reminded him.

'None of which helps us to decide what to do about unblocking the engines,' Klasvik pointed out.

'The machine,' Lannic said, 'the dream machine, did you call it?'

'Ace did.'

'What about it?' asked Klasvik.

'There must be some way it can help us.'

'Not unless it can create a diversion to draw the statues away from the engines.' Fortalexa was not convinced.

'Maybe it can,' offered the Doctor. 'It projects a lifelike image, it might fool them.'

'No chance. Without the activator key it won't project an interval, never mind any sort of performance.'

'Yet it was working in a sort of stand-by mode when Ace and I arrived.' The Doctor leaped to his feet and walked round in a small circle. 'Puzzling, isn't it?'

'But not very helpful Doctor.' Klasvik glared at him.

'This activator key, what does it look like?' asked Lannic.

The Doctor waved a hand vaguely round the room. 'Oh it's a magnetically encoded card. Plastic, probably. About so big.' He held his clenched hands so they touched at the knuckles and extended his index fingers.

'Like this?' Lannic pulled a small card from her breast pocket. It was plastic, about the length the Doctor had indicated, slightly narrower. It was etched with a cluster of small leaves splaying out from a central branch.

Fortalexa snatched it from her. 'Exactly like that,' he said.

He had watched everything, heard everything. The slave terminal from the same processing unit relayed the images that she brought up at the workstation. The camera in the simularity chamber relayed real-time images of her simulations.

When she first populated the auditorium with herself

151

and Hamlet, he had laughed out loud. But by the time she asked again whether she had all the relevant documents, he was less happy. As he watched her leave the latest simularity, he steepled his fingers and raised them so his forefingers touched his lips. He had not anticipated that she would move so fast.

She would re-examine the documents now. And he was not sure how much she could discover from those. Perhaps the investigation had gone far enough. He leaned back in his chair and put his feet up on the desk, crossing the ankles. It might be interesting to see how far she could get.

Klasvik stole a look round the end of the lander. He snapped his rain-soaked head back almost at once. Just as the Doctor had said, the three statues were standing motionless by the engine pods. They were completely still and silent, posed in tableau, the rain splashing off their shoulders and running down their face. They did not seem to have heard them open the door using the manual controls, were still waiting for the sound of a motor from one of the hatches before investigating.

'Satisfied?' hissed the Doctor in his ear.

Klasvik grunted. He still did not trust the Doctor, but at least he seemed to be helping now rather than offering silly pseudo-scientific explanations and preaching doom like some character out of *Black Vengeance*.

'Come on, let's see where they've got to.' The Doctor nudged Klasvik and turned away. Klasvik followed him down into the tunnel. They were well past the shored-up section before they met Lannic and Fortalexa wheeling the dream machine along the tunnel towards them.

The Doctor held up his hand, and they stopped where they were. 'That's good enough,' he told Fortalexa quietly. 'We don't need a direct line of vision, we can work out the calibration and project an image from this range, I paced out the distance on the way.'

'Sorry we took so long,' Lannic said. 'We had fun getting it up those steps.'

The Doctor smiled. 'Yes, I can imagine.'

They watched as Fortalexa slid the plastic card into a slot in the main panel of the machine and began programming in the distance information. 'Ready?' he asked eventually, his face tight with nervous anticipation. They all nodded. 'This should project the characters but not the scenery. With luck, they'll appear just like real people.'

The Doctor patted both Klasvik and Lannic on the back in encouragement. 'They're pretty slow, we should be able to avoid them in the confusion. And remember, we don't need to completely clear the engines. If we can get the bulk of the mud out, Ace can fire them and that will blast out the rest.'

They stood silent, looking round at each other. Fortalexa said, 'Right, I'll give you to a count of one hundred, then I'll cue in the machine. *Hamlet* all right for you?' Nobody bothered to answer.

The first indication that anything was happening was the sound of metal on metal – of swords crashing against each other. The Doctor exchanged glances with Klasvik, and Lannic. 'Right on time.'

Huddled under the Doctor's umbrella for shelter, they peered round the edge of the lander.

The Doctor recognized both Hamlet and his mother from their earlier encounter. But the other figures were unfamiliar. There was a crowd, gathered in a circle. It took a moment for the Doctor to realize what was happening. Then as he saw Hamlet dive forward in the middle of the ring, sword in one hand and dagger in the other, he knew. A glance round the faces of the observers confirmed it: Fortalexa had plunged them straight into the final duel between Hamlet and Laertes. A good choice – lots of action, movement, people.

The king and courtiers applauded and exclaimed as Hamlet and Laertes rushed headlong at each other, swords clashing as they rolled apart and rejoined for another bout.

And amid the choreographed confusion, the three statues – Lannic, the Doctor and Ace – milled round as if unsure of themselves, grasping at figures which evaded their clutches and failed to acknowledge their existence. The statue of the Doctor lurched into the middle of the fight. It reached out for Hamlet. Laertes ducked as he disappeared behind the grey figure, and Hamlet lunged forward, his sword slicing through the stone Doctor's waistcoat as it reached for Laertes.

The Doctor gasped, and clutched his chest.

'Are you all right?' asked Lannic, reaching out to help him.

He turned to her, his eyes wide. 'I'm glad that wasn't me,' he whispered. 'Come on, this is the best chance we'll get.'

Keeping close to the side of the lander, they darted along towards the engine pods. The lander afforded some protection from the rain as it angled in at them. Even so, within seconds they were drenched and dripping.

The four huge circular openings of the engine pods were jammed solid with dark mud. It dripped from them as if it had been hastily packed in, or as if it was trying to crawl in against the force of gravity. The Doctor plunged his furled umbrella into the nearest of the pods and gouged out a chunk of the sticky material. 'Mud pies,' he exclaimed in delight.

After a second's hesitation Lannic pulled her coverall sleeve back as far as it would easily travel, then pushed her hand and forearm into the opening, tearing out a fistful of mud and dropping it with a squelch to the ground. She looked round quickly to see if the statues had heard, but the noise of the rain splashing into the soft ground and the shouts of appreciation from the swordfight drowned out the noise.

Before long they were all three tunnelling into the side of the lander. Then the sound of the fight stopped, and they froze.

'Another hit, what do you say?' Hamlet's voice reached them clear and enthusiastic.

Laertes was less happy, deferent but resigned: 'A touch, a touch, I do confess't.'

The Doctor, Lannic and Klasvik breathed a collective sigh of relief.

'Doctor, I can't reach much further.' Lannic was up to her shoulder as she scooped out another handful of mud.

'You and Klasvik go back inside, tell Ace she can test-fire. If she keeps the burners running she should be able to clear the rest and keep them open.' The Doctor watched the play for a moment.

The King's voice floated over, commanding but worried: 'Gertrude! Do not drink.'

'Give me exactly five minutes to finish clearing the last one,' the Doctor told them, 'then I'll collect Fortalexa and catch you up.'

Klasvik checked his chronometer and started his surreptitious way back towards the safety of the hold. Lannic caught the Doctor's arm as he reached it into the last of the pods, umbrella extended.

'And the machine,' she said, her eyes wide with urgency and insistence. 'You must bring the machine too.'

'Yes, yes, of course.' The Doctor clicked his tongue irritably and went back to work. He did not think it would be long now before the statues realized what was happening and returned to guard the engines – particularly now that there was a lull in the action.

He had almost finished and had two minutes to spare when a hand closed on his shoulder, pulling him round. The Doctor turned slowly, not yet resisting, ready to dive to the side when his attacker reached out for his face.

'Need any help?' asked Fortalexa, releasing his hold on the Doctor.

'Yes,' said the Doctor, looking over Fortalexa's shoulder. 'Help getting out of here!'

Fortalexa turned and followed the Doctor's gaze. The statue of Lannic was lumbering heavily towards them, arms outstretched. Behind her Ace and the Doctor were detaching themselves from the court of Elsinore even as the fight was starting up again. The Doctor's statue was moving to the side of the lander, blocking off their escape route.

'Any ideas?'

The Doctor considered, pulling a gold pocket watch from his muddy waistcoat and flipping open its lid to consult it. He licked his grubby finger and stuck it in the air as if testing the wind direction. 'Yes. We wait here.' He folded his arms, leaned against the side of the lander and started to whistle what sounded like a military march.

'Is that it?' Fortalexa watched as the Doctor continued to whistle, twirling the watch round his finger on its chain. The statues were all but upon them now. The sticky mud was oozing from their joints as they lurched forwards.

'At this point,' said the Doctor suddenly, as if he had just remembered something important, 'we duck.' And he disappeared from sight.

Fortalexa joined him face down in the mud, hands behind his head, a second later. He too had heard the primary ignition at the back of the engine pods.

The Doctor rolled onto his back and watched with satisfaction as the last of the mud was blasted out of the holes in the lander's side. It was followed a split-second later by four jets of flame. They reached out like flame-throwers above the Doctor, singeing his eyebrows and warming his face, licking round the three statues which were bending towards their prey.

The Lannic statue was the nearest. It was engulfed in the blast, shrivelling as the dried outer covering was scalded away. The face collapsed inwards, a smoking mess, and the moulded clothing peeled away to reveal the lack of skin beneath. The sludge inside began to collapse once its rigid shell was removed, slowly running downwards in a huge viscous ball which bubbled and evaporated in the heat.

Behind Lannic, the Doctor and Ace were caught in a less intense heat. They staggered forward a step, dragged further into the blast by their own heavy momentum. Their faces blistered and burned away, dark liquid boiling as it seeped from their eyes and ran down their cheeks.

The statue of the Doctor lurched into the remains of the statue of Lannic and toppled forward, crashing in a steaming heap against the lander. It left a brown sticky stain where it slid down the side. The facsimile of Ace seemed set to stagger close enough to the Doctor and Fortalexa to reach them, but then its liquid knees gave way under its own weight and it collapsed down on itself. It jarred to a stop, its waist spreading out as it hit the ground. Steam hissed up from the wet surface. Slowly it seemed to sink into the ground as the weight of the statue combined with the heat to melt it from the floor up. The head stared accusingly at the Doctor for a moment through stained hollow eyes, then it too was gone.

'Good night, sweet ladies,' muttered the Doctor and he and Fortalexa crawled out from under the flames. The Doctor stood upright as soon as they were away far enough from the heat. He dusted himself down and doffed his hat to Hamlet who was busy ramming a goblet into his stepfather's face. 'Good night, sweet prince,' he called.

'You know,' the Doctor said to Fortalexa as they entered the hold, 'I think it may well have been Shakespeare who said "I love it when a plan comes together." '

It still made no real sense. But Bernice was not one to give up. She was going through each of the documents again, in random rather than chronological order this time. There was something on the tip of her consciousness that niggled. She was sure that somewhere in these documents – one perfect facsimile of a discoloured piece of paper, or hidden in words buried within an optical sphere – was the clue she was looking for.

The problem was, she had not the faintest idea what she was searching for. And what was more it was getting boring as well as frustrating. She realized she had not been paying attention to the sheet she had been reading, sighed, and started again. It was an especially pompous account of the reconstruction of part of the admissions block after a fire in the late twenty-third century. She got more and more frustrated with the stilted writing style as she went through. *In this correspondent's opinion, the admissions buildings have been eminently in need of profound attention for some considerable time now.* Bernice growled at the document facsimile, screwed it into a ball and threw it across the room.

It bounced off an ornate Herastian wall mirror and skidded to a halt under a Sequantil writing desk. Bernice was immediately on her hands and knees retrieving it, her mind in a whirl as it tried to work through the incredible conclusions it had leapt to while the paper ball was still in flight. She was sitting cross-legged on the floor with her velvet skirts spread out like an island round her, smoothing out the document again when the man came in.

He was wearing a close-cut grey suit which seemed familiar. Her mind tried to accommodate the distraction. 'Just a second,' she said, 'I've nearly got it.'

He nodded to show he had heard, then stood still and silent, waiting for her. But Bernice found this more distracting than if he had spoken, and her brain began to work through the secondary problem of who he might be. Tall, a little older than me, well chiselled features – that was it. He was the man from the Garden of Whispers. Though come to think of it, he also looked remarkably like the character of Hamlet the computer had generated in the simulated theatre.

'I didn't realize you worked here.' She pulled herself up off the floor and returned the straightened paper to the desk. 'But I am nearly ready for another carafe of the Kintampo Creek stuff, thank you.'

He raised an eyebrow. Probably more used to hunting out documents, thought Benny. 'Do you know anything about body language?' she asked, remembering how learned he had seemed when they last met.

'Body language?'

'Non-verbal communication, you know.'

'A little. People express themselves through gestures, postures, physical habits.'

'There's a theory that much of the research into *non-*

verbal communication can be applied to the verbal media as well, you know.'

He looked a little pained. 'I am *au fait* with the work of Plaquet and Frost. They make some valid points.'

Bernice nodded. 'Do you have a copy I could borrow, do you think? I'd like to try to apply some of those points to some of these documents.' She gestured at the piles stacked at the workstation. 'I think they could reveal quite a lot.'

'Ah.' The man nodded gravely. He walked slowly and deliberately across the room, flopping down on a *chaise longue* and breathing out heavily as if coming to a decision.

'Are you listening?' He said it so loudly that Bernice looked round to see who was behind her. But there was no one. 'Elliniko – wake up.' He paused for a moment, and smiled at Bernice as a faint ping came from the workstation as if in answer. 'Good, then you can stop listening. And you can send in tea.'

Bernice looked at him, her mouth open in surprise and anger. 'You've been bugging me – this room's wired.'

'Of course. They all are.' He leaped to his feet. 'But I'm forgetting my manners. I do apologize, Professor Summerfield. Or may I call you Benny – I gather your friends do.' Before she was quite aware what was happening, he had led her back to the *chaise longue* and she was sitting beside him, her hand held between both his. 'Allow me to introduce myself,' he said. 'I am Irving Braxiatel.'

Benny gulped. 'Nice place you've got here,' she said.

Lannic was waiting for them when they entered the hold. She was standing by the water cannon, which was strapped in ready for lift-off. 'Where is it?' she demanded before they were completely inside.

'What?' asked Fortalexa.

'Quite well, thank you,' the Doctor said, touching his hat. 'We got away unharmed.

'Where is the machine?'

Fortalexa was confused. 'It's down the tunnel. Where did you think it would be?'

'We're not leaving without it.'

'Like hell we're not.'

'What's the problem – can we leave yet, or what?' Ace was standing in the door to the main part of the lander. 'Klasvik's strapped in ready to go – couldn't hold him back. How was my timing?'

'Impeccable as ever, Ace.'

'Well, we'll have to go soon or the engines will burn off too much fuel. But I daren't turn them off in case they get the mud treatment again. Are you lot coming through?'

Lannic looked round at them all. 'All right.' Her teeth were clenched. 'I'll get it myself.'

She could hear footsteps close behind, but she did not turn back. At least someone had the decency to follow, to help. The machine had to be the top priority for the expedition – had to be.

It was standing exactly how Fortalexa had left it, lights flickering across its control panel. Lannic reached out and shut down the main function, running her hand almost reverently across the finish.

'So what's so great about plays?'

She turned quickly. It was the woman Ace – she had expected Fortalexa, or perhaps the Doctor. 'You obviously have no concept of how important this is.'

'True.'

'A programmed performance of *The Good Soldiers*. Never mind the technical capabilities of this thing, for that alone the Exec will grant me an audience.'

'And this Exec's some top dog is he?' Lannic looked confused, so Ace went on: 'Okay, let's get it back to the lander if it's so important.'

They began to wheel it up the tunnel. The machine was not heavy, just bulky. It was awkward to handle as it bounced along the uneven floor of the tunnel. When the hand touched Lannic's shoulder she assumed it was Ace

160

prompting her to move round so they could get a better grip.

Then she saw the other arms, greasy with wet mud, pushing their way out of the tunnel walls ahead of them.

'I hate "B" movies,' said Ace as a hand snatched at her hair. 'Ready to run for it?'

'I'm not leaving the machine.'

The walls beside them were alive now, arms writhing and grasping. They were hampered by their own slipperiness, the mud slipping as it made contact with the women. 'You're determined, aren't you – you and your infernal machine. Okay, we'll try it. But any problems, we ditch the thing, right?'

They ran, heads down, keeping low over the machine as they pushed. Occasionally it hit a bump and flew up in the air, catching them as it fell back, bruising and winding them. And all the time the hands reached out and tried to grab them. Ace lost a handful of hair to one. Lannic's coverall was ripped open at the shoulder by another. But somehow they kept going.

Then suddenly the attack was over. They were into the section of tunnel shored up with plastic sheets. They paused for breath. With a snapping sound, one of the sheets split, and torn dark fingers started to work their way through the crack.

Ace was looking back down the tunnel. Lannic could see them too – the arms were pulling free of the walls, whole bodies were detaching from the sides of the tunnel. An army of statues was pulling itself into existence and turning towards them. And all the statues looked like Lannic or Ace or the Doctor.

Lannic screamed and shoved the machine forward. Ace joined her and they raced for the tunnel mouth.

Ace was through the hold and onto the flight deck in a moment. She sat down and strapped herself in in one movement. 'I don't know or care where you all are,' she shouted over her shoulder, 'but I'm leaving *now*.'

'What about the glass of orange juice and today's

papers?' asked the Doctor from the seat behind her. She glared at him, then watched Lannic enter and start strapping in. Klasvik looked as though he was asleep, and Fortalexa was already at the communication console.

Ace plugged herself into the net and set the thrusters at full power. The noise of the motors built to a scream.

And nothing happened.

The Doctor leaned forward, scanning the instruments in front of Ace. 'The power's getting through,' he said. Then his eyes widened and he looked at Ace. 'It's holding us back.'

'What is?'

'Don't you see? It's not going to let us leave. We're stuck in the mud!'

'Not if I can help it.' Ace pushed the engines to maximum power. The force of the upward thrust and slight response from the lander's heavy body forced her back into the chair and forced the Doctor to sit down heavily. Ace kept the power output sliders hard up against the end-stop, the noise of the labouring engines thudding through her head.

And slowly at first, then more easily, the *Pride of Padrillion* began to lift. The aft scanners were soon clear, and Ace could see the mud clinging desperately to the underbelly of the ship. As the ship lifted off, the mud was elongating into sticky strings like recalcitrant cheese on a slice of pizza. With a final surge of power as the rear pods unblocked, the lander pulled free and leaped towards orbit.

Source Document 9

Extract from Heletian survey of the Schlaer asteroid belt

Heletian Survey Project: 92/88/4a

While the area is itself hazardous in the extreme, Mellor's sonic and optical surveying has established a possible channel through the main body of the Schlaer Belt. To reach the start of the Mellor channel is not difficult, and it emerges near the far side of the Belt, so could be used as a path through the asteroid field.

It should be stressed however, that the existence of the channel, although it is now marked on the standard charts, cannot be confirmed. Both probes collided with the side of the channel – an asteroid or space debris – before completing the run. Our expert opinion is that the channel *is* navigable, but only at low speed and with extreme caution.

Chapter 9

You Never Can Tell

Theatre was in effect provided by the technologists, and as such was treated as a technology. It was not until it was given back to the artists and designers – in much the same way as human-computer interfaces were given over to artistic development in the early twenty-first century – that the theatre was re-established as popular and accessible entertainment in a dramatic rather than a technological sense.
  Osterling's Legacy – Azcline Grigsen, 3498

Lefkhani saw the approaching ship on the *Icoronata*'s detectors almost as soon as it left the planet. He had been monitoring almost round the clock, initially out of boredom, but increasingly out of fear. He was not surprised they were on their way back – he had been tempted to break communications silence to check the lander crew knew about the Rippeareans' latest positions and advances. But he knew Bannahilk and Fortalexa would be cued in.

What did surprise him was the reading – only four life-forms were aboard. Or was it five? The reading seemed to be flickering between the two. So he thumped the side of the console unit, and it went dead. He snarled out loud in exasperation. Then he hit the console again, still to no avail. So he opened the outer doors to the hold and set off in search of his jacket.

Ace was feeling rather pleased with herself. She had managed to pilot the lander to its rendezvous with the

Icoronata with little difficulty. Even the Doctor seemed mildly impressed, although he had said little about it. He had even waited patiently for a few minutes when she ducked into a store-room and examined the stowed equipment – including some serious weaponry.

Now he and Ace were sitting opposite each other, drinking more of the Doctor's obnoxious tea. Lefkhani had given them a brief tour of the ship once Fortalexa had introduced them. He had left them in the rest-room and headed back to the command deck for a debriefing from which the Doctor had managed to get them excluded.

The rest-room was one of the largest rooms on the ship. The *Icoronata* was really a troop carrier, and the multitude of dormitories and the single rest-room were where the soldiers in transit would spend most of their time. At the moment it was empty apart from the Doctor and Ace. They sat opposite each other in one of the enclaves of seats grouped together across the room. The seats, like the rest of the decor, were bland but functional. They somehow managed to look more comfortable than they actually were.

'You remember what you said about the "B" movie?'

Ace took the opportunity to put down her drink. 'Yeah – sorry about that. More of a doberman than a poodle in the end, wasn't it?'

'I'm not so sure.'

'Don't worry, Doctor, we got out of it okay. Didn't we?'

The Doctor frowned. 'Oh yes, no problem.'

'Good.'

'No. No, I don't think it *is* good.' He leaned towards her, cradling his beaker in front of him so that the noxious steam went up Ace's nose when she leaned forward to join the conspiracy. 'You're super-intelligent mud, Ace – '

She sat back quickly. 'Thanks.'

'No, I mean suppose you were. Would you let some stray archaeologists drill down through you? And if you did, when you decided to fight back, would you go to the trouble of making statues of them or stretching arms out of walls?'

'Maybe. If I wanted to frighten them a bit first.' But she was not convinced.

'Why bother? Why not just ooze all over them without warning?'

'Or collapse the tunnel. I see what you mean.'

'It's all a bit melodramatic. We must be missing something.'

Ace twisted sideways in the chair, dangling her legs over the arm. 'We're safe now – we got away. I don't know what you're worrying about.'

'Don't you? Then tell me, Ace, why did the Menaxans die out apparently so suddenly, without leaving any of their belongings, just their architecture? How did they survive in the first place on a planet where the mud is apparently hostile?'

'Maybe the mud did get them. It ate everything up – just couldn't digest the dream machine.'

The Doctor nodded, his eyes staring into the middle distance. 'Yes. The dream machine. That has to be part of it.' He put his beaker down on the floor and was quiet for a moment, then suddenly he was on his feet and pacing round Ace's chair so quickly she could not swivel her head fast enough to keep up. 'Then there's the weather,' he said suddenly, stopping for a moment to punctuate his observation with a jabbed finger. Then he stepped carefully over the beaker and was off again. 'How did they cope with the changes in the weather – dry and dusty for half the time, then pouring with rain and awash with mud the other half?'

'They went to the theatre, Doctor.'

'What?' He halted suddenly, his feet coming to a dead stop but his body continuing, swaying forward then back again. Then he sat down and took Ace's hands. 'You still don't see the problem, do you Ace?' His voice was quiet with a tinge of sadness.

'No, I don't. So far: odd but not conclusive.'

'All right then, try this one. You're the sort of race that enjoys going to the theatre – lives for it, in fact.'

Ace nodded.

'Such fanaticism seems quite common in this part of the universe.'

'There could be lots of reasons for that.'

'So you build a theatre – a huge amphitheatre, the theatre to end all theatres.'

'Yes Doctor.'

He leaned back in his chair, tipped his hat over his face, and said quietly, 'But would it ever occur to you, Ace, on a planet where half the time it's raining cats and fifty-foot dogs, to make it an *open air* theatre?'

The debriefing proved to be of little help or interest to anyone except Lefkhani, and he found it difficult to believe most of what he heard. So he concentrated instead on keeping the ship on course and monitoring the comnet. He also kept a watchful eye on the detectors. Behind him Fortalexa, Lannic and Klasvik continued to argue over what to report and what to keep to themselves.

When Lefkhani interrupted they all seemed relieved. Until they heard what he had to say.

'Sir, there's a ship coming up on us from behind on an intercept course.'

Fortalexa was with him in an instant, punching up verification. 'Do we have the ident signal yet?'

'No, sir. Any moment now.'

'Is it one of ours – an escort?' Klasvik was optimistic. They all knew an escort would not be spared.

'Could be in retreat from one of the recent actions,' suggested Lannic.

'Got it – Gamma five zero nine slash four.'

Fortalexa was already checking the listings. A match flashed at him from towards the end of the list. '*The Hordes of Bastura*. It's a battle cruiser, Cluster class. And it's Rippearean.'

'They'll be in range in about thirty seconds.' Lefkhani checked the perceptor readings. 'They're locking weapons now.'

'Try to lose them – maximum drive.' Fortalexa turned to Klasvik. 'Find the specs on the Cluster class. See if we can outrun them.' He opened an intercom channel and his voice reverberated round the command deck as it was relayed through speakers on every deck and in every cabin. 'Doctor, Ace – to the command deck please. If you hurry, you'll be here before the torpedoes.'

There was a good selection of cakes and two pots of tea, but Benny was more concerned with finding out what was going on. She had described the problems she found with the theatre and with the documents, and Braxiatel had just smiled.

'What conclusions do you reach?' he inquired reasonably.

So she told him what she thought.

'And how is that possible, do you suppose?' he asked when she had finished.

'Well I don't really know. I suppose time travel must have something to do with it.'

He laughed. It was a quiet laugh, good-natured and genuine. 'Oh no,' he said, 'for once time travel has nothing to do with it.'

'Do you have another explanation?'

'First things first.' He leaned forward and surveyed the cakes. 'Help yourself, won't you? They really are as good as they look. I'll pour you some tea: there's a traditional Terran brew, and also one I had blended myself. Do you have a preference?'

Benny decided she preferred to try the traditional Earth blend. Braxiatel seemed not at all put out, excusing himself to answer a polite knock at the door.

It was Elliniko. While the two men exchanged a few quiet words, Benny sipped her tea, trying to think what Braxiatel's explanation might be. She was no wiser by the time he returned.

'Good news?' she asked.

'Perhaps. A Rippearean cruiser has encountered a Heletian orbiter *en route* between Menaxus and Heletia. We're linked directly into the net, but even so the original report will have taken a while to get posted.'

'That must be Lannic's expedition.'

Braxiatel nodded. 'They're just approaching the edge of the Schlaer Belt. My guess is they will run for it and try to hide in amongst the asteroids.'

Benny all but dropped her cup and saucer onto the table and leapt to her feet. 'But an old orbiter's no match for a cruiser.'

Braxiatel seemed mildly concerned. 'Careful – you'll spill your tea jumping about like that.' He dabbed at the table with a napkin.

'Oh forget the tea, we have to do something.'

Braxiatel smiled and gestured for her to sit down again. 'I'm afraid there's really nothing much we can do.'

Benny sat down. He was right, but she felt no better for knowing that. 'I suppose they'll be okay,' she said distantly and Braxiatel nodded sympathetically. 'After all, the Doctor's with them.'

The tea splashed into the saucer as Braxiatel turned sharply towards her. 'What?'

Compared with the rest-room, the control deck was tiny. It seemed even smaller to Ace since it was crammed to capacity with consoles and equipment. What wall space was left was dominated by the main screen, and what floor space there was had several additional flight chairs bolted to it.

Fortalexa was on the detector console, Lefkhani was piloting with Ace as his back-up. The Doctor had appointed himself navigator, staring at the charts on the main screen and doing the calculations in his head since that was quicker than using the computer. Lannic and Klasvik were strapped into crew seats, although they were close enough to see and hear what was going on.

'Why don't you show us what we're heading for?' Klasvik was annoyed that the main screen was dedicated to navigation charts he could not understand.

'If we can see it,' Fortalexa told him without looking round, 'then we've already hit it. At this speed we're wholly dependent on the detectors, so I suggest you don't interrupt the Doctor's calculations. If he's slightly off, we'll get scraped against an asteroid.'

Ace checked over the readings again. Lefkhani was linked in, but she was double-checking against the physical controls. 'Looking good.'

'Check.' Lefkhani had his eyes shut, his hand tight on the control stick.

Ace looked round at the others. Fortalexa had one earpiece of the headset pressed to his left ear, the other dangling free. The Doctor was holding his pocket watch like a stopwatch, counting off the seconds and tracing a line with his index finger across the chart projected on to the main screen.

'They're still with us.' Fortalexa had got a faint ping – Ace had heard it through the free earpiece of his headset. 'Their detectors are active.'

'Is that good or bad?' asked Lannic.

'Both. It's good that we know where they are. We can't afford to go from passive detect, they'd find us at once. But it does suggest they know we're no threat to them.'

The Doctor tapped a point on the chart and glanced at his watch. 'We're within the Schlaer Belt now. Can we decrease speed?'

'I'd rather not, Doctor. They're gaining on us if anything.' There was a louder ping from the headset – they all heard it. 'Right, that's it, they got us that time. They'll be locking weapons and preparing a salvo.'

The Doctor nodded, silently counting off the seconds. 'Come left thirteen degrees in five – four – three – two – one – mark.'

Lefkhani moved the control stick slightly and Ace followed the directional readings as the forward indicators shifted thirteen degrees.

'And down seventy six in three – two – one – mark.'

The chart shifted position as their perspective changed with the ship's bearing. There was a sudden flare of static from Fortalexa's console.

'Good work, Doctor – that was the detonation.'

'And right two degrees in three – two – one – mark. We should be in the channel now.'

The chart shifted again and a black line appeared across it, stretching forward from their current position. The Doctor looked at his watch again. Then he pulled a length of string from his jacket pocket and measured along the line with it.

There was another loud ping.

'Doctor – they've got us again.'

'And they know where we're going,' Ace pointed out. 'We have to follow the channel.' The asteroids were packed close along either side, a slight deviation would smash them to pieces.

'They may not follow us in – their charts aren't as detailed as ours.'

'But they will launch.'

'Yes. Doctor, we need to outrun them.'

The Doctor had his abacus out and was flicking beads furiously. 'Lefkhani, increase speed by twenty-five per cent in three – two – one – mark.'

The thrust pushed them all back in their seats. The Doctor staggered slightly, dropping his string. A moment later there as a ping from the headset – higher pitched this time. It was followed a second later by another. And another.

'They've launched.' Fortalexa was timing the gaps between the pings. 'The missile has acquired us and is locking on. Gaining.'

The Doctor's face was set, his eyes focused on the chart as his finger moved slowly up the black line. It was about a third of the way along it. 'Increase speed by ten per cent in two – one – mark.'

Ace checked the readings as the thrusters surged again. She was not sure she had ever been so fast in normal space. But if they tried to jump without calculating the shot they could end up anywhere. And this close, their pursuers could follow the trace themselves, or task a missile to do it.

The Doctor's finger was moving more quickly along the

line now. And the pings from Fortalexa's headset were coming faster and faster.

'Impact in eleven.'

Lefkhani's hand stiffened on the control stick, sweat breaking out on his forehead and his eyes still tight shut.

'Impact in eight.' Each ping was starting almost as the previous one finished. The gap between them shortened further, and they started to overlap, becoming a continuous sound with peaks and troughs rather than discrete pings.

The Doctor's finger traced its way painfully slowly along the line. It was almost at the top now. He checked his watch. 'Be ready to come right seventy degrees and up thirty on my mark.'

'Impact in five.' The sound was amost a single tone. Ace wondered how Fortalexa could tell how close they were now. Perhaps he was guessing.

'Right seventy and up thirty in three – two – '

'Impact in two.'

' – one – mark.'

Lefkhani's hand jerked across and up, almost in spasm. The ship trembled after it, throwing the Doctor off balance. And then the blast wave hit them, sending the control deck spinning and knocking the Doctor to the floor as it dropped away from him. The screen went blank.

'Impact – within one hundred meters.'

The Doctor was on his feet as soon as the ship stopped rolling. 'Ace – where are we?' he shouted across.

She called up the flight log. 'We rolled thirty-one degrees right and fourteen down.'

'Then come left twenty-eight and up seventeen – now.'

Lefkhani responded immediately. After a moment the screen came back on, re-oriented to their current perspective.

'Decrease speed by eighty per cent – two – one – mark.' The Doctor pulled out a paisley handkerchief and rubbed his hands and face with it.

'Are we through?' asked Lannic.

'We're still in the belt, but the asteroids aren't so densely packed here. And we've slowed right down.'

'But are we safe now?' Klasvik looked more shaken than anyone else.

'Probably,' Fortalexa said. 'You never can tell, but with luck they'll think they caught us in the blast. I doubt if they'll follow us through the channel. Even if they have a decent set of charts we're not worth the effort.'

In the silence that followed, they all heard the ping, clear and distinct.

'I wouldn't put money on it,' the Doctor said.

The sun was setting over the Mansionhouse behind them as they came down the shallow steps into the water avenue. Braxiatel was holding Benny's right hand in his left. He held it high, at about the level of her shoulder, his fingers around hers. She delicately made her way down to the path, the scarlet dress dragging slightly at the steps behind. As they reached the base of the steps, Braxiatel let go of her hand and gestured for her to continue. She realized with a silent smile that he had been holding her hand to support her if she slipped on the steps. He probably assumed she was wearing high heels under the dress. She wondered what he would make of the genuine antique Nike trainers she actually had on.

'Have you known the Doctor long?' he asked after a few steps.

'A while. Difficult to tell really.'

There had seemed no doubt in Braxiatel's mind that they both knew the same Doctor. 'I realized you must know him when you used his research ticket. But it never occurred to me that he might actually be on Menaxus.'

'Have *you* known him long?'

Braxiatel turned to her and smiled. The light from the setting sun lit his face, casting shadows across it which exposed an age and experience Benny had not noticed before. 'For ever,' he said.

'Yet you won't help him – I don't understand why.'

Braxiatel started walking again. She kept pace with him

as they passed the first of the small pools lining the avenue. In the centre two stone cherubs supported the base of a fountain from which white water cascaded around them.

'I think "won't" is a little unfair.' He did not look at her as he said it. ' "Can't" would be more justifiable.'

'But you won't even try.'

'You know, each of the fountains along this avenue looks the same from any point in the avenue. But when you actually get close enough to see through the water which splashes down around them, you find that each is different from the last, and no two designs are repeated. *Cherubs* back there,' he pointed back, 'and *Angels* next. Those are their names. They all have names.' He nodded across at a fountain diagonal from them. From where they were it looked like all the others, stone surrounded by a curtain of water.

'I assume there's some point to this – I mean, as a way of subtly changing the subject it does lack a certain finesse.'

He seemed not to hear her. 'That one is actually the god Neptune, trident in one hand, water jet raised in the other. From here he looks just like any other fountain, but unlike the characters and beasts in the others, he is absolutely in his element.'

'Of course.' Benny stopped suddenly and slapped her hand to her forehead. 'The *Neptune factor* – I should have known.'

But Braxiatel was not amused. He walked on in silence. 'Okay, okay. I do understand really. You're saying that the Doctor doesn't need your help anyway. And maybe you're right. But what if you're not? What if he's changed since you knew him?'

'I think that is extremely likely,' Braxiatel said. 'But he will still be in his element.'

'So you're not worried?'

'Yes, I'm worried. Because he won't have changed so much he can resist a mystery.'

'Why should that worry you?'

They were reaching the end of the avenue now. The

sun was dipping behind the Mansionhouse, lengthening the shadows around them.

'We'll cut back through the Orangery,' Braxiatel decided. 'We can be back in the Mansionhouse before it gets dark.'

'And then what?'

'Then we'll find you a ship.'

'You're getting rid of me? Sending me off before I can find out what's going on?'

Braxiatel laughed. His laugh was quiet, almost restrained, yet it rang across the grounds ahead of them. 'Oh no. I'm sending you off before *the Doctor* can find out what's going on. I want you to take him a message.'

'To Menaxus?'

'No, he won't be going back there. To Heletia.'

'Let me get this straight.' They had reached the end of the path. The last fountain was on their right and the path bent away to the left, doubling back through the Orangery. 'You want me to fly through a war and take a message to the Doctor.'

'We'll get you safely through most of it. Getting past the Heletian home defence lines might be a little tricky though.'

They had stopped again. Benny was talking loudly, partly in anger, partly to be heard above the sound of the fountain beside them.

'Oh thank you. Thank you very much. And what do I get in return?'

'In return? You get to help the Doctor – you were keen for me to help him, I assume you apply the same standards to yourself.'

She glared at him.

'I'll tell you what's going on, although I think you probably know a lot of it already, it's just that your brain won't let you believe it.'

'And what then? What happens after the Doctor gets your message?'

'Ah.' Braxiatel stepped aside and pointed at the last

175

fountain. 'I told you every fountain in the avenue was unique.'

'You did, yes. I can retain information for a whole hour sometimes.'

'I'm pleased to hear it. So what would you say this statue was?'

Benny stared at the water, trying to discern the shape beyond it. She could see what looked like a straight pillar of stone, but the fading light made it impossible to see any detail. 'It's just a piece of stone, isn't it?'

He laughed again. 'No, it's not *just* a piece of stone. All the other fountains were like this one before they were carved. This one is still the original plinth, waiting for the sculpter's chisel. One day it will be a statue like all the others – bird, beast, man, whatever. But at the moment it is unformed; potential; the real statue is still hidden within.'

'You said they all had names.'

'You remember that too?' He smiled. 'This one is called *Future.*'

Source Document 10

Extract from the *Heletian Weaponry Handbook*, section covering High-Impact Phason Bolters

The weapon rifles the shell for increased accuracy. The phason charge itself is covered with detonation bolters. Only one of these needs to make contact with the target for the detonating explosion to fire.

The main phason charge is exploded *within* the containment vessel. The heat and gas are restricted by the surrounding duralinium until the pressure exceeds the metal's limits or (more frequently) the casing joints give way. In either case, the vessel fragments, the pieces and the internal blast are channelled in the direction of least resistance. This is through the bolter cap which detonated – that is, the one in contact with the target.

The gases, now released from pressure, force the surrounding air outwards as they expand (if used within an atmosphere) at a speed of approximately 4,700 metres per second. In a vacuum, there is no atmospheric resistance to the blast.

Detonation of the phason is almost instantaneous, and has been timed at 11,000 metres per second.

Operated by an expert and fired directly at a point on the hull in direct line with the ship's magazine, a single charge from a high-impact phason bolter can bring down a battle cruiser. Given the range of the weapon and the extent of the resulting blast, in this situation the death of the operator is almost instantaneous.

Chapter 10

The Revenger's Tragedy

The few short extracts that do exist from The Good Soldiers *are almost certainly not original or genuine. The fact that the play was so widely acclaimed when first performed and has such a reputation now implies that it must have been of a considerably higher standard than those extracts exhibit.*

How and where these extracts originated cannot be confirmed, of course, but we can speculate. They are almost certainly from a copy-cat version of the play performed somewhere among the frontier worlds. A similar version of Hamlet *exists complete from such a performance contemporary with its original staging. In the case of* Hamlet, *the manuscript originates in Terran Germany. A travelling troupe of English players touring the German courts offered its usual repertoire to one German prince. He demanded instead to see a performance of* Hamlet, *of which he had heard good reports.*

The troupe duly wrote a script for Hamlet *that night, helped by the memory of one of their number who had actually seen the play, and by copious quantities of German beer. They then learned their lines and staged the forty-minute play the following evening. The version that has survived is actually an English translation of a German courtier's transcription of that performance. Since the performance was given in English, and the courtier transcribed it into German as he wrote, the manuscript itself is two trans-*

*lations removed from the second-hand interpretation
from memory.*

*One can suppose that a smiliar transition has
befallen the surviving remnants of* The Good Soldiers. *To get an idea of how different the original
may have been, we can compare the language of the
German* Hamlet *with that of Shakespeare's. Would*
Hamlet *have achieved the reputation it has if the
original had actually included such poetic lines as
Hamlet's 'To be or not – ay, there's the rub' or Marcel-
lo's fateful warning of the uneasy spirit of Hamlet's
father: 'My Lord, there is a ghost doth walk these
battlements every quarter of an hour'?*

Osterling's Legacy – Azcline Grigsen, 3498

The cruiser was gaining on them. Not fast, but little by
little it was edging closer. They had narrowly escaped
several missiles, but it was only a matter of time before the
Rippearean ship held the *Icoronata* within its detectors for
long enough to get an accurate shot. Unless it got lucky
enough to hit with a ranging blast first.

They had managed to go for several minutes without
even a faint ping from the enemy bouncing off their hull
when Ace finally snapped. 'Right – that's it,' she proclaimed, marching down to the door.

'Ace – where are you going?' Fortalexa called after her.
The Doctor shook his head silently and went on with his
calculations. Then she was gone.

It did not take Ace long to make her way back to the
store-room and find what she was after. She had just
finished her rushed preparations, adjusting the gauntlets
and slinging the shoulder strap over her head, when
another blast caught them and she was flung out of the
armoury and across the corridor, the heavy weight on her
back carrying her into the wall. Cursing, she set off back
to the control deck.

'Right, let's sort these drongos out.' The voice came from
the doorway. Klasvik had to turn to see. He was barely

179

aware of Lannic mirroring his movements as he twisted round in the chair, hands still clenched on the arms.

Ace was standing silhouetted in the doorway. She was wearing a spacesuit, carrying the helmet under her left arm. She had tied her hair back out of the way so that the helmet would not be impeded by it or catch it when she turned her head. Over her shoulder was slung a high-impact phason bolter, its huge muzzle rising high above her head.

'Ace, what are you doing?' the Doctor asked. Everyone else was still staring open-mouthed at her. Even Lefkhani had turned, sensing something was happening in the world outside the flight computer.

'I'm sick of this, Doctor. We're not going to outrun those guys or hide from them for long.'

'S'blood – ' Fortalexa was alerted by a warning bleep from his console. 'Incoming – looks close.'

'Drop seventeen, fast.' The Doctor spoke without looking at the chart. He was still watching Ace.

Klasvik felt his stomach heave as the ship dropped suddenly from beneath him. He and Lannic strained at the straps on their chairs, Fortalexa and Lefkhani leaned forward against their harnesses. Ace and the Doctor staggered slightly, then they were flung together as the blast caught them and the ship shuddered under the impact. They sprawled across the console next to Klasvik, arms locked as they each tried to prevent the other from falling.

'You're sure about this, Ace?' Klasvik heard the Doctor ask quietly as the shock-wave subsided.

'Doctor, I'm going to do it,' she told him.

'Are we safe for a moment?' the Doctor called to Fortalexa.

He listened for a second, checking the console. 'Looks like they lost us in the wake of that. We should have a minute or so.'

'Good.' The Doctor was at the chart, jabbing his finger at a blob which represented an asteroid. 'I'm going to bring us round the back of this one.'

'Why? That will slow us down – we should be getting

out of this sector before they quarter it, they're bound to see us when we emerge from occlusion.'

'Exactly.'

'I'm not with you.'

'Nor will Ace be. We'll drop her off as we round it – here.' He pointed to one edge of the blob. 'Then when we emerge, the Rippearean will come to here.' His finger traced back to a point where the cruiser would have a clear shot at them as they emerged from behind the asteroid.

It was also in direct line of where the Doctor had suggested they drop Ace. 'And then *blam*,' she said.

'You're mad!' Fortalexa was staring in disbelief at the chart. 'Even if the cruiser actually ends up where you say it will, there's no guarantee they won't get a shot off before Ace does. And if they don't, we'll all get blasted to bits when their magazine goes up anyway.'

'Do you have a better suggestion, Mister Strategy?'

Fortalexa said nothing.

'We are running out of options,' the Doctor pointed out.

Fortalexa shrugged. 'You want a suggestion? Aim for the aft thruster feed section, not the main body of the ship.'

'Oh great, now you want a trick-shot. And you tell us we're mad.'

Fortalexa grinned suddenly. 'Maybe. But at least I can tell a hawk from a handsaw.'

The section of the Mansionhouse they had entered from the Orangery was deserted. 'I keep these rooms and areas for myself,' Braxiatel confided quietly as they walked down a corridor lined on both walls with mirrors.

A never-ending reflection of Bernices turned to Braxiatel. 'Where are we going?' they asked in a single hushed voice.

'My drawing room. I need to check on the readiness of your ship. And there's one exhibit I'd like you to see.'

181

'You're not maybe considering telling me about the history of Menaxus?'

'Let me show you the exhibit first – it is relevant, I promise you. Then I'll tell you about Menaxus.'

'Fair enough.'

What Braxiatel called his drawing room would, Benny thought, have made kings weep with envy. It was huge, with walls made of inlaid marble. In the centre stood a mahogany writing desk, a simple office chair behind it. Alcoves along each wall were filled either with statues of Lavithian Graffs in full ceremonial armour, or with forced-perspective paintings of parts of the grounds of the house. These seemed to be substitutes for any windows, which suggested that the room was hidden within the depths of the building. For whatever reason, Braxiatel had ensured that he could not be overlooked from outside. Benny guessed that the room was also shielded.

Braxiatel walked across the room to the one alcove that contained neither a statue nor a mural. Benny followed, her feet ringing on the stone floor and her eyes fixed on the replica *Supremacy of Venus* which covered the high ceiling, the goddess sitting among the clouds surrounded by cherubs and maidens. She negotiated the writing desk, glancing idly at the blotter and silver fountain pen lying on it. The blotter was headed *Custodian of the Library of St John the Beheaded*, but before Benny could ask what that meant, Braxiatel called her over.

He had already opened the glass-topped specimen cabinet. Inside was an opened book. It was bound in leather with the pages edged in silver. A silk bookmark was laid down the margin of the left-hand page, its counterpart was the illuminated cover page.

Braxiatel stood back a little to let Benny see. She read the few lines on the cover page. ' "*The Good Soldiers*" – *a theatrical play by Stanoff Osterling.*'

'The original handwritten manuscript,' Braxiatel confirmed. 'It's all there.'

'Have you read it?'

'Oh yes.' He smiled. 'It's actually not terribly good. Grigsen was wrong about that.'

Benny reached out for the book. But she stopped herself before her fingers touched the page. 'May I?'

He waved a hand for her to continue. 'It's been treated; you won't damage it so long as you're careful.'

Benny turned a few pages, reading odd lines and sections as she went, holding her breath in awe. 'Why don't you publish it?'

'Because it's not very good.' He could see that his answer surprised her. 'I'm serious,' he went on. 'There is such a mythos about this play. If I publish it now that whole bubble of mystery and awe would burst.' He clicked his fingers sharply to illustrate the point. 'Imagine your greatest and best childhood memory – then go back and relive the moment. I guarantee it won't be the same. It can never live up to your expectations, so you would never go back to it. It is the potential that's important, like the statue for the last fountain. I can't deprive the universe of such a magnificent work of art, even if it never really existed.'

Benny thought of her diary. Even her recent past was covered with yellow sticky reinterpretations. Maybe he had a point. 'But it's a play. Maybe in performance it really is stunning.'

'Maybe.'

'Have you seen a performance of it?'

'In a sense.'

'And?'

'And you'll probably get the chance to judge for yourself.' He turned away and walked over to the writing desk, leaning back against it and waving Benny to the chair. 'Now then, the question of Menaxus. I just about have time before your ship is ready, and you will need to understand before you go. Not least so you can talk to the Doctor about it for me.'

Benny sat down, smoothing the velvet on her lap. She was eager to hear what Braxiatel had to say, to discover how close her improbable theories had been to the truth.

But she was also intrigued by Osterling's lost manuscript. 'Has it occurred to you that the Doctor might already know all about it?'

He seemed startled. 'No – how could he?'

'I don't know.' Benny glanced back at the specimen cabinet. 'But that manuscript is the original, not a copy?'

'Oh it's quite genuine, believe me. Is there a problem?'

Benny shrugged. Trying not to sound too concerned she said: 'I doubt it. It's just that I recognize the handwriting.'

The line detached almost as soon as Ace hit the ground. She fell on to her side, rolling with the momentum, and saw the line looping back towards the *Icoronata*. She checked the suit monitor which flashed up on the inside of the visor of her helmet at the tap of one of the buttons set into her left wrist, and breathed a heavy sigh. There was no loss of pressure, so she need not scrabble for the sealant tube in the pocket on her right thigh.

Ace waved to show she was all right as the ship disappeared round the back of the asteroid. She could not see the Rippearean cruiser, but it would have locked solidly on to their signal by now. The detectors had been pinging intermittently as she left the control deck. They would easily deduce that the Heletians were sheltering behind the asteroid, trying to hide. She just hoped they would bother to go round the back and make sure rather than simply blast the asteroid out of the way.

She stared at the distant stars for a while to get her bearings. If the Doctor was right, then the cruiser would come at her between Optron and Limnus Five. She looked around for a suitable outcrop to shelter behind and to sight the bolter. The Rippeareans would not be looking for her, but their laser radar might detect the metal of her suit and the energy charge of the phason bolts as they approached. And if she failed to cripple their ship then there was no doubt they would soon pinpoint her position.

'This could be a bad move, Ace,' she muttered to herself, secure in the knowledge that the communicators were not functioning for fear the enemy would pick up the broadcast. Then she set off for the largest ridge within sight, hoping that the Doctor's estimate of how far behind them the cruiser was could be trusted not to be too optimistic.

She jumped easily over the ridge and into the shallow trench behind it. Too easily – she almost overshot and for a moment feared she might go spinning off into space. She was grateful that the asteroid was large enough to have any gravity at all, but she should not presume on its hospitality too much. Once she had settled back into a comfortable position, and her heartbeat had settled back into a comfortable rhythm, she lined the bolter up against the stars, resting the angled legs on the end of the muzzle into a cleft in the rock. Perfect; from here she covered most of the sky in the direction from which the cruiser must come.

She was entirely dependent on her vision – no sound in the vacuum; no perceptors in case the Rippeareans caught an echo of the scansion fields. She began watching the most likely sectors of the starscape for movement, her eyes scanning slowly back and forth looking for the tell-tale movement of a star, or a point of luminance flickering brighter than the others as it caught and reflected distant light.

When it came it was quicker than she had imagined. She recognized the snub nose of the cruiser as it approached from the ident charts Fortalexa had shown her. But even so, it took a precious second to register that it was what she was looking out for. She fumbled the bolter slightly in her haste to align it, her visor knocking into the viewfinder as she tried to sight through it.

One shot was all she would get. If that – it looked as if the ship was coming straight at her, intent on smashing its way forcibly through the asteroid. Perhaps they intended to blast it after all.

Then at what seemed like the last moment, the enhanced image banked and shied away. Ace had to track quickly to keep up with it. But she was at last getting an angle on the flank. The huge metal bulk panned smoothly across her line of sight, slowed almost to a standstill in terms of its normal speed as it paused to manoeuvre round the asteroid. Ace's brain registered the landmarks along its hull as they passed: forward weapons arrays; auxiliary fuel and storage bays; armaments magazine – on no account hit *that*. So the next identifiable section should be the aft weapons pods, and then the aft thruster feed section.

She almost missed the cross-hatched piping which signified the start of the section she must hit, and the bolter jogged a little as she moved it to catch up as the ship rushed towards her. The phason charge was away almost before she knew her hand had flexed on the trigger-grip. She watched the circular projectile spinning towards its target, the projecting detonator bolts a blur in the viewfinder.

Too early – she had been over-eager. The charge was heading forward of the ideal detonation point. Heading for the weapons pod. If it hit that the resulting explosion might take out the magazine as well.

Ace muttered a well-worn military phrase she had often used in such times and ducked down behind the ridge, her hands shielding the back of her helmet in a futile reflex.

Two of the bolters on the charge's outer casing made contact almost together on the hull of the Rippearean cruiser. They were both plunged into the casing by the force of the impact and detonated virtually together. The main phason charge exploded in the centre of its double skin, the heat and gas forcing their way outwards through the joints of the containment vessel.

The vessel burst under the pressure, shrapnel and the initial blast wave exploding outwards through the holes left by the two bolter caps which had started the reaction. As a result, the detonation that ripped into the hull at 10,996 meters per second was dissipated to about half the destructive power that the designers had intended. Even so, the weapons pods were smashed backwards through the bulkhead into the feed linkages for the rear thrusters, crushing them beyond repair. The forward motion of the ship helped channel the explosion backwards, and the double-strength bulkhead screening off the magazine from the rest of the ship buckled but remained intact.

From initial impact to the complete destruction of the aft thruster feed linkage took just under one hundredth of a second.

A shower of debris and shrapnel splashed down on the ridge. Ace saw fragments of burning metal bounce along the top, and heard others scatter across her helmet. When the noise and yellow rain had stopped, she cautiously raised her head.

The cruiser was spinning slowly on its axis, the impact had knocked it round in a circle and stopped its forward motion. As the damaged side spun into view Ace could see the hole torn through the hull and the fires still burning in the thruster sections at the rear. As she watched, a mist of fire-retardant gas sprayed out along the aft of the ship, and then the damage spun away out of sight.

'Hasta la vista, baby,' Ace said with satisfaction. Then the warning bleeper started.

She stabbed at the buttons on her wrist and watched the read-outs scroll across the inside of her visor. Pressure was down – and still falling. But where was the leak? A red-hot particle of metal from the cruiser must have penetrated her suit, though there was no obvious damage. She slumped into a sitting position.

She checked the oxygen levels. Too low. She adjusted the pumps which were trying to make up the shortage of pressure. At least what oxygen remained would ebb away more slowly now. But most had already been efficiently pumped into space. She had to find the leak.

Ace started isolating areas of the suit and checking the pressure levels. She was looking for an area where the pressure was noticeably lower than other areas. Or should it be higher if that was where the oxygen was being forced out? Damn! She could hear her breathing becoming laboured within the helmet now. She had to concentrate.

187

She was looking for abnormal pressure: low or high, either would do.

Left leg – had to be. The figures were fluctuating all over the place. She stared down at the suit. Nothing to see, but the hole could be tiny. Probably was. Ace tugged at the zip of the pouch at her right thigh, forcing herself to stay calm and to pull steadily when her jerks failed to open it. The zipper tore silently across, plastic teeth grinning up at her as they parted and her vision started to blur.

She managed to get the tube of sealing gel out of the pouch, but she dropped it trying to unscrew the top. It bounced off the side of the rock her back was against and skidded just out of reach. With an effort she leaned forward, her fingertips scrambling to catch at it. The air was rushing in her ears and her heart was pounding within her head when she finally managed to pick up the tube. It seemed far heavier than when she had dropped it.

The top came off easily and she smeared a thin layer of gel on to her leg, squeezing a blob just above the knee and spreading it across with the palm of her hand. Almost at once, at the top of the area she had covered, a bubble started to form. It blistered outwards, thinning and stretching. Then it burst in a tiny shower of pale droplets, releasing a breath of Ace's life into the emptiness of space.

Her hand seemed to be seizing up as she reached across and squeezed a larger amount of gel over the point where the bubble had formed. She could feel the strain in her hand as she held the tube; she could detect the deterioration in her vision as the gel immediately began to blister before it had time to set. She managed to squeeze another lump of gel over the leak, but she could scarcely see what she was doing.

Ace's head lolled forward and she felt but could not see the tube of sealant slip from her limp fingers.

'All the evidence,' Bernice said, 'points to a civilization wiped out almost without trace. Whatever happened, it

188

was over very quickly – buildings completely destroyed and no other material evidence left intact.'

'And the Doctor sent you to confirm this theory?'

Bernice was not actually sure quite why he had sent her. 'Partly,' she hazarded. 'And partly because I think he felt there were some things that didn't add up.'

Braxiatel pushed himself forward off the desk and wandered over towards the cabinet containing the manuscript. 'Such as?'

Benny was not entirely sure about that either. But she had her own suspicions. 'The acoustics of the theatre are all wrong for one thing.'

Braxiatel clicked his tongue. 'Yes, we missed that.' He shook his head as if chiding himself for the mistake.

'You've been investigating it too?'

He ignored her question. 'What else?'

'Oh, I don't know. Lots of little things. It just seems weird generally. Then there's the problems with the research papers and source documents. And the computer's simulation of the way the buildings were destroyed.'

'Yes.' He nodded. 'It never occurred to us to run a simularity on it.' He smiled suddenly. 'Never mind. Is that it?'

'Yes. And no. There's this machine I found. It projects an image of a play. A sort of simularity. But there's more to it than that.'

'What sort of more? What does the Doctor think?'

'I don't know. But it worries him. He thinks – *we* think it's connected to whatever happened all those years ago.'

Braxiatel was pacing the room now, walking thoughtfully between the manuscript and the desk. 'Interesting . . .' he muttered. 'Very interesting.'

'You said you'd done some research as well – and you've implied you have some theory for what happened on Menaxus.'

He stopped and stroked his chin. For a moment he was quiet, then he seemed to come to a decision. 'Oh, I know what happened on Menaxus. That's why you have to get to the Doctor and warn him.'

'Warn him? What about?'

'About the machine; about an invasion.' He sat on the desk, shuffling backwards so his feet were just clear of the floor and stared intently into Benny's eyes. 'Let me tell you about Menaxus,' he said. And then he told her what had happened.

Fortalexa had set up a small workshop in one of the crew cabins. He had the control panel off the machine and was attaching various instruments and monitors to its internal circuitry when Ace found him. Lannic was leaning against the wall watching him, her arms folded. She pushed herself away from the wall as Ace came in.

'You feeling all right now?' she asked.

'Fine thanks. Throat's a bit sore still, otherwise no problems.'

'Good.' Lannic passed her in the doorway. Ace turned sideways to let her through. 'Good,' said Lannic again as she squeezed past, and she smiled and clapped Ace on the shoulder. Then she turned back into the room and called across, 'Oh, you might try linking the VR units to the projection system via the real world interface. Should get you something.'

Fortalexa looked up for the first time. 'Yes, it's a thought. Thanks.'

'Pleasure.'

After Lannic was out of sight down the corridor, Ace went over to Fortalexa. 'Thank you,' she said.

'Ah, forget it. Dragging unconscious women across asteroids and flinging them into airlocks is what I joined up for. It was the Doctor's idea I should go looking, anyway.'

She could see he did not want to make anything of it. 'Sure. But thanks anyway.'

'Pleasure,' he echoed Lannic.

'She seemed in a good mood.'

Fortalexa flicked a couple of switches and tapped a

recalcitrant read-out. 'Probably glad to be on her way home. I know I am. Where's your home, by the way?'

'Oh, in the Federation,' said Ace vaguely. That was a discussion she was not sure she was up to yet.

'I went to the Federation once, as a child – before the war.'

'Oh?'

'Yes. Went shopping with my mother. We got deported.'

'What? Why?'

'Silly mistake on my part. Bad choice of words. Mother was trying on necklaces on Alpha Centauri. I saw a really nice one and pointed it out to her.'

'What was wrong with that?'

'Well the sales assistant was just beside us, and I said "That's the one I'd get." He took it personally.'

It took Ace a moment. Then she laughed out loud. It made her throat hurt more, but it made the rest of her feel good. 'A bit unfair to our monocular friends,' she said when she had recovered. She said it not because she meant it, but to show she really had understood the joke.

Fortalexa shrugged, 'Oh I don't know, they've got a great sense of humour from what I've heard.' He frowned at the readings and flicked another switch. 'This thing's ancient.'

'Why bother with it then?'

'The technology's ancient, but what it does is remarkably sophisticated.'

'And what is that?'

'I wish I knew. There's some circuitry in here I just can't interpret, but it looks like serious function.' He disconnected a set of wires from one of his meters and reconnected them to another set on the controls. 'There's a lot of microcode hiding around as well. More than it should need.'

'Lannic said something about a "real world interface".'

He answered automatically, busy with the wiring. 'Yes. Might work.'

'I didn't realize she was a techie.'

'She's not. Probably just repeating something she heard

191

from someone. Hey,' he looked up, 'that's a point. Do you think the Doctor might have any ideas?'

Ace laughed. 'I'm sure he would. He's full of them.'

'So's everyone else. But unlike the Doctor, that's usually not all they're full of.' He disappeared behind the machine.

Ace tried to see over the top, but gave up and bent to look underneath instead. She could just make out the shape of Fortalexa's head through the tangles of wire and componentry which hung down out of the body of the machine. 'I'll get him for you,' she said. He did not answer, so she left to look for the Doctor.

'I'm determined to sort out this thing if it kills me.' Fortalexa stood up and smiled over at the young woman. But she had gone, so he returned his attention to the machine. Try linking the VR units to the projection system via the real world interface – yes, it should certainly give him some sort of result. Maybe he could display some internal diagnostic information through the interface.

The linkages were fairly straightforward, unlike most of the other rechannelling he had attempted. Fortalexa held his breath and pressed the operation key.

The result was immediate. A red glow formed in the centre of the room, an image within it. Fortalexa walked round it. It was vague and hazy from all angles, but seemed to be solidifying. The red glow was fading as the image within gained clarity. It was a group of figures, a tableau. He moved a little closer and concentrated on one of the figures. It was humanoid, but it was not human. Too bulky.

It was a robot. Two of the figures were robots. Taller than Fortalexa and much broader. They were constructed from reflective metal built into an exoskeleton. The skull head was riddled with fine mechanisms to drive the jaw and rotate about the neck. The eyes were glowing red bulbs set deep within their dark sockets. The rest of the body followed an almost human bone structure, but was left bare – no covering material at all, the joints and circuitry open to view. Fortalexa could see the tiny motors drive the knee joints as the metal figures stepped forward; could hear the whirr of the servos as the fingers flexed on the ends of the metal hands reaching towards him.

They were magnificent examples of precision engineering. Probably from the climax to *The Good Soldiers*. He would have examined them in greater detail if he had not at that moment recognized the figure standing between the robots as they stepped towards him.

Fortalexa backed away, his jaw slack, his head shaking from side to side in disbelief. He was preoccupied with the human between the robots that he hardly noticed when they stepped forward, out of the red field, and shimmered into reality. His brain was still wrestling with the problem, trying to relate it back to the events on Menaxus, trying to tie in the dream machine, when a metal hand closed round his throat and with a swift servo-assisted movement snapped shut.

'Here he is,' Ace led the Doctor into the room. 'He'll get you sorted.' She looked round; the room was deserted. There was just the machine in the centre of the floor.

'Fortalexa?' the Doctor called out.

'Can I help you?' Fortalexa stood up from behind the machine.

'I thought I was going to help you,' the Doctor told him.

'Thank you, but I think I can manage.'

'Hang on there,' Ace leaned across the machine. 'You said you needed the Doctor's help.'

'I think I can manage,' he repeated.

'Manage what?' asked the Doctor, his eyes narrowed slightly as he and Ace walked round the machine. The innards had all been packed away inside. It looked like Fortalexa was finished.

'Manage to get it working. We must be able to present a play on our return.'

The Doctor smiled. 'What a nice thought. You know, I haven't been to the theatre for centuries. What play did you have in mind?' Fortalexa did not answer. 'Could we get a performance of *The Good Soldiers*, perhaps?' hazarded the Doctor.

'That's the one I'd get,' Ace said immediately and grinned at Fortalexa.

But he did not react at all. 'I am quite busy, actually,' he said, his face impassive. 'Perhaps we could discuss this another time?'

'Of course, of course.' The Doctor was already on his way to the door. 'I quite understand.'

But Ace understood nothing. She followed the Doctor into the corridor. 'What's happened, Doctor? He was laughing and joking a few minutes ago, now look at him. What's he found out?'

'I don't know, Ace. But I'm pretty sure of one thing.'

'What's that?'

'That machine – it's the key to whatever is happening, and to a lot of what has already happened.'

'How?'

'I don't know.' His brow furrowed for a moment, then his eyes brightened and he said, 'But I think that whatever is being played out here is about to enter the final act.'

ACT 3

Source Document 11

From *The Techniques of the Actor*, article by Haga Nodena in *Theatre Today* issue 428, July 2049. An extract which survived the Bodleian Library fire

Braxiatel Collection Catalogue Number: 957JM

Balance of power on the stage is important. There is no point in casting a strong and forceful actor in the role of a weakling, especially if he is expected to play opposite a weak actor who is presenting a more powerful character, such as the play's *raisonneur*.

The Flannegan production of *Henry V* failed for exactly this reason. It asked the audience to believe in a frail and weak king leading his troops to victory and spouting hollow rhetoric with a lisp and a limp. By contrast, Keffley's portrayal of Bardolph as a forceful and intelligent manipulator not only played against Shakespeare's intentions but upstaged Grayton's King.

As a result it seemed to the audience that Bardolph was a more likely monarch than Henry, and several were heard to blame Shakespeare for not making it more clear that Bardolph was really the power behind the obviously ineffectual throne.

Chapter 11

The Doctor's Dilemma

*Osterling wrote primarily for the emerging techno-
logies and practices of the purpose-built theatres of
his day. He was able to make full use of an emerging
dramatic form and a new and less restricting set of
staging techniques.*

*That said, although most of his plays were written
for the public audiences of the theatres, some were
written – perhaps even to order – to be performed at
court. The Good Soldiers is unlikely to have been
one of these plays.*

The New Dramatists – Barbas Lothal, 3544

Locris Marlock had become Manact of Heletia through
political manoeuvring and liberal use of assassination. He
used those same techniques to keep his position. He also
believed fervently that knowledge was power, which was
why he was hurrying through the concrete corridors of
the palace to a meeting with the Exec. He knew that they
would not dare to start the audience without him, but he
knew also that if he arrived late he might miss a vital
comment or a telling raise of an eyebrow.

His two bodyguards kept in step as they followed on
his heel at an indiscreet distance. When they reached the
heavy wooden double doors to the green room he strode
towards them without slowing, knowing that the guards
within would see his approach on the monitor and open
them for him. Or they would die. Fear was such a useful
tool.

The doors swung open without warning and Ace turned from the throne. So far they had been kept waiting, the Exec sitting at his desk apparently oblivious to their presence.

The Exec was a small man, made smaller by the high ceiling of the drab grey windowless room adorned only with the green carpet leading across the stone floor from the main wooden doors to his desk. The room lacked even the playbills and posters which seemed to add colour to the featureless concrete of the rest of the palace. It was difficult to tell quite how small the Exec was since his desk and the chair behind it were raised on a podium. And he was surprisingly young. Ace did not reckon him to be very much older than herself. He had short, greasy black hair and his skin looked like it needed the attention of a good cleansing agent. His lips stuck out as if he were permanently preparing to burst into tears. His watery grey eyes had flicked across at her once, then returned to the papers on his desk. He continued his slow way through them, initialling one, discarding another.

But when the doors opened he immediately stood in greeting – almost in reverence, it seemed to Ace. 'Ah, Manact Marlock. Good.' He sat down again and waved a hand at the piles of paper in front of him. 'You know Marlock, I sometimes think a computer console might help organize my affairs somewhat.' His voice was high, as though nervous. The way it rose slightly at the end made it sound almost as if he were asking a question rather than making an observation.

Marlock growled his response. By contrast, the Manact's voice was firm and deep: 'You know that an engineer's tool would not befit your position. The pen is mightier than the console, and much more noble. No, Exec,' he continued with a slight bow, 'you would not wish to be burdened with the excess of data and useless information that a console would force you to endure. Far better that you see just those communications and orders which require your – ' he broke off for a second, as if in search of the right word, ' – *special* attention.'

Ace thought she understood the subtext of the conversation and wondered how many times it had been played out in similar fashion. If he were not such a wimp she might have felt sorry for the Exec.

Marlock got none of her sympathy. He sounded self-assured and frighteningly over-confident. Ace could see that others thought so too. The guards either side of the main doors were all but quaking in their boots, as were the few courtiers gathered for the audience. And the two men standing alert behind Marlock (their purpose starkly clear) had their hands firmly on the handles of their disruptors.

Had she not seen the recent display of power, Ace might have put Marlock's hold over the courtiers down in part to his appearance. He was a large man – she could imagine he towered over the Exec. His head had not a hair on it and his ears were flat against the sides. His nose was broken in the middle and his eyes were a piercing blue-grey. His right eye seemed set deeper than the other, but this might be a trick of the light coupled with the discoloration round it. The way the skin was pulled sideways across the edge of the socket where the wide scar ran in a vertical line from his forehead down to the right side of his thin-lipped mouth did nothing to help. He was dressed in the dark uniform of the Heletian fleet, the braid at his shoulder presumably signifying his position. Though Ace imagined that everyone on the planet would know him by sight.

The Exec sifted through his papers and eventually found the one he was looking for. 'This matter of the uprising on Arbela.'

Marlock found himself a seat on the stage beside the Exec's desk and slumped down in it, looking round the assembled courtiers. His eyes lingered on the Doctor, Ace and the archaeologists. Then they flicked back to the Exec. 'You have my recommendation there.' He pointed to a sheet of paper buried about half-way down one pile, identifying it by the visible corner.

The Exec pulled out the paper and scanned it. 'Is the commissionaire from Arbela here?'

One of the courtiers stepped forward. 'Exec.' He was a shortish man, fat and balding; what hair he had was slicked over in an attempt to make it appear he had lost rather less of it than was actually the case. The attempt had failed.

'Ah, good. The rising has been put down, I see. But a lesson must be taught.'

'The rebels and Rippearean sympathizers have been executed or shipped to the camps on Pulai Kompay.'

'Yes, yes. But we – I – feel a further lesson is necessary. You will select one thousand of the inhabitants of Arbela City at random, and execute them also.' The Exec licked his full lips with a pale tongue.

The commissionaire's face went white, 'But – Exec – '

The Exec was on his feet at once, his voice a histrionic screech. 'You dare question me? I shall have you flogged! Two thousand – you will execute two thousand of the population!' His face twisted into a schoolboy grin, his eyes acquiring an inner light. The commissionaire bowed stiffly and stepped back.

'My, my,' came a voice from behind Ace. 'That seems a little extreme under the circumstances.' Ace turned to see the Doctor stepping forward. Fortalexa was unmoved by the exchange, but both Lannic and Klasvik looked pale. Ace wondered if they had ever seen their Exec before. Obviously they had never seen him like this.

'Extreme?' screeched the Exec, once more on his feet, his face boiling an angry red.

'Under the circumstances,' offered the Doctor with a smile. 'After all, the plotters are already taken care of – isn't that right, Marlock?'

Marlock said nothing, but Ace could see his eyes glinting intently as they watched the Doctor.

The Exec stepped down off his podium, his bodyguards alert beside him. 'I don't know who you are,' he began.

'Oh, I'm sorry,' interrupted the Doctor. 'I'm the Doctor.' He waved his hat in a friendly manner towards his companions. 'And this is my friend Ace and my associates Fortalexa, Klasvik and Lannic.' The Exec watched open-mouthed and Marlock shook his head and sighed loudly. 'Our pilot, Lefkhani, went on somewhere I'm afraid – nice chap, but he had a war to get back to. So sad, don't you think – war?' His voice tailed away.

'Well, *Doctor*, I shall have you shot for interrupting me – for questioning my authority. You will be blasted into fragments.'

The Doctor clapped his hands together with glee. 'Oh such power and political acumen. Nothing like an execution to solve the problem, is there? Right, off you go then.' He clamped his eyes tight shut and folded his arms over his chest, his hat resting over one of his hearts.

Ace tensed, her hands balling into fists. They had been both searched and scanned for power sources when they came into the room. For once she had been right to heed the Doctor's advice and conceal her single remaining smartbomb in her room. Goodness only knew when she would have a chance to slip back to the TARDIS parked in a corner of a hanger in the spaceport.

The Doctor opened one eye cautiously. 'Come on, then. What's keeping you?'

'Take him away,' snarled the Exec. One of the door guards stepped forward. Ace tensed, ready to launch herself into them.

'No no no no. That won't do at all.' The Doctor threw his hat down on the floor and glared at the Exec. Ace relaxed slightly. She began to suspect the Doctor had things under control after all.

'So, you see the error of your ways. But too late, Doctor.'

'Error? Not at all. But if you are to execute me as an example to those who question your authority or who interrupt your ranting, then you should do it here and now.' He stuck his chin out and folded his arms, planting his feet firmly either side of his discarded hat. 'I insist.'

Ace watched surprised as the Exec took a step backwards. 'Here?' He sounded unsure, worried. 'Now?'

'Yes. In fact, to make a proper job of it, you'd best do it yourself.' The Doctor nodded to the door guard who had approached him. His disruptor was already drawn and inclining his head slightly he made to hand it to the Exec.

The Exec flinched as if struck and leaped back on to his podium, taking refuge behind his desk. 'No. I have – I have changed my mind.'

'Oh?' The Doctor sounded disappointed.

'Yes. Too many executions may be . . .'

'Counter-productive? Might begin to upset those loyal citizens who have no intention of rebelling or causing trouble?'

'Quite.' The Exec nodded quickly.

'I see.' The Doctor stepped back to join Ace. Almost as an afterthought he called back: 'So, you'll be repealing the execution orders on the good people of Arbela then.'

'What?'

Ace watched as the Doctor went into his *I'm-sorry-I-thought-it-was-obvious* routine. 'But surely you've decided that too many executions may be counter-productive and might begin to upset those loyal citizens who have no intention of rebelling or causing trouble?'

The Exec gulped and looked across to Marlock for help, but the Manact was sitting with his face in his hands, shaking his head slowly as if in disbelief. 'Quite, quite – see to it, Commissionaire,' the Exec said faintly when he saw there was no help coming. 'Er, the matter of the Menaxan expedition,' he went on quickly. 'A report, I believe, from – ' he hunted through the papers again, 'from Camarina Lannic.' The Exec looked round expect-antly, and Lannic stepped forward.

She bowed formal and low. Ace thought for a moment she was going to curtsy and suppressed a giggle of humour and relief. The meeting seemed to have changed direction.

'My lord Exec,' Lannic's voice was sticky sweet and submissive. Ace looked closely, but she seemed com-pletely sincere. 'It is my honour to report our excavations as a triumphant success.'

'Oh.' The Exec clearly was surprised that something had gone well. He also seemed smitten by Lannic's attitude. 'Good. Well done.'

Ace caught the Doctor's eye and mimed sticking her index finger down her throat. The Doctor shrugged: he clearly did not know what Lannic was up to either.

'At great risk and suffering heavy losses we have secured and brought back a wonderful gift.'

'A gift? For me?' A note of suspicion crept into the Exec's voice, 'What is it?'

'It is a machine – a dream of a machine. It presents virtual-reality-enhanced images of plays.'

Marlock snorted. 'You call that a dream? The Exec can order a real play any time he wishes. With a cast of his choosing. He has no need of a simple holo-projector. We might as well watch a celluloid for all the soul and immediacy of performance you offer.' He leaned forward in his chair and snarled: 'Or is this an audition for the starring role in *The Execution of Segestus*?'

Lannic bowed again. 'I meant no disrespect, sir. But the machine I mentioned is pre-programmed with several plays which may interest the Exec.'

'Such as?'

'Such as *The Good Soldiers*, sir.'

The room went quiet. 'Is this true?' asked the Exec in a hushed voice.

Lannic nodded. 'We believe we can operate the machine and present a performance. Perhaps in the royal theatre?'

'Have you seen the play this machine projects?' asked Marlock.

'We've seen *Hamlet*,' offered the Doctor cheerily. 'Well, bits of him anyway.'

Lannic answered to the Exec, 'We would not presume to watch Osterling's masterpiece ahead of yourself. Nobody should see *The Good Soldiers* until it is presented to the Exec of Heletia.'

'Quite – quite right.' The Exec still looked a little pale from the news. But his voice was regaining what little strength it usually had. 'No one shall see the play before we do ourselves. When can it be presented?'

Fortalexa answered stiffly. 'We can set up the machine tonight and have it ready for a command performance tomorrow evening.'

'Very well,' Marlock said before the Exec could respond. 'Tomorrow night in the royal theatre. See to it.' With that he stood up, descended the steps from the stage and went to the door, standing beside it as the guards swung it open. He made no effort to leave, but his meaning was obvious and the courtiers began to file out.

'This audience is at an end,' the Exec said, a little late and apparently a little surprised. Marlock smiled at him, the scar down his face stretching with the movement of the skin. 'Wait,' the Exec continued and Marlock's smile froze. 'Go and prepare for the performance,' he said to Fortalexa, who bowed and left. 'Lannic, will you and your associates stay and tell me more about your expedition?'

Klasvik looked worried at the prospect, but Lannic's whole face seemed to light up and her eyelids fluttered with joy.

'Come on, Doctor,' Ace nudged him. 'Let's go and help Fortalexa before we throw up.'

Marlock stopped them at the door, standing in their way as they tried to leave.

'Enjoy a good play, do you, Marlock?' asked the Doctor politely. 'Keeps the Exec out of your way for a while so you can get on with the war for him, I suppose.'

'Be careful, Doctor,' Marlock replied quietly. 'You may be too clever for our own good.' Then he stepped aside, his mouth set in a smile. But his eyes were harsh and humourless.

The Doctor and Ace had been allocated adjoining rooms. These rooms were as bland and functional as the green room. In common with all the other rooms Ace had seen they had no windows, just several framed posters announcing plays she had never heard of starring actors and actresses she had never heard of either. But despite the splashes of colour the posters offered she was beginning to think of the whole establishment as more of a bunker than a palace.

They were in the Doctor's room. The Doctor was sitting on the single upright plastic chair, which he had pulled from under the single plastic table, and Ace was lying on the bed, her hands behind her head. The smartbomb she had retrieved from her own room lay quietly in her pocket.

'Going to the play?' Ace asked.

'I doubt if we'll get any choice.'

'Oh. Is it any good?'

The Doctor smiled. 'Bit boring in the middle, I seem to remember. You'll like the ending though – very violent.'

'Should suit that screwed-up cretin Exec down to the ground.' She sat up suddenly, biting back her words and looking round the room.

'It's all right. I've already checked for bugs.'

'Phew – no bugs.' Ace settled back again.

'Oh I didn't say that. There are three actually.'

'What?' Ace leapt up.

'But they don't work,' smiled the Doctor, brandishing a small square-headed hammer.

Ace sat down on the bed with a growl and drew her knees up under her chin. 'I don't like it. There's still some weird stuff happening.'

'You're right there. I'd like to examine the machine again before they get too engrossed in setting up for tomorrow.'

'You think there's a problem?'

'Why is the circuitry so complicated? How did we manage to get caught up in its performance of *Hamlet*? How did you get scratched by a non-existent knife? And then there's the deaths on Menaxus.'

Ace was puzzled. 'But that was the mud thing, right Doctor?'

'Was it? You know, that's pretty improbable too. Living mud – still don't like it.'

'Spooky statues,' mused Ace. 'You know, I saw this

206

opera once on telly – God knows why or where – and this guy got talking to a statue of this bloke he'd murdered.'

'Did he invite it home for tea?'

Ace frowned. 'You've seen it too?'

'Yes I've seen it. The statue accepts the invitation and turns up.'

'Yeah, like I said – spooky. Must have been Channel Four.'

The Doctor tossed his little hammer from one hand to the other several times. 'But Menaxus was more like *Death's Bane* than *Don Juan*.' He froze, and the hammer clattered to the floor. He retrieved it with a frown, flipped it into the air and pulled open his jacket pocket for it to fall into.

'What is it?' asked Ace.

'Oh, just a thought. Probably nothing.' He rubbed his chin for a moment, then leapt to his feet retrieving his umbrella from where it lay across the table. 'But I have to see that machine again.'

They had given Bernice a delta dart. As she strapped herself into the single-person fighter she wondered where they had found it. It was strange finding anything other than antiques here. Obviously Braxiatel had clout with the armaments corporations of the Federation.

Now all she had to do was wait. Benny checked over the instruments again, playing back Braxiatel's reassurances in her mind: a small fighter could get through the Heletian lines undetected; the Heletian defences were nothing like as impressive or well implemented as they had been a year ago; of course the Rippeareans could get their own ships through, but anything bigger than a fighter would be detected and then stranded behind the enemy lines . . .

Braxiatel's face flicked into existence on a side screen, breaking in on her thoughts. 'You have the message, don't you?' his voice asked, tinny and distant.

'Don't fret, I've got it here.' Benny waved a plain white

envelope at the screen, then returned it to a pocket in her flight suit. I'm glad I changed, she thought. It would have been fun trying to wrestle her way into the tiny cockpit dressed in the full velvet skirt. Would have amused the launch crew too.

'One other thing,' said Braxiatel.

'Good luck?' she guessed.

'Of course. But as well as that.'

'I've memorized the route and the strategy for dodging the home defences when I get to Heletia if that's what you're after. And even if I hadn't, the navigation computer has it all sorted out.'

'I assumed that.'

'I also know the positions of the main battle lines, if you're sure the locations are accurate.'

'Don't worry.' Braxiatel smiled. 'I provide lines for all the best people.'

'Oh. What then?'

'You remember that you said Richard Mique gave the models of the Temple of Love and the Belvedere to Marie Antoinette?'

Benny did remember. 'Yes. What of it?'

'According to Pierre de Nolhac, she didn't keep them. I thought you ought to know.'

Benny laughed. She had assumed he thought she was bluffing. 'Well, you learn something new every day,' she said. 'Can I go now please?'

Braxiatel looked towards the back of the ship, at something or someone out of sight of the scanner. After a moment his gaze returned to Bernice. 'Yes, everything cleared the pre-flight checks. Whenever you're ready. Good luck.'

The scanner went blank. Benny hit the ignition button and pulled back on the control column.

The royal theatre, like the rest of the palace, was constructed of reinforced concrete. In many ways it was similar to the Pentillanian theatre on Menaxus. It was an amphitheatre in the old style: the orchestra or playing area slightly raised above the gangway around it and the front row of seats. The auditorium was raked in tiers, circling round the front half of the stage and soaring above it. Unlike the Menaxan theatre, it was roofed in with a heavy grey ceiling from which a lighting gallery hung.

High on each side was a private box. One of the boxes was reserved for the Exec and his entourage. The other had been screened off with one-way glass across the front and sides. It was in this second theatre box that Fortalexa was setting up the dream machine for the next evening's performance of Osterling's greatest masterpiece.

The Doctor watched from the stairway behind the box, Ace was behind him trying to see over his shoulder. Fortalexa continued tinkering with the machine, oblivious to the Doctor and Ace behind him. The Doctor silently shooed Ace from the stairway and they retreated down the steps to the corridor below.

'What we need is a guard, or a functionary of some kind,' he said.

'Why? Don't you trust Fortalexa?'

'Do you?'

'I don't know.' Ace considered for a moment. 'A day or two ago, yes. But since we left Menaxus – since you sent him to get me off the asteroid, in fact – he's been – '

'Not himself? Ah, hang on a second.' The Doctor had spotted a courtier crossing the corridor further down. 'You there,' he shouted. The courtier stopped in his tracks. The Doctor continued, waving his arms officiously and brandishing a pen: 'Where's Fortalexa? You know, the dream machine chap. The Exec wants to see him.'

The courtier was immediately flustered. 'Oh, er, I believe he will be with the machine – in the Queen's box. Not that we have a Queen, of course, but you know that. Er, I expect.'

'Well, don't stand there all of a dither, go and get him.' The Doctor strode off without waiting for a reply, leaving the courtier stammering and looking from left to right in confusion.

Ace followed the Doctor. As she passed the courtier

she said, 'I'd do as he says – he's the one who got Walter Raleigh executed.'

'Waltararlay – oh dear oh dear,' muttered the courtier, wringing his hands. Ace glanced back as she rounded the corner, and saw him making his diffident way towards the stairs.

'Dost know that waterfly?' asked the Doctor as they watched him leave their sight. 'And I did not get Raleigh executed,' he went on before she could think of a suitable answer. 'He was executed for being left over from the previous reign, not my fault at all.'

It did not take long for the courtier to reappear, still dithering, and closely following Fortalexa. They disappeared down the corridor the other way, the courtier struggling to keep up with Fortalexa's long and determined stride.

'Right, off we go.' The Doctor dashed for the stairs, stopping running two-thirds of the way there and skidding the rest of the distance on his heels.

Ace kept watch at the top of the stairs while the Doctor spent what seemed like an eternity examining the machine in silence. At last he said, 'Just as I thought – there's more to this machine than meets the eye.'

'You needed all this time to work that out?' Ace went over to join him by the machine. She was sure she would hear Fortalexa if and when he returned. Probably the Exec would keep him waiting for hours yet, and then there would be a non-battle of wits as they tried to work out who had really sent for whom.

'I meant it literally, Ace. There's more than just image projection going on. I think another reality is projected, and in some way merges with our own. That would explain how we came to get caught up in it. It's a world in its own right – many worlds, one for each programmed play.'

'You mean they really happen.'

'Absolutely. Well, I think so.' The Doctor looked uneasy for a second. 'Ace, there's a whole universe captured in there. People who think they're real but who are actually

210

just fiction are running about saying pre-written lines about self-will and never even realizing it.'

'Well, more fools them.'

'Yes,' but he seemed uncertain. 'I suppose so. Unless,' his face brightened, 'they are the real people, and it's we who are just imaginary.' He laughed and busied himself about the machine once more. After a few minutes with his arms stretched up to the elbow inside its innards he said, 'I wonder if we can deliberately muddle up the two universes.' He did not look up, but continued with his efforts. He seemed to be rewiring the circuitry for a particular switch at the edge of the main control panel.

'Like what happened by accident when we landed on Menaxus, you mean?'

'Yes. Did we lose *our* free will too, do you think? Were we doing things prepared for us by someone else? And if so, how did they know we'd be there?'

'Doctor, what are you on about?'

'Ace, in there,' he pointed at the machine, 'is a universe where there is a special providence in the fall of a sparrow.' He broke off and toyed with his upper lip. 'I must know what it's like!' He turned to her suddenly. 'Want to come?' he asked.

'I think I'll stick with what's really real, thanks Doctor. Once was enough.'

'Suit yourself.' He sounded disappointed. 'Oh well, wish me luck.' He reached for the switch he had been rewiring on the control panel.

'Doctor – what are you doing?' She rushed forward, but it was too late.

A red glow emanated like a mist from the machine and enveloped the Doctor. He smiled at Ace through the mist as it thickened into a fog, and with a raise of his hat disappeared within it. After a moment the red glow faded away, leaving Ace and the machine alone in the room.

Source Document 12

Extract from partly completed manuscript for *Beyond Osterling's Legacy*, by Azcline Grigsen. Date assumed to coincide with Grigsen's death – 3515. Manuscript never published.

Braxiatel Collection Catalogue Number: 883CR

In *Osterling's Legacy* I postulated that Stanoff Osterling's greatest work, *The Good Soldiers*, would be a disappointment, if it were ever to be recovered.

It seemed to me from the extracts that survive and the account of the plot that the play had some merit in terms of its storyline and overall theme, but was substandard in its treatment of character and dialogue. Despite disagreement from many experts and cries of 'Heresy' from the others, none has been able to refute this claim with any real evidence to the contrary.

Indeed, the greatest argument against my theory is the enduring reputation that the play has earned. While that reputation may be perpetuated through myth, there can be no doubt that it was initially built upon solid ground. However, while I am willing to accept from this premise that the play does indeed have some deep meaning and enduring quality, I maintain that it is not connected with the mediocre scripting.

In this book, I present my own theory on what this quality was. It was innovation.

I shall attempt to prove – through reference not to *The Good Soldiers* but to other plays of the twenty-third century – that the play did not gain its reputation through the quality of its script. However, it did introduce a single basic staging concept which provided a new vitality for the theatre and led directly to the form of the play as we know it today.

To discover what this innovation was, we must look not to the dialogue, but rather to the stage directions.

Chapter 12

The Master Builder

*To object to the voice of the author impinging on the
fiction is of course untenable. It is not only in the more
obvious asides where the author takes the reader into
his confidence that the writer begins to assert his own
point of view. The whole of fiction is actually intrusive
in this way. Unless scrupulously written from the first
person (and one can argue that nothing ever is),
the shift in viewpoints alone is enough to endow the
reader with insight which cannot 'really' be gained.
It is contrived, manufactured – a lie.*

*The stage may appear to bring us one step closer
to a representation of the real world. But this too is
an illusion. For while there is no direct link into the
thoughts and motives of any particular character,
the characters do take us – the audience – into their
confidence. Richard III leaves us in no doubt as to
his motives and plans, whereas by contrast, many of
Pirandello's characters only serve to disguise their real
intentions and feelings by their words. But whichever
happens, the audience is still granted a privileged
position – by the author and by the medium itself.*

*It is the author who decides which characters will
expose what information and offer what insights at
what time. The medium is more insidious. The whole
concept of theatre (and other performance arts) is to
present a picture to the audience, and it is a privileged
picture, a viewpoint that is unique in that it is not the
viewpoint of any person who is in the context of
the play 'real'. The author is always a character in*

his own right, and in the world of the theatre the audience becomes a character too. The difference is that the author is in control, and while the audience may draw what conclusions it can, it is always directed by the author and by the performance.

Fictional Voices – Booth Kitava, 2267

As the red mist faded from his eyes, the Doctor peered into the gloom of the castle.

Then suddenly, light. The glow was not intense, but it was bright enough to illuminate the characters standing beside him. He knew at once that they were characters, recognized them from his previous excursion into the world of the machine. 'Action,' he said, as the two figures jerked into life.

'So much for this, sir,' Hamlet said to Horatio, drawing his friend to one side, as if afraid the Doctor would overhear. 'Now you shall see the other. You do remember all the circumstances?'

'Remember them?' muttered the Doctor. 'I was probably there.'

But Hamlet ignored him. The Doctor slipped away through a side doorway. Hamlet's voice fading into the distance: 'There's a divinity that shapes our ends, rough-hew them how we will.'

The next room was the next world. 'Exits and entrances,' the Doctor thought and looked around him.

In front of him along the corridor, an arm was pushing its way through the rough stone wall. It was groping blindly for a hold on the whimpering young woman who tried to push past it. But the passageway was too narrow, and even if she escaped the clutches of this hand, another was already sprouting further along. But she struggled onwards, somehow forcing her way through the flailing arms as they clawed and tore at her clothes and face.

The Doctor watched her progress with interest. Things were becoming clearer. He was about to return to Hamlet, when the woman screamed – loud and long. At the far end of the corridor a figure had appeared and was making

215

its way towards her. The arms raised out of the way of the figure, as if in salute. The woman had given up her struggle along the passage, was watching the progress of her double as she approached.

The Doctor could see the cold stone features of the statue as it got nearer. '*Death's Bane*,' he muttered disparagingly. 'All spectacle and no plot.' He turned before the statue crushed its human image.

'But wilt thou hear now how I did proceed?' asked Hamlet, as the Doctor passed behind him, doffed his hat, and made his way across the room.

'I beseech you – ' Horatio called across, seemingly annoyed by the repeated interruption.

'Sorry,' said the Doctor, and swung open the heavy wooden door.

'Being thus benetted round with villainies – '

Hamlet's voice was cut off as the Doctor swung the door shut.

'This is more like it.' The Doctor swung his umbrella appreciatively and joined the party from Masterson's *The Croquet Match* on the lawn for tea. 'Thank you.' He smiled at the manservant who handed him a china cup and offered him a scone. Here at least was a civilized play with no animated statues or angst-ridden princes. On the trees in the distance, clusters of small autumn leaves splayed out in the breeze. The Doctor sipped at his tea and beamed round at the guests who accommodated him within their dialogue. When they dropped their croquet mallets and teacups at the blood-curdling scream from the main house, the Doctor helped himself to another scone. Yes, except for the murder this really was a *very* civilized piece of theatre.

The characters froze into tableau in horror as the act ended and, within the house, other images of the same characters began the next. The Doctor finished his scone and brushed imaginary crumbs from his shirt front.

It was just as he was putting down his teacup that he saw the man. He was the other side of the croquet lawn, standing by one of the flower beds on the main terrace.

In many ways he looked extremely ordinary: an old man with a white beard lengthening his already long face. But his attire, a one-piece white suit, was completely out of keeping with the Edwardian splendour of the guests on the croquet lawn. And he was still moving, shuffling his feet as he watched the Doctor brushing at his chest with his fingertips. The Doctor continued the motion, his brain already working its way through the possibilities, discarding all except his initial premise. Then the man shook his head as if in annoyance, turned and went into the house.

Immediately the Doctor was in motion. 'Wait,' he shouted as he dashed across the terrace. 'Wait – I'm real. Like you!' He launched himself through the open French windows and skidded to a halt in the drawing room.

'I love Albert,' wailed a tall thin woman, and the other house guests watched in sympathy.

The Doctor slumped into an empty armchair. The old man was gone. 'Stoppard!' he exclaimed in annoyance.

He wasn't coming back – at least, not immediately, that much was apparent. Ace was tempted to try every control on the machine, but she somehow doubted that would help. She was still trying to decide what *would* help when Fortalexa's voice almost made her jump.

'What are you doing here?' His voice was angry, his eyes sharp.

'Sorry,' said Ace despite herself. She was annoyed she had let him get so close without hearing his approach. She must have been very deep in thought, although she had to admit he did move very quietly. She watched as he crossed the room towards her, his feet barely seeming to touch the floor.

'You haven't been fiddling, have you?'

'I haven't touched anything,' Ace snapped back. 'I just came to see how you were getting on. In case you needed any help.'

'Thank you, but I have everything I need.' Fortalexa began to tap out a complicated sequence on the machine's keypad. He seemed to have forgotten Ace.

'And how's it going?'

'Fine.' He continued without looking up.

'So we'll actually get a performance of this play tomorrow, will we?'

Fortalexa's head snapped up and he fixed Ace in a steady stare. 'The performance will take place as planned. Everything is going according to plan. Exactly according to plan.'

'Okay, okay – keep your hair on.' Ace backed away, worried by the intensity of his response. 'I'll leave you to it, all right?'

Fortalexa watched her to the door, then his attention flicked back to the machine, almost as if a switch had been thrown in his mind.

Ace frowned and bit lightly at the inside of her cheek. 'I say,' she called over experimentally, 'my dog has no nose.'

'I am sorry to hear that,' Fortalexa replied without shifting his attention. 'If you will excuse me, I am rather busy.'

'Sure,' said Ace. 'Sure you are.' And she left him to it.

The honour was about the highest he could ever had wished for, and Klasvik hated every second of it. If he could have left, he would have done. As it was he tried to keep his face from betraying his feelings and his mouth from doing anything other than eat the food. Fortunately they each had a set of dishes, so he need not ask for anything to be passed.

Although its corners were hidden, receding into the gloom, the room was large, rectangular and featureless. So was the table where the main light was focused. It was obviously intended to seat far more than four people. There were more than four people in the room, of course – the unending stream of waiters, Marlock's bodyguards and the alert men standing behind the Exec's chair, hands permanently on the butts of their disruptors, eyes forever glancing round the room.

Klasvik sat at the middle of one of the long sides of the table, so he would have had to shout to make himself heard by the Exec or Marlock, who sat at opposite ends. Marlock had no trouble making his comments heard throughout the room – effortless shouting was an art that Marlock seemed to have perfected long ago.

Lannic had been sitting opposite Klasvik, but she had slowly shuffled her chair closer and closer to the Exec during the meal, until now she sat almost at his right hand. Klasvik had tried not to show his disgust at these manoeuvrings, while Marlock had all but leered down the table at Lannic.

Klasvik had to admit to himself that Lannic was an attractive woman. Especially since she had changed out of her coverall. Klasvik was more than conscious that he was still wearing his. He wondered where Lannic had found her new clothes – nobody had offered him any. He thought he was lucky to have found a shower.

Lannic was radiant. She was wearing a simple knee-length dress, sleeveless and with no flourishes or other adornment. The dress was a colour which seemed to alternate between black and silver depending on where the light caught it. The effect was to create artificial shadows at every contour and so emphasize the shape of the curves in Lannic's body. Klasvik might have been quite smitten, had he not been feeling so nauseated.

The effect on the others was easy to read. Marlock was amused by the whole thing, but at the same time could hardly keep from slobbering; the male guards and waiters were having trouble keeping a straight face when Lannic stretched or crossed her legs (both of which she did frequently). The Exec was head over heels in lust.

Klasvik was not sure what made him feel most sick, the way the Exec ate with his mouth open, dripping food and drink in equal quantities back on to the table, or Lannic's obvious fawning and flirting. He concentrated on his piksyassi, trying to tease strands of it from the uvinza sauce.

He tried not to look up as Lannic laughed loudly at yet another inane comment from the Exec as he questioned her about the expedition and Menaxus. He could imagine her leaning back, letting her hair hang to one side as she cocked her head and brought up a stockinged knee clasped between her folded hands. He could see the Exec from the corner of his eye as the greasy young idiot leaned obviously forward for a better glimpse of leg.

Klasvik looked away in disgust, and found Marlock watching him. The Manact had a wide grin across his face. He nodded down the table towards the Exec and Lannic, raising an eyebrow as he tried to draw Klasvik into the scene. Klasvik looked down at his food, embarrassed, and heard Marlock's laughter join with Lannic's and the Exec's.

The delta dart was certainly nippy. But even so, it would be another few hours before Bernice had to worry about the defence shields and sat-strikers positioned round Heletia. For the moment she had only to worry about avoiding units which might have strayed from a war which was being prosecuted parsecs away, but closing ever nearer. The Heletians would make their consolidated stand at Nichoria by all accounts. And by those same accounts, it would be a bloody affair drawn out over years.

She checked the charts again, looking for a more direct route which did not involve too much risk. But she knew there wasn't one.

All the corridors and all the rooms in the place looked much the same. Grey, drab, concrete, boring. Only the variety of posters framed in silver on the walls broke the monotony. Ace was just about to give up finding anything of interest and return to her quarters to wait for the Doctor to reappear when a short fat man bustled down the corridor towards her. He seemed familiar. Ace stepped aside to allow him plenty of room, but the man still managed to brush against her.

'Second door on the left ahead of you,' he whispered as his face passed close to Ace's shoulder. 'I'll be there soon.'

Ace tried to give no indication that she had heard. The

man obviously did not wish anyone to know he had spoken to her. Equally, Ace was not at all sure she wanted anyone knowing that she was being offered assignations with a short, fat, bald man who she hoped was too old to be her father.

Nevertheless, when she reached the second door on the left, she opened it and went through. She hoped it looked natural, as if she had been wandering aimlessly down the corridor with the single intention of entering this room.

Except that it seemed to be the Heletian equivalent of a broom cupboard. The light had come on automatically as she entered, and she wondered how the fat man would find room to fit in with her. She soon found out.

'Thank you,' the fat man breathed heavily as he squeezed himself into the small room beside Ace.

'I haven't done anything yet,' Ace told him, wishing she had not included the 'yet'.

'You are here. That is enough.' Even within the confines of the room, he was glancing nervously around.

'Wait a minute.' Ace realized where she had seen him before. 'You're the commissionaire of wherever it is, aren't you?'

'Arbela, yes.' He glanced round again, licking his dry lips and swallowing. 'I really wanted to talk to your friend the Doctor – he intervened with the Exec to help my people.'

'Yeah, he does that sort of thing. But I'm afraid he's, er, unavailable right now.'

The commissionaire nodded as if he quite understood, though Ace was certain he didn't. 'Never mind. You can take a message to him.'

'Now wait a minute, I'm not his secretary or anything.'

'Please – please, we want him, both of you in fact, to join us.'

'Doing what?' asked Ace, but she thought she could guess.

'Not all of us are in favour of prolonging the war. Or even of having a war at all. If only we can speak to the

221

Exec, make him see reason, we can sue for peace.' His eyes were large and watery as he looked up at Ace.

'He didn't look the peaceful type.'

'He's only a boy. He was seven when this war started. Marlock is the real power.'

Ace laughed. 'That much should be obvious even to a seven-year-old.'

'But not to the Exec. If we can get to him, talk with him, without Marlock being there – better still, if we can have Marlock sent away somewhere on a fool's errand – then maybe we can reason with the boy.'

'And you want the Doctor to help?'

The commissionaire nodded.

'Sorry,' said Ace. 'We're strictly neutral. Non-intervention is the Doctor's middle name.' She considered for a moment. 'Might be his only name,' she added.

The commissionaire shook his head sadly. 'I am sorry. I had hoped that the Doctor was a man who understood what was happening here – knew something of the evil and how to fight it.'

'War is hell.' She tried to keep a straight face as she said it.

'No.' He shook his head again. His eyes were firmly fixed on Ace now, no longer darting furtively in search of hidden cameras and microphones. 'No, not just the war. The occupations, the terror, the oppression, the camps.' He struggled to turn back to face the door. 'I am sorry you will not help. But I had to ask. Any hope for us has to be explored.'

'Heh, look – if it's serious – ' Ace was starting to think maybe they should consider the situation. She was not sure quite what he was talking about, but he was certainly sincere. 'I'll talk to the Doctor, tell him what you said.'

The commissionaire's face broke into a smile and he grabbed her hand and shook it as violently as the space allowed. 'Thank you.' He calmed down at last and let go of her hand. 'Thank you,' he said again.

'Yeah, right. But no promises. We'll just see what's going on, okay?'

'Then go to Marlock's office, in the war room. If your stomach is up to it.' He described briefly where it was located, then opened the door and stepped nervously into the corridor. 'Good luck, and thank you,' he called back to Ace, then set off down the corridor, head swaying slightly as he bustled about his business.

'Okay, doctor,' said Ace to the empty room. 'What the hell have you got us into now?'

The Doctor had completely lost track of the route he had taken. He had no idea how to get back to *Hamlet*, or even if he needed to in order to escape from this world. He was more concerned at the moment with finding the mysterious character who had been watching him on the croquet lawn. He had seen the man a couple of times – amidst the confusion of the ending of *A Splash of Red*, and ducking out of *The Dumb Waiter*.

As he chased through the seemingly never-ending series of stages, each abutted to the next, the Doctor reflected that Pinter was an interesting playwright to find under these circumstances: how could he tell if the characters were frozen by the machine or by a scripted pause? But compared to some of the other thoughts whirling round in the Doctor's head, this puzzle was not a priority.

A rather more worrying thought occurred to the Doctor as he caught a glimpse of the man hurrying past Faustus. He could have eluded the Doctor several times – in the drawing room right at the start of the chase, the Doctor had completely lost him until he stuck his head round the door, saw the Doctor, and ran off. Maybe, considered the Doctor as he waved cheerily to Sergeant Musgrave, he was himself being led a dance.

He skidded to a halt. The room next to the northern mining town was more familiar than most. It was the great hall of a castle. The rough stone sprayed with heat-resistant sealant, the plastic flooring and the blast-proof doors all suggested a variation on Scott Bailey's designs. Bailey had started with hydrogen plants and moved on to fortresses, and the Doctor was sure that this was a representation one of those fortresses – the fortress of Limlough. He knew of only one play set in such a room, and the positions of the six characters, seated round the banqueting table, confirmed this. He was on the main set for *The Good Soldiers*.

Judging from the fact that the characters were still at the table, and that the makeshift stage required for the play within a play had not yet been constructed, he was at the very beginning. The performance had not yet started.

The Doctor took a tour round the table, tapping each of the motionless men on the shoulder as he passed. 'Remek, Spidler.'

He murmured their names, as if they were old friends – and in a way they were.

'Prator, Freppon, Teel.'

They looked almost exactly as he had imagined. He had Osterling's detailed stage directions to thank for that – they left almost no room for interpretation. The Doctor smiled: they had been extremely boring to transcribe from Osterling's dictation. But the creeping restioparothis had taken the playwright's ability to hold a stylus or tap on a keypad. And they neither of them trusted a computer to get the transcription correct. Besides, it was *Art*, and they had both considered *that* the province of the sentient rather than the machine.

The Doctor reached the head of the table and clapped the final figure on the shoulder. 'Jorvik,' he whispered to the cloaked man. 'The only one who held true to his beliefs. The only "good soldier" here. Philosopher, traitor and murderer.'

He turned away at last. There were two doors out of the room, excluding the one he had just come through. He went immediately for the door stage left, the door through which the players would later arrive to enact Jorvik's cruel play within a play.

Outside the door was a void. Blackness, like the Doctor and Ace had seen beyond the limits of *Hamlet*. And as far as the Doctor could see, away into the darkness, stretched the line of players waiting to come on stage.

They were all cloaked in purple, their faces partly obscured by heavy hoods. From beneath the hoods glowed the red of their electronic eyes, throwing shadows down the reflective metal of their skull-like faces and the exposed sections of exoskeleton which showed from beneath the cloaks.

That the players were robots did not surprise the Doctor. That was totally in keeping with the play. But while Osterling had been uncharacteristically remiss in not explicitly stating how many robots there were, it was generally assumed that there were at most a dozen. Five players would fit with Jorvik's description of the mime play they were to perform. Five players would mirror the characters whose deaths they would portray. Add to that another six or seven to burst in at the climax of the play, and twelve was more than ample.

But here there were hundreds. And the Doctor could think of only one reason to swell their ranks.

There was a movement in the shadows beside the Doctor. An area of the dark void shimmered within the overall mass. The old man he had been chasing through the worlds of the machine stepped from the shadows and stood beside the Doctor. And as they surveyed the ranks of mechanical troops, the Doctor at last believed he knew what had happened on Menaxus.

The look of disdain on Klasvik's face was almost completely undisguised. Marlock smiled to himself at the old man's envious disgust as Lannic curtsied to the Exec, her hand outstretched. The Exec took it and wiped a greasy kiss over her knuckles. Klasvik turned away.

'Until tomorrow, then.' The Exec barely acknowledged either Klasvik or Marlock when he spoke.

'Until tomorrow,' echoed Lannic in a voice more husky than usual.

The Exec's bodyguards followed him from the room, close on his heel. Lannic followed them. Marlock inclined his head slightly as she passed him, but she seemed not to notice.

Klasvik made to follow, but Marlock held up a hand. 'Wait. A word, if I may, Leontium Klasvik.'

'Marlock.'

'My title is Manact.' Marlock's voice was like a thunderclap.

Klasvik took a step backwards. 'Er, yes – Manact. My apologies, I did not intend any, er, any disrespect.'

'And none is taken.' Marlock opened his arms to show how forgiving he was. Then he made a point of turning to look at the door through which the others had just left. 'You know,' he said without looking back, 'I think we shall be seeing a great deal more of Camarina Lannic.' Suddenly he spun round, his finger pointing at Klasvik's head. 'What do you say to that?' he demanded.

Klasvik blustered for a moment. 'The Exec chooses his friends wisely,' he eventually managed to say.

Marlock threw his head back and let out a single snort of laughter. 'He does not.'

Klasvik looked puzzled. Marlock explained. 'The Exec is an adolescent idiot who couldn't choose where to sit down if we didn't give him a special chair. You saw how that Doctor made a fool of him earlier today. It is a constant struggle for all of us who serve him so loyally to – how shall I put it? – to emphasize the better parts of his character and abilities.'

Klasvik gulped. 'Yours must be a very special talent,' he hazarded.

Marlock glared at him. 'It is. Now, Lannic.' He strode up to Klasvik and stood in front of him. Marlock's guards kept close behind. 'You were as revolted as I was by the display this evening. But you show too much of your feelings. Suppress them.'

'Yes, Manact.'

'I do not know what your colleague is doing, any more than I see you do. I doubt very much if she is as taken with our Exec as she would like us, and him, to believe. But whatever power-play she thinks she is making, I wish her to continue.'

'To continue?'

Marlock snorted again. 'Yes, to continue. She will not gain any real power through a liaison with the Exec, but while he is – occupied, shall we say? Yes, while he is occupied, I can concentrate more of my energy and time on matters more important than acting as nursemaid.'

Klasvik nodded nervously, and Marlock went to the door. Without turning back he said to Klasvik, 'You will ensure that the relationship between the Exec and Camarina Lannic is not . . . interrupted.'

'Of course, Manact.'

'And I shall see if we can't still salvage something from this glorious war which our esteemed Exec has all but lost for us.'

'I see from the change in your expression that you have come to some conclusion – perhaps you now understand what is happening here?'

The Doctor looked at the man who had joined him. From close up, he could see that the old man's face was wrinkled and pale with age, but his eyes were full of experience. 'Oh yes,' the Doctor said. 'It's all become very clear. Ingenious, I suppose. Although it would only work with a civilization like that on Menaxus – one devoted to theatre.'

'The plan was of course written for the target audience.'

The Doctor frowned. 'You said "was" – you mean that you know that Menaxus is now a dead world, a world where civilization was wiped clean?'

The man nodded. 'There's nothing on Menaxus now. But it's an automatic cycle, you see. Once started it must run its course, like all good theatre.'

'And it's running now?'

'It is. And since I have indulged your interest, perhaps you will indulge mine?'

'In what way?'

'A simple matter. I was merely wondering who you are and how you came to be in a universe where all the characters are fictitious.'

The Doctor switched his umbrella to his left arm and

227

extended his right to shake hands. 'I'm dreadfully sorry, how remiss of me. I'm the Doctor, and I'm here to stop your machine before things go too far.' They shook hands. 'And you are?'

'Why, Doctor, I thought you had guessed when you said it was my machine.' The man gave a short bow. 'I am Aronholt, inventor and builder of the machine you are now trapped within. Welcome to my universe.'

Source Document 13

Extract from status report made by Japara
Ikyen, commissionaire of the Heletian camps
on Temenos

Stored in the Rippearean Imperial Archive.

Should the Rippeareans break through the Nichorian
Line, then we shall need to know immediately if we are to
sanitize before their advance troops arrive. I have already
authorized a thirty per cent increase in the throughput to
the chambers and incinerators, but even working at full
capacity we shall need prior warning if we are to
implement a final solution to the problem of the indigen-
ous populations.

Chassemy's experiments are proceeding to plan, but
have not yet yielded the lasting results that we had hoped
and anticipated. The implants become unstable after a
maximum of three days, and the subject reverts to normal.
Control cannot be re-established either with surgery or
with more traditional forms of coercion, and there is no
option but to have the subject chambered or incinerated.

Morale is generally low, as we had expected given the
status of the campaign. We are allowing the garrison to
'pre-process' about ten per cent more of the physically
sound prisoners, and this is alleviating some of the tension.
This number cannot be increased further however without
impacting Chassemy's work – once the garrison has
finished with a prisoner, particularly a female, that subject
is no longer equipped either physically or mentally to
survive an implant and associated education.

Chapter 13

Justice

Although it is said that Naturalism is a depiction of life as it is, whereas Realism shows life as it really is, neither of these is true. And yet, there is a sense in which 'real' life is as much an act, a performance, for those of us who live it as anything played in the theatre.

Reality – An Overrated Concept
– Rankin Alduss, 2876

Aronholt led the Doctor back onto the set for *The Good Soldiers*. They stood beside the banqueting table, the characters around it still motionless, the food undisturbed.

'If you know that Menaxus is dead,' the Doctor said, 'then you must also know that your machine has lain dormant for centuries, possibly for millennia.'

'Has it?' Aronholt seemed indifferent as he surveyed the scene, obviously pleased with the design of his set. He paced the room, running his hand down a wall, smiling with satisfaction at a detail in the carvings on the door.

'But the machine is now working again,' the Doctor continued. 'There is to be a performance of *The Good Soldiers* within the next day.'

Aronholt turned from his examination of the wood carvings. 'And what of it?'

'It is unnecessary. Your plan has already run its course and Menaxus is in ruins. There is no need to continue with this.' The Doctor waved his arm in a semicircle to indicate the whole of the room they were in. 'You – the real you outside this machine-world – have been dead for a thousand years or more.'

Aronholt stopped his pacing and joined the Doctor by the table. 'Doctor, you are a clever and intelligent man.'

'And you're an excellent judge of character. Now can we stop the machine? Change the plan?' He was getting tense, shuffling from foot to foot while his hands played with the handle of his umbrella.

But Aronholt shook his head. 'But I fear you may have rather missed the point. Perhaps you had better tell me what, exactly, you think the plan is – what the machine is for.'

The Doctor took a deep breath, sat on the edge of the banqueting table and began his story. 'Many years ago, a thriving civilization existed on the planet Menaxus. It was a civilization which placed great store in its admiration for the theatre and for dramatic art. It was a civilization which built a great theatre in which to present the very best of drama to a huge audience.

'I don't know how long the civilization lasted, I must confess I had never heard of it until recently. But Menaxus was a society with enemies. One in particular devised a plan to invade and lay waste the planet. Why the plan was so complicated, I also don't know, but perhaps it was difficult to penetrate the Menaxan defences any other way. But what they did was to build a machine, a machine that presented drama – plays – as a projection.

'The technique was not technologically innovative. The attraction lay in what plays the machine could perform. The Menaxans were given the machine, or perhaps it was contrived that they should find it. But whatever, they discovered that this machine could present one play in particular – Osterling's lost masterpiece, *The Good Soldiers*. So, predictably, the Menaxans arranged a great performance.

'I imagine everyone of any importance, and a great deal of other people, were present when the play was performed. And I imagine they loved it. Right up until the end.

'You see, the machine – this machine – is more than just an image projector. The plays, the characters and situations actually exist inside it. And with the inclusion of a real-world interface and a crude dimensional osmosis damper it is possible for people from the real world to get inside the machine. And for characters from the plays within the machine to escape into the real world.'

Aronholt nodded. 'Go on, Doctor.'

'We both know how *The Good Soldiers* ends.' The Doctor pointed to the door they had come through earlier. 'The machine destroyed the entirety of the civilization on Menaxus. And its job done, the machine slept. Until now.'

'And now?'

'The machine has been woken. Probably by Lannic's excavations. It has survived undisturbed on Menaxus perhaps for thousands of years, and in that time I think the dimensional osmosis damper has de-phased. As a result we've had some bleed-through from the plays within the machine. Elements of *The Good Soldiers* and *Death's Bane* have appeared within the real world, have interacted with it. And now the machine has started its program again. And a performance of *The Good Soldiers* is scheduled for tonight.

'But this machine doesn't know or care that its job has already been done, that it is now on another world, that it will destroy another civilization that did not even exist when it was built.'

Aronholt was silent for a while, stroking his beard slowly as the Doctor waited for a response. Eventually, he spoke: 'An interesting theory, Doctor. And one which certainly fits the available evidence.'

Most of the huge building seemed deserted – almost everyone was off fighting the war, she assumed. Occasionally Ace came across clusters of activity, like a set of rooms grouped together which were being used as offices or for accommodation. But whether occupied or not, all the rooms seemed almost identical. Only the posters changed, and most of those seemed to depict scenes of incredibly handsome and beautiful people killing each other on stage.

Now she found herself back at the theatre, standing at the foot of the staircase that led to the box where the dream machine was installed. She paused. Should she go back to the machine? The Doctor might have reappeared by now. Since she was here she might as well have a look. And she could ask Fortalexa what was going on – if he had regained his sense of humour.

Even while she was still thinking it through, Ace had started to climb the stairs. She went slowly, making an effort not to make a sound. If Fortalexa was still in a mood, then she would be happy to slip away unobserved. She reached the top of the stairs and peered round the corner into the room.

Fortalexa was standing by the machine, apparently making still more adjustments to its internal circuitry. But he was not alone. There were two other figures standing in the shadows at the edge of the room, watching.

Ace could tell they were watching, because although their features were shadowed, their eyes were glowing a dull red. Ace leaned closer, her foot crunching slightly on the loose concrete where the new prefabricated wall met the structure of the staircase. Two pairs of red eyes swivelled towards her and she ducked back out of sight, hearing the whirr of the motors which powered the mechanics of the eyeballs.

What was going on? She had seen no other robots in her exploration of the palace – had these been specially assigned to help Fortalexa?

'See what that was.' Fortalexa's voice was hard and emotionless. It was followed by the sound of footsteps. Ace didn't wait to confirm her guess that one of the robots was coming over to the staircase. Nor did she wait to see if there was a legitimate reason for the robots to be there at all. She ran down the stairs, all attempts to conceal her presence forgotten. Behind her the pace of the footsteps increased.

At the bottom of the staircase, Ace pushed open the

main door into the theatre, closing it quietly behind her. She did not wait to see if her pursuer would guess where she had gone, but ran immediately down towards the stage. She almost made it. But before she was across the circular dais and out of sight behind the backdrop, the door crashed open and a metal figure stood framed in the opening. Its skull-head swung evenly round as the electronic eyes surveyed the auditorium.

Ace ducked through the wings and looked back up the tiers of seats. The robot was starting down the main gangway, eyes fixed on the point where Ace had left its view. Its movements were inhumanly smooth as the skeletal metal form made its way to the stage.

The obvious escape route was down the corridor towards the dressing rooms. So Ace discounted it immediately. She looked round for an alternative. 'Come on, come on,' she muttered to herself, fists clenched. Then she saw it – a small door in the wall to the side of the backstage area she was in. She tiptoed over, prayed it wasn't locked and pulled on the handle.

The door opened to reveal a narrow, dusty staircase beyond. Ace was getting sick of stairs, but behind her she could hear the robot crossing the stage. She pushed the door almost closed, leaving a slight gap through which she could see when the robot passed her and went up the corridor. Then she could escape back through the auditorium and leave the way she had come in while the tin man searched the backstage rooms.

But the robot never crossed her line of vision. Ace was on the point of opening the door a little further and sneaking a look round when the door handle leapt out of her hand.

She yelped in surprise, and looked up into the robot's face. The tendon-like supports rising from its shoulders to the back of its head stretched as it looked down at Ace, its body leaning towards her. Then its arm shot out.

Ace jumped back as the heavy fingers of a huge hand snapped shut where her throat had just been. 'We're obviously not going to be friends,' she said as she took the first three steps in one go. Behind her the robot's head shifted slightly to reacquire its target. The exoskeleton straightened up and it started up the stairs after her.

The staircase seemed to go on forever, winding back on itself as it snaked up inside the wall of the theatre. Eventually, Ace arrived at the top. She bent forward and rested her hands on her knees, taking deep breaths. At least the robot was not as quick as she was. Although, as she realized where she was, she could see that might not make any difference.

She was standing in a small opening almost at the roof of the theatre. The auditorium was almost a hundred feet below. In front of her was the mesh of the lighting gantry, perhaps six feet wide with a low support rail along the sides. It stretched across the width of the theatre. But there was no door at the other side, no escape route at all. And behind her she could hear the scrape of the robot's feet on the steps.

Ace sighed. Well, she had at least tried to escape rather than make a mess. She reached inside a pouch in her combat suit. Only one smartbomb – still, that would do. She whispered instructions to it as the heavy tread of the robot got steadily louder and closer. The bomb bleeped its understanding, rose quietly from her hand and disappeared round the bend in the staircase.

The noise was exaggerated by the confined space and the concrete walls. The force of the blast was enough to ruffle Ace's hair. She smiled and started back down the stairs. But before she got to the first turn, she stopped. From just around the corner came the unmistakable sound of metal on concrete. She turned and hared back up the steps.

When interrogated by the defence system, the delta dart gave an outdated clearance code. Not programmed for either tolerance or generosity, the system did not ask again. Instead it allocated a kill-sat and listed the dart as destroyed in the daily log.

Determining the size and speed of the delta dart, the

satellite let loose a single distronic sat-to-ship missile. The STS locked on to the flare-trace of the engines almost immediately and closed steadily on the dart as it tried to weave and jink past the detectors. To no avail.

The next-to-last thing the missile did was to inform its parent satellite of the launch of an escape pod. The last thing it did was to impact with the delta dart and discharge its energy wave through the engine housing, blasting the small fighter into more pieces than the satellite could count.

The satellite monitored the escape pod, targeting another STS. But the pod showed no sign of slowing, so the satellite concluded that it was a 'dumb' lifeboat with no powered support, and left it to burn up in the atmosphere of Heletia or break apart when it hit the ground. It tracked the pod for long enough to be certain that nothing would survive, then resumed station.

Inside the escape pod, Bernice was getting uncomfortably hot. She closed her eyes, crossed her fingers and hoped that the shielding which Braxiatel's men had attached to the outside of the pod would protect the retro-rockets they had installed sufficiently for them to lower her gently to the ground. She also hoped that her calculations were accurate enough for her to land within sight of the main city. But as considerations went, that came a poor second.

The robot's chest was blackened and it was limping slightly, but otherwise it appeared undamaged by Ace's bomb. She backed away across the gantry, feeling behind her for anything to use as a weapon. She had already established that the lights were fixed in position and she doubted that a robot which could survive one of her smartbombs would be much distracted by a spotlight flung at it.

The robot started across the gantry towards her, its arms outstretched. The gantry began to shake under its weight and the sound of its footsteps on the metal mesh rang across the theatre.

Ace looked up. No chance of the gantry giving way, it was solidly attached to the ceiling by metal chains encased in plastic sheaths. They reminded Ace of the chains Midge had used to secure his motorbike. She backed away further, her head connecting painfully with a low spotlight, and found her back was against the wall.

In desperation, Ace grabbed at the spotlight. It swung and rotated easily in the chassis, but there seemed to be no way to remove it from the pole. She cursed and swung it round. And saw the small button in the back of the housing.

The robot was almost on her now, limping its way closer, fingers snapping and opening as they reached for her. Ace edged round the back of the spotlight so that it was between her and the robot. They had their backs to opposite edges of the gantry, the wall was on Ace's left. One of the heavy chains rose from near the corner beside her to its retaining hook in the ceiling.

The robot took a step towards her, ignoring the spotlight and reaching past it at her face.

Ace pressed the button on the lamp, hoping it was the on/off switch. It was, and a bright beam of light cut across the robot's face, burning into its eyes. The robot froze for a moment, its head snapping back slightly as if in surprise. Ace knew it would not be confused for more than the second it would take for the electronic eyes to adjust.

In that second, Ace pulled herself up on the chain with her left hand, her right pushing up on the top of the spotlight. It was already getting hot and she almost slipped as the light and the chain took her weight. She brought her legs up, knees bent and kicked with all the force she could at the robot's charred chest. Then she let go of the chain and pulled her hand from the painfully hot casing of the spotlight, falling heavily to the mesh floor of the gantry.

The robot staggered back, its weakened leg giving way slightly, and clanked against the guard rail at the edge of the gantry. The rail caught it near the top of its legs, and its head swung back over the edge. It froze for a moment,

237

arms stretched forward to balance the distribution of weight. But then the damaged leg gave way as it tried to brace against the rail, and the robot's chest slowly swung backwards as it pivoted round the guard rail and fell.

Ace watched it the whole way down through the mesh floor, its arms still flailing and head twisting to keep her in sight. When it hit the ground, far below, the back of the robot shattered across a row of seats, its chest, head and arms falling one side, legs the other. The head rotated slowly as it stared back up at the gantry and Ace could hear the laboured grating of the servos. Then there was a loud snapping sound and the motors ground to a halt. The red glow of the eyes dimmed slowly and a single outstretched arm dropped heavily to rest across the chest.

Ace breathed out slowly and sat up, rubbing her arm where it had connected with the gantry floor. As she turned, she realized that she could see over the top of the one-way glass covering the box where the dream machine was housed. The gap above the new walls was covered over with ordinary glass and she could see inside.

Fortalexa was staring out through the front of the box, his gaze fixed on the remains of the robot below. Beside him, the second robot turned smoothly and made its way to the stairs.

Ace pulled herself to her feet and ran.

The pod lay ruined and smoking in the wasteland surrounding the city. Its exterior was streaked with scorches and the feeder line for one of the retro controllers was burning.

The hatch jerked half open, then stopped. After a moment it swung the rest of the way out of the housing and clattered down the outside of the pod before crashing to the ground.

Bernice's face appeared at the opening. She reached through the hatchway to pull herself out, and yanked her hand suddenly back inside the pod as she felt the heat given off by the shell. She considered for a minute, and threw out her kit bag. Then she dived through the opening

238

without touching the sides. As she hit the ground, she bent her knees and rolled forward, head tucked in. After two complete revolutions she had exhausted her momentum and lay sprawled out on the ground, arms and legs spread out as she lay on her back and stared at the sky. Her flight suit was ripped and muddied from the fall.

She lay there for a while, feeling bruised and flustered. Then she pulled herself to her feet and retrieved the kit bag. She started to sort out some sensible clothes.

She couldn't go back to her quarters – that much was obvious. Fortalexa or his surviving pet robot would look for her there first. Ace's options were disappearing as quickly as her hopes of ever finding out exactly what was happening. The only person who had tried to explain anything to her recently was the Arbelan commissionaire, and he had made very little sense.

But he had suggested one line of action – to investigate the war room.

She found it easily from the commissionaire's directions. She was helped by the fact that the level of activity increased as she got closer. This seemed to be a central point of the palace.

There were two guards on the door, checking people in and out. Most they knew by sight, but some they stopped and inspected their I.D. cards. Ace hesitated in the corridor outside. Oh, what the hell? she thought and marched up to the door.

One of the guards stopped her with his hand on her shoulder as she reached for the door control.

'Yes?' demanded Ace.

The guard seemed taken aback for a moment. 'Identification,' he said when he recovered.

She laughed, raising her eyebrows in mock frustration so that both guards could see. 'Get serious,' she said. 'I've only been gone five minutes, you just saw me leave.'

'I'm sorry,' the guard was confused but insistent, 'but I do need to see your I.D.'

'I'm sorry too,' said Ace. 'Sorry that you will have to

explain to Marlock that you delayed his special emissary with this pathetic show of officious bureaucracy.' She turned to the other guard who hastily concealed the beginnings of a smirk. 'Perhaps you would like to go and fetch the Manact and explain to him that your colleague is keeping me waiting at the war room door.'

The guards seemed undecided. A couple of other soldiers were now waiting behind Ace, shuffling impatiently as they too waited to be admitted.

'You,' Ace pointed to one of the soldiers, 'tell these goons who I am.'

'Er, well – I – ' he seemed unsure.

'I don't believe this,' Ace fumed. 'I shall report you all to the Manact when I see him.' She pushed her way past the guard and went into the room, listening for the shout from behind, waiting for the sound of a disruptor pulse ripping through the air towards her. When the noise came she almost threw herself to the floor. But she realized in time that it was just the door sliding closed behind her.

The war room walls were lined with charts. Where there were gaps between the marked-up star maps it was to allow space for a terminal screen which showed similar charts and schematics, but animated to show the movement of troop positions and ships. The room was full of people, but they were dwarfed by the information around them.

Even the centre of the room was dominated by a huge simularity which presented a three-dimensional image of an engagement. The ships of the opposing sides were represented by their transponder codes as they moved ponderously across the scene. The scale had to be huge to keep the relative speeds of the attack-ships so slow. Ace wondered if she was looking at a real-time image of what was actually happening somewhere, a computer prediction of a battle yet to be fought, or an analysis of one long since lost or won.

At the far side of the room was another door. From the shape of the walls projecting into the room in that corner, space in the main room had been allocated to an office. Ace made her way across the room to the door.

A couple of Heletians were standing just outside, discussing a series of figures and co-ordinates being relayed to a screen not far from the office door. One of them turned his watery grey eyes to watch Ace as she passed. She glared back at him and he looked away hurriedly. Ace knocked quietly on the door, hoping there would be no answer. After a moment, she tapped the opening control. The door hissed open.

'Ah – Manact, I have the report you wanted,' said Ace loudly enough for the men outside to hear. And she closed the door behind her.

'What's wrong with you?' snapped Marlock. The guards on the war room door had come to attention just too quickly, had put just too much enthusiasm into it for his liking.

'Nothing, Manact.'

Marlock considered for a while. 'Nothing will come of nothing,' he said quietly. 'Perhaps you would like to revise your opinion?'

The guards exchanged glances, and the second guard gulped. 'I must apologize, Manact. I fear we – I – may have offended.'

'Really?' This was getting more curious by the moment. 'And what, pray, have you done to give offence?'

The guard looked even more uncomfortable now, and Marlock could imagine the two bodyguards behind him suppressing their amusement. 'Your special emissary, sir.'

'My what?' His eyes flared.

'We delayed her, sir – an error.'

Marlock rubbed a hand across his scarred cheek. 'My special emissary was here?' The guards nodded. 'And you delayed her?' They nodded again. 'How did you delay her exactly?'

'We asked to see her ident, sir – we didn't realize she was on an errand for you.'

'Let me see if I understand this,' Marlock's eyes

narrowed and his voice became quieter, almost reasonable. 'You made my special emissary show you her identification, yes?'

'Well – '

'Well, yes or no?' shouted Marlock. 'Did you see her ident?'

'No, sir.'

Marlock's voice was quiet again. 'No. No you did not see her ident. Where did she go?'

'Inside, Manact. She is still there.'

'Good.' Marlock smiled. He turned to one of his bodyguards. 'Have these idiots removed. I'll decide how to deal with them when I see how much damage has been done.'

It had been relatively simple to hack into the terminal in Marlock's office and bypass the security measures which purported to protect his private data. Now Ace was reading through another of the reports locked within. Each seemed more horrendous than the last.

She had read of the planning and construction of the death camps; had examined the initial specifications for the genetic experiments; had almost cried in anger and frustration at the statistical analyses of the throughputs of the incinerators and rad-chambers on a dozen worlds. Now she was reading a report about the camps on Temenos. Although she considered herself to be a hardened soldier, although she had seen more death than she cared to remember, although she had watched countless numbers of her friends killed in action, Ace was close to tears.

'So, you are my special emissary?' Ace had not noticed Marlock enter the office. 'I see you have been doing some research – have you found anything interesting, I wonder?'

'You inhuman monster!' She launched herself across the desk at Marlock, her nails reaching for his good eye. He smiled and did not flinch. For a moment Ace thought her anger and emotion would carry through her attack,

242

but the moment before her fingers reached him a hand closed round her wrist and dragged it aside. She collapsed across the desk, and the bodyguard dragged her over it so she crashed to the floor, disks and papers scattering round her. Then she was yanked up again, her feet leaving the floor for an instant as the bodyguard pulled her to her feet in front of Marlock.

Marlock seemed amused by the whole thing, a thin smile creasing his distorted features. Then suddenly his lip curled at the end untouched by his scar and his hand lashed out. It caught Ace across the cheek.

The force of the blow knocked her from the bodyguard's grasp and sent her crashing into the wall. Her head was in a spin and she could taste salt. She slumped down the wall and lay in a crumpled heap. From far away she could hear Marlock and wondered who he was talking to.

'The problem with performance is that it is all an act. In real life, of course, an act is a lie. And liars have to be punished – *The Good Soldiers*, if the accounts of the plot are to believed, will teach us that very clearly.'

The Manact's voice seemed to be receding, as if he were falling away from her. Ace tried to concentrate on his words, but they slipped away.

'Another problem we can easily solve, I think. Yes, even the Exec will approve of that. An execution, on stage immediately after the performance. A fitting way to round things off.'

The rest was silence.

Source Document 14

Extract from the examiner's comment on final doctoral thesis by Fardal Konin (3931)

Reproduced with the kind permission of Fardal Konin's estate

But despite these points, which taken alone would certainly merit a first-class review, there is one major problem with the thesis as it stands.

You do not acknowledge your sources.

This is especially unfortunate, as your own ideas and theories are ably presented and supported by well chosen facts and statistics. But without the clear distinction between what you are arguing on your own account and what you are merely reiterating from previous research and theory, it is impossible to give proper credit to the original thinking that you have undoubtedly done.

The bibliography you have provided and the footnote acknowledgements which are included fall far short of the level of research that is expected for a thesis at this level. They are also obviously incomplete.

The result, I am afraid, is that while your arguments concerning the development of forced perspective Palladian scenery in the Zouxian Empire are undoubtedly worthy of merit, it is impossible to conclude that it is new work of your own rather than lifted piecemeal from an unacknowledged source. This is especially true since it follows directly from the section about the staging techniques of liturgical drama on Earth in the tenth century

– which is so obviously lifted directly from Wadan's interpretation of the Bishop of Winchester's *Concordia
Regularis.*

Leontium Klasvik (Examiner)

Chapter 14

Man of Destiny

When looked at objectively, the whole notion of performance is, after all, absurd. The performer has very little to do with it. He interprets the words and actions written for him by an author. Even when the author and performer are one and the same – even in improvization – the actor is slave to the part he must play. In a Stanislavskyan interpretation this is even more the case. The actor may feel he is in control, is bringing something of himself to the performance. But if this is so then the point is lost, for the actor should be striving not to involve himself but rather to exclude all of his own personality and character from the role.

The role of any character within a performance work is dictated entirely by the author's words, by the character's words and actions within that text. The world of the performed character is a world of predestination. When Stoppard calls his play Rosencrantz *and* Guildenstern are Dead *he is not merely quoting* Hamlet, *he is predefining the end point of his play. Or rather, he is making it even more apparent that Shakespeare has already done so. However an actor interprets either Rosencrantz or Guildenstern their final destiny is already set, defined three hundred years before the play was written, and reiterated in the title.*

The characters in any play are men of destiny – the ultimate existentialists.

The Absurdity of Performance
– Wanlek Ackman, 2044

'Everything you say is certainly sustainable by the facts, Doctor,' Aronholt said. 'However, your interpretation of those facts is lacking in one important respect.'

'And what's that?'

Aronholt shook his head, smiling. 'Oh no, Doctor. I am the guardian of the plan as well as the creator of the machine. My very purpose here is to ensure that the machine's program runs its course.'

'But on Menaxus, surely.'

Aronholt went to the banqueting table. He stood for a while leaning forward on it, palms resting flat on the wooden surface, his back turned to the Doctor. 'No, Doctor, I am sorry.' He straightened up and turned to face the Doctor again. 'You must return now to your world. And let destiny run its course.' He pointed across the room to the door in the corner behind the Doctor – the door he had abandoned in favour of the one opposite which had led to the void.

The Doctor walked in silence to the door. His hand rested on the handle for a second, then he pulled the door open. Through the red haze beyond it he could see the converted theatre box where the machine was installed, the stairs leading down from it directly in front of him. 'Thank you,' he said, turning back to Aronholt, 'for what help you have given me so far. But I'm afraid it's not enough.' He closed the door.

Aronholt spread his arms, palms outwards. 'I can do no more, Doctor. Everything to do with these worlds, everything involving the machine, is almost by definition an act. I do not exist – have never existed. I too am a fiction. I can offer only the words and actions that have been devised and defined for me.'

'But your programming is somewhat more sophisticated than that of the other characters. You have powers of thought and reason.'

Aronholt shook his head. 'No, not really. I can operate within the slightly broader parameters of a programmed existence, as you say. But I am still limited, can still only

247

perform what has been scripted for me. Only my author can alter my lines or change my mind.'

The Doctor smiled widely. 'But that's the nature of a performance. As good old Wanlek used to say – ' He stopped suddenly, his smile resolving into a more thoughtful expression.

'Doctor?'

The Doctor's face brightened again. 'Aronholt,' he said, marching across the room and slapping his friend on the back, 'I've got the most terrific idea.'

Bernice had managed to push her way almost to the front of the crowd when it started to disperse. Typical, she thought as the lines of people before her started to drift away.

Across the square Benny could see a line of soldiers. As she watched, the officer shouted an order that could have been in any language for all the guttural sense it seemed to make, and the troops wheeled round in unison. They shouldered their ceremonial disruptors and marched out of the square.

Above the departing soldiers, on a balcony jutting out from the tallest of the monstrous concrete buildings in the square, stood another group of people. This was a smaller group, mostly military but in the middle stood several civilians. There was something familiar about a couple of them. Bernice pushed closer through the few people who were still waiting around or dithering. She tried to get a better view up at the people on the balcony, but it was difficult as they were shielded by a transparent screen which caught the sun as she craned to see.

Bernice had just found the ideal place to stand so she could see in clearly when the group began to file off the balcony and back into the building. But she had seen enough – she had recognized the old man as Klasvik.

Benny watched the last of the party disappear from sight, then she started to walk round the huge building. If Klasvik was inside then it seemed a fair bet that the

Doctor and Ace were not far away. At any rate, it was a good place to start looking.

Marlock had not been intending to bother with the inspection, but he needed time to consider. His options were fast dwindling as the Rippeareans closed on their sector. If the final lines of defence looked threatened, he might have to consider leaving Heletia and establishing a base of operations elsewhere. But there was no immediate worry. The Rippeareans had to take the long way to Heletia – they would never manage to negotiate the satellite mines in the Alterberg Gap.

As he left the balcony and made his way back to the green room, Marlock reflected that the inspection had not afforded him the thinking time he had hoped. He had been distracted by the Exec and Lannic. They had spent the whole time in hushed conversation. Klasvik shuffled uncomfortably nearby, loath to miss anything but biting back his repugnance. The whole thing really was quite pathetic.

But it kept the Exec busy and occupied. He had not asked for more news about the progress of the war since meeting the woman and Marlock doubted if he had even read through the anodyne reports which were his daily source of information.

In the green room the Exec climbed the step onto his dais and sat behind his desk, surveying his subjects. The scene brought a smile to Marlock's twisted mouth.

'Continue, my dear.' The Exec's voice was husky as he beckoned Lannic up to the stage, waved for her to sit at his feet, pretended he had not heard Klasvik's snort of revulsion as she did.

Lannic smiled and in a honeyed voice said, 'That was when I first realized that the statues were not stone at all.'

'Really?' The Exec was enraptured, immediately drawn back into the story. As Lannic went on, Marlock shook his head at the even more improbable direction Lannic's narrative was taking. In a way it was a shame she was so absorbed with the Exec. She was sitting on the dais beside the Exec's chair, her legs pulled back and tucked under her body, her bare knees and a hint of thigh visible from under her dress. The dress itself was white, belted at the waist and slit up the side. It opened in a wide V at the neck and was pulled tight across her breasts. Marlock didn't know where she had got it, but he could see immediately why she had chosen it.

Marlock was just drifting into reverie when Klasvik's outburst echoed round the concrete room.

The old man had been fidgeting and getting more and more disgruntled since they had returned to the green room. Now it seemed he could contain himself no longer. 'S'blood!' he shouted.

The effect was startling. The Exec sat bolt upright, his indiscreet examination of Lannic's cleavage forgotten. The Exec's guards were almost as fast as Marlock's own as they spun round, disruptors already aimed at the source of the noise. They could all blast a knife out of the air as it hurtled towards them without prior warning – it was a test they had to pass every week in training, and effectively removed any whose reactions had become too slow.

Klasvik ignored the effect his exclamation had had. 'Exec – sir. I cannot allow this to continue.' The Exec gaped, but made no sound of protest as Klasvik went on: 'I have listened to Lannic's account of our expedition in your service, and apart from the basic outline it bears no more than a passing resemblance to the actual events. She has totally exaggerated her own part in the story, has claimed to be responsible for every major discovery or theory.'

'You wish to make some point, Klasvik?' Marlock's voice was cold and hard.

But Klasvik ignored the warning. 'I do,' he continued, the adrenalin keeping hold. 'I have listened for long enough to this woman whose intentions here are as obvious as they are demeaning. I can tolerate – just – a common harlot trying desperately to ingratiate herself with her betters, but this – a distinguished archaeologist

250

taking credit where it is not due, failing to acknowledge the contributions of others, putting ego and reputation above the facts – this is too much.'

He pointed at Lannic. She shrank away, her arm encircling the Exec's legs for protection and support.

'You go too far, Lannic,' Klasvik shouted at her.

'And so do you.' Marlock's words cut across the room like a disruptor.

There was sudden silence. Klasvik still stood, arm extended towards Lannic. Then he seemed to comprehend Marlock's words and his arm dropped lifeless to his side and the colour drained from his face. His shoulders slumped and he turned towards the Manact, his features sagging. For a while he had seemed dynamic, vivacious. But now he looked old and tired. Drained.

'You had your chance.' Marlock clicked his fingers and the two guards beside the door snapped to attention. 'Take him away.'

'Please,' Klasvik whimpered as the guards took his arms. 'Manact, I'm sorry. Forgive the outburst of an old man.' He strained to turn his head towards the dais as the guards led him out. 'Exec – forgive me, I meant no harm.'

The Exec had not moved. But now he reached down and ran his hand through Lannic's hair, shaking his head. His mouth opened and closed soundlessly as his head moved, then suddenly he shouted, 'Take him away.' It was almost a squeal, high-pitched and emotional. The scream of a child.

Marlock nodded to the guards. 'No harm?' he spat in Klasvik's face as they dragged him past. 'You raise your voice in anger in this room, call into question the competence of our ruler to distinguish between truth and fiction, and you insult the Exec's friend . . . And you have the gall to say you mean no harm?'

Klasvik sagged and the guards took his weight, dragging him from the room.

'My apologies, Exec, for this unfortunate incident,' Marlock said quietly. 'And to you, madam.' He bowed to both the Exec and Lannic. The Exec looked relieved. But

Marlock was not sure quite how to read the emotion he saw deep within Lannic's eyes. 'You may rest assured that this geriatric fool will not bother you or anyone else again.'

The small courtyard seemed to be a sort of dumping area for the rubbish and waste of the palace. The smell was enough to put Bernice off investigating further, but as she looked round and wrinkled her nose, a pair of double doors opened.

She ducked behind a stinking skip, slipping alarmingly on something she decided not to examine too closely. Two men struggled into the doorway, carrying a large and obviously heavy plastic box. A third man appeared in the doorway behind them, supervising the operation. When she saw who it was, Benny broke from her cover and went over to join him.

'Am I glad to find you,' she said standing clear of the doorway so the other two men could bring their load through.

'Professor Summerfield.' Fortalexa seemed neither surprised nor interested.

'So you made it back all right then,' she observed needlessly.

He ignored her, watching as the two men with him deposited the crate in a corner. One of the men dropped his end down too quickly and the top of the crate jumped up, landing at an angle. Some of the contents of the crate were also unsettled and stuck out of the gap at the top. The other man lowered his end of the crate more carefully, then pushed the contents back inside and resealed the lid.

'What are you doing? Dumping something?'

'Some componentry I no longer need. It is defective.' Fortalexa's eyes still did not meet hers.

Benny was not convinced. This did not seem to be even a remote relative of the man she had met on the expedition to Menaxus. It must have been one hell of a journey back. Benny was suddenly very keen to find the Doctor and Ace, but she wasn't sure she wanted to involve Fortalexa in her search. It might indeed be electrical components of some sort he was dumping. But what had appeared from inside the crate, although obviously made of metal, had looked suspiciously like a hand and forearm.

She smiled. 'Well, I can see you're very busy, so I won't keep you any longer.' She stepped into the building.

She spent the next hour searching through the palace corridors, looking into any rooms she found unlocked. She navigated, as far as she could, by the changing posters along the way – *Two Gentlemen of Verona* at this junction, *The Fifth Sermon* at the next; *The Eumenides* opposite one room, *The Silent Partners* outside another; *Black-Eyed Susan* here, *The Playboy of Aspallon* there. At first she tried to hide when she heard anyone coming, but after several courtiers and soldiers had passed her without comment she decided that skulking about in shadows and frantically struggling with locked doors was pointless and gave up the effort.

So when she saw Klasvik coming down the corridor towards her she almost greeted him like an old friend. But then she saw how close the two soldiers at his side were marching and noticed that they were discreetly but firmly holding the old man's arms pinioned. Klasvik was stooped, more so than usual. He was shuffling slowly, being propelled largely by his captors. His feet were only just scraping the ground. His head was bowed and he seemed not to notice Benny as she waited for them to pass.

When they were a safe distance away, Benny set off after them. She had no idea where they were going, but she might as well follow as continue her aimless wandering.

Aronholt shook the Doctor's hand warmly. 'The fact that I can agree to your proposal suggests that it is acceptable to others.'

The Doctor wasn't convinced. More likely he had hit on a scenario which had not been anticipated or played out by the real creators of the machine. But he said nothing, just smiled. He swung his umbrella out in front of him and marched up to the door back to reality.

'Till we meet again Doctor.' Aronholt raised his hand in a gesture of farewell.

The Doctor paused for a moment and looked back round the banqueting hall. 'Of all the people here, Aronholt, you are the one I shall not meet again,' he said. And he raised his hat to the good soldiers round the table, nodding deferentially to the cloaked figure of Jorvik whose features were obscured beneath the wide brim of his hat.

Then the Doctor opened the door and stepped back into the real world. Behind him the tableau remained unchanged as his voice floated back to the still, silent characters: 'Adieu, adieu. Remember me.'

The pounding of blood in Ace's head had almost subsided but she could clearly feel the point where the skin was broken; feel the anger at Marlock for striking her and at herself for allowing it to happen. She had tried to clean the wound with water from the basin in the corner. There was no mirror to indicate how good a job she had done, but if she stood at an angle to it she could just make out her reflection in the glass covering Hazor Kolonna and Julu Ozette in *Balance of Power*.

As cells went, Ace's was pretty basic. There was no electronic lock on the heavy metal door, just bolts. There was no window, just solid walls of rough concrete. There were no bars, except for the small grille in the door. And there were no guards, except at meal times when a plate of unpleasant mush was slid through a small hatch at the bottom of the door.

All in all the whole set-up was basic. But it was also escape-proof – no lock to pick; no guards to bribe or trick.

The commotion at the other end of the line of cells was something of a novelty. There was some scuffling of footsteps, the sound of bolts being drawn and then a heavy clang as the door was slammed shut and the bolts were pushed back into place. Two sets of footsteps retreated across the room outside and faded away down the corridor beyond. Another guest checking in to Hotel Death Row.

After a short pause, Ace heard more noise. A faint tap of someone tiptoeing across the room. She had to strain to make it out. There was a whispered conversation from the far end, although Ace could only make out one voice and she couldn't hear what that said. It seemed to get more frustrated as it went on.

After a while the whispering stopped and the cautious footsteps started again, slowly edging along the cells towards Ace's. Ace backed away from the door and sat on the edge of the shelf that served as a bed. The footsteps stopped outside her door.

'Practising the hard cell?' a familiar voice asked through the grille. Then the bolts were pulled back and Bernice gave Ace a self-satisfied smile.

'What kept you?' asked Ace.

'Charming. I'm pleased to see you too.' Benny stepped back to let Ace through the door. 'You look like you've been in the wars,' she added as Ace emerged into the better light.

'I have.'

'Me too. I'll tell you about it some time.'

Ace smiled back at Benny and slapped her on the shoulder. 'Well, better late than never, I suppose. Have you seen the Doctor?'

'No. Is he down here too? It's Klasvik up the other end – not very talkative though. I left him there, seemed best. Where's Gilmanuk, by the way?'

Before Ace could think of a tactful way to reply, a voice came from behind them. 'Ah, both of you together. How fortunate. That will save us some time.'

They turned towards the voice. And the Doctor stepped out of the shadows at the end of the row of cells, smiling broadly.

Source Document 15

Extract from security memo issued from Manact Marlock's office

From an original print-out preserved in the Rippearean Archives

- The front-of-house barrier will be manned at all times by two of the garrison.
- All persons wishing to pass the barrier must be checked against the guest list provided (on attached optical disc). Name and picture verification is required.
- The barrier will incorporate energy-detection units. Any guest found to be carrying an energy weapon or device to be detained.
- Only the Exec and his immediate entourage to be admitted to the royal observation box.
- No late-comers to be admitted.

Chapter 15

A Game At Chess

Quite a lot is known about the construction *of the*
Globe *theatre. It was built by Cuthbert Burbage in*
1599 using timber from The Theatre *(London's first*
playhouse).

From contemporary accounts and from document-
ation about other playhouses of the time, we can make
some assumptions about the Globe. But in fact, the
only direct documentation for what an Elizabethan
theatre looked like is a copy of Johannes De Witt's
impression of the Swan Theatre *as it was in 1596.*

Shakespeare's Playing Space
– Michael Campling, 1998

They had managed to make their way through the palace
without incident. Once in his quarters, the Doctor sat
down at the desk and motioned Ace and Bernice to make
themselves comfortable. Bernice flopped down on the bed
and Ace sat on the edge of it. Her head had stopped
aching but she was still seething deep inside at what she
had found in Marlock's office.

'So,' said the Doctor, 'what's been happening to you
two?'

Ace and Benny exchanged glances. 'Okay,' said Ace.
'I've discovered that the way the Heletians treat their
conquered people makes the Nazis look like *Dad's Army*,
and I've been attacked by Fortalexa and C3PO's big
brother. I've also been thumped by Marlock for raiding
his office, and I've been sentenced to death. Sentence to
be carried out after this play that Fortalexa and his metal

chums are hell-bent on getting sorted out.' When this provoked no immediate reaction, she added, 'So nothing much to report, I'm afraid. Just a typical day in hell.'

'I saw Fortalexa earlier,' Benny offered. 'He did seem very odd. Not himself.'

'I don't think he is himself,' said the Doctor. 'I think he's been replaced by a projection from the machine. I was right about the machine, Ace, about what's inside.' He turned to Benny. 'You see –' he started.

But she interrupted him at once. 'It's all right, Doctor. I know all about the machine.'

He was put out. 'Do you? Oh, I see. Well then. Hmmm.' The Doctor pondered for a moment. 'Well, for Ace's benefit then. The machine is a weapon.'

'I knew it!' Ace almost jumped to her feet. But she saw the Doctor's expression. 'Sorry, Doctor. Go on.'

He cleared his throat and then sniffed. 'The machine is a weapon. I don't know all the details – the nice man I spoke to about it was a bit vague on some points. But it was the machine which wiped out the civilization on Menaxus.'

'Doctor –' Benny interrupted again.

But the Doctor was in full flow. 'There is a play – *The Good Soldiers* by Stanoff Osterling – in which there is an army of robots.'

'Robots?'

'Yes, Ace. That play is programmed into the machine. And its performance on Menaxus led to the destruction of the planet. Now it seems that the machine is functioning again, and the play is to be performed tonight.'

This time Ace did leap to her feet. 'Then it will happen again – the machine will massacre everyone here.'

The Doctor nodded slowly. 'It seems likely. The fact that you've seen one of the robots outside the machine suggests that the program is already running. Probably we're too late to stop it now.'

Ace was already at the door. 'But we have to try. Marlock and his cronies may be murderers and war criminals, but there are loads of innocent people here too. We have to stop the massacre.'

But the Doctor made no effort to move. 'I'm not sure, Ace,' he said.

Ace almost laughed in surprise, and was about to remonstrate with him when Benny spoke.

'There is just one small point I'd like to make before we continue the discussion,' she said. 'Menaxus wasn't destroyed by the machine. There never was an invasion of Menaxus – no performance, no massacre.'

The outburst by the pathetic old man had frightened the Exec. He was acutely aware of his own mortality already. The sudden force of Klasvik's verbal attack had heightened his fears. He stroked Lannic's hair as he worried. The performance of *The Good Soldiers* – that was an obvious place for an assassin to strike. The audience was composed entirely of specifically invited courtiers and senior officers, but even so.

'Is it worth all the fuss,' he asked Lannic, 'this performance?'

She looked up at him, running the underside of her smooth chin over the palm of his hand. 'The greatest play ever written? The chance to host the first performance of *The Good Soldiers* in millennia – worth it? The universe will talk of nothing else for years.'

He nodded. 'I suppose so,' he said glumly. 'I suppose so.' He was silent for a while. Lannic nibbled his fingers playfully, but he seemed not to notice. 'I suppose nothing can go wrong? With the machine, I mean.'

Lannic took his hand and squeezed it gently. 'Fortalexa will make sure everything's fine.'

The Exec nodded, but he felt little better. He beckoned one of his bodyguards over. 'Have the theatre searched. Make sure everything is – is safe.'

Mutina Nuranjo had been cast in the Palace Guard Troupe after seeing active service in three campaigns. She had been lucky to survive the advance on Veterov: the troop carrier was shot down over Bostra and all but seventy three of the passengers were killed in the initial missile-hit; another sixty eight burned up on the way down or were fried on impact. Three of them survived the twenty-nine days until they were picked up.

After that she had been assigned to light duties to recover, in the camps on Phaselis Minor. But despite her front-line action, her stomach was not up to the job and she requested a transfer. She was lucky to get assigned to the palace rather than have her tour extended.

Now that the tide of the war had turned, her feelings were ambiguous. A part of her longed to return to the front – to do what she could to defend the territory she had fought so hard to gain. But a part of her liked the easy life of palace duties: the parades and inspections, the politics and the gossip. And if she dared to acknowledge it, a part of her felt that a people who could condone what she had seen in the camps – what she had *done* in the camps – deserved to be defeated, and wanted no part in the military decision.

But whatever her inner mental turmoil, her physical reactions were trained beyond her control. So when she saw the outline of the figure shrouded in the shadows at the top of the stairs, rather than ignore it and check on Fortalexa and the machine as her body and her commander wanted, she leaped back and drew her disruptor.

On Bostra similar reactions had saved her life. At the top of the stairway to the Queen's box of the royal theatre, the result was quite different. She loosed one bolt before the huge figure grabbed her and smashed her against the wall. Nuranjo's body mocked gravity for a second, splayed against the concrete. Then it slid slowly to rest, slipping down several steps and leaving a dark sticky trail across the grey of the wall.

Sub-direkter Hacilar and his team had found nothing. Exactly as Hacilar had expected. He ordered another sweep of the auditorium just in case, but he knew what the result would be. Hacilar sprawled in a seat in the back row and watched the useless search. He could hear the detectors bleeping their frustration as the soldiers swept them to and fro as they retreated up the aisles and pushed their way between the seats.

'Anything?'

Hacilar pulled his feet down from their rest across the back of the seat in front and stood up briskly. But it was just the technician from the box above – Fortalexa. 'No, nothing.' He sat down again. 'Boring as a mid-week matinée.'

'Good.'

'I told them we'd be wasting our time. Should be on an interval now – we were due off duty ages ago.'

'Best to be safe.'

Hacilar heard the technician's footsteps behind him as Fortalexa went back to the door. He heard the door open, and the steps paused.

'By the way . . .'

Hacilar twisted round in his seat. 'Yes?'

Fortalexa was standing sideways in the doorway, leaning against the frame with his legs braced against the door to hold it open. 'You sent a trooper up to check the box.'

'Yes – Nuranjo.'

Fortalexa shrugged. 'Whoever. I asked her to run a couple of errands while she was there. Hope that's all right.' He pushed himself upright, the door started to swing closed behind him.

'Yeah, fine,' Hacilar called after him, turning back towards the stage. 'Tell her she can go off duty when she's done.'

Benny made the most of the attention she was getting. 'I'm talking about what I found at the Braxiatel Collection,' she said. 'What I discovered about Menaxus and its history.'

'And what was that?'

'Well, first of all, there are no documents relating to any aspect of Menaxan life which doesn't directly involve the theatre itself.'

The Doctor leaned forward in interest, balancing his chin on the handle of his umbrella. 'Really?'

Benny nodded. 'And all the documents there are were donated to the collection on the same date. About six years ago. Just before Lannic found them.'

'They could have been donated by the same person – someone only interested in the theatre so he kept nothing else,' suggested Ace.

'I thought of that. So I cross-referenced with all the documentation on other planets in the sector.'

'And?'

'And there's no reference to Menaxus at all. Not to the theatre, not to anything.'

'Strange.' The Doctor tapped the umbrella on the floor, his chin rising and falling with it. 'Very strange. You'd expect something.'

'Yes, you would. But just being strange didn't help much. Especially with all the other strange things about Menaxus.'

'Such as?'

'Such as a theatre which is great when it's a ruin, but has appalling acoustics when it has an audience of any size in it. Like piles of rubble which the Braxiatel computer insists can't possibly have ever been part of any actual structure.'

'Like an open-air theatre,' suggested Ace, looking at the Doctor, 'on a planet where it pours with rain half the time?'

'Yes. Yes, I missed that one,' admitted Benny. 'But I did wonder why the walls that *are* lying flat – the ones which really *were* walls – seemed to have been knocked down by a bulldozer.'

'What?'

'And then there are the documents – that was what really got me worried.'

'What about them?'

'Well, it took me forever to work it out. I knew there was something wrong. Not with any particular document, you understand, but with all of them. As a collection. I think it was when I cracked that one that Braxiatel decided to tell me what was going on.'

'Braxiatel?' The Doctor's chin left the umbrella and his demeanour changed from brooding consideration to alert intelligence. 'You met Irving Braxiatel?'

'Oh yes. Nice guy.'

'Look, when you two have stopped name-dropping, could one of you please tell me what was so odd about these documents?'

'Sorry, Ace. Well, I saw it eventually, and of course it was obvious once I'd worked it out.'

'Worked what out?'

'The phraseology was odd. The documents – there are several hundred of them – are centuries apart in terms of original dates. But the same pompous phrases and vocabulary keep turning up in them. Almost as if they were written by the same person.'

'But how can that be?' asked Ace.

'Well, it's obvious really. But I missed it. The reason the rubble seems never to have been part of any real structure is because it hasn't. The reason the theatre works better as a ruin than as a theatre is that it was *built* as a ruin. The reason the walls seem to have been knocked down by a bulldozer is because they *were* knocked down by a bulldozer.'

The Doctor continued the progression: 'And the reason that the documents seem to have been written by the same person is – '

'Is that they *were* written by the same person. Yes.'

'But why?' Ace was stuck for words for a moment. 'I mean – well, yes – *why*?'

'I think, Ace – and Benny will know for sure – because there never was any civilization on Menaxus. No people, no theatre, no machine and no massacre.'

Benny nodded. 'That's right.' She laughed. 'We should have spotted it much earlier. The whole place made no sense. It was laid out as an archaeological dig, not as a place people actually lived or worked. The whole supposed history is based on precedents stolen from other people's real history. I think some of them are included as a sort of one-upmanship – I mean, the supposed sketch of the theatre which Lannic worked from was apparently drawn by someone called De Witte, for goodness sake! Even the curse on the monolith was a kind of joke – I gather from Braxiatel that they were never expected to find it.'

'Hang on, hang on.' Ace held her hands up for silence. 'So the whole thing was an invention, right?'

The Doctor nodded. 'Yes, Ace. An act.'

Benny smiled. 'In a way, Doctor, but there again everything turned out to be exactly what it seemed.'

'Fine. But I still don't understand why.'

The Doctor looked at Benny, and she signalled for him to go ahead. 'Because I think what Benny is telling us is that the catastrophe I thought finished Menaxus hasn't happened yet. The machine wasn't built centuries ago to destroy a planet now long-dead. That planet was never alive. And the machine was left there only a few years ago. It was built to enable the Rippeareans to invade and destroy Heletia – here and now.'

'That's right,' confirmed Benny. 'The whole history and archaeology of Menaxus was divised just to get the Heletians to excavate and to find the machine. They knew that Lannic would take it back to the Exec, and they knew he wouldn't pass up an opportunity to stage *The Good Soldiers.*'

'But they're winning – the war's all but over. Why go to all that trouble now?'

'Lannic's initial expedition was five years ago, remember, Ace,' the Doctor pointed out. 'The situation in the war was very different then. Even now it could drag on for several very nasty years.'

'So what went wrong?'

'According to Braxiatel, who seems to have masterminded the whole thing, the machine was programmed to make conditions on the dig as unpleasant as possible so that Lannic and her team would pull out quickly. Otherwise they might spend forever excavating and never get

264

the machine back here at all. It seems to have done its job too well on the first dig, and they left before they even found the machine.'

'I should have guessed,' mused the Doctor. 'Braxiatel was always a grand master of political chess. A formidable actor too, though a little melodramatic – hence the extraneous trimmings, I suppose.'

Ace gaped as a thought struck her. 'The mud monster!'

The Doctor nodded. 'Yes, it would explain a lot if that were also part of the act – part of the machine's repertoire. It certainly seems to owe more to the imagination than to science. I think the machine lifted elements from *The Good Soldiers* which includes some nasty executions in the play-within-a-play, and from *Death's Bane* which involves homicidal statues, amongst other things. It used them to scare us off.'

'I don't know what monster or statues you're on about, but that would fit with what happened to me when I found the machine, and with what Braxiatel said.'

'And now the drama will be played out as written. Five years late.'

Ace looked from Bernice to the Doctor. 'And you're just going to sit back and let it happen?' she asked, appalled.

The Doctor got as close to a shrug as he could while leaning forward on his umbrella. 'I don't know, Ace. It might be best.'

'What?' She could not believe what she was hearing.

'Perhaps this will help you decide, Doctor.' Benny pulled the envelope Braxiatel had given her from a pocket. It was crumpled, and she tried unsuccessfully to smooth it out a bit before handing it to the Doctor.

'From Braxiatel?'

Benny nodded.

The Doctor slid his index finger inside the ungummed corner and ran it along the top to rip open the envelope. He pulled several sheets of paper from inside and unfolded them. He read them in an instant, refolded them and pushed them back inside the envelope. Then he put the envelope in his jacket pocket, transferring a large paisley handkerchief to the pocket on the other side to make room.

Ace and Bernice watched the Doctor closely. He stood up, dusted himself down and made for the door.

'At last,' said Ace. 'Action.'

'Action?'

'We're going to stop the performance – yes?'

The Doctor shook his head. 'No.'

'No?'

'No. I was just thinking we ought to get there early to make sure we get good seats. It wouldn't do to be stuck at the back. Behind the woman with the beehive hair-do.'

'Or the man with the extremely wide head and sticky-out ears,' Bernice offered.

Ace glared at them. Then she shook her head, pushed past the Doctor and stormed out.

'She could ruin everything.' The Doctor followed her into the corridor, but Ace was already out of sight.

'Then we'd better stop her, before she stops Fortalexa.'

The Doctor nodded sadly. 'Yes, Benny. Always so impulsive,' he murmured as he stared down the empty corridor.

They set off after Ace, Benny struggling to stay with the Doctor rather than run on ahead. He swung his umbrella as they walked. 'Benny, when we've found her, and while the performance is going on, would you do something for me?'

'And miss the play?'

The Doctor stopped. 'It is quite important,' he told her.

'All right then, Doctor. Just tell me what it is.'

So he told her. 'And now I think,' he said as they reached a corner, 'we had better rescue Ace.' And he ran off down the corridor, umbrella hooked over his arm.

It was later than Ace had realized. As she approached the theatre, the number of people milling about in the corridors of the palace rose from near zero to a much higher number. It seemed as though all the courtiers and most of the guard contingent were converging on the place. They seemed to be helping to make final preparations rather than jostling for seats.

In the corridor outside the main door to the theatre, a group of guards was laying out a plush green carpet. There was a barrier set up a few yards in front of the door and two soldiers stood on sentry duty outside. Ace waited at the far end of the corridor. Partly she wanted to keep out of sight of the courtier in case he recognized her, and partly she wanted to see what happened to anyone who tried to pass through the barrier.

She did not have to wait very long. The carpet was soon smoothed out to the satisfaction of the courtier, and the group disappeared to carry out another vital mission. The sentries, however, maintained their vigilance. One of them was holding a clip-pak, Ace noticed, and he idly tapped his fingers on it. Ace assumed he was checking through a guest list.

She took a deep breath and marched up to the guards. 'I need to get into the theatre. I'm on a special mission for Manact Marlock,' she said pompously, hoping Marlock had not warned his guards to look out for anyone claiming to be his special emissary. She reckoned she was pretty safe: it was unlikely they had even noticed she was no longer in her cell.

'Name?' snapped the sentry with the clip-pak.

So it *was* a guest list. Ace tried to peer over the top of the clip-pak in the hope of catching sight of a name, but the guard glared at her and raised the pak up so she could no longer see it. She had, however, been able to catch a glimpse of the list – beside each name was a small picture.

'Name,' he repeated. 'If you're not on the list, you don't get in. No matter who you say sent you.'

The other guard's hand was poised near the handle of his disruptor. Ace doubted if she could just apologize and walk away.

'Lannic,' she said. 'Camarina Lannic.' And she hoped that if gossip and rumour travelled round the Heletian barracks as fast as round any other she had visited then they might not even bother to check Lannic's name – they might already know who Lannic was.

But the guard examined his clip-pak, tapping on the bottom of the screen to page down the list. Ace watched him closely as he read down, ready to make a run for it at the first hint of trouble – best to wait until the moment of most confusion.

'Right,' said the guard, and Ace braced herself ready to run. But the guard stood aside and saluted.

Ace hesitated. Were they more clever than they looked – were they luring her into a trap? She didn't have much option though, the second guard had closed in behind her. She nodded and stepped past the sentry with the clip-pak, trying to catch sight of the screen as she did so. Her eyes lingered on the energy-detectors built into the ends of the barrier – lucky she wasn't carrying any weapons, they would set the detectors off instantly.

One line, which Ace assumed was Lannic's name, had no picture against it, just a blank square. Of course, Lannic must be the one guest for whom they did not have complete record. After all, she had only just arrived.

'Thanks,' said Ace, resisting the temptation to congratulate them on the fine job they were doing. They were still watching her, so she went into the theatre through the main double doors.

Once inside the theatre Ace glanced round. People were stacking piles of programmes or adjusting the lighting. She immediately turned back to the doors and pushed one of them open a crack. The guards had turned back towards the corridor. Probably they would not have worried if she had gone straight up the stairs towards the box, but it was best to be cautious.

Ace pushed the door open wide enough to slip through and made her way quietly to the stairs leading to the box where the machine was installed.

She knew what she wanted to do once she reached the top of the stairs, but she wasn't sure exactly how she might do it. If Fortalexa was not there then it was simple – smash the machine with whatever came to hand. If Fortalexa was guarding the machine, then that might complicate matters slightly.

At the top of the staircase she paused. The lamps were dimmed in the box, but she could see the main control panel of the machine lit by its own read-outs and lights. The machine was silhouetted against the one-way glass which let in the brighter lighting in the theatre. Ace listened for a few moments. Silence – it sounded as if the room was empty. She stepped quietly over the threshold.

And Fortalexa stood up from behind the machine.

'Last-minute adjustments, eh?' Ace smiled. 'You shouldn't have wasted your time.' She looked round for something heavy to use as a cudgel. A baseball bat would be ideal, but she doubted the Heletians would have such a thing. In the far corner of the room, in the shadow cast by Fortalexa and the machine, she could just make out the gleam of something metal. It looked cylindrical, like a pipe propped up against the wall. If it were heavy enough it would be ideal for the job she had in mind.

But before Ace could reach it, the cylinder moved forward into the light. It resolved itself into the metal forearm of a robot – the twin of the robot Ace had destroyed earlier.

Ace backed away as the robot stepped towards her. 'Sorry,' she said with a nervous half-laugh, 'I was looking for the Ladies, must have taken a wrong turn.' As the robot reached out towards her, Ace spun round, ready to race down the stairs. But Fortalexa had already worked his way round behind her. He was standing in front of her, cutting off her retreat.

Out of the corner of her eye, Ace could see her shadow cast on the side wall of the room. And she could see the shadow of a skeletal hand reaching out for her neck.

Source Document 16

Extract from partly completed manuscript for *Beyond Osterling's Legacy,* by Azcline Grigsen. Date assumed to coincide with Grigsen's death – 3515. Manuscript never published

Braxiatel Collection Catalogue Number: 883CR

Shakespeare was almost certainly on hand to give advice to the actors when his plays were rehearsed. Rehearsals for what was in essence a repertory company, expected to provide different plays every week, must have been short and infrequent, so the actors would have welcomed what notes were offered.

By contrast, Osterling was not involved in the production of his plays at all. He delivered the manuscript, and went to the first night. His way of maintaining control was to issue explicit and detailed stage directions within the text of his script. These directions he expected to be followed meticulously (witness his famous argument with Hanrich Endersyn over the colour of the carpet in *Death by Mirrors*).

Shakespeare's stage directions however – perhaps because of the liaison between writer and actors – are virtually non-existent.

That is not to say there are no instructions to the actor in the plays of Shakespeare. But unlike Osterling, Shakespeare constantly gives instructions to the actors *within* the body of the text, using the speech of the characters to define and identify the important details of movement and action. 'See it stalks away,' Barnardo says of the ghost of Hamlet's father. At once he instructs the ghost how it should move, and draws the audience's attention to this detail.

Osterling's text is too often starved of the poetic detail of action with which Shakespeare's lines are imbued. His directions are stark, straightforward and, in an epoch where the action of the play largely happens off-stage and is merely alluded to by the characters, would seem to be totally inappropriate. If *The Good Soldiers* is ever rediscovered, I think we shall find that Osterling's approach to the presentation of the drama, in this play at least, is completely different from that of his contemporaries. It will vindicate his attention to the detail of action which the staging techniques of his era, with its post-Greek inclination, would seem to make a superfluous liberty.

Chapter 16

The Crucible

At some time in the distant past, Thespis (according to tradition) stepped out of the choral Dithyramb and spoke alone. He became the first actor, and his dialogue with the chorus formed the basis for tragedy.

By the time Aeschylus came to the theatre, the ancient Greeks had evolved a ritual which allowed for two speaking actors: the protagonist and the deuteragonist. There were other characters in the plays, but only two speaking actors. So the speaking actor would change his mask and replace one of the dumb actors when a new character spoke. But because there were only ever two of them in any one scene, all dialogue was two-way. The two actors spoke, and the chorus interpreted and commented on their dialogue. The action happened off-stage, and they all described and commented on that.

The ritual was set, established, unchangeable. The stichomythia – the exchange of single lines of dialogue like a hammer hitting an anvil in the central emotional argument of the play – was defined and understood. The two characters engaged in the debate would get no help or hindrance from elsewhere. And the audience knew it.

When Orestes returns to avenge the death of his father Agamemnon in The Libation Bearers, *the central argument is between Orestes and his mother Clytaemnestra. His mother has murdered Agamemnon (ostensibly for sacrificing their daughter to the gods in the hope of good fortune in the siege of Troy). His choice is simple but harrowing: he can appease the gods and murder his father's killer, or he can renounce them and let the mother who suckled him live.*

When the argument takes place, Orestes' companion Pylades is witness to it. Throughout the play, Pylades has not spoken, and the audience is aware that he cannot intervene now as the two speaking actors have taken the roles of Orestes and Clytaemnestra. So when Orestes falters in his resolve and asks Pylades what he should do, we know that his companion can offer no advice.

Aeschylus's innovation was to introduce a third speaking actor. He does this not from the outset, but towards the end of the play. Imagine the tension among the thousands in the audience when Orestes asks his companion whether he should kill his own mother. And imagine the shock and the drama when his companion – the companion who the audience knows can offer him no advice – tells Orestes to appease the gods. Orestes, like the audience, is swayed and Clytaemnestra's fate is sealed.

Tragedy and drama in general took another innovative leap forward with Pylades' only speech throughout the play. 'What of the future?' that speech begins. What indeed?

The Greeks had a Play about It
– Peter Hinton, 2012

When they arrived at the barrier and were greeted by the two sullen soldiers standing at the only point they could pass through it, Bernice assumed there would be trouble.

She was disappointed.

Once the Doctor had pointed out that he was in fact on their guest list and that his assistant Professor Summerfield must therefore have been omitted by mistake, they became very helpful. Not so helpful that they would actually let Benny through the barrier without further questioning and obstinance, but they did not actually shoot

Benny and the Doctor out of hand – which had to count for something.

'Shall I wait here while you see if you can find her?' Benny asked.

The Doctor was stupefied. 'Certainly not – it's the principle of the thing.' He turned back to the guards. 'Now then, we are needed to get the machine running properly so the play can actually be performed. I assume from your overtures that you will not allow Professor Summerfield through the barrier, so we shall remain here. And we shall explain to the Exec when he arrives why the performance cannot take place. I'm sure Marlock will be very interested too.'

The Doctor sat down on the floor by the barrier and crossed his legs. The guards muttered quietly to each other. The Doctor started to whistle.

After a few moments of hasty haggling a compromise was reached. The Doctor and Benny could pass through the barrier, provided they only went to the box where Fortalexa was setting up the machine. One of the guards would accompany them as far as the bottom of the staircase. In the meantime, the other guard would send a message to Marlock to get proper authorization for Benny, who had obviously been left off the guest list by mistake.

From the way the conversation ended, it seemed as though this compromise was entirely the initiative of the sentries, although Benny was certain the Doctor had worked most of it out before they even started to negotiate. As they climbed the stairs, she tried to work out at what point the guards had been given control of the conversation. But before she succeeded, both Benny and the Doctor heard the noise. It sounded as if there was a small war going on in the room above them.

'Ace!'

The Doctor nodded, and they ran up the stairs.

At the top of the stairs, Fortalexa was standing with his back to them, looking back into the room. His hands were on his hips and he was watching intently what was happening on the other side of the box. The Doctor reached him first, took one look at the scene in the room, dropped his shoulder and without slowing his speed crashed into Fortalexa. The Doctor's shoulder caught the man in the small of the back and sent him sprawling across the room. The Doctor continued for a few paces, then skidded to a halt.

Bernice was just behind him, and like the Doctor took in the scene at a glance. Ace was backed into the far corner of the box, almost pressed up against the glass wall. A large metal figure was walking slowly but steadily towards her, robotic arms extended, servos whirring as its legs smoothly inched forward. The whole construction looked like a man the size of an Ice Warrior had been stripped to the muscle and bone, then encased in metal and sent on a body-building course.

Ace was throwing anything to hand at the robot – which now meant very little. But judging by the trail of electrical components and broken furniture, she had been holding off the inevitable for a while. Now she was almost out of ammunition.

The Doctor used the weapon he had immediately available: his umbrella. He smashed the robot across the head with it. His umbrella bent almost double; the robot seemed not to notice. Its right hand closed on Ace's neck.

'Stop,' shouted the Doctor, but his cry had no effect. The robot's fingers were touching the glass wall, its palm and the crook between thumb and forefinger tight against Ace's neck. Benny could see Ace's eyes begin to glaze over as the robot arm moved slowly up the wall.

Benny ran over and grabbed the robot's arm with both hands, trying to pull it away from Ace's throat. Ace was on tiptoes now. Another inch and her feet would leave the floor. The robot's left hand connected with Benny's head as it swatted at her, and she went spinning across the room, crashing into the wall and collapsing in a heap on the floor.

Fortalexa was watching, silent. He had picked himself up after the Doctor had knocked him over, but he made no attempt to help either the robot or Ace. His lips were curled into a set smile.

'Do something!' Benny screamed at him, but he didn't move.

'Stop.' The Doctor's voice was quieter this time, but somehow more authoritative. He was standing beside the machine, his bent umbrella poised above the main control panel. 'Stop, or I destroy the machine.'

The robot froze. One of Ace's feet was off the floor, braced against the glass wall. The other was on its toes, ballet-style.

'That's better. Now let her down – slowly. Then release her.'

Ace collapsed to her knees as soon as the pressure of the hand was released. She gasped in air and clutched at her throat, pulling open her collar. Benny could see her neck beginning to discolour as the bruising surfaced.

The robot remained frozen in position, its red eyes glowing but otherwise inanimate. By contrast, Fortalexa was exasperated. He stayed clear of the Doctor and the machine, but his hands were clenching and unclenching, his head swaying to and fro.

'Now,' said the Doctor, holding his umbrella above the machine with one hand and adjusting controls with the other. 'Let's see just how good this dimensional osmosis really is, shall we?' He winked at Benny and jabbed at a final sequence of buttons.

A red glow seeped across the room from the machine. It wafted towards the silent metal figure by the wall, paused, then slowly surrounded it. It spread like a mist over the area of the room where the robot stood. Ace crawled away as it expanded, enveloping the robot completely, thickening until the shape of the figure was no longer discernible. Then it faded, thinned and disappeared. The robot was gone.

'I wish I'd known about that,' croaked Ace.

The Doctor smiled and shouldered his battered umbrella. 'All part of the service.' He turned back to the panel.

But before he could operate another control, Fortalexa was on him, dragging him away. Benny ran across to help, aware of Ace pulling herself to her feet behind her. Fortalexa pulled the Doctor clear of the machine and hurled him at Benny. They collided and fell in a tangle of limbs and umbrella. Ace, just behind Benny now, tripped on the Doctor's thrashing arms and joined the mêlée.

'You're clever, Doctor,' Fortalexa was tapping a command sequence into the machine. 'Clever, but too late.' And for the first time since they had arrived on Heletia, he laughed.

Benny, Ace, and the Doctor were managing to extricate themselves from their scrum on the floor. Now they all watched in amazement as Fortalexa's body rocked with mirth. Tears began to roll down his cheeks and he gasped for breath between bouts of laughter.

'You can't stop it now,' Fortalexa gasped between snorts of laughter. He wiped a tear from his eye. 'The programme's running on the timer – the reality envelope is already forming down there, in the theatre. There's nothing even you, Doctor, can do to change that.'

'Hmmm – big joke.' Benny pulled herself to her feet and helped Ace up. 'Is he right, Doctor?'

The Doctor nodded. 'Yes and no. He's right that I can't stop it. But then again, I don't want to.'

Ace was still wheezing and rubbing her neck, as she staggered towards the machine. And Fortalexa's laughter turned to a cry of pain.

The red mist drifted out of the machine again. Ace was silhouetted against it as the thin cloud curled round Fortalexa, seeming to grab at his arms and legs. He was screaming now, his cries muffled by the mist as it pulled at his limbs, dragging his arms and legs apart, seeming to snap his head backwards.

'Doctor?' But the Doctor shook his head in answer to Benny.

The red of the glow deepened, becoming more opaque. Ace stepped back, away from it, affording Benny a clear view as it closed over Fortalexa just at the moment it looked like his arms and legs must tear away from his body. His screams became more distant, then suddenly they cut off. When the red mist cleared, he was gone.

'Fascinating.' The Doctor seemed not at all worried by the strange events.

'What – where did he go?'

'Go, Ace? Back inside the machine.' The Doctor wandered over to where the last vestiges of the mist were dissipating. 'In a sense, you see, he was never *really* here – he was a projection of the machine.'

'No, Doctor.' Benny shook her head. 'He was on the mission before we even reached Menaxus.'

'Oh I've no doubt the real person was on the mission, and we met him and joked with him. This Fortalexa, the one who faded away so dramatically, was a copy. At some stage on the journey home, the machine replaced him with its own version.'

Ace nodded. 'That would explain why he lost his sense of humour.'

'Yes – he had to follow a script written to accommodate his character. The instincts and wit were not a part of the role. Though judging by the surprise he showed at the end – you saw how he screamed – I don't think the copy even realized he wasn't real. He actually believed he *was* Fortalexa.'

'Must have been quite a shock when he found out he wasn't.' Benny had another question: 'Doctor, how did you know that threatening to destroy the machine would stop the robot? Lucky guess?'

'No, Benny. You told us.'

'I did?'

'Yes. Remember when you first found the machine, it tried to kill you; you thought someone had grabbed you from behind. But when you were about to damage the machine, it stopped. The machine stopped attacking you in order to defend and protect itself. It seemed reasonable to expect the same behaviour again.'

'Well, whatever the explanation, thanks Doctor.' Ace joined him by the machine. 'Now can we destroy this thing

278

and get out of here?' She reached out for the control panel, but the Doctor slapped her hand away.

'You're forever trying to destroy things, Ace. This time I think it's better for all of us if we leave it be. Besides,' he went on, 'I doubt we can stop it – I think Fortalexa was right about that.'

The Doctor reached out to the control panel and experimentally pushed a button. Almost as soon as it touched the control, he whipped his finger back with a cry. Benny heard the faint crackle, like a static discharge, from across the room. 'What is it, Doctor? Static?'

'I don't know.' He held his hand up level with his eyes, palm facing down. 'It's made the hairs on the back of my hand stand on end – look,' he laughed. Then he cautiously jabbed at the button again. This time there was no noise, and he rested his hand on the panel. He thought for a moment. 'Probably a residual energy image of Fortalexa. The machine retrieved him in something of a hurry; bound to be something tangible left behind.'

'I still say we smash it up.' Ace was hunting through the mess of broken equipment and furniture on the floor. Benny assumed she was looking for a suitable implement to break up the machine. Ace worked her way across the floor, head down, scanning the debris. As Benny watched her progress towards the door, she realized that there was a figure standing in the doorway, watching the proceedings.

But before she had time to comment, Ace had picked up the broken metal leg of a chair and returned to the machine. The Doctor rushed round from behind it, but he was not in time to stop Ace bringing the leg clanging down on the side of the machine. It connected with a flat area of the side plate, denting it and deflecting off sideways and downwards. Ace raised the metal bar again, but the Doctor caught her hands as they reached the top of her upswing. His eyes were level with Ace's and Benny could see them burning with anger.

279

Marlock coughed. 'Smash it up? So, sabotage as well as espionage.'

Ace was startled, dropped her weapon and backed away towards the machine.

The Doctor stepped forward and grabbed her wrists. 'Perhaps, Marlock, you would be good enough to lock her away again before she can do any more damage?'

Act looked startled. The other woman, who Marlock had not seen before, stood her ground. He thought for a moment she might cause trouble too, but a look from the Doctor stayed her. The Doctor – Marlock was still not quite sure about him. But Ace certainly needed attention. Marlock stepped into the room and gestured for his bodyguards to restrain her.

'It is unfortunate that we cannot execute you twice, so I suppose once will have to make do for both crimes.'

The bodyguards dragged Ace over to him. She was strangely passive, staring at the Doctor with a mixture of surprise and worry. Eventually she looked away from the Doctor and stared at her feet.

Marlock grabbed her chin between his thumb and forefinger and pulled it upwards so she was forced to look him in the eye. 'You really should stop pretending to be things that you are not. Such deceptions are always detected.' He chuckled; it was a chilling, throaty vibration. 'Had Lannic not been with the Exec, she might have had considerable difficulty getting to see the performance. But you will be pleased to know that I have arranged for you to have no such problems.' He raised his voice and threw the Doctor a quick glance. 'Or you, for that matter, Doctor.'

'Thank you, Marlock. Got us good seats, I hope.'

'The best in the house. Although I was not aware that you had another colleague with you.' He gestured at the other woman.

'My name's Benny,' the woman offered. 'But you can call me Professor Summerfield.'

Marlock nodded to her in mock gratitude. Another insolent friend of the Doctor's 'I think we can find seats

280

for all three of you. But quite what I am to do with you *after* the performance is another matter.'

'Why not just let us go?' Ace suggested.

Marlock ignored her. 'As I said, Doctor, I have reserved seats for you. In the front row in fact. That should afford an excellent view of the play, which I am assuming will go ahead with no problems.'

'Oh yes.' The Doctor patted the machine affectionately. 'No real damage done. The timer's set so it will start right on cue. All running according to plan. Tickety-boo.'

'Good. I've also ensured that you and Professor Summerfield will have an excellent view of the execution that will take place immediately after the performance, Doctor. I doubt you will want to miss that. Your friend Ace will of course have a somewhat more prominent role to play then. For that reason I fear that while yourself and the Professor here will be able to avail yourselves of the excellent refreshments service both before the play and during the interval, Ace will have to be restrained. I hope that will not be too much of an inconvenience and will not mar her enjoyment of this unique occasion too much.'

'She's a bit old for ice-cream and popcorn,' the Doctor observed. 'She'll live with it.'

Marlock waved for the Doctor and Professor Summerfield to precede him down the stairs. The bodyguards dragged the protesting Ace after them.

'I doubt it, Doctor,' Marlock said as they descended. 'I doubt it very much.'

Ace had rarely been to the theatre, but the seat she had was wider and more comfortable than any cinema seat she had tried. But then again, she had never been strapped into a cinema seat; her wrists tied to the arm rests and a leather band holding her round the waist. Even her feet were restrained. Coupled with the threat that if she did anything to disturb the performance – whisper even – then she would be shot somewhere painful but not fatal by the guard positioned three seats away for precisely this purpose.

The upshot of this was that Ace was not about to disturb the performance. Not unless and until she could get free. They would have to release her to get her up on stage to be executed at the end of the play anyway. And at that point she would be released from the chair, and she would have precious little to lose.

It had occurred to her that the Doctor had some master plan up his sleeve. But he was sitting, apparently sulking, in the next seat. She reckoned he was just as stuck for ideas as she was. She guessed he had only prevented her from smashing the machine because he realized Marlock was watching.

On the other side of Ace, Benny was looking back up the auditorium. 'I shouldn't worry,' she said, turning round to look at Ace. 'Something will turn up – relax and enjoy the play.'

Ace glared at her. 'You try relaxing strapped in like this.'

'No thanks. Anyway, I must be off – things to do. Right, Doctor?'

The Doctor nodded without acknowledging in any other way that he had heard.

'Not staying for the historic performance? Who knows what that crazy machine will throw at us?'

Benny laughed. 'Not a lot, I think. It feeds on action, mainly. Dialogue isn't its forte.'

Ace didn't follow. 'So what?'

Benny sighed and put on her professor's voice. 'All right, there's just time before I have to go, I guess.'

Ace pulled at the cord holding her right wrist. Then she caught the eye of the guard, smiled innocently and relaxed back into the chair. 'Don't feel you have to spend any time here on my account,' she told Benny.

'No, no – I insist. Now then, by the start of the twenty-third century, Earth and her colonies were getting pretty depleted in terms of technology and the recession was well under way. The Dalek invasion and the Cyber wars hadn't helped any. And all this had a serious effect on the theatre – no money, no spectacle. And no spectacle meant the scripts had to be rather better and what action and excitement there was in the story had to be pretty basic and cheap.'

'Great. This'll be dead boring.'

'Probably,' Benny conceded. 'But follow me carefully, it may prove a comfort. Come Osterling's time – mid to late twenty-third century – drama had found a solution. It had reverted, broadly, to the Greek model.'

'Of course – obvious solution.' Ace was not at all sure she was any encouraged by Benny's lecture.

'Absolutely. So, loads of dialogue and in-depth argument going on. But the action all happens off-stage. In ancient Greece, Agamemnon goes off-stage to be murdered and Clytaemnestra comes out afterwards to describe the scene in vivid detail. They even wheel out a tableau for extra effect. But you don't actually see it. The action isn't in the play. Same in Osterling's *The Mercenary* – the whole play is about the battle, but the audience is stuck in a wood nearby with the women from the town and gets to hear reports from messengers. Great dialogue and description, but no action.'

Ace considered. 'This is supposed to make me feel better, is it?'

'Should do. What do you think will happen if the dream machine brings the play to life? In the worst case some guy in armour will come over and shout at you about how terrible things are getting in the next room.'

Ace considered again. 'I can handle that,' she said.

'Good,' said Benny. 'Got to dash now. If I'm back in time, I'll buy you a drink in the interval.' Benny gave a cheery mime of raising a glass and an exaggerated point towards the refreshment area at the back of the auditorium. She aimed it at the Doctor, but it was really for the benefit of the guard cradling a disruptor two seats away. Then Benny stood up and left.

The Exec scanned the audience below him, the theatre

was packed. Only the front row was almost empty. By tradition it was reserved for visiting dignitaries from foreign worlds, and Marlock had accorded the strange Doctor and his companions that privilege. One of the women was secured by a seat restraint brought specially from the interrogation suites, and the other had already left. There was a guard watching the Doctor and the restrained woman. Three less people to worry about.

'That guard,' Lannic whispered in his ear, 'he has a disruptor, so he must be trustworthy. And he can see if there is any trouble.'

The Exec agreed. Then a thought struck him. 'He is one of Marlock's guards.'

Lannic smiled. 'So we have nothing to worry about.'

The Exec nodded glumly. Of course there was nothing to worry about – just a guard with a gun. In the theatre, where no weapons were allowed. Even Lannic had been scanned for energy sources. The detectors in the barrier had only been switched off for the Exec himself. Although Marlock had kept pace with him as they passed through.

Lannic leaned closer and took his hand, patting it gently. The Exec took the opportunity to admire her blouse. Above the simple black skirt she was wearing a low-cut blouse of tight black gauze. It showed off her figure to its best. Only the strategically placed patterns woven into the diaphanous material obscured the view. He examined one of the patterns closely – it was identical to the others, a cluster of small leaves splaying out from a central branch.

The Exec looked back down at the audience, recognizing the tops of the heads of people whose brothers, sisters, parents and lovers he had had executed. He sat back in his chair and tried to think about something else. The performance would start soon. He had been looking forward to it.

Benny made her way back to the Doctor's room. She needed a few minutes to decide how exactly to achieve her objective. She would not be back in time for the interval – she could not even start until the performance was well under way. Her action had to coincide with the climax of the play, that was the whole point.

Benny hoped her short lecture had soothed some of Ace's fears. She also hoped Ace would forgive her if they survived the evening – after all, nothing Benny had told her was untrue. Two days ago she would even have believed it herself.

'Ace?'

When he said her name the second time, Ace deigned to look at him. The Doctor was leaning towards her in a theatrically conspiratorial fashion.

'What is it, Doctor? Words of comfort from you too?'

'Sort of. Everything's under control, if that's what you mean.'

Ace snorted. 'Oh yeah – whose control? Benny says not to worry anyway, the whole thing will be a non-event.'

The Doctor looked hurt. 'She said that?'

Ace nodded.

'She should know better. It will be superb.'

'Ancient Greek dialogue, Doctor – no action. Boring.'

'Ah.' The Doctor looked round as if checking to see if anyone was trying to overhear. 'You know a bit about the theatre history of the twenty-third century, then?'

'A bit. Recently acquired knowledge.'

'Well, here's some more, something long forgotten. Something the people here don't yet appreciate. Osterling wrote poor dialogue – convuluted and pompous. And *The Good Soldiers* is a rotten play.'

'So why all the fuss?'

The Doctor shrugged. 'Reputation.'

'Yes, but something has to lead to a reputation in the first place.'

'Innovation. Osterling changed the course of theatre history, though as I said, that's long forgotten by now – lost with his play.' He leaned even closer, his voice getting quieter. 'That was the whole point. Osterling's innovation – a stroke of genius really. Can't think where he got the idea. In Osterling's time, the action all happened off-stage and was then reported. An interesting but archaic dramatic convention, largely left over from the leaner years of theatrical parsimony.'

Ace's stomach suddenly felt empty. Her hands were clenched on the arms of the seat and there was a tightness in the muscles in her calves. 'So what did he do? What was the innovation?'

The Doctor grinned. 'He wrote a play – this play, in fact – where the final action was an invasion. A group of people in a fortress are massacred by an army of robots. But unlike the other plays of his era, even his own plays, *the action happened on stage.*'

Ace could feel the colour draining from her face as she strained at the straps and the lights began to dim.

'At the end of the play, an army of robots burst on to the stage. The audience saw the invasion first-hand. Actually witnessed the massacre.' He settled back into his seat and clicked his tongue in appreciation.

'Doctor!' Ace's voice was almost a shout. She heard the guard flick off the safety features on his disruptor, and clamped her mouth shut. She bit her lip and strained towards the Doctor as a red glow paled into existence on the stage in front of them, resolving itself into the banqueting hall of a fortress.

Just as the last of the light in the auditorium faded, the Doctor turned back towards Ace, He winked and put his finger to his lips to signal for silence. Then he turned his attention back to the stage, resting his elbows on the arms of the seat and his chin on his steepled fingers. And the performance began.

Source Document 17

Bolvadin's retelling of *The Good Soldiers*.
From *Stories from the Theatre*, first published
2294

*Braxiatel Collection Catalogue Number of surviving first
edition: 002CH*

Far far away, both in space and time, there is a town
called Limlough. On the hill overlooking the town stands
a mighty fortress. And then one day, the war comes to
Limlough.

As the armies approach, it becomes clear that there will
be a great battle. The townspeople flee in fear for their
lives and the soldiers camp around the town in readiness
for the battle. In one of the camps of the Ragussan army,
six comrades banquet together on the eve of the battle:
Jorvik, Remek, Spidler, Prator, Freppon and Teel.

They are looking forward to the fight and boasting
of what they will accomplish. Only Jorvik is quiet and
philosophical.

The next day the battle is fought. The robot armies of
the Samrong destroy the men of Ragussa, and the
defeated survivors retreat into the fortress of Limlough.
The Samrong lay siege to the fortress and many of the
survivors die trying to escape or to send for help and
supplies.

Two months later, with the outer wall of the fortress
penetrated by the enemy, the six comrades meet up again,
survivors all – now trapped in the fortress, the last bastion
of their empire. They share stories of old times and of

their heroism in the battle as the enemy comes ever closer to their door. They are all boastful, apart from the tall, imposing figure of Jorvik.

During the night, as they feast, they watch a play arranged by Jorvik. The play concerns five comrades who meet and share a banquet before a great battle, and who die during or shortly after it. So, in this play a character called Kemer mirrors the real Remek, and dies at the battlefront; Teel is appalled as the character Leet is executed as a war criminal. At the climax of the play, the enemy – an army of robots – wins through.

Then the players reveal that under their costumes they are themselves soldiers of Samrong. At the same moment, the Samrong robots break through the final defences of the fortress of Limlough.

Jorvik's speech as the robots attack makes it clear that in fact all the 'good soldiers' were deserters: they never got to the battle of Limlough. The exception is Jorvik, and he is a traitor. The players, smuggled in by him, attack the comrades from the rear.

The soldiers defend themselves, and are killed according to their scenes in the play. Jorvik sides with the enemy robots with whom he was always allied, as anyone who was at Limlough would have known.

And so, as the Samrong robots achieve their final victory, only Jorvik the traitor survives – still true to his beliefs, however misguided.

Chapter 17

The Good Soldiers

Hamartia *is not, as many think, a tragic flaw. It is rather a character trait which happens, under certain circumstances, to lead to the downfall of the character. Othello's jealous disposition would be of little note were it not for the circumstances under which it comes to the fore.*

Similarly, the states of anagnorisis *and* perepeteia *need explanation before we can continue. Perepeteia is the moment at which the hamartia leads to the character's downfall. For Oedipus, the moment of perepeteia is when he kills an old man on the road. Recognition that this was his perepeteia comes much later. In fact things seem to be going his way – he discovers the old man was a king and Oedipus now replaces him. What is more, he gets to marry the former queen.*

Recognition of the fall, when it comes, is anagnorisis. And it comes late to Oedipus. The recognition that his impulsive character has been his downfall is dependent on a simple piece of information missing in the first instance: that the old man he met was his father, and the queen he has married is therefore his mother.

When the audience realizes the perepeteia – achieves anagnorisis – before the character, then we have the makings of dramatic irony. When hamartia leads to perepeteia and then (inevitably) to anagnorisis, we have tragedy. They are dramatic notions which will drive a man to murder a loving wife, or to gouge out his own eyes.

The Greeks had a Play about It
– Peter Hinton, 2012

Ace could tell that the audience was loving it. She could see the Doctor's point though – the dialogue was stilted and opaque, and the plot seemed extremely simple. Six characters left over from a battle they had lost, holed up in a castle boasting and starting to watch a play. Ace was finding it boring, and her left leg had already fallen asleep.

There had been one interval, and the Doctor had disappeared before she could talk to him. He had returned with a drink which he held up to her mouth, since she could not move her arms. The liquid tasted of overripe melons mixed with brandy. She had not drunk much of it.

'It's a winner so far,' she told the Doctor as she tried to push the beaker away from her mouth. 'Can't wait for the film.'

The Doctor muttered something about Philistines, handed the remains of the drink to the surprised guard who had been watching them intently, and sat down again in the seat next to Ace.

'How do you like it in there?' the Doctor asked without looking at her, and without seeming to move his lips.

'Not at all. I'm getting cramp,' she whispered back.

'It livens up a bit in the second half. We may need to leave in a bit of a hurry towards the end.'

Ace laughed out loud, and the Doctor risked a warning glare at her. But the guard was busily trying to drain a last drop from his melon brandy. 'Flex your muscles a bit. Get yourself ready just in case.'

Ace was about to protest: she could hardly flex a finger. But then she realized that there did seem to be more play in the straps round her ankles. She shifted her leg experimentally and found its movement unrestricted. She looked down at her wrists and saw that the cords still lay across them but they were unfastened – positioned rather than tied. She frowned at the Doctor and he smiled back.

Before she could question how he had managed it, the lights dimmed again and the characters frozen on the stage jerked suddenly back into life, picking up the script at the moment they had abandoned it.

'You'll enjoy this act,' the Doctor said to her, ignoring the angry shh-ing from the row behind.

Ace tried to pay a bit more attention during the second half. Now it was dark she also flexed her hands and legs. She did not dare to move her hands too far – the guard was too close to risk it, even though he seemed intent on the stage.

The Doctor was right, it was picking up a little. Complications in the plot arose when it became clear that the main characters were beginning to recognize themselves in the play as their counterpart characters were killed. As Benny had told her, this happened off-stage. A cloaked guy called Jorvik described it for the audiences both on the stage and in the auditorium.

Jorvik was the most interesting of the characters. The rest were hardly more than two-dimensional. But Jorvik was a philosopher who pondered the validity of war and the virtues of heroism. He was also something of an eccentric, judging by the way he kept his wide-brimmed hat on, his face perpetually in shadow. His slight body was forever swirled in a long heavy cloak. He seemed to dominate the play, organizing and chiding the other characters, despite his seemingly unimposing nature and his diminutive stature. His comrades all stood at least a head higher than he did, but still they seemed to shrink away in fear as he described the deaths of their counterparts in the play within a play.

'The *Spirit of Samarra* reports another three Rippearean cruisers closing on the Alterberg Gap.' The operator listened for a few moments longer, scrawling notes on a clip-pak. 'That's confirmed by the *Repercussion*.'

Petralona didn't like the sound of it at all. She had only started duty a couple of hours previously, and it had been relatively quiet then. Now everything was happening at once. 'How many ships is that so far?' she asked the technician entering the information onto the main display.

He checked his notes and counted off the transponders already marked. 'Ninety six. Almost two-thirds of the Rippearean fleet are now concentrated round the Gap and the sectors bordering it.'

'Where are the others?'

'We don't know – the only ships we have contact with are those near the Gap.'

'So they could be on their way there as well.'

The technician nodded. 'Could well be. We won't know till one of our ships or a sat-station makes contact.'

'Great. Let's hope they're just regrouping. At least the kill-sats will keep the Gap secure.' Petralona was not in a position to take much counter action. The commanders in the field would have more up-to-date information and would be co-ordinating their response through the local net. Only the Exec or the Manact could send a direct order.

'Another two,' the com-net operator called across. 'One of them is a mine destroyer.'

'S'blood. They're going for the Gap.'

'But the kill-sats are proximity devices, a destroyer won't get close enough to wipe them,' the technician pointed out. 'And if it sends probes the sats will trace them back to the parent vessel and take it out anyway. The mines would have to be deactivated before they could clear a path through.'

'That may be,' Petralona told him, 'but there's no other explanation.'

'Then we should tell the Manact,' the operator said.

'Who asked you?' Petralona was beginning to panic. It didn't help that the rest of the staff in the war room were paying close attention to what was happening by the situation display.

'What else can we do?'

'He'd kill us,' the technician said, and he meant it.

Petrolona agreed. If they interrupted the all-important performance of *The Good Soldiers* with some vague notion that the Rippeareans might be about to risk two-thirds of their fleet by driving it through a minefield, he might very well execute them all for their trouble. But if the Rippeareans were about to deactivate the field somehow, and they did not raise the alarm . . .

She made her decision. 'The field commanders will handle it. Have their communications relayed direct through the net. We'll lag behind, but we should get warning of what's happening if anything goes wrong. Warn the fleet protagonist of our concerns, and monitor the status of the sats positioned within the Gap. If anything more happens, I'll contact the Manact.' ,

'If anything more happens?' The operator was on his feet, headset abandoned at his station. 'What more are you waiting for – an advance in force? Never mind trying to hold them on the perimeter and forcing them to take months negotiating a path round the Surralian system, if they come through the Gap they'll be here in hours.'

'Sit down,' Petrolona shouted. She could feel a nerve ticking by her right eye. 'The field commanders will handle it. They're just regrouping – all right?' She looked up at the status display. Another three transponders joined the mass on the other side of the Gap. The area was almost whited out with their tiny lights. 'They're just regrouping,' she repeated. 'They can't get through.'

The communications suite was a relatively small room off the same corridor as the war room. All that happened there was that messages to and from the war room were relayed through a booster and directed to or received from the appropriate satellite orbiting Heletia. The process was automatic and computer-controlled. As with all automatic processes, it required the presence of someone to monitor it and ensure that everything worked.

That someone was at the moment Junior Technician Chassada. He was not yet eighteen, and had just completed training. He was due for a posting any time now but was hoping the war would be over before he got to it. They were talking months rather than years in the barracks, but even so he would probably still see action. If he was lucky he would live to regret it.

The door behind him opened and he turned to see who it was. He was not due to be relieved for another few hours yet. It was a woman: tall, slim, with short dark hair and a wide smile.

'Hello,' she said. 'I'm fascinated by technology. Mind if I sit in?'

Chassada was at a loss for words as she pulled up the spare chair and joined him beside the main monitor. 'I'm not sure you should be here,' he eventually managed to say. And he quickly checked his disruptor was in its holster on his hip.

'Oh nonsense.' She leaned forward and pointed at an area of the screen in front of them. 'What does this do?' she asked. The woman's chest was perilously close to his face as she leaned across, and he could not help but notice that the top few buttons of her brushed denim jumpsuit were undone.

Chassada had to lean round her to see what she was pointing at. Strangely it seemed to be a blank area of screen. He was confused and distracted, so did not immediately appreciate the significance of the slight tug at his waistband as the woman smiled warmly at him.

He recalled just too late that his holster was on the same side as the woman, and in a sudden panic he reached for his side-arm. His holster was empty. For a split second he wondered where his disruptor had gone. Then it hit him.

The play had finished. The actors were taking their bow. They still wore their masks and cloaks. In many ways they presented a similar profile to Jorvik, except that all the players were tall and well-built. Jorvik was slight and noticeably shorter.

The reaction from the six comrades was mixed. Jorvik clapped loudly and stood up to join the players as they faced the other survivors of Limlough. But his comrades were less appreciative. Teel and Spidler exchanged glum looks. Prator and Freppon clapped without enthusiasm. Remek sat staring at the stage. He made no attempt to applaud, his face was emotionless.

Jorvik held up his hands for silence, and the desultory applause died out. 'My friends,' he said, arms outstretched – open and giving – and his face still hidden in the shadow of his hooded cloak. 'The final act.' And he stepped out of the way of the makeshift stage.

In a single movement the players pulled off their masks, threw off their cloaks. The comrades leapt to their feet, Teel already running towards the door. Only Remek remained seated, nodding sadly as Jorvik's laughter rang round the great hall of the fortress of Limlough and the Samrong robots who had performed the play stepped from the stage. Prator drew his sword and sliced at the nearest of the robots. The blade splintered on the robot's metal frame and Prator staggered back, his arms ringing from the blow. The robot advanced on him, the heavy pike it carried lowered and ready to strike.

Teel reached the door just as it gave way. The heavy wood split across and crashed to the floor. He staggered to a halt just short of the debris, his eyes widening as the Samrong warriors charged in at him, the firelight from the torches round the walls reflected off their burnished limbs.

Before he could get clear, the first two robots through the door grabbed his arms, twisting them up behind his back. His head was thrust forward over the back of a chair. Then, from the line of robots marching into the room, the executioner stepped forward. His eyes were burning holes in the metal skull as he raised the axe high above his head. Teel's screams echoed round the hall as the axe began to swing slowly towards him. For a moment it paused at its apogee, then gravity gave it one more little pull and the blade continued over and down. It gathered momentum as it went and slammed into his neck with a slapping squelch that echoed round the theatre, adding to the sound of Jorvik's laughter.

Ace almost rubbed the back of her neck in sympathy,

but caught herself just in time. She need not have worried, the guard – along with the rest of the audience – was transfixed by the action on the stage.

In moments the massacre was over. The Samrong robots gathered round Jorvik at the edge of the stage. The audience waited for Jorvik's famous soliloquy: many of them knew the first few sentences as reconstructed from Findlater's parody. But before he spoke, the Samrong robots who had performed the play stepped from the stage.

The guard near to Ace drew his disruptor, worried, and staggered back in surprise. The robot advanced on him, the heavy pike it carried lowered and ready to strike. The guard fired, but the energy bolt shattered and dispersed across the robot's metal frame.

Ace pulled free of her restraints; the audience behind her was already starting to panic. She could hear the sound of the people pushing along the rows of seats, trampling across each other trying to escape before she saw the chaos.

Through it all the Doctor sat calm and silent, watching the stage.

The guard turned to run, but before he could get clear the first two robots off the stage grabbed his arms, twisting them up behind his back. His head was thrust forward over the edge of the stage. Then, from the line of robots marching into the auditorium, the executioner stepped forward. His eyes were burning holes in the metal skull as he raised the axe high above his head. The guard's screams echoed round the theatre as the axe began to swing slowly towards him. For a moment it paused at its apogee, then Jorvik stepped to the edge of the stage and spoke.

'The play is spent; the act is done.'

The effect of his first words was immediate. The robots stopped their advance, staggered forward slightly and then swayed back. The few people still fighting to get out of the theatre stopped and listened to Jorvik's voice despite their panic. Some began to sit down again, believing the whole thing to be a clever staging technique, but most were already trying to put as much distance as possible between themselves and the theatre.

'Time makes honest brokers of us all. And Time in turn brings in his revenges. Now am I naked, my soul laid bare. My deeds are all confessed. Time has undone me as it destroys everything.'

The robots remained frozen. The small audience slowly calmed, the remaining people either returning to their seats or stopping where they were. Ace could hear several of those familiar with the reconstruction of the speech exchanging hushed whispers – this was nothing like it should be.

A single spotlight illuminated Jorvik now. The shadow of the brim of his hat still hid his eyes, but his mouth was visible as his speech continued, a single area of pallidity in his dark figure.

'Like the innocent and the beautiful, we have no enemy but Time. And we cannot call back yesterday, nor bid Time return. We talk of killing Time, while Time quietly kills us. Time watches from the shadows, antiquates antiquities; coughs when we would kiss. Time fells the mighty and quells the dragon's wrath.'

The theatre was silent apart from Jorvik's voice. His words were clear despite the slight slurr in his voice. The Samrong robots at the foot of the stage began to sway as if in time to his words. It seemed to Ace that as the speech went on they were getting older, their metal frames tarnishing. As she watched, a patch of rust began slowly to form on the shoulder of the robot nearest her. The executioner's axe, still held aloft – poised at its highest point – swayed and fell heavily to the floor. It buried itself in the fabric of a seat and the guard tore himself free of the two robots still holding his arms. He ran from the theatre, his disruptor clattering to the floor as he went.

Nobody watched him go. They were entranced by Jorvik's words and enthralled by the effect they were having.

'We are all dwellers in eternity with but a short time to separate our beginning from our ending – our light gleams an instant, then is gone. All is come to naught.'

The rust had spread across the robot's torso. It was a brown stain across the chest and down one leg. As Ace watched, the leg gave way under the weight of the robot, and it collapsed sideways, smashing to the floor.

'Now is the very witching time. Now churchyards yawn and Time itself breathes out contagion to the world. Our act is done, our roles fulfilled. The script is ended and our useful lives have come to this – a handful of sand blown crazy by the winds and whims of Time.'

As Jorvik continued speaking, one robot after another keeled over and fell around him. The others were swaying ever more violently. Only Jorvik stood calm and straight, his arms stretched wide as the figures round him toppled over with age and began to decay.

The robot which had fallen near Ace had all but rusted away. The main body was eroded completely, exposing the decaying mechanisms within. Another robot collapsed forward off the front of the stage, landing in a heap at Ace's feet. Its eyes stared into hers. She watched as the red glow within paled and faded, as the skull-like metal face browned and lost its sheen. A ball of rust rolled down its face. Another welled up in the eye and then slowly made its way down, an open tear in the metal in its path. It paused for a moment half-way, then cried its way down the lower half of the torn cheek.

'Only through time is Time conquered,' said Jorvik, his voice almost a snarl now as the last of the figures round him fell to its knees, then pitched forward, its face cracking on the concrete floor of the stage. Jorvik pushed at the broken head with his foot and it detached from the body and rolled across the stage. It paused for a moment at the edge, then it continued over and down. It gathered momentum as it fell and slammed into the floor below with a metallic crunch that echoed round the theatre. The head shattered on impact, leaving a rusty star-shaped stain at the point where it landed.

Jorvik looked round at the broken remains of the Samrong robots and sighed. 'I will show you death in an hourglass,' he whispered.

For a while there was silence. Then the cloaked figure stepped over the wreckage in front of him and stood on the very edge of the stage. The spotlight was still full on him as he threw aside his hat and pulled off his cloak. The slight figure of Jorvik, revealed for the first time, smiled at his twin in the front row of the auditorium. He raised the umbrella that had appeared from under the cloak, signalling his appreciation to the audience for their indulgence. He held it by the end so that the question mark of the handle was silhouetted against the back wall of the banqueting hall set.

In the front row the Doctor leapt to his feet. 'Bravo!' he shouted, and his alter ego on the stage smiled in thanks. The Doctor in the front row began to clap. After a moment Ace joined in, and then the theatre erupted in a storm of applause. The spotlight faded and a red glow set in for a few seconds on the stage. Then it too faded, like mist in the hot sun.

'I suppose you think that's terribly funny – or at least terribly clever,' Ace said to the Doctor when the applause eventually died down enough for him to hear her.

'Now you come to mention it, I suppose it is,' he replied with a grin. 'It was also terribly well written, especially given the tight deadline.'

'Who did you nick it from?'

'Nick it? I am not a plagiarist, Ace.' The Doctor looked annoyed for the briefest of moments. Then he smiled. 'But I did take the opportunity to pay homage to several great poets and playwrights.'

Only the Exec had not heard Jorvik's words. His teeth were chattering with fear and he gripped Lannic's hand tightly in his own. His head began to shake uncontrollably and he allowed Lannic to lead him to the back of the box and down the steps to the corridor beyond. His bodyguards, disruptors already drawn, were a step behind. He could still hear Jorvik's words in the theatre behind him as he almost ran towards the green room, dragging Lannic with him. He was barely aware of Marlock watching them dash along the corridor – making no move to follow them, shaking his head as he answered his communicator.

'They wage war on me now through the theatre,' he gasped to Lannic as they ran. 'My enemies are even here, all around me. I can trust no one.'

'Trust *me*,' she said and he slowed for a moment, squeezed her hand and attempted a smile.

When they reached the green room, the doors opened for them. The guards inside the door saluted as the Exec ran in, Lannic close behind. The bodyguards were already taking up position behind the Exec's desk as he tried to get his breath back.

'Leave me,' he said as soon as he could speak.

Nobody moved.

'You mean – ' Lannic started to ask.

'No! No, not you.' He waved his arms wildly. 'The rest of you – all of you – leave me. Leave me alone,' he stamped. The guards looked round, confused. Then one of the door guards cautiously left the room. The other one followed. The bodyguards waited slightly longer, but the Exec's glare and a further shout of rage was enough to send them from the room. The Exec followed them to the doors, then slammed them shut behind the last soldier. He slid the heavy bolts into place, turned and leaned against the doors. Slowly he slid down until he was sitting on the floor.

He was aware that Lannic was standing in front of him. She knelt down, and as he started to weep she cradled his head in her hands and ran her fingers through his hair. His whole body shook as the sobs took hold of him.

The equipment was straightforward, and Braxiatel had written out the routing codes and a brief set of instructions on the sheet of paper the Doctor had given her. Benny sent the coded phrase to him first – *Tell passenger Irving Braxiatel*, she sent to the Rippearean flagship, *The good soldiers have finished their banquet*. She laughed out loud when the confirm acknowledgement came back from the satellite stationed above Heletia. It included the name of the ship she had addressed with its transponder ident. Braxiatel had not told her that the flagship was called *Jorvik*.

The next process was less simple. Braxiatel's instructions were clear, but the sequence was complicated. She put the message on the net first, then set about the deactivation protocols. She knew the message would take a while to reach the Heletian fleet.

Benny managed to program in the deactivate sequences without a hitch. She rubbed her hands in self-congratulation and stepped over the unconscious body of the young technician. She paused to bend down and give him a cheery slap on the cheek, then set off across the room with a self-satisfied spring in her step.

But before she reached the door, it opened anyway.

'Ah. I think perhaps we might have found a little fault in our communications systems.'

Marlock's face split into what he might have described as a smile. His two bodyguards stepped past him. One took Benny by the arms and twisted them up behind her back, the other jabbed his disruptor into her ribs. Marlock stared into Benny's face from what seemed like only an inch away.

'A simple retraction message should undo your handiwork, and if you were working in concert with the Rippeareans we may well be able to arrange a small surprise for whoever is hoping to take our surrender.' He ran a finger down Benny's cheek and across her lower lip. 'And then we shall find something *exquisite* to do with you, my dear.'

Source Document 18

Extract from a personal letter from Irving Braxiatel to the Doctor

Braxiatel Collection – not catalogued

But if you must interfere, and I know from experience that you must, then I hope you will consider my suggestions and advice. I am sure we are agreed about the ends, only the means – as ever – may be in dispute.

Despite our past differences, however, I hope you will understand my motives now even if you cannot condone the means. If it will help you rest easier, they were and probably still are the only means available to me.

If all goes well, we may meet again shortly. But if you choose not to wait, I shall understand.

Good luck, my friend. May Time be good to you, and you to it.

Chapter 18

Endgame

> *Acting is of course by no means confined to the
> theatre. Many people spend their entire lives acting,
> for whatever reason. For some the act is a charade to
> hide innate diffidence. For some it is to impress and
> win over others. But whatever the reason, acting is a
> means to an end rather than an end in itself.*
>
> *When presented with out-of-character behaviour
> ask not* What is being presented? *but rather* What is
> being hidden?
>
> **Verbal Non-Communication** – Vyse Plaquet and
> Hughes Frost, 2137

The program which Benny had run in the communications
suite sent a single pulse to the nearest kill-sat in the
Alterberg Gap. The kill-sats were in a pyramid formation,
fanning out in three dimensions from a single point. The
single kill-sat at the point was the closest to Heletia, and
it was the one to which Benny's message was directed.
The pulse passed the satellite three instructions.

The first instruction was to deactivate itself. Which it
did, after checking the origin triangulation of the carrier
message.

The second instruction was to relay the same instruction
set, pulsing it out at three distinct and specified angles. It
did this too, and the three killer satellites at those angles
received and acted upon the same program. Because of
the precise formation of the thousands of kill-sats defend-
ing the Gap, the program rippled through them without
a hitch, at the speed of light. At the edges one or more

303

of the signals sped off into space since there was no satellite positioned to accept it.

The third instruction was the simplest of all. It was to ignore all further instructions.

The reasoning behind the complex instruction set rather than a simpler pulse sent to each satellite in turn was twofold. The first reason was that once the formation was analyzed and the angular relationships calculated, the program itself was fairly simple and needed only to be sent once. The second was that the Heletians were less likely to detect a single pulse from their own communications suite than a stream of thousands.

In fact the pulse did go undetected. The Heletian war room was in an uproar as the operators tried to decide whether the surrender order was genuine.

Then the first kill-sat discontinued its function and went off line.

'So why the grand finale?' Ace asked. The Doctor was picking his way through the debris which littered the stage. The set had faded and gone when Jorvik had disappeared. So, mercifully, had the bodies of the good soldiers. But the Samrong robots had already entered the real world, and their remains were now dissolving to dust.

'This insubstantial pageant – faded,' muttered the Doctor. 'Still, it made an impression – quite spectacular,' he told her. The theatre was deserted apart from the two of them. The people who had stayed to the end had quickly dispersed. 'The stage directions were very tricky to write. Didn't quite get it right, I think – that's why these bits and pieces are still here.' He frowned, deep in thought. 'There must be a way, a form of words. Forta-lexa's fictional double faded away when his work was done. Oh well,' he brightened, 'can't be expected to get everything right first time, can we?'

'But why bother? Why wait till the end before changing the script? Why let the robots in at all – you could have ended the play early and avoided all this.' Ace waved her arm round at the metal limbs and plastic components which were rotting around them.

'As I said, it made an impression.' The Doctor stopped his inspection of the mess strewn over the stage. 'Braxiatel's plan was to create a diversion. He wanted the Heletian court in an uproar, totally disorientated and chaotic. Then the Rippearean forces could take advantage of the confusion and press home their attack.'

'That was five years ago.'

'True, they were far stronger then. And in his letter he gave me an alternative. He still needed the diversion, but now Braxiatel has an agent planted here. An agent who can deactivate the minefield which forms the main obstacle between the Rippearean fleet and Heletia.' He resumed his inspection of the remains, calling back over his shoulder, 'So I substituted *my* ending for Braxiatel's rewrite of Osterling's. Rather than a massacre and a force of killer robots rampaging round the place, I managed a diversion which cost just a few bruises and the odd broken arm.'

'It also caused that poor guard Marlock left us to need a clean pair of trousers, I should think.'

The Doctor laughed. 'Dramatic licence.'

'So who is Braxiatel's agent? Anyone we know?'

'Yes – Benny. Let's see how she's doing, shall we?'

Marlock had taken a length of electrical cable from a store cupboard in the corner of the room. Benny watched as he cut across the end of it and stripped back several centimetres of plastic insulation. He started to splay out the copper wire inside, wrapping the other end of the cable around his hand.

'Hold her still,' Marlock told the bodyguard behind Benny. 'Let's see how strong some of these antique fibres really are, shall we? Denim, for example, has a reputation which could usefully be put to the test – don't you think?'

Benny tried to pull away, but the guard had her held tight. The other guard stepped aside, but he kept his disruptor levelled at Benny's stomach.

Marlock nodded his approval. 'If she flinches, shoot her in the arm.' He swung the cable to and fro. Benny watched its regular motion, transfixed, trying to empty her mind of what was to follow. 'Just a short burst.' He raised the cable above his head. 'I want her to retain consciousness for as long as possible.'

Marlock's bleeper sounded as his hand reached its apogee. He lowered the cable. 'Always when you're having fun,' he observed with a smile and flicked open a channel on his communicator. 'Yes, what is it now?'

The answer was a woman's voice. It was far from calm. 'Sir – the kill-sats in the Gap are deactivating.'

'What? How?'

'I don't know, sir – there's no signal from this end. They're just off-lining, one after another.'

'Check it,' Marlock snarled to the guard holding the gun. He gave a short nod and started to inspect the communications equipment where Benny had been sitting.

'Well?'

The guard shook his head. 'Nothing, sir – no pulse sending from this end. The source must be elsewhere.'

'They wouldn't acknowledge a signal from anyone other than us.' Marlock spoke into his communicator again. 'What are the Rippeareans doing?'

'Nothing, sir,' the tinny voice responded. 'They're still on station the other side of the field.'

'Good. They can't know what's happening – the satellites are passive, so they won't know that they've shut down. Tell me if there's any movement.' He turned off the communicator and stared at Benny. 'You sent the surrender signal,' he said after a while. 'But although you are not deactivating the mines, I think you know who is.'

The frayed cable swayed in front of Benny's face for a moment. She swallowed. This would take very careful timing and pretty good acting on her part.

'Very well,' said Marlock with a sigh. He raised the cable again.

This time Benny stopped him as the cable was about to come flailing down at her. 'The Exec,' she said, shouted probably, she could not tell. 'He was panicked by the performance. It was the Exec who sent me to call the surrender, it must be his orders that are deactivating the satellites too.' She hoped the fear had sounded genuine – it should have done, because it was.

Marlock paused. His good eye narrowed as he watched Benny. She could almost see the thought process inside his head.

After what seemed like forever, Marlock dropped the cable. 'Bring her,' he said to the guard holding her. 'It's time I sorted out this mess.'

The outermost line of kill-sats in the Gap deactivated themselves and threw out a program message pulse into the space ahead of them. There were no satellites there to receive it.

But the mine destroyer *Wild Fire* was positioned to receive it from two different satellites in the link. The signals arrived within a second of each other. The second in effect confirmed that the Gap was safe, and the *Wild Fire* began to despatch handler probes to clear a path through, dragging the kill-sats aside so gently that if their motion sensors were still on-line they would not detect it and detonate.

The *Wild Fire* also sent a coded signal to the flagship *Jorvik*: 'Final Curtain.'

When Marlock arrived at the green room with his two bodyguards and his prisoner, he found the doors closed and bolted against him. The two doorguards and even the Exec's two bodyguards were standing outside, evidently somewhat confused. They recounted the events which had left them locked outside, and Marlock sent them back to the barracks to await his wrath.

'It seems you may be telling the truth,' he told Benny. 'We shall soon see.' He hammered on the doors with his fist and shouted, 'Exec – open up. It's me, Marlock. The invasion is defeated and we are safe. *You* are safe. Do you hear me? Open the doors!'

They waited, but there was no response from inside.

'I'll watch her.' Marlock drew his disruptor and motioned for the guard holding Benny to release her. She flexed her shoulders, they were stiff. Marlock kept her covered with his gun. To his two bodyguards he said, 'Get those doors open. Now.'

The Exec's sobs had subsided and he was beginning to recover. Lannic was still holding his head, still had her hands tangled in his greasy hair.

'You don't know how I've waited for this moment,' she said. 'How I have dreamed of having some time alone with you.'

He looked up at her, his face smeared with the stains of tears. 'You wish to be my consort.' It was not a question. He ran his hands down her back, feeling the uneven mesh of the gauze of her blouse.

'I was married once,' she said. Her hands had stopped their tugging and she was staring into empty space. 'It was long ago.'

The Exec's hands had reached her waist. The adrenalin of panic began to give way to other stimulation and emotion as he followed the curve of her body and squeezed her thigh.

But Lannic seemed not to notice. 'It was sunny – a lovely sunny day. I was in the kitchen when I heard him scream. Funny how you remember, how immediate it still seems. It was the day after we were sure, the day we were going to celebrate.' Her voice cracked slightly. Her eyes were still unfocused, staring into the past. 'I ran out, but by the time I got there – ' She blinked suddenly and her head lolled forward. Then she recovered herself and continued, '. . . got there – it was too late.'

At last she turned and looked at the Exec. He could almost feel the intensity of her gaze, and his hand tightened on her thigh, rubbing downwards, feeling for an edge of her skirt. She still gave no sign of having noticed. 'They had him strung up in the yard. I didn't hear them arrive, didn't hear his first screams – he must have screamed more than once.' A tear welled up in her eye and rolled down her cheek. She made no move to wipe it away, her hands were still tangled in the Exec's hair. 'I couldn't run – couldn't leave him. He was still alive. Just.'

Her body began to shake with inner sobs, her voice was distorted with emotion and her head swayed slowly from side to side. 'I didn't try to stop them, how could I? I just kept looking at him, hanging there in the doorway, burned and bleeding. And they made sure he could see me – could see what they did. They weren't fit to be called men, let alone soldiers. They left me there, in the yard, crying by his dead body. They wouldn't cut him down even when he was dead.' Her voice faded away. She seemed calmer now, her fingers tying themselves into his hair again.

'The Rippeareans,' murmured the Exec. 'We'll make them pay.' His hand had felt its way into the split in her skirt. Now it rubbed up her right thigh. 'What's this?' He had felt a strip of material, thought it to be a garter, but it held a pouch strapped to her leg.

Lannic's hand closed on the Exec's, drew it away, and pulled the skirt aside. Her other hand was still in the Exec's hair and it pulled savagely, yanking his head up so that he was forced to look into her face. She was shaking her head, her eyes wide and her jaw set. 'Not Rippeareans,' she said, and her voice had become hard and determined.

Startled, the Exec pulled his head free. He flattened himself against the back of the doors, watching in horrified fascination as Lannic unclipped the flap over the top of the pouch at her leg. He gave a squeal of panic as she drew out a small percussion pistol.

'They were Heletians,' she said. 'Your troops.' And she raised her hand as if pointing at him, the percussion pistol nestling in her palm, the barrel protruding.

He pushed himself back, away from her, with his feet – tried to crawl out of the way. But her hand pointed after him even as he scrabbled his way across the floor towards his desk.

'You killed him. Killed both him and our child.' The words were almost spat across the room.

The Exec rolled over, faced her. He had to reason with her. Somehow. 'No – no, not me. I never killed anyone, never. I – '

But she wasn't listening. She was standing above him now, the tears staining her cheeks, the pistol grasped firmly in both hands. 'You murdering bastard!' she screamed as the sound of the detonation echoed round the room.

The thermite charges rocked the doors on their hinges. For a moment it seemed they had no other effect, then the doors swayed inwards and began slowly to fall. They crashed to the floor amid a wrenching of metal and shower of dust from the door frame.

Benny was the first to recover her senses when the dust cleared. She dived away, down the corridor, and ran. Marlock made no move to stop her. His disruptor disappeared behind his back as he peered through the thinning dust and clearing smoke from the blast.

Inside the room, Lannic was standing with her back to the door. As she turned to face Marlock and his guards, they saw the body on the floor. The Exec was sprawled on his back, his arms and legs spread out. His robes were dishevelled and in disarray. His head was a mess of bone and congealing blood.

One of the guards stepped forward, raising his disruptor. But the shell from Lannic's pistol felled him before he could bring it to bear. She shot the second guard before he had a chance to move, his stomach exploding as the shell pierced his body armour.

Marlock made no attempt to escape. He knew he could never outrun an old-fashioned bullet. He held his hands open in front of him.

'I mean you no harm, Lannic,' he said, walking slowly towards her.

She levelled the gun.

'A percussion pistol – very clever.' Another step closer. 'Just gunpowder, no energy source, so it wouldn't show up on any detector.' He wasn't walking directly towards her now. He wandered apparently at ease across the room, hands thrust into his jacket pockets. 'In future we shall have to scan for metal, I suppose.' Inside his pocket, Marlock's right hand felt carefully for the trigger guard on the disruptor as he prepared to reorient the gun. 'What do you say?' His finger tightened on the trigger as he turned the gun so it pointed forwards. But he hesitated for a split second – suddenly worried that he would need a new jacket.

Lannic said nothing. The report ricocheted off the concrete walls. The shot caught Marlock in the chest. It lifted him off his feet and slammed him across the room into the wall.

The shell was deflected by the duralinium mesh woven into his jacket lining, catching him in the right shoulder, lodging behind the shoulder-blade. His hand clenched in a spasm of pain, pressing and holding the trigger. The blast seared through the front of his jacket, burning its way upwards as he fell, drawing a charred line up his body. It reached the underside of his chin before he managed to release his hold. His face blackened as the phason burst ate into his skull. It drilled its way through his chin, diffusing into the bone structure and seeking the line of least resistance. His brain had already evaporated in the screaming heat before the shock-wave reached his eyes.

As his body slumped down, Lannic sat down heavily on the floor beside the Exec's body, cradling the pistol in her hands. She rocked to and fro slowly, and the pistol slipped to the floor with a clatter.

'Are you sure you want to come with us?' Ace asked. 'You seemed very keen to stay and see Braxiatel again.'

Benny stuck her tongue out. 'We're just good friends. Anyway, I'd have thought the Doctor would want to wait and see him.'

'Yeah, what is this, Doctor? He'll be landing within the hour. The commissionaire from Arbela was very impressed you knew him. Now he's taken over you might get a reward – he was happy to release poor old Klasvik with no questions asked.'

The Doctor unlocked the TARDIS and ushered them in. He took a last look round the hanger. 'Poor old Klasvik will be fine. But I'm not sure I want to meet young Braxiatel just now,' he said as he followed them inside.

'What, because you spoiled his plan?' Ace laughed. 'It came out all right in the end, you know.'

The Doctor nodded. 'Yes, it did. But I'm not sure it didn't all go according to Braxiatel's plan after all.'

'What do you mean?' asked Benny.

'I told Ace that Braxiatel had an agent planted on Heletia, Benny. I meant you.'

'So?'

'I'm not sure he didn't have another agent too. It's quite a coincidence that the very person who led the expedition to Menaxus and brought back the dream machine should want to assassinate the Exec.'

'You mean Lannic was working for Braxiatel – that the whole thing was to get at the Exec? She *was* very keen to meet him right from the start.'

The Doctor nodded glumly. 'Well, it's a possibility. In which case, the play was always intended as a diversion – as a way for Lannic to get to the Exec, to corner him alone.'

Benny laughed. 'I can see why you don't want to face Braxiatel, then. Wouldn't do for the arch-manipulator to have to admit he was manipulated himself, now would it?'

Ace joined in the laughter. 'Actually, I think *I'd* quite like to meet this guy – surely we can stay for just an hour or two, Doctor?'

But the Doctor was already busy at the controls. 'Yes, well – as I said, it's almost certainly a complete coincidence. So let's consider the matter closed, shall we?' He pulled a paisley handkerchief from his jacket pocket and wiped his face with it. Then he screwed the handkerchief up again and dropped it on the TARDIS console. Through the distortion of the rising central column, the swirling paisley patterns looked like clusters of small leaves splaying out from a central branch.

Curtain Call

Braxiatel was not surprised. 'I really wouldn't waste too much time looking for them, Commissionaire.'

The commissionaire of Arbela, now acting-Exec of Heletia under the programme of the state of emergency, was apologetic nonetheless. 'I am so sorry – they were here not very long ago, I'm sure.' He wrung his hands in dismay. 'I feel we are not doing so very well – having lost the assassin already, we have also mislaid your friends.'

'I'm sure the Doctor and his friends are quite safe.' Braxiatel smiled. 'Or at least, as safe as they ever are.' He stood and put down his empty glass on the commissionaire's desk. 'Now, before we arrange for the final acceptance of your surrender and start on the peace negotiations, I should like to see the green room for myself.'

'Of course.' The commissionaire led the way from his office. 'It's still cordoned off, but I think there is probably little value in keeping it off-limits. Perhaps the surrender should be signed there?'

'A nice thought. And I agree, the assassin will by now be melted into air – into thin air. Which is probably just as well: I feel she has done us all something of a favour.' He followed the commissionaire from the room, hands clasped behind his back, nodding to the Rippearean troops lining the corridor outside. The landings and troop deployments had been remarkably easy, but with three star destroyers and a battle cruiser directly over the city, and the gunships visible on station within the atmosphere, there was little to encourage the confused and despondent Heletians to resist. Their fleet was already disarmed and moored on the edge of the Piriquatai cloud, awaiting a Rippearean escort back to their home ports. If anything, the Heletians seemed relieved – except for those who knew about and had seen the camps. And that would make them all the easier to track down.

The green room was empty. A Rippearean guard stood outside. She saluted as Braxiatel and the commissionaire arrived. Inside the room seemed normal, except for the stains down one wall and the outlines painted on the floor where the bodies had lain. They looked surprisingly small.

'I gather there wasn't much left of either of them,' the commissionaire offered. 'I've always disliked this room. Here of all places we had to keep our real thoughts suppressed. What a place to have to meet your destiny.'

'Yes.' Braxiatel smiled. 'We are all slaves to destiny. We are driven like clusters of small leaves by the winds of time, directed through the summer of our lives to an ever-closer autumn.'

The commissionaire coughed, embarrassed. 'There was no sign of Lannic. Except for the pistol.'

The percussion pistol was lying on the floor beside the spread-eagled outline of the Exec.

Braxiatel bent to pick it up. 'May I?' he asked, looking back at the commissionaire for permission. The commissionaire waved a dismissive hand.

The pistol was quite heavy for its small size. Braxiatel let it lie in the palm of his hand for a moment, admiring the antique workmanship: the carefully milled barrel, the percussion chamber, the leaf design etched on the butt.

Then he dropped the gun into his pocket, wondering if the commissionaire had heared the faint crackle, like a static discharge, as he had picked it up. 'I think I'll take this back to the Collection with me,' Braxiatel said.

He wondered briefly where the Doctor was now, if 'now' was a useful term. 'Thank you for your help, old friend,' he murmured as he straightened up.

Braxiatel held his right hand level with his eyes. The hairs on the back of his hand were standing on end. He smiled, and clasped his hands behind his back once more, smoothing the back of his right hand with the palm of his left.

'Be cheerful, sir,' he said to the commissionaire. 'Our revels now are ended.'

'I'm sorry?' The commissionaire followed Braxiatel out into the corridor.

'Be not disturbed,' Braxiatel reassured him. 'I was just paying homage to a great poet and playwright.'

Already published:

TIMEWYRM: GENESYS
John Peel

The Doctor and Ace are drawn to Ancient Mesopotamia in search of an evil sentience that has tumbled from the stars – the dreaded Timewyrm of ancient Gallifreyan legend.

ISBN 0 426 20355 0

TIMEWYRM: EXODUS
Terrance Dicks

Pursuit of the Timewyrm brings the Doctor and Ace to the Festival of Britain. But the London they find is strangely subdued, and patrolling the streets are the uniformed thugs of the Britischer Freikorps.

ISBN 0 426 20357 7

TIMEWYRM: APOCALYPSE
Nigel Robinson

Kirith seems an ideal planet – a world of peace and plenty, ruled by the kindly hand of the Great Matriarch. But it's here that the end of the universe – of everything – will be precipitated. Only the Doctor can stop the tragedy.

ISBN 0 426 20359 3

TIMEWYRM: REVELATION
Paul Cornell

Ace has died of oxygen starvation on the moon, having thought the place to be Norfolk. 'I do believe that's unique,' says the afterlife's receptionist.

ISBN 0 426 20360 7

CAT'S CRADLE: TIME'S CRUCIBLE
Marc Platt

The TARDIS is invaded by an alien presence and is then destroyed. The Doctor disappears. Ace, lost and alone, finds herself in a bizarre city where nothing is to be trusted – even time itself.

ISBN 0 426 20365 8

CAT'S CRADLE: WARHEAD
Andrew Cartmel
The place is Earth. The time is the near future – all too near. As environmental destruction reaches the point of no return, multinational corporations scheme to buy immortality in a poisoned world. If Earth is to survive, somebody has to stop them.

ISBN 0 426 20367 4

CAT'S CRADLE: WITCH MARK
Andrew Hunt
A small village in Wales is visited by creatures of myth. Nearby, a coach crashes on the M40, killing all its passengers. Police can find no record of their existence. The Doctor and Ace arrive, searching for a cure for the TARDIS, and uncover a gateway to another world.

ISBN 0 426 20368 2

NIGHTSHADE
Mark Gatiss
When the Doctor brings Ace to the village of Crook Marsham in 1968, he seems unwilling to recognize that something sinister is going on. But the villagers are being killed, one by one, and everyone's past is coming back to haunt them – including the Doctor's.

ISBN 0 426 20376 3

LOVE AND WAR
Paul Cornell
Heaven: a planet rich in history where the Doctor comes to meet a new friend, and betray an old one; a place where people come to die, but where the dead don't always rest in peace. On Heaven, the Doctor finally loses Ace, but finds archaeologist Bernice Summerfield, a new companion whose destiny is inextricably linked with his.

ISBN 0 426 20385 2

TRANSIT
Ben Aaronovitch
It's the ultimate mass transit system, binding the planets of the solar system together. But something is living in the network, chewing its way to the very heart of the system and leaving a trail of death and mutation behind. Once again, the Doctor is all that stands between humanity and its own mistakes.

ISBN 0 426 20384 4

THE HIGHEST SCIENCE
Gareth Roberts

The Highest Science – a technology so dangerous it destroyed its creators. Many people have searched for it, but now Sheldukher, the most wanted criminal in the galaxy, believes he has found it. The Doctor and Bernice must battle to stop him on a planet where chance and coincidence have become far too powerful.

ISBN 0 426 20377 1

THE PIT
Neil Penswick

One of the Seven Planets is a nameless giant, quarantined against all intruders. But when the TARDIS materializes, it becomes clear that the planet is far from empty – and the Doctor begins to realize that the planet hides a terrible secret from the Time Lords' past.

ISBN 0 426 20378 X

DECEIT
Peter Darvill-Evans

Ace – three years older, wiser and tougher – is back. She is part of a group of Irregular Auxiliaries on an expedition to the planet Arcadia. They think they are hunting Daleks, but the Doctor knows better. He knows that the paradise planet hides a being far more powerful than the Daleks – and much more dangerous.

ISBN 0 426 20362 3

LUCIFER RISING
Jim Mortimore & Andy Lane

Reunited, the Doctor, Ace and Bernice travel to Lucifer, the site of a scientific expedition that they know will shortly cease to exist. Discovering why involves them in sabotage, murder and the resurrection of eons-old alien powers. Are there Angels on Lucifer? And what does it all have to do with Ace?

ISBN 0 426 20338 7

WHITE DARKNESS
David McIntee

The TARDIS crew, hoping for a rest, come to Haiti in 1915. But they find that the island is far from peaceful: revolution is brewing in the city; the dead are walking from the cemeteries; and, far underground, the ancient rulers of the galaxy are stirring in their sleep.

ISBN 0 426 20395 X

SHADOWMIND
Christopher Bulis

On the colony world of Arden, something dangerous is growing stronger. Something that steals minds and memories. Something that can reach out to another planet, Tairgire, where the newest exhibit in the sculpture park is a blue box surmounted by a flashing light.

ISBN 0 426 20394 1

BIRTHRIGHT
Nigel Robinson

Stranded in Edwardian London with a dying TARDIS, Bernice investigates a series of grisly murders. In the far future, Ace leads a group of guerrillas against their insect-like, alien oppressors. Why has the Doctor left them, just when they need him most?

ISBN 0 426 20393 3

ICEBERG
David Banks

In 2006, an ecological disaster threatens the Earth; only the FLIPback team, working in an Antarctic base, can avert the catastrophe. But hidden beneath the ice, sinister forces have gathered to sabotage humanity's last hope. The Cybermen have returned and the Doctor must face them alone.

ISBN 0 426 20392 5

BLOOD HEAT
Jim Mortimore

The TARDIS is attacked by an alien force; Bernice is flung into the Vortex; and the Doctor and Ace crash-land on Earth. There they find dinosaurs roaming the derelict London streets, and Brigadier Lethbridge-Stewart leading the remnants of UNIT in a desperate fight against the Silurians who have taken over and changed his world.

ISBN 0 426 20399 2

THE DIMENSION RIDERS
Daniel Blythe

A holiday in Oxford is cut short when the Doctor is summoned to Space Station Q4, where ghostly soldiers from the future watch from the shadows among the dead. Soon, the Doctor is trapped in the past, Ace is accused of treason and Bernice is uncovering deceit among the college cloisters.

ISBN 0 426 20397 6

THE LEFT-HANDED HUMMINGBIRD
Kate Orman

Someone has been playing with time. The Doctor Ace and Bernice must travel to the Aztec Empire in 1487, to London in the Swinging Sixties and to the sinking of the *Titanic* as they attempt to rectify the temporal faults – and survive the attacks of the living god Huitzilin.

ISBN 0 426 20404 2

CONUNDRUM
Steve Lyons

A killer is stalking the streets of the village of Arandale. The victims are found each day, drained of blood. Someone has interfered with the Doctor's past again, and he's landed in a place he knows he once destroyed, from which it seems there can be no escape.

ISBN 0 426 20408 5

NO FUTURE
Paul Cornell

At last the Doctor comes face-to-face with the enemy who has been threatening him, leading him on a chase that has brought the TARDIS to London in 1976. There he finds that reality has been subtly changed and the country he once knew is rapidly descending into anarchy as an alien invasion force prepares to land . . .

ISBN 0 426 20409 3

TRAGEDY DAY
Gareth Roberts

When the TARDIS crew arrive on Olleril, they soon realise that all is not well. Assassins arrive to carry out a killing that may endanger the entire universe. A being known as the Supreme One tests horrific weapons. And a secret order of monks observes the growing chaos.

ISBN 0 426 20410 7

LEGACY
Gary Russell

The Doctor returns to Peladon, on the trail of a master criminal. Ace pursues intergalactic mercenaries who have stolen the galaxy's most evil artifact while Bernice strikes up a dangerous friendship with a Martian Ice Lord. The players are making the final moves in a devious and lethal plan – but for once it isn't the Doctor's.

ISBN 0 426 20412 3